RESTORATION

Book 3 of the Verity Fassbinder Series

ANGELA SLATTER

Jo Fletcher
BOOKS

First published in Great Britain in 2018
This edition published in 2019 by

Jo Fletcher Books
an imprint of Quercus Editions Ltd
Carmelite House
50 Victoria Embankment
London EC4Y 0DZ

An Hachette UK company

A CIP catalogue record for this book is available
from the British Library

PB ISBN 978 1 78429 437 3
EB ISBN 978 1 78429 436 6

10 9 8 7 6 5 4 3 2 1

Typeset by CC Book Production
Printed and bound in Great Britain by Clays Ltd, Elcograf S.p.A.

To my parents, Betty and Peter,
for their unfailing love and for helping to make me who I am.

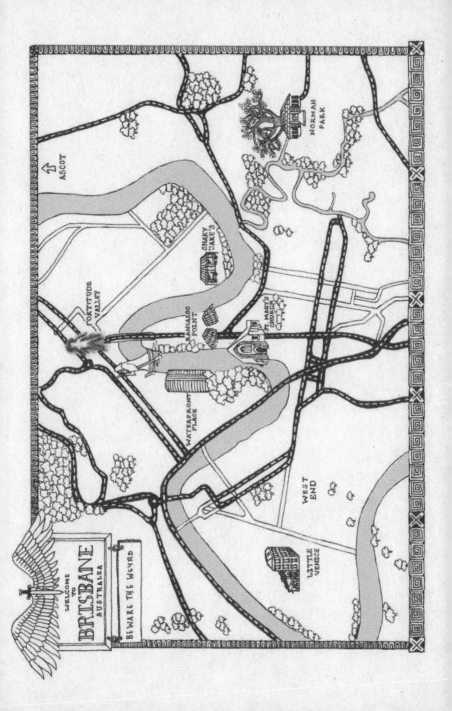

Author's Note

Greetings, dear reader, and welcome to the last of the Verity books in the first trilogy!

I wrote at the beginning of *Vigil* that the city was not the city. It still isn't: the Brisbane of Verity's world is always a strange reflection of the real Brisbane I inhabit. Sometimes the walls between the two, though, are pretty thin and you can hear noises from the other side.

A note on the mentions of the University of Queensland: I did my undergrad degree at UQ, and part of an abortive law degree. Professor Bob Milns was one of my favourite lecturers in Ancient History so it delights me to set part of this book in the Antiquities Museum, which was named after him – and where I spent many hours leaving nose prints on the glass of any display cases that contained shiny things. Some of those very same nose prints have been left in some of the finest museums around the world, most recently the British Museum.

Also, for the keen-eyed: yes, I know there is no level 9 in the Michie Building – I made it up, that's what I do. But there *are* some most excellent grotesques around the Great Court and I suggest you take a walk around it one day and see if you can spot the ones voted Most Likely To Be Weyrd.

In the beginning . . .

. . . God created the heavens and the earth, *thought the archangel, and had to stop itself from giggling. Now the earth was formless and empty, darkness was over the surface of the deep, and the Spirit of God was hovering over the waters.*

Although not today, it wasn't. Today it was firmly seated on a mountain top, watching the world go by, big bare feet planted in the snow of Musala Peak in the Rila Mountains, rough sack robe thin against the cold – not that the freezing temperatures would have any effect on either angel or The Deity.

A deity.

If the angel had learned anything at all in its very long life, it was that there was more than one god on this planet, this plane, this place, and their powers and influence waxed and waned according to the belief of the mortals worshipping or ignoring them – and the angelic choir's own strength, much to its chagrin, also depended on this ratio.

Ramiel the Archangel, the Thunder of God, felt the tremors each time a heresy, be it Albigensian, Nestorian, something new from the Fraticelli or whatever, arose amongst the Faithful. Questioning brought doubt, a weakening of the creed and a concomitant dwindling of its own puissance. One of the high and holy, one of The Deity's chosen, its purview was to watch over those who rose from the dead. It had been made a lord of resurrection in its own right by the hand of the one who sat before him. Ramiel knew what it – he – had to do to rescue them all, be they heretic, mortal, angel. He must marshal what was being allowed to stagnate: take it by whatever means and become something new himself, rise higher to ensure that the faith, the belief, the credence did not fade or fail.

He had been loyal for such an age! He had believed so utterly: been resolute and steadfast for aeons. He had stood by The Deity even as the Shining One made his own play for power. This was not a treason he'd come to lightly.

It had taken the archangel a long time to find what he needed. The thing had had many lives and passed through many hands. It had been found and lost and found, over and again. It had borne myriad names, but two had stuck: the Dagger of Wilusa, for the Bronze Age settlement sometimes mistaken for Troy, although it was far older than that. Some said it had been wielded by Zeus to kill Kronos; with it, Abraham had intended to sacrifice his son; Incan priests had used it to cut hearts from chests. It belonged to the Amazon queens of old, passed from mother to daughter. Latterly, it been in the possession of the Brotherhood of Boatmen.

Its true history was of no concern to the archangel, and in any case, Ramiel preferred the other name, although he certainly did not whisper it as he strode the vaults of Heaven or the planes of the Earth. He'd kept its possession secret, avoiding the temptation to boast of its finding to his brothers — he had never even mentioned his search for the thing, fearing that no one else would understand his duty, his obligation, his need to set matters right.

The archangel pulled the God-Slayer from its sheath; the metal whispered the merest song, but Ramiel felt the weapon heating up. He watched the cold sunlight glint on the sharp edge, almost distracted by the watery sheen before remembering his purpose.

The All-Seeing, All-Knowing didn't even turn around: too trusting, too weary, too long past its time — nothing like it was meant to be.

Ramiel raised the dagger and plunged it into the surprisingly slender back.

Jagged shards of fire poured forth, silver and savage, from the rent in Godly flesh. If The Deity made any sound, Ramiel couldn't hear it over his own screaming, for the light was burning him as surely as molten mercury. It seared *and scorched, an inferno of strange heat and eldritch flame that appeared to fracture The Deity, although that might have been Ramiel's fevered mind playing tricks on him in those few seconds that lasted an eternity. At last, though, it felt like his agony had ended. He broke away from the conflagration of God and archangel, of melting mountaintop that would be recorded as an unexpected volcanic eruption in the histories of the monks who lived in the Rila Monastery not so far away. The intensity of the pain was such that he ceased to feel it; he could no longer see the splitting of the Godhead – indeed, he ceased to have much grip at all on his sanity (although, if asked, his brethren would have ventured that to attempt what he had, his reason had clearly already departed).*

Ramiel turned and spun as if released from an oppressive grip.

Then he fell.

And continued to fall.

Chapter One

I woke on the couch, stiff and sore and shivering and roundly cursing the bastard beeping a car horn outside my house. Alas, that person's identity was no mystery to me. She could just have phoned, but apparently she was hardwired for shitty behaviour. I was already regretting – well, everything, frankly. I fired off a fairly curt text, which might have contained a threat, and the *honk-honk-honking* ceased. So far, this day was sucking harder than any Monday had a right to.

If I could get warm, I could squeeze another five or maybe even ten minutes before the summons started again. I closed my eyes, curled into a ball and reached down to find the doona that had deserted me in the night, but my fingers came up empty. I grudgingly re-opened an eye and peered blearily around until I spied the thing just beyond my grasp. *Damn.* I'd had nightmares again last night, although I couldn't recall the specifics, but clearly they were enough to have had me tossing and turning and shot-putting my blanky across the room.

No real surprise there.

It was, after all, my first night without the comfort and joy of David and our daughter Maisie in the house; the first night without my mother Olivia making herself useful and indulging in all the domestic tasks she'd avoided for almost three decades. Not that I was complaining, since it meant *I* didn't have to do them. She might have been a new presence in our lives, but we'd very quickly got used to her.

And it was the last night I'd been officially employed by the Weyrd Council and answered to Zvezdomir 'Bela' Tepes, and the last night that Ziggi Hassman, newly revealed as my uncle, had chauffeured me around the city of Brisbane and joined me for our final work-related cake'n'beverages at Little Venice. That had been right after I'd confronted Sandor Verhoeven, head of the Council of Five, to give him one last opportunity to yell at me and tell me what I was doing was a very terrible idea – and not just a terrible idea but, in the whole history of terrible ideas, easily the *most* terrible . . .

And today was the first day of my new job.

Said job, I noted, didn't come with a key to any executive washroom, nor was there a plush corner office and there was definitely no employer-paid superannuation, holiday pay or sick leave, but I did get a replacement assistant-cum-driver – which would have been fine, had Ziggi's replacement not wanted to kill me. Oh, and did I mention? My new boss was a psychotic, broken-arsed archangel who insisted he was the Guardian of the Southern Gate of the Underworld.

So why would I take such a job when my previous position had sweet benefits like Ziggi as my back-up, reporting to my ex (in as much as I ever reported to anyone) and the chance to get punctured in increasingly creative fashions?

Well, mostly because that was the price of the lives of those I loved: the price of rescuing my mother from the dreadful bargain she'd made many years ago with the aforementioned broken-arsed archangel, and the price of some breathing space while I figured out how the Hell I was going to get myself out of the equally dreadful bargain I'd made myself about a month ago with that self-same heavenly representative.

Unsurprisingly, last night I'd had myself quite the little pity party. I'd *obviously* fallen asleep on the couch unintentionally, and the presence of the doona certainly didn't suggest *any* premeditation . . . but I *really* didn't want to sleep in a bed that smelled of David, not when I didn't know when he'd be back in it. And while it hurt to think of David, that pain was almost bearable. Turned out, the lack of our daughter was not. As her nursery had been surrendered to Olivia, Maisie had been sharing our bedroom pretty much since her birth and the space was now redolent of talcum powder and lavender creams for soft baby skin. Maybe it was harder to let go of your own flesh? In any event, I couldn't endure the haunting sweet scent of my baby girl or the sight of the empty cradle.

I wouldn't be spending any great length of time in our bedroom until I'd restored my life to what passed for normalcy in Verityworld.

Maybe I'd move some clothes into Olivia's room . . . surely that wouldn't be quite so bad? I missed her too, but my feelings about my mother were complex, with a lot of ambivalence and resentment in the mix. She wasn't really a standard kind of mum – well, maybe that wasn't quite fair: her cooking skills were great, exceeded only by her assassination skills, which was kind of cool – and even though she was in large part the reason I was in my current predicament, the shape of her absence hurt. As a child, I'd been too young to really remember her, or feel the loss; now I knew her, or at least something of her.

She'd fallen in love with my father and paid a heavy price. She'd had to cut off contact with her own parents – and then she'd discovered what her exotic new husband Grigor truly was: a *Kinderfresser*, a child-eater, butcher to the Weyrd population of Brisbane, back when such things were still allowed. In her despair, she'd tried to drown herself, but her grief and anger had acted as a beacon for things tuned to such pain and she'd been pulled back to life. The Guardian of the

Southern Gate of the Underworld had offered a bargain: her service in return for revenge on Grigor, the man who'd promised so much and brought her so low, and she'd accepted.

Olivia had had a long time to regret that choice.

Covenants based on hatred seldom work out for the best, however, and all those years of doing the Guardian's bidding had taken their toll. Grigor had been dust for ages, but Olivia, still in servitude, finally couldn't take it any more and fled. She'd deserted me as a child, then come back to me, bringing a fucking great mess for me to clean up as an adult – but she'd protected my family for me when I couldn't, and it turned out, that counted for quite a lot, actually.

We would still have to have words when things had returned to normal, but for now, that could wait. I was horribly aware that I'd just sent my own child away and couldn't help wondering if one day I'd be having the same kind of uncomfortable conversations with Maisie. What if it took me years to sort out this shambles? How long before my daughter began to forget me?

I gave up on sleep, rolled off the couch and stretched, listening with displeasure to the cracking of my joints; surely I wasn't old enough for undignified old-person noises? Soon I'd be farting when I bent over: oh joy. Something new to look forward to.

My shower took considerably longer than it probably should have, given someone was waiting outside for me, but there was the washing of the hair, the conditioning of the hair, the exfoliating of the skin, the trimming of the nails, the brushing of the teeth, the blow-drying—

Okay, maybe that was taking the piss. I changed into jeans, Docs, a long-sleeved T-shirt and a leather jacket.

I was just considering making tea – my tastes had changed, apparently irrevocably, since Maisie's birth, which *no one* had warned me about – when the *honk-honk-honking* started up again. Even I was smart enough not to push matters too far.

'You took your own sweet time.'

Joyce dressed like a librarian – or at least my idea of a librarian – with a taste for Mary Janes of the Fluevog variety (quirky, architectural, more expensive than my pocket preferred) and frocks in tan, murky grey or muddy green, so as not to draw attention. As I climbed into the relatively new bronze Honda CRV she'd sourced from who-knew-where I saw that today was no sartorial exception. I guess camouflage is kind of important for an assassin, especially a *kitsune*. This morning, with her black hair swirled into a tight bun and her thick-rimmed glasses, the fox-girl assassin looked mostly harmless, which she most definitely was not.

The gods know Ziggi could be idiosyncratic in his observance of the Road Rules, but for someone who looked so law-abiding, her driving was incredibly careless, and not helped in the least by her apparent belief that hands were better used for gesticulating than holding the steering wheel. Joyce had taken me for a quick orientation the previous day and in that first twenty-minute trip I'd experienced more narrow squeaks and heard more horns blaring in anger than in all the *years* of Ziggi's chauffeuring. Still and all, I'd either become more Zen about stressful situations or better at hiding my conviction that I was going to die horribly in a hard-to-explain car accident. Or maybe it was just that since I'd lost my taste for coffee my nerves were no longer anywhere as jittery as they had been.

'You took your own sweet time,' Joyce repeated as she turned the key in the ignition.

I was doing up my seatbelt as quickly as humanly possibly, but she beat me, tearing onto the road without bothering to check for oncoming traffic seconds before I heard that faintly reassuring *click*. 'I had to iron my clothes.'

She didn't bother acknowledging my standard state of rumpled-ness, just floored the accelerator.

Approaching warp speed, Captain. It took an enormous amount of willpower not to grab whatever I could find and hang onto for dear life.

'You should give me a house key.'

I laughed out loud. 'Nope.'

'In case of emergency.'

'Joyce, you with a key to my house? *That* would be the emergency.'

'At least remove the fetish.'

'No fucking way.' The last time Joyce had visited, she'd left me a welcome home gift: the body of my delivery guy, Len. She'd also inadvertently left behind a hank of her fur, which I'd used to make a ward specifically tuned to keep her the Hell off my lawn. 'Perhaps you'd just like me to sit here while you slit my throat?' I offered as a compromise.

'Well, the boss wouldn't like that, so you're safe for a while,' she sneered, then jerked a thumb over her shoulder. 'He's sent something for you.'

'What?' I looked around at the back seat and spotted Joyce's brown satchel. A small white box, tidily decorated with a green ribbon, peaked out from under the flap. With more than a touch of envy, I asked, 'Did you do that? Because you have missed your true calling, Joyce. Gift-wrapping is a real art.' I briefly considered a universe where I could hand over all birthday and Christmas-gift-preparation to my new co-worker. *Briefly.*

'Just open it.'

Much though I loved presents, that was not going to happen, and it was not going to happen because I had a theory, albeit possibly a thoroughly wobbly and baseless one.

When Olivia was in his service, the Guardian had given her a sword and a strange kind of compact, a mirror through which to watch me. Mike Jones, one of the Weyrd security team who'd tried to protect me and mine, whose partner Jerry had died doing so, had found a pocket watch he had no recollection of buying. Joyce herself had carried a fine tantō, which had also come from the burned hand of her employer. The first time I'd travelled to the Underworld – *zero out of ten, would not willingly go again* – to find my mother, the Guardian had offered me a gift, of sorts: a reliquary, a piece of blindingly white bone inside an ancient locket of crystal and gold, something it – *he* – said I would need when I was hunting the things I needed to find.

I'd sent my mother back up topside but I'd hung on to her sword, planning to use it on the Guardian if I could. But the archangel just laughed and, at a gesture, the weapon had crumbled to rust and dust, which was inconvenient, I'll grant you, but revealing. The Guardian, drunk on his own cleverness, had declared, 'Do you think I have no control over the gifts I lend to my *menials*? Do you think I cannot destroy what was forged by my own will?'

See, the Guardian had a magic mirror in his lair to watch the minions, but my theory was this: the mirror only worked if his hapless slaves were carrying some kind of transmitter – *that's* why he was so keen on the present-giving. It was actually nothing to do with generosity, or providing the best tools for the job, and everything to do with staying in control.

I'd accepted the reliquary because it was essential to my task, but it was secured in a shoebox in a cupboard in the library at home. I'd made my mother throw away the compact, and Mike's watch was currently being stored in a lockbox in the Weyrd Archives for safekeeping, which I considered a comforting show of faith in my abilities: *someone* believed they'd eventually be able to examine it without risk. I wondered if the antique-looking copper bracelet on Joyce's right wrist was another tether.

'Go on. Open it,' she repeated.

'Maybe later.' *Like Hell*.

Joyce was smart enough not to insist, because nothing said *Drink from the poisoned chalice!* like starting an argument about it. Still, I thought it might be a good idea to provide a distraction. 'Those are nice, although they'd be nicer concealed.'

On the seat next to her bag were some new weapons: a set of *sai*, shiny and sharp as all get-out. Not nearly as pretty as the tantō had been, but she needed to replace it after something happened to it. Well, *I* happened to it.

'Not enchanted yet,' she said shortly. That meant they couldn't be shrunk down to nothing to fit neatly inside the satchel. Then she said, 'The boss wants to see you.'

'Nope! ' I said quickly, and in case she might have misunderstood me, 'Nope, nope, nope. I saw him yesterday – you know that, you were there. You drove me. In fact, yesterday's little tête-à-tête is the only reason you're here, remember?' I was *not* going down that hole again; there were ways into the Underworld other than death (the majority of folk, Weyrd and Normal) or stupidity (me), cracks and fissures, and I was no more keen on them than I was on taking another trip with the Boatman.

The archangel and I had done some fine-tuning of our bargain: he'd agreed that I needed to be able to speak with the Weyrd community (although my former colleagues, i.e. Bela and Ziggi, were off-limits, especially as, technically speaking, Ziggi was also family).

In return, I'd agreed to be accompanied by Joyce, even though I'd specifically demanded she be kept away from me.

'But—'

'It can wait until I've got something to report,' I said now. 'I am not being summoned every fucking day to play power games. Besides, I haven't had breakfast yet.'

In truth, I wasn't that hungry, but I *was* keen to procrastinate. I was no further along in my researches than I had been yesterday – and besides, I *really* hated the trip down to its lair. I had nothing to report and couldn't imagine the Guardian would have anything new to tell me – he was just trying to remind me who was in charge.

To her credit, Joyce didn't grit her teeth and/or swear out loud.

'Head towards Little Venice.'

'You know the Guardian doesn't like you going there.'

'I went over this yesterday! I will do this job, but I will do it *my* way. You both know that Little Venice is a hive of information' – besides, how else was I going to be sneaky and start circumventing the limitations placed on me if I didn't go to Little Venice? – 'so frankly, you can sod off.'

That kind of put paid to any chitchat for a while, until I noticed Joyce looking in the rear-view mirror with a frequency that my admittedly brief experience suggested was utterly foreign to her.

'What are you doing?'

She hesitated, then said, 'We're being followed.'

'You don't say?' I might have sounded flippant, but somehow I was not surprised.

'A black Mercedes GLE 350d, four-wheel drive, with super-tinted windows.'

'Terrible taste – very gangsta.'

'You don't sound very worried.'

'Oh, I'm worried, but I know I can't do much about it at the moment.'

'Don't you care? Doesn't it make you nervous? Just a little bit?'

'Hey, I'm working for a bastard who's considerably crazier than my usual boss. My family are in exile. I had to quit a job I didn't entirely hate. I've lost my delight in cake and coffee, and I'm in a car driven by someone who's plotting to kill me as soon as I finish this mission.' I ran a hand through my still-damp hair. I sighed. 'Besides, I know who it is.'

'Friend of yours?'

'Yeah – no. Let's just say she is well ahead of you in the "Let's kill Verity Fassbinder" queue.'

She paused, considering, then asked, 'What did you do?'

'Killed her family.'

'Wow. Like mother, like daughter.'

Chapter Two

One thing Joyce did have over Ziggi was the ability to find a parking space in West End. I was so used to being dropped halfway up Boundary Street and having to walk the rest of the way that the whole experience of getting out of a vehicle right outside Little Venice felt so uncanny that I wondered if she had some spell that simply removed anything in her path. Was there a pile of cars somewhere that had been in the wrong place, at the wrong time? Cars with befuddled folk sitting inside thinking, *How the Hell did I get here?* After a moment trying to work out exactly where her car-dump might be, I recognised I was being overly paranoid. Probably.

'Get a move on,' I urged, waiting impatiently for Joyce to catch up, but when she finally stood beside me on the footpath, I noticed she'd wrapped both hands around the strap of her bag and her knuckles were white. She was looking distinctly nervous.

I peered around, trying to spot the danger myself. 'What's wrong?'

'I don't feel . . . comfortable.'

'You're a bad-ass fox-girl assassin with a sea of blood on your paws and you don't feel *comfortable*?'

'What if they . . . ?' *Don't like me?* was the unspoken implication.

She fidgeted, scuffing the ground with the toe of one cognac-coloured Hope Promise, which kind of made my heart skip: those

14

shoes were too expensive for such treatment. Then I felt I was being disloyal to my Docs.

'They'll love you! Who doesn't love a *kitsune* as long as she doesn't drink so much she loses her shape, kills someone who looks at her sideways or steals a soul?' I rolled my eyes. 'Look, you'll be in good company: the Misses Norn have thought about injuring or giving me an atomic wedgie at least once.' I leaned close. 'You might not have noticed, but I'm *very* annoying. You'll barely register on the scale.'

To prove my point – and to hurry her along – I snapped my fingers and headed through the dark entranceway into what had once been my happy place before I lost my taste for rocket-fuel coffee and diabetes-inducing cakes.

Little Venice was variously a café-bar, a residence, a place to get your fortune told, and the spot where I'd taken out an angel who was trying to kill one of the Sisters Norn who ran the place. There were four big rooms downstairs, serviced by surly emo-Weyrd waitresses and one or two of the Sisters. The walled courtyard at the back was empty; it was too cold to sit out there and too early for the braziers to be lit. I couldn't see the small, colourful snakes – Aspasia's newest babies – that usually lurked in the foliage, so I guessed they were still curled up somewhere warm. The smell of last night's incense and this morning's coffee beans permeated the air.

Theodosia was behind the main bar, wearing jeans and one of the most unaccountably ugly sweaters I'd ever seen: a mangled mix of puce, asparagus green and yellow. Titian corkscrew curls piled haphazardly on top of her head looked set to tumble every time she rubbed the cloth over the marble bench, yet somehow the 'do stayed aloft. The quadrate cross scar left by the angel's ring at the base of her throat was still livid against her pale skin, even though it had been healed months ago. None of the Norns tried to conceal the marks, as if wanting the reminder of what had *almost* happened.

'Hey, Theo. That jumper – did you lose a bet?'

She looked up, lifted her middle finger and smiled, but her gaze very quickly slid past me and I watched as her grin became wider; her shoulders squared and her chest pushed out a little.

See, Joyce? Told you they'd love you. I almost felt miffed, but not quite.

'Fassbinder. Shouldn't you be politer to someone who catered your wedding? For free?'

'Very probably,' I agreed as she came out from behind the bar and enfolded me in a hug.

'Who's this cutie?' she whispered.

'Theo, this is Joyce, my' – *sidekick? friendly neighbourhood assassin?* Then I remembered I didn't actually have to be subtle about it – 'murderer-in-waiting.'

'Wow. Long line.'

'Truth.'

Theo was one of the Council of Five, who more or less ran the Weyrd community in Brisbane, so she knew why I'd quit working for them; that meant her sisters did too. But most of the Weyrd community didn't, and I was discovering that some of them saw my act as a betrayal; no matter how much my half-bloodedness, my interference, my very presence were resented, they had grown used to me. It certainly explained the looks I was getting from customers currently taking up real estate in Little Venice: glares, surprise, a dash of disdain and even downright hostility, none of which I troubled myself about.

'Joyce, this is Theodosia.'

Theo dropped me like yesterday's prawn shells and offered one slender hand to Joyce, who hesitated a moment, then blushed an astonishing shade of pink as she touched those long manicured fingers.

I bit down on a grin and settled onto one of the barstools, waiting patiently.

Of course, my patience always was a short-lived thing. 'Any chance of toast and tea?' I asked.

Reluctantly, Theo released Joyce and went back around the counter. She stuck two slices of bread in the toaster and started to prep a peppermint tea, then smiled at Joyce. 'Anything for you, lovely?'

Joyce shook her head and clambered onto a seat next to me; it was a rare treat to see her speechless.

'Oh, no. Joyce, you've got to try the Angel's Blessing.' One of the Norns' specialties: a three-layer thing of lemon mascarpone, mead jelly and marshmallow, sandwiched between the thinnest slices of sponge top and bottom.

'For breakfast?' Joyce clearly objected, but I would not be denied my vicarious eating.

'She'll need a coffee to wash that down.'

Theo began the making of Joyce's involuntary repast. 'So, Verity Fassbinder. How's the new job?'

I shrugged. 'Too soon to tell. Is Aspasia around?'

'What am I? Chopped liver? It hurts when you don't want to talk to me,' she said, but it was the merest of resentful glances.

'I *am* talking to you, Theo, but I also need to talk to Aspasia.'

She let out a high-pitched whistle, and I checked my ears to make sure blood hadn't started flowing.

'Wow. That's how you're communicating nowadays? Bet she loves that.' And as if to underline my point, a stream of profanities came from the direction of the kitchen, some of which were unrepeatable. Even I was impressed.

'How many fucking times do I fucking have to fucking tell you not to fucking whistle at me? I'm not a fucking dog!' Aspasia rocketed through the doorway, her black locks twisting into snakes that hissed and bit at the air. She pulled up short when she saw me – then she spotted Joyce and her eyes widened a bit more. The last time the *kitsune* had been here, she'd been having a drink with one of her now-deceased sisters as they tried to track my runaway mother. Aspasia knew exactly what those fox-girls had done in the meantime – and what Olivia had done to two of the three – so her surprise was quite reasonable. 'Hey.'

'Hey.' I rose and crossed over to her and as Theo engaged Joyce in a *So-tell-me-all-about-yourself* conversation, I was able to hug Aspasia and whisper, 'Friday night ten p.m., St Stephen's Cathedral.'

She slid a hand into and out of my back pocket; it wasn't like Aspasia to get touchy-feely – that was Theo's purview – so I didn't take it personally. When I felt the thick square of paper she'd left behind, my heart beat a little faster.

'Any news about our friendly neighbourhood sorceress-on-the-warpath?' I asked loudly.

She shook her head. 'Only a few sightings, but she hasn't contacted anyone that we know of – or anyone who's admitting to it, at least.'

'We don't know who her flunkies are nowadays,' I pointed out, 'so I'm not sure where she'd have found new ones, not when the Nadasy name is pretty much a dirty word.'

Dusana Nadasy might have money and power, but she'd made herself an outlaw amongst the Weyrd – not that anyone really blamed her for her actions. After all, Eleanor Aviva, disgraced member of the Council of Five, purchaser of illicit wine made from the tears of children, collector of exquisite handbags and secrets, powerful witch and all-round mercenary, had been the one to cast the spell that'd kept Dusana wrapped up in a bronze mermaid statue for fifteen years. Dusana, understandably peeved at this, had taken revenge by murdering Aviva in the Bishop's Palace (the Council's HQ), then fled the country.

Now, however, she had returned.

'Plus, everyone knows what you'd do to anyone who offers her succour.'

'Big word.' I sighed. 'Did she hang out with anyone when she was in disguise as Galina?' She had been glamoured to look like a short, stocky Eastern European bodyguard. *My* short, stocky Eastern European bodyguard.

'Bela and Mike and Jerry.'

'None of them count, do they? Jerry's dead. Mike had another master.' I pursed my lips. 'Only Bela knew who she really was, and what she did landed him in a bloody big pot of poo. I can't imagine he's nursing much of a soft spot for her nowadays.'

'And Bela does hold a grudge.'

'Yes, he does.'

'Not against you, though.'

'Oh, give the man time.'

She gave a concessionary nod, then said pointedly, 'There's *you*.'

'Yes, but she wants to *kill* me, not ask for my help.'

Even though I'd been the one to discover Dusana's predicament and get her set free, I had also killed her mother, her father and her son – all in self-defence, mind you, and *technically*, her son had killed her father, but that didn't matter because, well, dead is dead. While acting as a bodyguard for my family, she'd saved me from the machinations of a lovesick *smågubbar*, which had effectively wiped out her debt to me and left her free to kill me in revenge for that whole family massacre thing. It was quite straightforward, really.

I had to admit I'd thought I'd have had more time before she came for me, which might have simply been insane optimism. I thought I might at least get the current Guardian-related crisis off my plate before I had to worry about the last of the Nadasys calling me out, but just in case, I had made a point of warding the house against her in the same very specific manner as I'd done against Joyce (Bela had brought me an old locket of hers) and I was glad I'd gone to the trouble when, just a week ago, she had shown herself. I was wandering down the Queen Street Mall, clutching a huge bag of clothes I'd bought for Maisie to grow into while she was away from me, when I saw a tall, elegant woman standing on the spot where everyone in Brisbane arranges to meet, outside the Hungry Jack's at the crossroads of Queen and Albert. Her long blonde hair was teased into loose curls; her slim-fit indigo jeans looked tailor-made; they were teamed with a plain white T-shirt and low-heeled expensive leather boots. I recognised her posture, the tilt of the head, before I did the face and the blue-blue eyes.

My first thought was, *Shit. Not now.*

As if she'd heard me, she melted away – I'd never seen a more graceful transit – before a fuckwitted idea like rugby-tackling her in the crowded mall had even begun to cross my mind, which was probably for the best. For a while I wondered if I'd imagined her, then I decided her intention was just to let me know I was on her list. I still texted Bela to tell him she was back and warn him that he'd have to make some contingency plans with whoever was taking my place – *temporarily* – as the Council's enforcer/peacekeeper/fight-fin-isher-and-occasional-starter.

'Got anything for me to pass along?' asked Aspasia, interrupting my musing.

'I've seen her a couple of times. She's driving a black Mercedes

GLE 350d, with the license plate cunningly obscured – it's probably glamoured. I don't imagine she signed a nice, traceable rental agreement on it, and if she did buy it, it would've been sourced by some flunky or other. I doubt there'll be any paper or e-trail of her.'

'Toast's up,' Theo called, and I heard the sound of a knife being scraped over the surface.

'Don't be skimping on the butter,' I said, ignoring Theo poking out her tongue as she cut it into neat triangles, then wrapped it in greaseproof paper before brown-bagging it. A takeaway cup of tea waited beside it and Joyce waited beside *that*, giving me an impatient glare.

Theo pointed and said, 'This might well be the saddest breakfast known to man.'

'You're telling me.' I asked, 'How's Thaïs?'

'Melancholy,' she replied as she started polishing glasses. Her gaze was still fixed on Joyce.

'She's not getting sick, is she?' I said. 'Or ready to sleep again?'

Thaïs, the oldest sister, the most powerful of the Norns, was known to drop off for very long naps on occasion – astral travelling, she claimed, but who really knew? One thing was certain, and that was that it was generally at a very inconvenient time.

'Nah,' said Aspasia, joining Theo on the service side of the bar, 'you know her, she's got her moods.'

'Yeah.' I'd need to talk to Thaïs at some point, but only when I'd managed to drop my little shadow. There was a limit to what I was prepared to let the Guardian's spy know about, so I was already trying to work out a delicate balancing act of appearing to feed her information while withholding the important stuff. I noticed she'd polished off her breakfast cake, but didn't say a word.

'And not that it isn't always *lovely* to see you, of course, and to provide you with free food,' began Aspasia, adding her own bit of cover, 'but is there an actual reason for this visit?'

'A more sensitive soul might feel unwanted, you know.' I grabbed the cup and bag. 'A heads-up, really: I'm going to be asking questions about grails.'

'As in holy ones?' Theo grinned.

'As in all kinds: holy, unholy, metaphorical, et cetera. So I'd be grateful if you'd put your collective Nornly heads together and see what you can come up with. I'll be back.'

'When?'

'Probably when I'm hungry.' I raised the cup in salute. 'Say hi to Thaïs for me.'

'What exactly did that achieve?' asked Joyce as she unlocked the car.

'Well, I got breakfast.'

'Why didn't you ask about grails when we were there?'

'Thaïs was feeling out of sorts.'

'What does that matter?'

'Clearly you've never met Thaïs. If she's not in the mood, it's like pulling teeth from a very irritable bear. Besides, if I give them some time, they'll get me better intel.'

She rolled her eyes. 'And?'

'They'll have something for me in a day or so.' I pointed back at the shadowy entryway. 'If there's a scrap of knowledge that doesn't flow through there, it's not worth having. They collect everything, whispers, gossip, truths disguised as lies, lies that become truths, rumour, information, hints, certainties, possibilities, you name it. In a couple of days they'll have distilled whatever they can find about grails, and *that* will give me a place to start.'

I opened the door of the Honda, put the bag of toast on the

dashboard, tucked the tea securely into the cup holder, then climbed in, attempting the complex manoeuvre of buckling my seat belt before my bum even hit the soft leather seat – which was fortunate, because there was a screeching of tyres on asphalt and I was surprised not to feel the impact of a major crash as Joyce pulled out with her usual gay abandon. To her credit, she slammed on the brakes immediately and the black Mercedes GLE 350d swerved past us, the wind created by its passage making our vehicle rock. Before I could start swearing, Joyce gave what I could only describe as a primal snarl. Her shape shifted and flowed and for a moment all I could see was the fox that lived inside her human suit, surfacing on a rage that was entirely bestial.

Just as quickly, she was Joyce again: a pissed-off Joyce who floored the accelerator, sending us shooting out onto Boundary Street to a symphony of angry horns, profanities and the distinctive smell of burned rubber. Once I'd caught my breath and managed not to swallow my tongue I started cursing, but it was pretty obvious that my tantrum was having no effect whatsoever.

I forced myself to say calmly, 'Joyce? Hey, Joyce? You're not going to catch them and you're drawing attention to us.'

We squeaked through lights showing only the barest hint of amber at the intersection where Boundary Street sort of but didn't quite cross with Browning Street and sped up the hill; soon it would meet Cordelia Street and that was going to be ugly. I was about to try yelling again when a siren sounded, loud and up close, which finally succeeded in snapping my driver out of her mood. The foot came off the accelerator and our breakneck speed bled away as she pulled obediently off to the side like the good little librarian she so wasn't. I was fascinated by the effect the constabulary had on someone I knew for a fact had slit another's throat just to send me a message.

Eyeing the flashing red and blue lights of the cruiser behind us, I said the only reasonable thing I could think of under the circumstances. '*Fucking Hell*, Joyce!'

'I'm . . . sorry.' Strangely, she sounded quite genuine.

'What the Hell are we going to do? Do you even have a driving licence? Let me do the talking—'

Before she could reply there was a simultaneous tapping on my window and hers: one cop was standing on either side. I pressed the upsy-downsy button; Joyce did the same. As I listened to the hum of the electric window descending, I prepared my best what-seems-to-be-the-problem-officer? smile – which pretty much died when I saw who was standing beside me. Honestly, I should not have got out of bed that morning.

Constable Lacy Oldman, her blonde hair hanging in a perfectly straight ponytail from the back of her police cap, gave me the grin a crocodile gives a slow-moving tourist and said, 'Well, well, well. Verity Fassbinder.'

Chapter Three

It might come as a shock to some that I'm not at all familiar with the inside of the Watch House at Roma Street. The cells, I'm happy to report, were clean and tidy, but there's only so much you can do about nasty smells. Bleach provides its own challenges. I did my best to breathe shallowly for a couple of hours, which made me feel lightheaded. Sure, I *could* have pulled the door off its hinges, but that would have created more problems than it solved, and I couldn't imagine McIntyre admiring that little stunt.

We might have got away with the various traffic offences if it hadn't been for the shiny set of *sai* in full view on the back seat. Joyce went from being pretty damned mouthy to mousy in an astonishingly short amount of time. Oldman's brother-in-blue rested a hand on his Glock 22 as if we were likely to lean over and pluck one forth. 'Your Honour, it was our considered opinion that the suspects were about to start some shit.' And sure, we were, but not right at that particular juncture. It was all very unfair.

They'd housed Joyce a few doors down and although I would have gladly shared my opinion with her about fox-girls with impulse control, I thought it probably best not to share that particular opinion with those unfamiliar with the Weyrd underbelly of our fair city. Just because I wasn't working for the Council any more didn't mean I was going to expose its secrets. When we got out – if we ever did – I'd happily make my feelings known, but until then I fumed in silence.

When we'd been brought in, I'd asked the sergeant on the front desk to contact Inspector Rhonda McIntyre post-haste, which caused some eyebrow-raising but he nodded all the same . . . and two hours later I was still waiting, which made me wonder if maybe McIntyre wasn't talking to me or perhaps she was getting some amusement at my expense – she'd been no more pleased than Bela that I was leaving the employ of the Weyrd. Or maybe Constable Oldman had managed to thoroughly knobble me, telling the sergeant not to worry, she'd let McIntyre know then buggering off for a long lunch, sniggering all the way. Seriously, I wasn't the driver of the vehicle, so what the Hell was I even doing in there?

At last, however, the door opened, revealing Detective Inspector Rhonda McIntyre, a barrel in a navy suit, leaning against the door-frame. She grinned. 'You know, *this*' – she gestured to me, the cell, her – 'has occurred much later than I thought it would, Fassbinder.'

'Not in the mood for jokes.' My stomach growled.

'Oh, c'mon! Do you really expect me to pass up a chance like this?' She strode in and sat beside me on the thin bunk; she smelled faintly of a citrusy cologne. I glared at her until she shrugged and said, 'You're no fun.'

'I've got a few things on my mind at the moment, Rhonda.' I crossed my arms, looking, no doubt, like a sulky three-year-old. I sniffed again. 'You're very perfumed today.'

'I had a thing.'

'That makes you break out in oranges?'

'You're an idiot. Who's your friend?'

'The current millstone around my neck. Has she even got a licence? Oh, please tell me the car's not stolen.'

Rhonda shook her head. 'The car's registered to a Concord Holdings. Joyce Miller has a driver's licence registered in Victoria with an address in Coburg. No previous record.'

'That is some cover,' I muttered. 'The company isn't registered to her, though?'

'Nope, leads back through a series of shelf companies. I assume you want some digging done?'

'Well, since you're offering . . . Remember the delivery guy I found stuffed in the jacaranda tree in the back yard?' When she looked intrigued, I told her, 'That was her handiwork.'

'And I'm not arresting her *because*?'

'Because I need her for a while. And I *do* like being driven around.'

'The new job?'

'You know, the more I hear that phrase, the less I like it. Let's call it a *secondment*, shall we?'

'Right. Anything else you want to tell me?'

'Not at the moment. Anything you want to tell me about Constable Oldman and why she was in a position to put me in here? Also, make her find out who owns Concord Holdings, please.'

'I'm making her do a month in traffic for the experience. Putting you in here was her own idea of fun.'

'You keep that little turd away from me.'

'Now, now. Venting your spleen on Constable Oldman is quite unfair. She really couldn't do much else after any number of witnesses watched your vehicle committing a fairly impressive traffic violation – and that's before we get to the *very* pointy things on the back seat.' She clicked her tongue. 'Besides, that guy she's partnered with? He's a stickler. No way she could have let you off with a warning; he'd have made noise.' She patted my knee. 'So, you should be thanking Constable Oldman, as she had the good grace to tell me about your incarceration here a good couple of hours before the desk sergeant deigned to do so.'

'Then where the Hell have you been?'

'I had a thing – a Normal scene, not a Weyrd one, for a change. I do that sometimes.' She sounded wistful as she pulled from her pockets my house keys, wallet, mobile and the letter, all of which I'd had to surrender when 'checking in'. I paid proper attention to the handwriting on the envelope at last and swallowed. Rather than react in front of anyone, I stuffed it back in my jeans.

'Thanks. Anything interesting?'

'Probably a very cold case: a partial skull and some ribs discovered over at Teneriffe when an old commercial property was knocked down. Don't quote me but I reckon they've been there forty, fifty years at least.' She sighed. Even if you could solve a case so old with modern forensic techniques, it didn't really matter; that far down the track oftentimes both murderer and the victim's family were already dead. 'Now, would you like to get out of here? Or is the ambience so delightful that you'd prefer to make it a long-term booking?'

'Honestly, what I'd like is for you to keep Joyce in here for a couple of days, but I'm not sure any walls can hold her,' I grumbled as she stood and ushered me out into the corridor. 'How's Ellen?'

McIntyre's girlfriend Ellen was the morgue tech who took care of the Weyrd bodies which ended up there. I liked her.

'The hormones are making her pretty sick.'

'*Hormones?*' I stared at her.

'We're trying for a baby,' said McIntyre reluctantly.

That information was new and terrifying. '*You? Children?*'

'Shut up.'

'I seem to recall you using the words "vermin", "dirt magnets",

28

"ankle biters" and "tiny terrorists" in regard to other people's off-spring,' I pointed out helpfully.

'Shut up.'

'You know you can't take them back to IKEA and exchange them for something useful, right?'

'Shut up.'

'Were you not the woman who said, and I quote, "Thank Christ for my barren womb"?'

'Shut up.'

'Who are you and what have you done with Rhonda Caligula McIntyre?'

'That is *not* my middle name.' She sighed. 'Younger partners, Fassbinder. They want kids.' She shrugged again. 'Look, we earn good salaries, we're secure and I want Ellen to be happy, so we're doing the IVF thing. Who knows, maybe it'll be someone to look after us in our dotage.'

'Be nice to them, they'll be choosing your retirement village.'

'Christ, Fassbinder.' Another door opened for us and we stepped into a lift lobby. 'Can't you be a little positive?'

'You do remember what I just had to do to my family, right?'

I could see that was the moment she did.

'Yeah, okay, you get to be pissy – just this once.'

I took a deep breath. 'I'm happy for you, Rhonda,' I said, and I was, but I also had to bite back comments about how having kids would make you feel vulnerable *for ever*. That was my shit to deal with; she'd have her own in good time.

'Oh, hey. Your friend Joyce?'

'*Friend* is a very strong word.' The elevator pinged its arrival. 'Yeah, let her out. I guess. But hey, maybe give me a head start?'

'Thirty minutes? Three hours? Six?'

Tempting though it was, I went with three. 'Can I leave a note for her?'

'Anything else you'd like the Queensland Police Service to take care of for you? Shoeshine? Pick up your dry-cleaning?'

'I'm sensing some sarcasm, Rhonda.'

'It's like you're psychic.'

We got in the lift and she dropped her voice low, as if embarrassed. 'But hey, are you doing okay? Without the family . . . ?'

'Ask me on Friday when I've had to eat my own cooking for a week.' I was pretty sure the Norns were unlikely to consent to taking on that task. I sighed, thought about going back to my empty house and felt the bottom drop out of my stomach. 'I'll be okay, Rhonda. I don't have the luxury of falling apart.'

She patted my arm. 'Let me know if you need anything, okay? I'll tell Oldman you send apologies for thinking the worst of her.'

'Sure, you do that.'

She led me out through the brightly lit foyer of Police Headquarters so I didn't look completely like a common criminal. I thought for a moment, then asked, 'Oh hey, Rhonda? Check something else for me?'

My curt note told Joyce I'd see her at nine the next morning. It was only early afternoon, but the day's capers had sheered my nerves very thin and I didn't think I could maintain a calm demeanour while explaining to my chauffeur-cum-guard dog where she'd gone wrong. I assumed she'd head back down to face the Guardian and explain my absence and I felt a bit uncomfortable about the possible unpleasant consequences – right up until I remembered the kidnapping of my mother, threatening me and my unborn child, killing Len. I didn't feel quite so bad after that.

After I left the hospitality of the QPS, I headed for the Roma Street Parklands. I was starving – meanly, they hadn't allowed me to bring my breakfast into the cell – so I located a terrible tea and a slightly stale bagel. I'd planted myself on a bench and was contemplating the envelope when my mobile rang. I was tempted to ignore it, but I glanced at the number and my innate curiosity got the better of me. I tucked the letter away.

'Verity Fassbinder,' I answered, as if I didn't know who it was.

'Ms Fassbinder.' The tone was formal, clipped and decidedly unfriendly.

'Why, Eurycleia Kallos, fancy hearing from you. Am I to assume that Hell is soon to freeze over?' Eurycleia was the head of Brisbane's nest of sirens. I'd investigated her daughter's murder, saved her granddaughter and done my best to keep the siren death toll as low as possible when a gang of crusading angels was doing its best to wipe them out. Even so, Eurycleia was unaffected by any kind of gratitude; she saw me only as the person who'd prevented her from having custody of her granddaughter, Callie. I was not merely an impediment, I was an active annoyance, so her calling could only mean she wanted something.

As it turned out I was a little bit right and a little bit wrong.

'We missed you at our wedding,' I said cheerily. We hadn't.

'I'm calling on behalf of my mother,' she said frostily. 'There's no other reason.'

Now, her mother Ligeia, I liked, her former tendency to eat humans notwithstanding – gods, I hoped it was still *former*.

'Ah ha. So no brunch dates.' It was clear Eurycleia hadn't worked out that whole 'catching more flies with honey than vinegar' thing – or maybe she just didn't care. 'Out with it, Eurycleia; no need to prolong the agony for either of us.'

'Ligeia wishes to see you.'

Jeez, quit one job and everyone assumes you're at their beck and call. 'Look, Eurycleia—'

'My mother is sick, Ms Fassbinder.' Her voice began to tremble, and that shocked me more than anything. 'She is dying.'

'Oh.' I stared at the flowerbeds in front of me without seeing them; instead all I saw was Ligeia, sword in hand, dancing through a pack of angels, cutting them down as if she was harvesting poppies. She'd looked immortal then, eternal. 'Are you sure?'

'She is very old, Ms Fassbinder, very old indeed. As a young woman she saw the walls of Troy fall. All . . . all the signs are there, all the signs that show one of our kind is not long for this world. Although she is strong, I do not know when the end might come.' There was a pause. 'Will you attend upon her? Please?'

That last word must have cost her dearly. 'Yes. Of course.'

She gave me the address, then hung up without saying goodbye.

Day One without my family hadn't even finished and already I felt exhausted.

Chapter Four

The place proved to be less a cosy two-up-two-down and more a rambling mansion with several turrets. It was perched on a reach of the river high enough to add a few more zeros to the resale value, not quite Bulimba, not quite Balmoral. Last time I was in the neighbourhood it was to search the home of Eurycleia's dead daughter, Serena. There was a high red-brick wall, older than the current residence, running around the perimeter, with lots of trees poking over the top.

The taxi driver dropped me at a reinforced iron gate painted silver; when we'd arrived he'd looked around with an expression that said he couldn't recall seeing this place before, and he wouldn't remember it afterwards either; the glamour worked that way on Normals, which was handy as you didn't want someone returning out of curiosity and trying to poke around. The gate slid open silently before I even got my finger to the intercom; I stepped through and it closed right behind me with the softest of clangs. There must be a camera somewhere, but damned if I could find it. The driveway meandering through the grounds was long and windy; indeed, it seemed to be considerably longer and windier than the block of land should have allowed, but a lot of Weyrd things were like that.

As I followed the path, I noticed movement in the gardens: women with wings unfurled, their glamours forgotten for the moment, some sitting on the grass or on benches, idly eyeing me as I passed, or reading books, playing chess, talking, and others who flew effortlessly amongst the trees. Sirens don't like to think of themselves as 'Weyrd' even though they are. Mostly they tend to stay apart except to breed, and although Weyrd blood generally runs wild, in one of those rare instances of predictability siren genes tend to dominate. I wondered how many of Brisbane's winged conclave lived here and how many had just dropped in because Ligeia, the oldest of them, was dying, and it was an event that must be witnessed.

As I stepped out from the foliage I caught my first sight of the house: an old white jumble of verandahs and trellises, tall windows and heavy dark wood doors, never-ending extensions pushing the place back and back, and turrets that reached up and up. It wasn't entirely unlike the house at Ascot where Dusana Nadasy's mother Magda had plied her grisly wine-making trade. That thought didn't cheer me up much at all.

The front door was opened by a tall brunette siren who appeared to be in her twenties, which meant she was probably a thousand years old, but at least she smiled when she saw me. That was not a completely new experience, having a siren smiling at me not as if I were food, but rare enough to feel that way.

'The Matron said you would be visiting.' She gestured for me to come in. The foyer had a high ceiling and a mosaic-tiled floor where more winged women (looking more avian than they did nowadays) flew. 'I'm Thelxiope.'

From the distant days of my university degree with a double major in Classics, I dredged up the knowledge that her name meant 'eye pleasing', which she was, although I had yet to see a siren who wasn't. 'Thanks. Is Eurycleia around?'

She shook her head. 'She had other matters to attend to, Ms

Fassbinder.' Which was clearly code for *She didn't want to see you*. 'Please follow me.'

The house, like the grounds, was bigger on the inside, with lots of twists and turns and staircases. There were lots of doors, too, some open, and when I peeked through those I saw different styles, not just décor, but also time periods. I wondered if Eurycleia woke up thinking 'You know what? Today I'm feeling a bit a Jacobean. Sitting room number four, methinks.'

We went up and up and by the time we reached a thick oak door with a leaded glass panel in it (again, the winged woman motif), I was a bit out of breath and I reckoned we must be in one of the turrets I'd seen from the road. With one hand on the ornate silver doorknob shaped like a woman's head, Thelxiope said quietly, 'She tires quickly and sometimes she wanders in her memories.'

She opened the door to a snarl from inside. 'I heard that! I'm neither dead nor senile, not yet! You . . . you *egg yolk*!'

Thelxiope paled at what was obviously a deep insult for sirens, then with a rueful grin said, 'She probably won't bite. She likes *you*.'

I chose not to mention that time Ligeia had looked at me the way a drunk looks at a 2 a.m. kebab but thanked Thelxiope. As she quietly closed the door after me I could almost smell her relief. I found myself in something like a suite in a very expensive hotel, with arched windows from which rock stars would doubtless be throwing televisions sets.

The interior design screamed nineteenth-century French brothel, made of mahogany and velvet, ebony and silk, with everything in shades of crimson and black and gold. There were armoires, a chaise longue with an ermine throw and embroidered cushions, a dressing table, a roll-top desk. All that was missing was Alfred de Musset draped across a fainting couch.

The statement piece was an elaborately curtained four-poster bed, in the middle of which, beneath a brocade coverlet, sat the old siren Ligeia, propped up on a lot of pillows, her white cotton nightie at odds with her surroundings and making her look positively ghostly. The Exile had no truck with the manicuring most of the conclave went in for, and she didn't fight against her age – indeed, she had let it settle its full weight upon her: long grey-white hair, furrowed skin, feathered eyebrows, cracked lips, ancient eyes. Her teeth were unreasonably white, as if she'd always taken pride in *them*, the tools of her trade. She'd never shown any interest in integrating with humankind; she lived in shadow, fed on darkness and mortals, uncompromising in her tastes, even when they'd got her banished from her tribe. I'd made it a condition of seeing her granddaughter that she stop eating human flesh and that she obey the directives of the Weyrd Council. I didn't know if she still hunted in secret or if she'd held to her word, but there'd been no reports of any disappearances that might be connected to her, so I chose to have a little faith.

She'd never swaddled her wings, either, but I knew from past sightings they were now skeletal, the silver plumage grubby and sparse. Today she had covered them with a concealing glamour like the other sirens did when they walked the Normal world. I wondered at that.

'Girl,' she said, and grinned at me.

'Ligeia. You're looking very sprightly for someone supposedly on their death bed,' I said. She cackled.

'Don't be deceived by appearances, girl. My daughter doesn't want me to look like I'm dying, for all she may well want me gone.' So saying, Ligeia threw back the covers.

Sirens pretty much appear like human women, except for their legs, and even those are pretty fine if the feathers are removed by either waxing or electrolysis. It's mainly the feet with their three clawed toes at the front and one to the back that give them away. But Ligeia, devoted as she was to the old ways, had always kept her legs fully feathered.

The limbs she showed me now, however, were like burned twigs, blackened and shrivelled, bare of any kind of feathering, withered.

'Jesus,' I blurted before I could stop myself.

'Indeed,' she drawled. 'But *this* is the worst.'

And in a blink there were her wings, entirely naked chicken skin, and *charred*. As I watched, flakes of ebony sloughed off and floated away to be lost on the dark linen. Death was chewing at her from both ends.

'Oh. Oh, shit.' I swallowed. 'Is this . . . is this because I made you stop . . . ?'

'Eating people?' She laughed heartily, then shook her head. 'Ah, little strangeling' – that was Thaïs' nickname for me and I wondered how often I might have been the subject of their discussions – 'much though I'd enjoy tormenting you, no. No, this is old age pure and simple. When it comes for one like me, it is swift and ugly.'

'I'm sorry, Ligeia.' And I truly was. I'd always thought her eternal; just over a week ago at my wedding she'd looked fine.

'Chat to an old woman.'

'You called me here,' I reminded her and sat on the edge of the bed. 'What do you want to talk about, Ligeia? Sports? Fashion?'

'I wonder if I'll miss you when I'm gone? Will I even remember this world?' she mused. 'You know we only get one ride with the Boatman, we full-blood Weyrd?'

'Indeed I do.' It was one of the things I'd learned when I went to rescue my mother and found none of my friends could – or would – come with me to the Underworld. Only Normals and mixed-bloods like me could pass back and forth. The Weyrd got a one-way ticket and that was it.

'There will be a journey with my old friend.'

The Boatman ferried us all, Weyrd and Normal alike, to the Underworld. We drank from the Waters of Forgetting to let our memories go, just for a while, to make us light enough to pass on. It was temporary; it didn't mean you escaped your sins. You just checked your baggage for a bit, and when you moved on to wherever such things happened, they were returned to you so your heart might be weighed and all your deeds judged. Or that was what I'd been told. After that? Well, it was anyone's guess.

'Will it hurt, do you think? The judgement?' she asked, but there was no self-pity in her voice, no fear.

'I don't know, Ligeia. I guess it depends on the good you've done to balance out the bad.'

'Have I done enough, do you think?' She frowned and I recognised that it wasn't really a question for me. She reached out and waited politely for me to take her hand. It was cold, so cold and so very thin. I felt like I was holding frozen twigs, and I was nervous about gripping too hard lest I break anything.

'I would ask a favour of you, strangeling,' she said softly.

I should have known a trap was in the offing, what with the sadness and the softly-softly. I gave her a stern stare; I wasn't going to rush in where angels had regretted treading. 'Mmmmm?'

'Ah, ever the pragmatist.' She cackled again, but she didn't let my hand go when she began to cough. It took a long while to stop, and when it did, her lips were spattered crimson. She spat something scarlet out onto the bedspread where it was lost in a pattern of the same shades.

'Aw, jeez, Ligeia.'

She shrugged. *She* didn't have to clean it up.

'Can I call someone? Get you water?'

'There's no help for me now, girl, but do something else for me, lay my mind at rest.'

The trap snapped shut.

'Sneaky, old chicken. Ligeia, if I can do it in good conscience, I will.'

'What would we do without your fine conscience, Verity Fassbinder?' She grinned, then sobered. 'My great-granddaughter.'

Calliope Kallos, the child of a siren and a deadbeat angel called Tobit, a double-winged creature of prophecy a fanatical archangel had believed was the key to locating his missing god. Ligeia had taken out the arch and I'd removed Callie's wings so she couldn't be prophecy-fodder any more.

'Yeeees?'

'She is so young. My daughter is very set in her ways; she loves the girl, but not as much as she loves her own strictures and rules. Eurycleia has learned nothing from the loss of Serena. When I am gone Calliope will need someone to watch out for her, to temper Eurycleia's influence. Will you be my great-granddaughter's shield?'

What the Hell, Eurycleia didn't like me anyway. 'That I can do.'

With my agreement, she let my hand go. Those dreadful wings faded from view and she pulled the covers over her legs. Sure, it was emotional manipulation, but I would have agreed to look out for Callie no matter what and if it made the dying siren happy to have outwitted me, then fine.

Besides, *quid pro quo*.

'Do you feel up to answering some questions?'

She grinned. 'What, an ulterior motive? You're here for something other than the pleasure of my company?'

'What can I say? You're dying, so I need to take my shot while I can.'

Ligeia cackled. 'If the choice is listening to my daughter perform her grief and speaking with you, then I choose the latter.'

I paused, then said, 'You know I'm no fan of your daughter, Ligeia, but she does love you. She just has a . . . a different way of showing it. She'll be lost when you're gone.'

'I was gone for many years and she survived,' she said tartly.

'But then, she knew you were alive. Even in exile—'

'—which she ordered—'

'In all fairness, you were putting not just the sirens' conclave at risk, but all of Brisneyland's Weyrd.'

She grumbled under her breath.

'As I was saying, even in exile she knew you still breathed, still walked the earth, soared in the heavens, snacked on the unsuspecting populace.' I licked my lips. 'When you're gone, there'll be no hope for her of . . . a reunion, a reconciliation, whatever. There's only knowledge of the end of things as they once were.'

'How strange for you, then,' she said wonderingly, 'to have been certain of your own mother's death and then have her returned to you. How very strange to have that certainty removed.'

'The older I get, the less certain I am of anything.'

We sat in silence for a few moments, until she said softly, 'You were kind to say such things of Eurycleia. I will repay you with whatever truth I may own. I'll not tease you, little strangeling, although it amuses me to do so.'

'When we fought the angels?'

She nodded, grinned at the memory.

'You remember the archangel?'

'His heart was sweet. Delicious.'

'Okay, focus. Everything I've read says there aren't many of them left in the grand scheme of things, the arches at any rate. Angels feed on faith, right? Archangels need more than your common or garden angel, right?' I pressed out a breath. 'But, Ligeia, in the Underworld there's a thing hiding out, a burned, blackened thing, and it's another arch.'

She gave me a slow blink.

'You were the only reason we won that day. None of the other sirens had weapons beyond teeth and talons. Your sword made short work of it. You . . . the way you *moved* . . .' I couldn't keep the admiration out of my tone.

Still she said nothing and I wondered just how honest she was going to be.

'Ligeia, there's an archangel below us. He calls himself a Guardian, but as far as I can tell, he's squatting. He's hiding.'

'What need has such a place of a Guardian? The Boatman and his brotherhood are all that's needed.'

'Did you ever hear of another arch? One like I've described?'

She said nothing.

'He's insane, Ligeia, and he's looking for things – more specifically, he's got *me* looking for two things: a grail and a tyrant.'

Still nothing.

'Any ideas? About anything? Anything at all?'

She looked away, staring out the windows. At last she said, 'There are tales. Something . . . fell.'

I held my breath.

'Not the first fall, nor even the second, not the Shining One and his legions, but something different. Something about which the angelics do not speak. Something fell, but not here, somewhere in Europe. They whisper that a great sin was committed' – how strange to hear such a word on her lips! – 'and something fell in fire and smoke and blood. I know no more than that.'

'Shit.'

'But if there's anyone who might know, it would be the Reprobate.'

Tobit. Calliope's biological father. Serena Kallos' lover, who let her down. A slacker, a deadbeat: an angel out of step with his brethren.

Ligeia grinned. She liked him despite the interspecies enmity angels and sirens had turned into a fine art.

'Also, you might speak to the woman Aviva, with all her little spiderwebs.'

'Yes, except she's dead, remember?'

'That's never stopped anyone before.'

'But she's Weyrd – she can't come back.'

'No, but . . . we leave shades behind. Not ghosts, precisely, not the way the Normals do, but when you write on a notepad, the imprint goes through . . . we leave a kind of tracing on the skin of the world. You can summon that, the shade, the memory.' She said slyly, 'Titania Banks is *very* good at that sort of thing.'

Ligeia knew, though she'd pointedly not mentioned it, that I no longer had access to the Council's range of esoteric services, and she also knew I wasn't one to let that sort of thing stop me. I bit my lip, considering. It was Aviva who'd stolen my mother's body from the morgue and arranged for her delivery to the Guardian – not to mention the cryptic message Aviva had left for me when she lay dying in her cell in the Bishop's Palace.

I did indeed have a whole bunch of questions for her.

The old siren was looking weary; our time was coming to a close.

'Ever hear of any stories of a grail in Brisbane? Or a tyrant, perchance?'

She raised both eyebrows, their feathers fluttering. 'If such a thing came here – and I have not heard of it' – she paused, frowned in concentration – 'if . . . you might begin by looking for a cluster of miracles. Healings, and those who rise from the dead for no good reason. The churches keep tight hold of such items and record such marvels. Amongst the Weyrd they are seen as a source of position and prosperity. That is all I have for you, girl.'

'Not to worry.' She was tired, but I'd come and see her again, have another dig.

'Will you return?'

'Promise not to die before I do.'

She laughed through a wide, sharp-toothed smile.

I hesitated then said, 'Ligeia, if I were to find a grail? Would it help you?'

'Oh, undoubtedly.' Her smile faded. 'But I would not want it to. I have done with this world, little strangeling. I have done.'

Chapter Five

At home I picked at a Chinese takeaway in front of the television for a while before I remembered the letter from Aspasia again. It was crumpled and slightly damp from being sat on for lengthy periods, but that didn't matter. The handwriting on the front, just my name in blue pen, made my heart hurt.

There was supposed to be no contact, no communication. If the Guardian found out, he'd think I was playing him, and with Joyce hanging around like a bad smell, the risk of discovery was high. And I was in no way certain about what the Guardian could and could not see in my life. My half-arsed theory about him needing me to carry around something he had given me had not been field-tested.

What had been so urgent that David had written, and not just so soon, but at all? Sensitive New Age nappy-changing bloke though he was, he wasn't the type to send long epistles to the Romans, the Ephesians or me. Unsurprisingly, the letter was brief.

His spidery script told me he was well, that Olivia was also well and a great help, and Maisie was doing basically the same stuff she'd been doing at home one day ago: eating and pooping and cooing. And she was also growing at a rate of knots, which he could only assume was the result of Weyrd blood and not some form of gigantism (I made a mental note to check into that). My family were holed up at Ocean's Reach, a sort of Weyrd B&B/spa not far from Byron Bay.

The owner, Wanda Callander, a witch of some repute, had helped us when Maisie was born prematurely; of course, she'd also caused some problems by not being entirely upfront about a few things, not least her knowledge about a certain murderous, lovelorn *smågubbar* called Wilbur Wilson. So she had some good will to claw back if she didn't want to spend eternity on my shit-list. Providing sanctuary to my family was her first big step. David wrote that she and Olivia were getting on fine; that Wanda had produced both a kitten (Bitsa: bits of this, bits of that) and a puppy (German shepherd), who was apparently spending a lot of time licking Maisie. Gross. Devoted, but gross.

He told me that he loved me and he missed me.

That was all.

Such a small thing to be so breathtaking, so painful, so risky.

So *everything*.

Ocean's Reach was warded up the wazoo. My mother was one of the deadliest creatures I'd ever seen. Wanda could whip up a storm in a moment. And two very large Weyrd, Sulla and Jacquetta, were on duty. I had the Guardian's promise that he would leave my family alone, but that depended on me keeping my part of our bargain and not dividing my loyalties. *This* was skirting the boundaries, and when I say 'skirting' I mean, stepping over the line, dropping trousers and giving it the dark side of the moon. My only defence was that I'd not *asked* for the letter.

Flapping the page around in a combination of annoyance and frustration I saw the PS on the other side.

And yes, I know you'll be pissed off that I've written, V, but you need this. You need to remember we're here, that you're not alone at a time when you most feel it. Stay grounded, V, stay safe. Remember you're loved. Bring us home.

It took me a while to stop crying, and by the time I did the ink on the already-damp letter had run in places. My family was so newly made, this thing I'd never thought to have – suddenly I had it, and then even more suddenly, I didn't. That loss, even though I told myself every day it would not be a permanent one, hurt like Hell.

It made me think again about Dusana Nadasy, who'd lost her entire family for ever. Despite the fact her parents had been Evil with a capital E, and by all accounts she'd had too much attention from her father and not enough from her mother, they were still her parents. She'd been helpless, trapped inside a metal mermaid while she'd watched her son grow up lonely and neglected by his own father.

At least when I'd lost Olivia it was before I could remember her. My father, Grigor – also pretty Evil, let's face it – had loved me, and when he was gone Albert and May Brennan, my maternal grandparents, took me in and raised me and didn't make me feel bad about my mixed blood or my enormous strength. When the Weyrd community had maintained its distance from me, my grandparents had been there, keeping me grounded and normal, if not entirely Normal, and let me know that I was loved.

Dusana hadn't had anything like that. I pitied her, which was a weakness likely to get me killed. It wasn't lost on me that I was now almost as isolated as she'd been. *Almost.*

On the couch beside me, my phone bleeped. Just two words from Mel Wilkes, my next-door neighbour and one of my embarrassingly small number of Normal friends.

He's here.

Time to saddle up.

*

It was dark by the time I slipped down the back stairs and climbed over the spot where the fence between our properties sagged low; David had already made a point of hammering any stray nails into submission. Mel's daughter Lizzie had considerately left a bike out for me to trip on and I had to bite off a stream of profanities because nothing ruins covert ops like dropping the f-bomb at the top of your lungs in a nice quiet suburban back yard.

I limped up the steps to the back door. It took rather too long for my quiet knock to be answered; the sight of a slightly mussed Jost Marolf with smears of lipstick on his neck and collar told me why. Mel, behind him, was flushed and grinning. Signs of someone else's domestic happiness did nothing to improve my mood, but I was grown-up enough to recognise it as jealousy and managed not to snarl, 'Get a room.' I *did,* however, say meaningfully, 'You took your time.'

Jost hung his head and nodded, which was really his only option apart from saying, 'My apologies, I was sucking face with your friend!' which would have been way too undignified for Jost Marolf. His name meant 'border wolf' and the stubble of hair on his palms that occasionally grew through gave a hint why. Don't get me wrong: this was no hulking were with eyebrows joining in the middle and the stink of old meat on his breath. No, this was a *most* civilised Weyrd.

Marolf, current Archivist for the Weyrd Council, was utterly, ridiculously handsome: big blue eyes, chiselled jaw, thick blond hair, pouty lips and cheekbones so perfectly architectural you'd have thought someone had genetically engineered them. A charcoal-grey suit with the kind of exquisite cut that only a butt-load of money can buy hung from his gym-sculpted physique. I had to admit that looking at him made me sigh every time, just a little, and think, *Pretty, so pretty!* He had a perfect Archival pedigree too, having done his apprenticeship in the Great Library of Alexandria, followed by stints in the Great Archives of Prague and the Great Edinburgh Necropolis Archives. So, basically anywhere that had 'Great' in the title, he'd been there. What the Hell he'd done to get sent to Brisneyland remained a mystery.

Unusually, he was looking a bit tired, but maybe that was due to holding down a job and a burgeoning relationship. But when I squinted a bit I could make out his glamour was slightly wavery, unstable. I'd noticed that the first time I'd met him, but I'd put it down to the lighting in the Archives.

'Sorry, Verity,' he mumbled, interrupting my chain of thought.

Mel just poked out her tongue as she gave me a hug. 'How are you doing?'

'Tired, lonely and grumpy.'

'Okay, hot chocolate for you.'

I sat at the kitchen table and said a little wistfully, 'Lizzie in bed?'

'Yeah, school night.'

That made me sad, because I loved Lizzie and she was still young enough to have that whiff of baby about her. Mind you, that would've reminded me of Maisie, and of course, *that* would have made me cry, so it was probably best she'd already gone to bed.

I fixed my gaze on Jost as he took a seat across from me. 'So, how are things?'

'Well, thank you.' He glanced at Mel and an involuntary smile lifted his lips.

I sighed. 'Look, I could take you outside and discuss this, but that would require a degree of subtlety we all know I do not possess. So let's just go with this: Marolf, if you hurt my friend, I will hunt you down and force that very expensive and rather fetching tie down your throat.'

'V!' Mel gasped, but Jost just grinned, almost as if he was relieved.

'It's okay, Mel. It's a fair warning.' He gave me those blue, blue eyes and said, 'Verity Fassbinder, I promise that I've no intention of harming your friend. You'll find I'm loyal, faithful and reliable.'

Sounds like a golden retriever, I thought but didn't say.

He went on, 'I've been hurt myself, I've suffered loss . . . there was my Lady . . .' He pursed his lips, blinked, regrouped. 'I would not willingly visit that upon another.'

'Well, okay then.' I rubbed my face.

Mel put the mug of hot chocolate in front of me, saying, 'Have you eaten?'

'Would it surprise you to know I have?'

'Yes.'

I gave her an unfriendly stare, then said, 'Takeaway. So, what have you got for me, Mr Archivist?'

He looked nervous as he reached down to pick up a bulky-looking black leather portfolio from a kitchen chair beside him. 'Photocopies only; it wouldn't do for the clerks to notice anything out of place, but . . .'

'. . . but still important and highly confidential and I will take the very best care of them, I promise.' I softened my tone. 'I do appreciate it, Jost, and I am very aware of the risk you're taking to help me.'

Since I was no longer working for the Council of Five I had no way of accessing the Archives. Lucky for me Jost Marolf (a) liked me, (b) thought the work I did was important and essential, and (c) was trying to impress his new girlfriend. I was okay with that. I wasn't proud when it came to getting an advantage.

'Thank you. These are some brief histories of Weyrd families who are reputed to have owned grail objects and descriptions of those objects. At the top are the ones who live in Brisbane, but I included the others because I know you like to be thorough.'

'Aren't grails a little . . . Christian-y?' Mel knew bits and pieces about the Weyrd – how could she avoid it with me around? – and at some point I'd stopped trying to keep her in the dark for her own (and Lizzie's) protection because I figured a bit of knowledge might go a long way to safeguarding one or both of them some way down the track.

'Strictly speaking, there are all sorts of grails – and the term "grail" is just the one that's gained the most currency due to Christian mythology, Arthurian Romances, et cetera.'

'And Indiana Jones movies,' I contributed.

Quite rightly, Jost ignored me.

'So, there's the holy grail or *sang real*; some legends say Joseph of Arimathea brought it from the Holy Land to England. But before that there were the Irish legends of the Dagda's Cauldron of Plenty, or Undry, which supplied never-ending food and drink. The Welsh goddess Cerridwen is the Keeper of the Cauldron of Knowledge; there is the cauldron of Annwn, the Otherworld of the *Mabinogion*, also a sacred vessel, and Bran's Cauldron of Rebirth. Medea of Greek myth claimed to have one, but she lied.'

'Well, strictly speaking, she only lied to the daughters of King Pelias and gave them the wrong recipe. She did manage to reinvigorate Jason's father by putting him into a rather large Crockpot.'

It was worth mangling the myth to see the pained look on Jost's face, but he continued valiantly, 'In the romance of Peredur, the grail is actually a salver with John the Baptist's head on it. Tales of the Knights Templar say their grail was actually a stone, the *Lapsit Exillis*, which fell from Heaven. And the term "greals", which may nor may not be related to "grail", refers to brews of wisdom.' Jost handed over the folio. 'Those are just the highlights. There are a few others but I didn't worry about giving you grail histories; I figured you had your own books on the subject.' He hesitated. 'There's one thing I couldn't find, an old journal article by an Oxford academic who's been out at the University of Queensland for some years. It's noted in there; maybe you can track it or him down?'

It felt wrong that he'd give me work to do when I'd specifically hoped to avoid it, but I couldn't really complain. He'd saved me several days of research and I was grateful for that. 'How many Brisneyland families on the list?'

'Three.'

I could tell from his tone that none of them were going to be simple. I didn't feel strong enough to open the folder, so I asked for something that might just be easier. 'How does Titania Banks feel about me nowadays?'

Titania, long-time member of the Weyrd Council and huge fan of Stevie Nicks gypsy skirts, had never done me a bad turn.

'She always has a sly grin when you're mentioned.'

'That's a positive. I need her to meet me.'

'Why?'

'I need to talk to Eleanor Aviva.'

'But she's . . . oh.' He sat back, looking both admiring and stunned at the same time. 'If nothing else, that will get Titania's attention.'

We spent a few minutes discussing what would be needed if I could convince Titania Banks to stump up a bit of light necromancy – or not even really necromancy if you didn't think about it too hard: really just the eldritch equivalent of rubbing a pencil over a sheet of paper to see what someone had written on the missing top sheet.

Finally, I steeled myself and asked Jost about the three families who'd had grail objects. I felt vaguely ill when he gave me their names, although admittedly it did cut down the list a bit further.

'Oh, and Verity?'

'Mmmm?'

'That other thing you asked about? It should be here tomorrow.'

Chapter Six

'How are you doing?' I asked Joyce when she collected me the next day, right on time. There had been no undignified beeping, but she wasn't especially talkative or noticeably more friendly. At least there was no sign of the *sai*; I assumed she'd got them back from the cops and managed to get them enchanted overnight. I wondered how much of a hard time the Guardian had given her; there were no marks that I could see, but that meant nothing.

I took a deep breath. 'Look, I apologise.'

Her mouth dropped open and she glanced over at me, which meant we started to drift into the other lane on Lytton Road, which was bad.

'Joyce!'

The swift direction correction made my breakfast swirl in my stomach in an unhappy manner and I begged, 'Please, Joyce, concentrate on the driving.'

She mumbled something.

'No, *I'm* sorry,' I said again. 'I'm sorry that I sent you back to him on your own. I'm sorry if he punished you for my no-show.' I *didn't* apologise for leaving her in the lock-up, however.

I'd been kept awake last night wondering how the Guardian might chastise Joyce, an attack of conscience I neither needed nor wanted, but it didn't let me sleep until I acknowledged it and decided I had to make amends. Maybe it was the result of my musing about Dusana and how the loss of family scars you. Joyce had had two sisters until my mother took them out – admittedly in self-defence, which seemed to be the Fassbinder refrain – but that didn't diminish her grief. And when Olivia fled the Underworld, I suspected Joyce lost the only mother figure she remembered. Not to mention, I was annoyed at having failed to extract anything personal from Joyce about her life with the Guardian.

There was a long pause, then she said, 'No. No punishment this time.'

'Well . . . good.'

'You know, you're just like your fucking mother, the teacher's pet.' When she spoke it was with a petulance so bitter it might have stripped paint.

'You're . . . you really hate my mother, don't you?' She didn't answer. 'That kind of suggests to me that once upon a time you really liked her.'

Nothing.

'Joyce, I heard you call her *Mother*. Twice.' I spoke softly. 'She told me you'd put her heart back in when the Guardian took it out to show her who was boss.'

Still nothing. *I know you're out there, I can hear you breathing.*

'Whether you believe me or not, Olivia didn't kill your parents. I asked the Guardian straight out, and he admitted that he'd only sent her to collect you and your sisters. Whatever happened to them, it wasn't her doing.'

She grunted. Well, that was something. Then she asked, 'Why are we going to East Brisbane?'

'McIntyre called early this morning.'

'Fassbinder—'

'Hey, it's not working for the Weyrd Council. Joyce, it's pure

Normal, at least until proven otherwise. Look, she asked me to do this as a favour.' I sighed. 'Just let me take a peek. You can come in too, make sure I'm on the level.'

'Great,' she said, but her tone said otherwise.

'Take the next left onto Eskgrove Street. Detective Inspector McIntyre's found something nasty and unusual, which is, ironically, usual. Or rather, someone else did so and it landed on her desk with all the charm of birdshit from on high. Now turn right. It's over there somewhere.'

Behind us was Mowbray Park, the frequent habitat of international students from the nearby private college enjoying barbeques by the river, hipster parents and their designer offspring playing on the swings and canny undines doing their darnedest to steal from picnic baskets. Ahead was Laidlaw Street, one of those peculiar roads you get when an area has been long settled but developers have gradually moved in and started buying up the old fibro shacks and Queenslanders. Soon enough they're knocking them down, either to instal blocks of units remarkable only for their feature-lessness, or faux Mediterranean villas painted cappuccino outside and in, the perfect blank canvas for people's equally personality-free furniture.

There were still some holdouts: the big, venerable places built by those with a lot of money, thank you very much, who had no interest in any kind of upgrading or helping the lower orders into *their* suburb. Then there were the little old houses, generally tenanted by elderly folks who bought there when it wasn't a desirable locale and it was the best they could afford; they were hanging out until they died, then their kids could sell up and make a hefty profit. At the far end of the street Norman Creek let out into the Brisbane River, disgorging all manner of crud that people thought it okay to chuck into bodies of water; litter has never been any great respecter of class or land values.

'You reckon that'd be it then?' Joyce's voice was deadpan as she pulled us over into a magically appearing parking space. The three police cruisers, the SOCOs' van and the ambulance suggested she was probably right.

The place we'd pulled up in front of was old even for the neighbourhood: a one-storey affair of sandstone bricks and a pitched corrugated tin roof, with a wide, railing-less verandah on all sides. The white-painted supports and the window frames, which appeared to have no glass in them, were all peeling. A leaning picket fence that had lost the will to live demarcated a property that was set back amongst a lot of trees and a lot more overgrown grass. The front path, however, was clear, which suggested it got a fair bit of use, enough to make regrowth a slow affair. Of course, that might have had something to do with it being overshadowed on two sides by enormous modernist monstrosities that probably housed two adults and one point five kids in seven bedrooms, nine bathrooms, eleven car spaces, a media room, a family room, a home theatre and a pristine kitchen, all of which would be full of water and surprisingly noxious mud the next time the Brisbane River rose and did its best impersonation of the Nile.

What struck me immediately was that we could see the place quite clearly, so there was no glamour (*ergo* not a Weyrd home). McIntyre had been cagey this morning about details; I'd agreed to come as much to shut her up as anything. But now I was properly curious as to why she'd call me to a Normal crime scene.

A flare of light from the darkened doorway startled me, until I realised it was most likely a portable spotlight being set up so the Scene of Crimes Officers could take photos, collect evidence, and yell at people to watch where they were walking.

'There's your friend,' said Joyce, her tone hovering somewhere between resentment and glee. Spotting Constable Oldman, I understood: resentment because of the whole getting arrested thing, glee because Oldman had also arrested *me*.

'You know, a lot of people are telling me how many friends I've got and I'm starting to think they don't actually know what that word means,' I remarked as we climbed out of the car and headed towards the hole in the rickety wooden fence where a gate might once have been. 'Try not to aggravate dear Lacy and please don't offer her any deals with the devil; she doesn't like you anymore than she likes me. She'd probably have at you with her nightstick and I might not be able to bring myself to assist you.'

Truth be told, Joyce would probably have something pointy out of her satchel in a trice and the good constable would quickly find herself wondering where her skin had gone and why she felt a bit sting-y.

Lacy Oldman was waiting under the shade of the verandah roof. She wasn't stupid enough to try to stop me with the old, 'You'll have to stay back, this is a crime scene' line, but she was grinning ear-to-ear.

'Constable, may I compliment you on the cleanliness of your cells?'

'I'm sure you'll have more opportunities to get to know them even better.'

Losing patience, I said, 'You know, I might suggest to McIntyre that you should clean them with your toothbrush every now and then.' I pushed past her and stood on the threshold, taking in the scene.

The front room had been a kitchen. Doors in three of the walls led to bedrooms, a lounge of sorts and a bathroom. It was pokey and there wasn't much in the way of furniture, just the broken remains of a chair or two and a vintage Kelvinator fridge with its door hanging askew. Dust, dirt, twigs and leaves had blown in and there were little mounds of scat, probably from some marsupial or rat-related creature.

McIntyre was standing next to the only other item in the room: a single stained mattress in the middle of the floor. On that mattress was a body.

I focused for the moment on what the woman was wearing: a towelling dressing gown over, incongruously, a pair of vintage embroidered silk pyjamas in Schiaparelli pink, decorated with butterflies and flowers. The legs were wide and the top was fastened with gold Chinese-style knots. On her feet were the sort of towelling slippers everyone steals from five-star hotels in revenge for the cost of anything from the mini-bar. Her long hair, brunette streaked with silver, was tangled on the mattress beneath her, but I could see it would probably reach past her bottom if she stood. At first, I thought her middle-aged but as I got close enough and crouched at her head I realised she didn't look so much aged as *mummified*: a bizarre mix of too smooth and too wrinkled. She could have been anywhere between twenty or a hundred. And her mouth was . . . well, her lips and stumps of her teeth were blackened, as if someone had set fire inside her mouth; there were even traces of soot on her nose. Her eyes, wide grey-white marbles, were staring up at the ceiling.

'Well, that's . . . different.' I rose, looked at McIntyre and said, as if we'd not just chatted the day before, 'Hello.'

'Fassbinder.'

'Not that it isn't always a pleasure, Rhonda, but why am I here?'

'Does this look weird or Weyrd to you?' she asked, pointing at the body at our feet.

'*Well*, the house isn't glamoured, so not Weyrd, but *this*' – I made a sweeping gesture – 'looks like it's Council business.'

'What if she'd just been doing something dumb, like drinking accelerant or some kind of moonshine, which did not go well for her?'

'Have you ever seen *this* from drinking meths?' I asked, then offered, 'Localised spontaneous human combustion?'

'Is that even a thing?'

I shrugged. 'In her pyjamas? *Vintage* pyjamas? In an otherwise abandoned house?'

'Look up,' Joyce said from the doorway.

'Huh?' McIntyre and I replied simultaneously.

'The opposite of down. *The ceiling*.' Joyce pointed to direct our attention, just in case we'd forgotten our arses from our elbows.

Sure enough, across the ceiling was a fan of the same black soot. It must have been sprayed as she arched in her death throws. It hadn't been an easy parting with life.

'Definitely Weyrd,' I said. Flicking a look in Joyce's direction, I added, 'I can't touch this, McIntyre.'

'Nope.'

'There's a wedding ring on her left hand. Maybe there's an inscription?'

'I'll make sure Ellen checks it out.' McIntyre sighed. 'Well, I'd just better wait for your replacement to arrive.'

'My *what?*' I was probably more offended than I had any right to be.

'Oh, is that not the right word? How about . . . um . . . *locum?*'

'Who is it, Rhonda?'

'Your Uncle Ziggi.'

Ah. Well, who else was Bela going to get on short notice? And I had deliberately made a point of not asking because I had more than enough on my plate. Replacing anyone in any official sort of position in the Weyrd community generally took ages because there had to be checking out of affiliations, interviews and assorted political jostling. My half-Weyrd blood meant I'd been able to walk between worlds. At least Ziggi was well-known, and he was on the side of right, or whatever the Weyrd side was. Almost right. Slightly left of right. He could handle himself. But the idea of my uncle investigating things without me – without back-up – made me sad. And uncomfortable. And worried. And annoyed at Bela, but that was par for the course.

'It could still be spontaneous . . . no, it couldn't.' I pouted. 'Okay, then. Say hi to Ziggi for me.'

I gave her a meaningful glance I could only hope she interpreted as, *Keep me posted*.

In the car I tapped my fingers on the dashboard for a few moments, thinking, before Joyce cracked and said, 'Well?'

'Have you ever seen anything like that before?' I asked.

'Nope. And I've seen a lot of stuff.'

'Stuff indeed.'

'Where to now? Unless you've got any more Weyrd Council-adjacent jobs planned?'

'My, what an acidic little tongue you've got on you, Joyce. We're going out to the University of Queensland, so set sail for St Lucia.'

'We're in a car, not a boat.'

'Don't be so literal.'

As we pulled out, I caught sight of a disreputable-looking purple gypsy cab in the rear-view mirror, turning into the street behind us: Ziggi, arriving to do my job for me. I didn't wave. I didn't want Joyce to notice, or to notice me noticing.

Chapter Seven

Since making my ill-considered agreement with the Guardian I'd discovered a lot about grails. As with most things there was nothing new under the sun; what Jost and I had discussed with Mel was pretty much the executive summary, yet the article Josh mentioned made me curious. It was relatively modern – written in the 1960s rather than the 1460s, which was refreshingly, well, fresh – but as the Archivist had said, it was impossible to find a copy. There was only one mention of it, in another obscure journal article, a throw-away reference that was snide in the way only academics can manage, and nothing could be found in any database, not for love nor money, nor could I track down a brittle yellow hardcopy from some second-hand book dealer or other such purveyor of venerable stuff. Even Project Gutenberg let me down, and that was a major bummer.

Jost had suggested the author was still out at UQ, but he'd have to be pretty aged by now. Academics of a certain vintage don't generally move around a lot; there's the occasional Fellowship here and sabbatical there, but as a rule, the majority tend to finish out their careers in the same place. As the world of scholarly endeavour slowly contracted and senior administrators became less willing to pay for tenured professors when they could get away with abusing a pool of hungry sessional staff, the older generation of lecturers clung to the spots they knew best.

It was unlikely that the author would still be breathing – although the only natural enemies of the academic are management consultants and other academics – but if left unmolested in their natural surroundings, they did tend to live long and relatively happy lives. Imagine my delight and surprise to find Professor Tiberius Claudius Ulysses Harrow *was* still listed in the UQ Experts Directory.

I was also in luck because it was semester time, which meant there was not a parking spot to be had anywhere near the Great Court and apparently Joyce's powers didn't extend beyond out here, so I had no choice but to have her drop me outside the Forgan Smith building. I waved her off her with instructions to drive around the 114-hectare site and keep out of mischief. She might have made rude gestures as she sped away, almost running over three slow-moving international students. I wanted to keep some secrets in reserve, which was going to be difficult if the little snoop was with me all the time.

I walked in under the lintel inscribed with *Great is truth and mighty above all things* and into the foyer and the dry cool only sandstone can give. Above me was a void. The atrium spread to left and right becoming corridors with the apparently indestructible faux parquet floor that had been there when I was a student . . . and possibly also when the building was opened in 1949. There was that strange quiet that comes about when everyone's either in lectures or tutes or hiding in their offices enjoying the brief periods when no one is knocking on the door, begging for extensions with tales of how homework had been eaten by ravening packs of dogs.

I moved out into the Great Court to take in the grand vista of a semi-circle of sandstone buildings, cloisters and carefully placed trees on a sward of greenery suitable for the throwing of Frisbees or the sitting upon and eating of lunch. The jacarandas were decidedly unpurple, which meant exam time was a decent way off. To my left, what had once been the Central Library, now renamed the Cybrary for reasons which escaped me, and to the right, the Michie Building, which was where I was headed.

Around the cloisters were the grotesques, my favourite things, created by a series of sculptors over the years. In amongst the carvings of coats of arms, flora and fauna were the heads of famed academics, literary characters and various so-called mythical creatures. I'm fairly sure that at some point in every student's life you look at one of your lecturers and think, 'Gotta be an alien/werewolf/vampire/random monster.' There's always one who *only* lectures at night; another's office always smells like burned sugar; yet another who fails to turn up to classes on nights with a full moon. When I was an undergrad I liked the carvings because they reminded me of my childhood (before things went south), when I'd seen the real versions of those self-same mythical creatures: my father's friends would come to our house, let their glamours go and just *be* what they actually were for a while. There were the books, too, chiselled into the stone with such cunning craft you could almost flip their pages . . . an interesting contrast to the *other* carven books, the ones that were decidedly closed, with three clawed locks (always three) to keep whatever knowledge was in there from getting out.

The Michie Building directory listed Dr Harrow's office as being up on Level 9. The lifts were as slow-moving as I remembered them, although they were better lit and smelled less like wet dog. When I stepped out into the corridor it took a few moments for my eyes to adjust to the alternating wells of shadow and light; the fluoros only penetrated so far. Downstairs there'd been signs of renovations since the 1970s; up here it looked like gentrification hadn't quite made it this far. The passages were narrow, some of the office doors were actually wearing cobwebs and the carpet was a student-resistant brown (although that might have just been an International University Standard). I looked around. Maybe no one came up here much and this was where they stored the adjunct professors prior to death? But nowhere had I seen the word 'adjunct' (which basically means 'We don't pay you') attached to Harrow's name. Not to mention, I'd not seen any other professorial names on the directory downstairs – so maybe he taught Ph.D. students in his dotage?

Professor Harrow had a corner office, which takes quite some effort to acquire and is hard to hang onto, unless you're around so long that no one actually remembers you've got a prime piece of university real estate. I knocked and waited for about thirty seconds, then put my ear to the door. Someone was definitely rustling about in there. Once again, I could have viewed this as an opportunity to rip the door from its hinges, but I regarded it as a sign of personal growth that I did not choose that option. Even I had learned that wasn't the best way to start a conversation. Also, I didn't want to give an elderly academic a heart attack. Besides, I could stand there for an age just knocking quietly and being really, really annoying.

I knocked again.

And again.

And again.

Until a *sotto voce* profanity sounded from inside – admittedly less on the *sotto* side of things – and the unmistakable heavy flutter of paper falling from a desk. Probably a thesis or a stack of marking or filing that someone had been meaning to get to since 1983. I replaced my grin with an expression of wide-eyed innocence as the door was unlocked and pulled open about six inches.

A woman – young, brunette, short and with the unsurprisingly harassed look of a second-year Ph.D. student – frowned out. Behind her I could see a sliver of the room, chairs and desk piled high with papers, overflowing bookshelves. A fan of paper covered the floor, presumably the one that had recently been a cataract.

'What? I'm in the middle of marking?'

'I don't wish to bother you, but I'm looking for Professor Harrow. You're not him, I guess.'

She made an irritated noise. 'I'm Sophie, his research assistant. What do you want?'

'I'm interested in an article of his and I haven't been able to find a copy – there's not even a listing in the library system.'

She barely managed not to roll her eyes, then said with ill-concealed impatience, 'What's it called?'

'"The Healing Vessel: Grails, Chalices and Cups of Plenty".' I'd memorised the title, it was catchy.

Her eyebrows knitted together like a pair of mating caterpillars. 'I've never heard of that one.'

'It's from 1964. His first published article.'

'I don't remember seeing that one.'

'The now-defunct *Journal of Critical Mythology*? Volume 5, issue 2?'

She frowned a bit more, then shrugged and poked a thumb at the mess behind her. 'They've hired me to catalogue everything and I'm still working on it, so it's entirely possible that's one I've yet to come across. He's pretty prolific, or was, at any rate.'

'He's not dead is he?'

'Oh, no. Just not here.'

'If not here, then where?'

An eye-roll, a proper one this time. 'Where he always is: downstairs.' I must have looked blank because she followed up with, 'In the Antiquities Museum.'

'And how will I recognise him?'

'Look for someone with the air of a man who's forgotten where he's put the other half of his ham sandwich.' With that she shut the door. She'd obviously had the comment locked and loaded for some time. I was glad she'd finally had a chance to use it.

I took the lift back down to the ground floor and brighter, wider corridors.

The RD Milns Antiquities Museum was very fine. It was on an upper level in my day, but had been rehoused into a considerably better location. It was a well-thought-out maze of display cases containing awesome old stuff: red and black figure vases, verdigris-encrusted figurines, shiny things in the form of rings, necklaces, earrings and bracelets, glassware, chunks of rock that only an expert could identify the significance of (and maybe not even then) and coins. Lots and lots of coins. I wandered through it as though I had no goal, leaving nose prints on cases whenever anything caught my eye, until I found in a back corner a gentleman who matched Sophie's description.

His age was anywhere between 'farting dust' and 'might have done carpentry on the Ark'. Long grey hair was mostly held back in a ponytail; like his eyebrows, it held no trace of whatever its original colour had been. His jeans were that shade of blue and cut generally seen only on aged dads, uncles and granddads: saggy in the arse and pulled high in the direction of the armpits. A battered leather belt held them up. His shirt was blue too, battered chambray, and he'd kicked off his brogues, which hadn't seen polish in quite some time. He sat in front of a glass case, staring intently at a grave-marker, a stela engraved with a rather rotund-looking goddess Diana and a hunting dog.

'Professor Harrow?' I said.

He startled as if I'd woken him, blinking at me with very brown eyes.

'Professor Tiberius Claudius Ulysses Harrow?'

'That's me, isn't it?' he said with a beatific smile and a beautiful English accent undiminished by years in Australia.

'Gods, I hope so. I'm Verity Fassbinder, Professor, I was hoping to ask you a couple of questions.'

'Oh. Certainly?' He said it as if it was a question he needed to know the answer to.

'Your research assistant said you'd be here.'

'That'd be Sophie,' he said, then, 'Isn't it?'

'Yes, sir, indeed it is. May I sit with you?'

He shuffled across the padded bench and gestured to the vacant space. This close I caught the aroma of mothballs and Old Spice, a bit like my grandfather, although Albert Brennan had been rather lighter on the mothballs; my grandmother wouldn't have allowed anything else. Professor Harrow smiled and said, 'How can I help? I should warn you,' he added, tapping at his forehead, 'sometimes I forget things.'

'That's fine, Professor. I was wondering if you might have a copy of an article you wrote about grails.'

'"The Healing Vessel: Grails, Chalices and Cups of Plenty"!' His smile was brilliant. 'My first published article. It made my name. Mind you, it was easier then. Or maybe it was harder. I'm not sure.' He frowned, all doddery academic lovey.

'It's awfully hard to find.'

'Oh, I'm sure there's one upstairs somewhere. Sophie will find it. Can you give me a way to reach you?'

I fished out a business card and handed it over. His eyes moved across my name curiously, before he slid it into the top pocket of his shirt, tapping the place over his heart twice as if to make sure he'd remember. I suspected I'd need to follow up.

'I don't suppose you can give me an executive summary?'

'Of course: it's all about grails, you see, and the different forms they might take. Some were great vats or baths that the dead would be immersed in to be brought back to life. Like the Gundestrup Cauldron. The problem was that such resurrections left the returned without voice. Then there were cups or bowls that provided an endless supply of food and/or drink so no warrior went away hungry – exceptionally useful on the campaign trail, don't you know. An army marches on its stomach!'

Fascinating though all that was, it was nothing new, so I prodded, 'But what precisely was your thesis, Professor? What put you on the fast track, so to speak?'

'Oh. I know that. I *should* . . .' He bit his lip, thinking. Tears of frustration pooled in his eyes but I was already patting his arm.

'Not to worry, Professor. I shouldn't have troubled you.' He grabbed my hand and held it with surprising strength. 'I'll be in contact with Sophie.'

'You do that, Ms Fassbinder. Sophie's a gem, she'll be able to help you.' He smiled gently. 'I'm feeling very tired.'

'Can I help you back to your office?'

'Oh, no – I'm not that doddery! I'll just sit here quietly for a while. It's my favourite spot.' He pointed at the stela. 'A father had this made for his daughter's grave. She was only eight. Such a dreadful thing, to bury a child.' He paused, and I wondered if he'd done that very thing.

'Do you have children, Ms Fasssbinder?'

'A daughter.' I swallowed. I couldn't imagine having to lay Maisie in the ground. I shook myself.

My companion glanced at me as if he knew why. 'How fortunate. A daughter's a blessing, they say, don't they?'

'I think so. I think my grandmother used to say it.' She'd said no such thing, but I didn't want him to think me entirely disagreeable. 'Thank you for your time, Professor Harrow.'

'Goodbye, Ms Fassbinder. It was a pleasure to meet you – I hope to see you again.'

I took a proper turn around the Great Court after I'd left the professor, then I texted Joyce, politely asking for her to collect me from the spot she'd dropped me off. While she took her time turning up – which, let's face it, came fairly low on the scale of vengeful acts – I thought about what the old man had told me.

Specifically, I thought about this: he'd talked about grails being used on Normals. The items might well be eldritch, though not necessarily Weyrd or Weyrd-crafted, but the effect they had was on Normals. Yet Weyrd families kept grails as marks of status, so could they use them? If yes, then why was there not a fecund black market in grails? What if a Weyrd returned to life in such a fashion became . . . worse? Unrecognisable to themselves and their own kind? Harrow'd said that those (Normals) immersed in renewal cauldrons returned voiceless – what if the effect of resurrection, for want of a better word, on the Weyrd was too terrifying to be countenanced? Was that why Ligeia hadn't been interested? Maybe that was why the Old High Weyrd still clung to their grails, their vessels of power: *We're too scared to use this, but we've got it anyway.* Like nuclear weapons?

Weyrd didn't get a second chance after death . . . even those who loved me had been so terrified of the journey, of not being able to return, that they'd refused to come with me to the Underworld to rescue my mother . . . yet Joyce and her sisters had *lived* there. I assumed the Guardian had caused some breach in the everyday, created some kind of exception for the fox-girls . . . but what if . . . ?

The beeping of a horn interrupted my thought process.

'Get anything?' asked Joyce as I buckled in.

'I made an old man cry.'

'Why am I not surprised?'

'You're very cynical.'

My mobile bleeped with a text from Jost: Titania Banks was happy to see me and help out, provided I could be discreet: *Could I?* He gave me the address, a time and a list of things I should bring.

'Anything important?' Joyce asked.

'Just McIntyre, reminding me that Constable Oldman hates me.' That appeared to allay her suspicions; anything close to the truth is the best kind of lie you can tell. 'Hey, go left here on Coldridge, then again onto Carmody. Then right onto Hawken at the roundabout.'

'Where are we going now?'

'Highland Terrace. Joyce, do you know much progress the Guardian had made in his search for the grail before I came on board?'

'We didn't know anything about it until . . . after your mother ran. He . . . didn't trust us with that task.' She waited for the traffic to clear the Chancellor's Place Roundabout then swung around it, heading towards the Ville.

'Nor Olivia.' When I'd confronted the Guardian he had maintained he'd been *waiting for me*. Waiting for me to be in pain and angry; to be suffering from the betrayals of my nearest and dearest. He was used to dealing with people who were broken by their lives and their griefs. Sure, I was pissed off at Olivia's desertion of me as a child, at Bela and Ziggi for keeping secrets from me – especially about Ziggi's relationship to me – but that was it; I was just cross. Maybe if it had all happened before David, before Maisie, the Guardian *might* have got some traction – but it hadn't and so he'd over-played his hand. It wasn't that I was better than anyone else, but I *knew* what he really was, even if he'd forgotten.

Joyce added, 'I don't know all of his soldiers – it's not like we go away for team-building exercises.'

That made me laugh harder than I thought I ever would at Joyce. 'You know what, if you weren't so determined to kill me we'd probably get along really well.'

'You're dreaming.'

'Yeah, probably. Go right here.' We turned into a small lane running between Highland Terrace and Ninth Avenue; on our right was a cute spook shop, with *Third Eye Books* emblazoned in an easy-to-read font. Outside there were a lot of plants in big expensive terracotta pots, a mass of pink and white flowers, in spite of the cold weather. Merrily Vaughan knew enough magic to get them to bloom all year round, even if she wasn't great shakes on a lot of other stuff. The shop looked terrific and she did a roaring trade in the area, telling fortunes and selling herbs, smudge, floaty skirts and books on New Age strategies for everything from wealth to better sleeping patterns. I didn't have to like Merrily to acknowledge she stocked good-quality merchandise – including the stuff Titania needed. Plus, I was in the vicinity.

I looked at Joyce. 'You'd better stay in the car.'

Chapter Eight

There was an envelope lying on the doorstep when I got home, your standard buff A4 thing, not overly fat. First of all, I made toast with Vegemite and cheese (brain food) and a cup of peppermint tea, then I took the envelope into the lounge room and planted myself on the couch. Turning the television on for the sake of background noise was a new habit, but it helped cover up the fact I was alone in a house that had only recently been filled with the sounds of a happy family learning how to live with each other. I scoffed dinner while the cheese was still gooey enough to offset the beefy bite of the Vegemite, then tore open the envelope.

The folder was a little smaller than A4 and made of some kind of fine pale leather. A note from Jost was tucked in the front of a sheaf of papers folded into folios and sewn roughly together with dark thread. The Archivist's handwriting was as precise as his dress-sense: a lovely, looping copperplate script so exquisite that I made a mental note to never let him see my psychotic chicken-scrawl.

Verity,

This is all I could lay my hands on at short notice. It is the translation of an older document, but gives you a history (of sorts) of your family's Jägers, or their beginnings, at least. I will continue to seek further.

Jost

The pages were onion-thin and freckled with brown spots; there were crossing-outs, ink blots, and the occasional doodle of cats with wings, pigs with human feet, and a man's body with an ass's head. There was no illumination, however, no big caps, and the script was mostly readable: possibly done on the scribe's day off as a practice-piece. I was grateful for the translation into English; if it had been in its original German I'd have been there for ever.

Ziggi had said his – *our* – family had been bound to the dark Queen of Thuringia back in the day, which had made me wonder, *What about now?* My father, Grigor, had served until his death, working for Vadim Nadasy, one of the queen's sons. Ziggi had fled rather than become a *Jäger*, one of the queen's huntsmen, which begged the question, who was serving her now? Was she even alive? Did I have an army of cousins (some with eyes in the backs of their heads so they would be better hunters, others who acted as butchers, *Kinderfressers*, who dressed what had been slaughtered by their siblings who rode to the hunt)? I knew Ziggi's defection had put my family at risk of being wiped out; my father's subsequent swearing of fealty to Vadim Nadasy had saved the clan, but his getting caught had almost exposed the Brisbane Weyrd to the gaze of the Normals, so it felt like we might have reached zero sum again – or at least right up until I'd taken out most of the still-extant Nadasys in Brisbane.

I'd asked Jost to do some digging mostly because I had a child now, and my history was hers. It didn't matter how much I wanted to avoid looking too closely at the strange fruit of my family tree; I needed to be prepared for my daughter.

I sipped the tea, bracing myself for a family history that did not promise to be either warm or fuzzy. It started with a list of names, a bunch of *begats* and the position they held in the Weyrd society of the time, and my eyes glazed over until I got to this part:

The true origins of the Jägers can be traced to a calumny and an atrocity.

I felt a bit bad about thinking, 'Some excitement at last!'

Berhta, the daughter of Gotfrid and Bertrâdis, was born late to their marriage: an only child, and beautiful, with hair of red-gold, creamy skin and eyes of blue, the heir to her parents' considerable estates and fortunes. This made her a much-sought-after bride for princes and merchant-lords alike, both Weyrd and Normal, but Berhta refused them all. Her parents begged her to make some concession to this intransigence and she agreed: she would marry the man who could match her in the hunt.

Now, Berhta was a notoriously fine horsewoman; she'd never fallen and never failed to take her quarry. It was said she had hunted down the Great Hart of Harz, though it took five days; she never left the saddle and all her companions dropped behind. Indeed, some gave up on her rather than wait and returned to her parents' castle to report her loss, her death, for surely there could have been no other fate? She had ridden off a cliff, had tumbled into a fast-flowing river, had thrown herself into the deepest lake, been taken by spirits of the forest . . .

And yet there was a homecoming: Berhta, triumphant, the body of the enormous hart slung across the backs of her four fierce black hunting dogs. Berhta, filthy, scratched, her hunting habit ripped, her hair wild with twigs, and blossoms sprouting there. Berhta, inexorable and indomitable.

She could not be unseated. She rode the roughest terrain, the subtlest trails. She lived for the chase, for the heating of her own blood, the feel of the prey's red warmth on her forehead for she wore it each and every time, claiming that every hunt was a new blooding, a new challenge, a new milestone, and the death of each beast deserved such a tribute.

Berhta was primal, terrifying, atavistic.

Yet suitors thought her worth the challenge: she was beautiful and clever and rich, so why would they not?

They came from all over Europe, the high and the low, the rich and the poor, those with ancient breeding and those without, those with the ink barely dried on the Letters Patent of their Ennoblement. Those who could barely sit on a horse and those who'd been born in the saddle, they all came to try their luck.

Many died, but that deterred none of them. They still tried to keep up, though Berhta took the narrowest trails, the highest jumps, swam her white horse through raging rivers that gave no quarter to man nor beast. Those who survived were often maimed in body and mind. Their terror of the hunt was exceeded only by their terror of Berhta, she who was without fear — for if a woman had no fear of anything, how could she ever be a good and dutiful wife?

Eventually, the flow of suitors trickled as her reputation as a cause of death began to outweigh the potential of her fortune as the source of an easy life. Berhta herself was delighted - what need had she of a husband? She took what pleasure she needed from village lads and stableboys, and girls too, for that matter. She produced four daughters out of wedlock, fulfilling the need for heirs, and they were good girls and true, or so she believed. If they shared their mother's love of hunting far too much, well, their grandparents were prepared to tolerate it. Berhta's parents had long ago passed from despair to despond, then finally reached neutrality. Their daughter would have her own way.

Then came the mage, seeking Berhta's fortune and hand.

And Berhta, who could predict which way any creature she might hunt would jump, had not reckoned on this sort of man: a prince, and proud, a mage and malign. He came with charm and gifts, he was handsome, beautiful almost, his words honeyed and wise. Her parents took him to their hearts — and three of her daughters too; maids and stableboys, servants and free folk, all fell under his spell.

All but Berhta.

He asked for her hand in marriage.

She offered her usual challenge.

He smiled, though its warmth did not reach his eyes, and accepted.

The hunting party set off bright and early. Hour after hours they roamed, and the group grew smaller and smaller with each passing, until even Berhta's daughters were left behind, until at last there were only Berhta and her suitor.

Then, at last, only the suitor was left to tell the tale: that Berhta had fallen from her mount, and thus she had forfeited and was obliged to become his bride. And he had left her in a clearing by a great oak tree to wash his face in a nearby stream — he had not been gone for so very long, but when he returned, he found his unwilling bride hanging from a branch of the oak tree by a knotted girdle, her final decision as to her state of un-matrimony made most clear.

And when the stragglers caught up, they did indeed find Berhta's body hanging thus — her suitor had not seen fit to take her down, deeming it right and correct that everyone should see for themselves what she had done.

Returning to her parents' castle, he told his tale with grief, distressed that she would be so adamant in her refusal of a husband. And in the days to come, when he'd recovered sufficiently from his distress, he asked that he might be allowed to marry one of her daughters. Legitimacy or otherwise mattered not a jot to him, he wanted but something fine to remember his Berhta by.

Berhta lay in state, not in a chapel, for the Weyrd did not worship in that fashion, but on an altar of the old religions in a cave beneath the castle. But when the day of her interment came, her corpse was nowhere to be found. Her suitor did not allow this to interfere with his plans: the very next day he stood ready in the castle grounds to marry Berhta's oldest daughter. But weddings are strange things, open to all manner of guests.

During the wedding feast, as the happy couple celebrated, Berhta returned to the world.

Berhta wore the skin of a deer, the one they'd been hunting. The great antlers had sunk into her forehead and now grew there. She told a different tale to the one her suitor had spun: that she had herself taken down the beast, that the mage had fallen from his mount, that she had laughed at him and told him to return to his own house, and then foolishly turned her back on him. He'd used his own belt to strangle the life from her, then taken her girdle and hung her high to cover what he'd done.

She had spent her days in between, refusing to pass over, fighting the terrible forces that pulled the Weyrd down to death and their final ride, until the god of the hunt came to her and demanded to know what she wanted. She was haunting his sacred places, keeping his animals in a state of fear, pulling at the fabric of the world by defying the laws of Weyrd death.

Life, she told the god. She wanted life and revenge. The hunt, for ever.

The god tried to reason with Berhta: she could hunt in the Beyond, new creatures, new prey.

But she knew as well as the god did that no one knew what was in the Beyond for the Weyrd, and Berhta replied that she would go nowhere. She would remain as she was, doing what damage she might until her way was given.

And purely to get rid of her, the god acquiesced, returning to her life and breath, all the while warning her of the consequences of such an act.

As she told this tale to her audience, Berhta lifted two fingers in the direction of the mage, moving from his toes to his head, and he was lifted off the ground. Two fingers of the other hand pointed from his crown to the tips of his boots — and his entire skin came right off. It took him quite some time to die. By right of vengeance she could have taken him as a serf, made him work out his debt to her for ever, or until such time as she might have felt merciful, but Berhta had been reborn in blood; she took the red price due to her.

Berhta came back with knowledge of other things, such as that of her four daughters, the mage had taken three to bed. Those were the daughters she turned into hunting hounds, with fur of the reddest hue. The fourth, the youngest, had remained loyal; she rode by her mother's side and inherited her place as the Dark Queen's Jäger when the time came for such passing. No one knew what became of Berhta after that. Some say she hunts still in the deepest, darkest parts of the forest.

This was the blood that ran through Ziggi's veins.

My veins.

My little girl's veins.

The blood of my however-many-greats-grandmother or aunty, Frau Berhta, so brimful of attitude that a god had given in to her demands. I thought about apples and trees and felt sort of proud but sort of terrified. None of this boded well for Maisie's teenage years.

I couldn't help but note that Jost's account had been thin on the ground about the consequences of a Weyrd returning. Pretty clearly Berhta hanging around showed a good whack of power on her part in the first place, to defy death, and not give many fucks about any ructions she caused in doing so. It was hard to know if her ruthless destruction of her killer was something new, or something she'd have done anyway. I was prepared to bet the latter: Berhta did not strike me as a particularly gentle, forgiving soul.

Idly, I ran a finger over the folder, feeling the texture, how strange it was – then I stopped and looked down. What I'd been touching was a mole with a hair growing out of it. It wasn't just leather: it was skin. Human skin.

I'd seen terrible things before, even done terrible things, but somehow pondering whether or not the skin belonged to the mage . . . that's when I felt Vegemite and cheese bubbling at the back of my throat and ran for the bathroom. I had a long shower afterwards, and took some small comfort that maybe I wasn't as bad as my blood suggested I should be.

Chapter Nine

'It's so good to see you, Verity!' Christos Alexander, casually but perfectly dressed in charcoal-grey trousers and a vibrant green shirt, his long dark hair flowing casually over his shoulders, led us into a warm, sunny lounge. A Royal Albert Regency Blue tea set waited on a coffee table, the fragrance of Lady Grey wafting upwards with the steam, and there was a plate of lavender-iced cupcakes that made me salivate – maybe not the way I used to, before Maisie's birth and all the life- and taste-changing hormones that had come with that, but in a satisfying way that suggested I might yet again, at some point in the future, be able to consume cakes like a champion.

'You just saw me at the wedding,' I reminded him.

'Yes, but it's *always* nice.' His look implied *not* always, and we grinned. Then he looked at Joyce and said, 'I'm sorry, lovely, I didn't get your name?'

'That's because she didn't give it. I'm Joyce.'

'She's appalling, really.'

'I'm right here, people.' I chose a comfy chintzy chair. 'You're adults, you can introduce yourselves.'

'Work experience?' he asked in a fashion that suggested he knew the state of affairs, and offered Joyce the plate of cupcakes first. He talked to Ligeia often enough to be up on the news – she'd overcome her distaste for his humanity as soon as she realised how much he loved to gossip.

'Not precisely,' I hedged. 'Joyce is a . . . colleague.' I'd find the right word one day, if I lived long enough. 'Who's minding the shop, Christos?'

Christos lived in a cosy cottage in Oxford Street in Paddington. His jewellery store, Facet, was up on Latrobe Terrace, a brisk walk away, just enough to keep him fit, he said, and out of smelly gyms. He'd been best friends with Serena Kallos, she'd put him on her daughter's birth certificate as the father and he'd been her dad in all the ways that count since the day Callie had been born. I wish I could say the same for her biological father, Tobit the deadbeat dad angel.

'Nicholas, my new assistant. He opens up in the morning, which means I get to have breakfast with Callie and take her for a walk, then get some paperwork done before I head up.'

'And where's the munchkin now?'

He poured tea. 'Vicki's taking her for a walk. Normally I go with, but since I knew you were dropping in . . .'

'And who's "Vicki" when she's at home?' I worked hard to not sound strident.

He clicked his tongue in reproof. 'You *know* her. She used to work at Dinky Darlings.'

I blanked for a moment, then remembered a pretty girl with excellent taste in vintage clothes: the only person at the day-care centre who'd been at all helpful when I'd been looking for Callie. 'Vicki Anderson!'

Christos nodded. 'We'd kept in contact. I needed someone reliable and she needed a new job – she wasn't getting on with the new owners – and you know she used to babysit Callie for Serena, so our interests dovetailed nicely.'

I sipped at the Lady Grey, then bit into a lavender cupcake. Raspberry jam glooped out and I licked my hand like a bear with its paw in the honey jar.

'Dignified,' said Joyce.

I ignored her. 'So, someone reliable . . . which implies Tobit isn't any more? Also, where is he?'

'Hasn't been around much for a couple of months,' he said curtly. 'And your guess is as good as mine.'

I narrowed my eyes; everything had appeared to be fine a little over a week ago. 'You didn't say anything . . .'

'Perhaps you've forgotten but your last nine months or so have been occupied by pregnancy, dry-land drownings, a reunion with your mother – lovely woman by the way, but needs some styling, bit like you – and the last time I saw you, as you so correctly observed, was at your wedding.' He put a slim, well-manicured hand to his chest and declared, 'I might be a drama queen but even I know there are times when it's not *all* about me.'

'Hmmm. Ligeia didn't mention anything about him either.' Never one to mince words, our Ligeia; she called Tobit 'the Reprobate' to his face.

'She, like you, has other things on her mind.'

'True.' I rubbed at my face. 'So, Tobit?'

'Oh, for fuck's sake, *who's* Tobit?' Joyce snapped.

I casually pointed to the wall opposite us, hung with family photos. 'In the middle? That's Tobit.'

If you didn't know otherwise, the photograph, taken maybe a year ago, could pass for extremely good fancy dress or top-class cosplay: Tobit, enormous wings spread, black curls framing his face, was holding his tiny daughter in hands the size of footballs. He was staring down at her, disbelief filling his silver eyes; amused adoration filled her mother's violet gaze. It had taken Christos *ages* to get him to agree to pose for that one, to unfurl his wings and take on his true form, letting his natural attire, the white chiton and black armour – bracers and greaves shining like jet, sable boots with pale pearl lacings – appear. There was no breast plate, however, like the one the first archangel I'd met had worn, with a burning heart, a mosaic made of twelve precious stones, at its centre.

Angels and sirens were long-term enemies, and yet Tobit had fallen in love with one, fathered this child – then let both of them down. I'd thought Tobit was working through all that and had come out the other side, but Christos was suggesting I was wrong. Well, it wouldn't be the first time, and truth be told, I was kind of getting used to it.

'Well, Christos?' I asked.

'He's been distracted for ages – he managed to pull it together for your wedding, but he's been MIA this last week. Although he's still answering texts.' Christos held up a mobile. 'This one is for strictly Callie-related stuff. He responds to that, at least.'

I was listening carefully, but also keeping my eyes on Joyce. She'd stopped in front of the wall, focused on the photo I'd directed her to and gone very, *very* still. All that nervous energy that practically sparked from her had apparently drained away.

That picture was one of the reasons I'd wanted her to come with me on this visit, although actually seeing Tobit in the flesh would have had more dramatic impact.

The archangel who'd threatened Brisbane almost a year ago had been different to the common-or-garden variety, the rank and file. His kind were bigger, more powerful; they had commanded the legions of Heaven, marshalled them in battle and driven back the darkness when Lucifer made a play for the throne. But something had gone wrong in the Middle Ages, when their particular god had gone AWOL. They'd wandered ever since, fading away as conviction weakened and the world grew increasingly secular. They fed on faith of any sort – Christian, Muslim, Judaic, Baha'i, Hindu, Buddhist, whatever; it was about the *credence*. As that lessened, they starved and diminished. Angels hung around cities and slurped up the dregs of piety, eked out subsistence, but they no longer massed the way they once had, because there was not enough faith for them to feed on.

But I digress.

Tobit might have the habit of making himself appear smaller – a more reasonable six foot three – but he was the same size as that archangel Ligeia had killed, the one who'd wanted to sacrifice Calliope. And they were both the same size as the ruined, burned creature who called himself with utter belief the Guardian of the Southern Gate of the Underworld. And Tobit had been avoiding my calls since my wedding.

Joyce had worked for the Guardian all her life. My mother had mentored her and her sisters. None of them knew they were dealing with an angel. Joyce, despite her losses, remained unquestioning of the Guardian, at least as far as I could tell, although perhaps that was as much due to fear and habit as any great belief. But here was proof of something she'd never expected: she couldn't help but notice the similarities to her boss – the size, the *wings*. She reached to touch the image and stopped a couple of inches from it, but her fingers remained outstretched.

Christos raised his eyebrows. *Is she okay?* I nodded, even though I knew she wasn't. But Joyce needed to process what she was seeing. It had to sink in.

'Did anything in particular happen?' I asked, dragging him back to the subject at hand. 'Anything you can recall set him off?'

He shook his head. 'He's always been moody. It's hard to tell.'

'Do you think he's depressed?'

'Do angels get depressed?' He looked surprised.

'Well, as it's been amply demonstrated that they can go insane, why wouldn't they suffer the rest of the ills mortals do?' I sighed and reached for another cupcake. 'I need to talk to him.' Perhaps he could give me a lead on grails and on tyrants who might have annoyed an archangel beyond endurance.

'So that was your only reason for coming here?' He looked offended, sipping his tea and clutching at invisible pearls at his throat with the other hand.

I grinned. 'Of course not. I also came to eat your food, enjoy the delights of your company and hug your child while mine is away.'

As if on cue there was a noise at the door, the rattle of keys and a dulcet voice talking low to a child, who answered in even sweeter tones. Pram wheels rattled along the polished wooden floor and soon a stroller bearing an exquisitely lovely little girl came into the room, followed by a young woman with chestnut curls and big dark eyes sporting a full-skirted navy vintage 1950s frock (or a really good Hearts & Roses imitation), with a mustard-coloured swing coat open over the top. Completed by a pair of red Mary Janes, the look convinced me that nannies were paid too well, or at least the one in this house.

'Hey, Vicki.'

'Ms Fassbinder! How are you?' She sounded genuinely pleased to see me and came over for a hug, ignoring the hand I'd offered. Then she swung away immediately and began unbuckling the straps that held Calliope Kallos in place. The little girl had waited patiently, not plucking at her bonds but staring at the adults with those startling violet eyes. She smiled at each of us as if we were her subjects. I wondered if that was Eurycleia's influence, or perhaps she was just genetically disposed towards regal.

I'd cut off her wings, but she didn't appear to hold it against me. As soon as Vicki had her out of the pram, the pudgy little hands reached for me like pale pink starfish. She wasn't my little girl, not by a long shot, but I'd saved her and I was fond of her, and who knew how long it would be before I got to hold Maisie again. There wasn't much by way of baby smell because Callie was floral-scented like her father. But as soon as I took her into my arms, I knew it was a mistake.

The closeness as she curled against my chest made every part of me ache, bringing tears, hot and stinging, to my eyes. I instinctively tightened my grip on her, but she felt *wrong*. It wasn't her fault, but she wasn't mine and couldn't replace what was missing. It was stupid of me to think I could take comfort in her; I was just torturing myself. I'd tried by sheer force of will to put Maisie out of my mind, and sometimes I succeeded for an entire five seconds. I'd been diligently taking the herbal mix Wanda Callander made for me to dry up my milk, unneeded sustenance whose production would be an inconvenience, but it couldn't dry up the well of pain in my heart.

It was obvious I was going to cry. Vicki hurriedly took Callie from my numb grip, announcing loudly that the baby needed her morning tea. As she was borne off to the kitchen, the little girl watched me over her nanny's shoulder with a gaze centuries older than she was. I blinked, a lot, and eventually the tears went away, though the ache didn't.

I cleared my throat. 'Well, I guess we'd best be off. Anything you need from me, Christos?'

'Eurycleia.' He gave a mock shudder but I could see the truth behind it. He wasn't a brave man, the darling, but he was kind and good. I understood his concerns: if Tobit wasn't around and Ligeia was dying and I was working for someone else, who was going to stand between him and the leader of the nest?

'She hasn't thawed at all? After all this time? I mean, she still hates me, I get that. But you? You're delightful.'

'I know! What's wrong with the woman?' He laughed, then sobered. 'Honestly, V, I'm terrified of her. When she comes to visit, she barely speaks to me, just to Callie, and she whispers to her in a language I don't understand. I really am worried – who's going to look out for us?'

I threw a glance at Joyce, who was still standing motionless in front of the photograph, then said quietly, 'I'll talk to Bela.'

Christos nodded, satisfied.

When I'd cut off Calliope Kallos' wings – two sets, black closest to her skin, silver nestled between – in the lee of St Mary's Church just after the sirens had defeated the Arch and his cronies, I'd taken what marked her out as a child of prophecy. I'd given her the chance to change, to find her own way in the world. But the wings were only what the *archangel* had valued; she remained the object of her grandmother's obsession. Eurycleia had tried to mould her daughter Serena into a pleasing shape, but Serena had rebelled: she'd loved an angel, an enemy of her kind, and had his child, then died to save that child, let down by both her mother and her lover. Eurycleia wanted a second chance – not to be a better mother but to forge Callie as she'd failed to do with Serena. Ligeia didn't believe Eurycleia was capable of changing and I wasn't convinced Ligeia was wrong.

'Leave it with me, Christos.' I wiped my hands on my jeans. 'Joyce? C'mon.'

Chapter Ten

After leaving Christos' place we spent part of the day in the State Library, trawling through the stacks. I sent Joyce off to find every cat-alogued book that mentioned grails, then I read them – even though I already knew most of what was contained in those very ordinary vanilla tomes. I had far better, far *deeper*, information in my own library, but the aim of the exercise was to wear her down, bore her senseless – it certainly had that effect on me – and most importantly, give her something to report to the Guardian.

When she complained, I told her piously that ninety-five per cent of investigation was reading shit, and the other five per cent was chasing shit, although that wasn't strictly true. I figured that if I kept pushing repetitive tasks like this at her, she was going to get blasé, and if she got blasé, she'd stopped paying such close attention to me and then I might just get away with a few things. She hadn't mentioned the Guardian's gift again, which I took to be a good sign.

Looking through the piles of books reminded me that I'd not heard from Sophie the Research Assistant, so there was a good chance Professor Harrow had forgotten his promise somewhere between the elevator and his office door. He'd probably looked at my business card with surprise, then binned it. I'd ring in the morning, see if Sophie answered phones with more enthusiasm than she did doors, and ask her very nicely to find that article.

Just to compound the boredom, I made Joyce drive around the city for a while without bothering to tell her why we were going where we went. We drove past St Stephen's Cathedral, where I'd last encountered a bunch of the angelic choir supping on skerricks of faith. It was unlikely I'd spot Tobit, especially if he'd chosen to make himself invisible, and even if I could, it probably wouldn't be wise to speak to him in front of Joyce. Besides which, the Guardian had been quite specific about the forbidden nature of holy structures, which meant I wouldn't be setting foot anywhere near one, at least, not when Joyce could see me. But I did hope I might *sense* him . . .

. . . which was, of course, nothing but wishful thinking. All I could do for the moment was hope he'd respond to Christos' text on the Callie-phone in a reasonable period of time.

When we pulled up outside my place in the almost-dark of dusk, I rubbed my eyes, then rested my hand on the door handle.

'Joyce?' I'd been thinking carefully about my next words.

'Hmmm?' She didn't look at me, just stared straight ahead; she'd been pretty uncommunicative since she'd seen the photo of Tobit, apart from the complaining bit.

'I know you'll find it hard to believe coming from me, but here's a friendly word of advice: don't tell the Guardian you've seen an angel.'

The fox-girl gave me a glance then: resentful, but there was also something complicit about it.

'Don't ask him about angels, and sure as shit don't mention *arch*angels. I did once and it almost burst my eardrums.' I opened my door and slipped out onto the footpath. 'Whether you believe me or not, it's forgotten what it once was. They're dangerous enough when they *remember* what they are.'

She gave me a long look, but eventually she nodded and I felt like a conspiracy had been entered into. Or maybe not. Maybe she'd go back to the Underworld and blurt it out, confess all to Daddy. But somehow, I didn't think so. I was happy to let it fester in the back of her mind.

Inside, I feasted on a couple of wizened apples and an orange that probably should have gone to God a while ago, then napped for a couple of hours. Around eleven, after showering and making myself presentable, I called a cab. While I was waiting, I called Professor Harrow's office; I had no expectation of an answer but listened to the message in Sophie's dulcet tones, then left a gentle reminder.

I grabbed the plain hemp bag from Third Eye Books that had cost me an extra five bucks, left lights on in the kitchen to fool people I was still there and slipped down the back stairs. The temperature had dropped considerably and I was glad I'd had the forethought to wear my thick coat, which had the added bonus of being black, so handy for not being seen at night. I clambered over the fence into Mel's yard, crossed to the other side of the plot (carefully looking out for stray bicycles) and headed up the drive – until a piercing whisper stopped me in my tracks.

'Verity!'

The sound of Lizzie's voice was unexpected and almost the cause of an embarrassing trouser accident. 'Sssshh! Lizzie, you should be asleep—'

'Where are you going?' She sounded hurt. 'I've hardly seen you.'

'I know, baby. I'm sorry, but I've got a rotten job to do.'

'I miss Maisie.'

Lizzie had been an almost constant presence in the house since she and Mel had returned from holiday, and rather sweetly, she'd taken to calling Maisie her little sister.

'Me too.' I swallowed hard. 'Go back to bed, Lizzie. The sooner I get this done, the sooner Maisie will come home, sweetie.'

I pressed on up the driveway and turned a sharp right, hoping it was enough to avoid any watchers there might have been in the darkness – Joyce, Dusana, anyone. The taxi driver waiting at the bottom of the street was quiet, didn't say much except for *Hello*, *Goodbye* and *Thank you*, which was just fine by me. Even better, he didn't complain when I gave him directions. He got a good tip when he dropped me off thirty minutes later.

The address Jost had given me was in Wynnum, a nice bayside suburb with escalating house prices. I wasn't sure what I'd really expected, but it hadn't been an oddly narrow, blue-and-white faux-Cape Code with a covered garage to one side and a lap pool on the other. A streetlamp barely illuminated the front yard behind the high wooden fence.

It was all very simple . . . except that there were a lot of shadows, which always made me nervous. I stood in the middle of the road, staring, waiting for whatever or whoever was making my Spidey-sense tingle to show it/themselves. I took my hands out of my pockets, unzipped the coat and rolled my shoulders, loosening the muscles in case I had to fight. It had been a while since I'd hit anyone (sucker-punching Joyce in the Underworld didn't really count) and I wondered if I should get a workout bag for home. I didn't really need one, though, I just had to get my hands on them and unleash the Weyrd strength that had popped more than one head off its shoulders. It was a messy business, not much in the way of subtlety, but usually quite effective.

Shadows shifted.

I waited.

The tension built in my chest until I felt something would surely snap.

Still I waited.

In the end, the watcher lost patience with our game of chicken and a tall, thin young man with a wispy beard and long dirty-blond hair stepped into the light. He wore black leather trousers – he'd cook in them in a Brisbane summer – and a black Rammstein T-shirt. No coat against the cold, and I could make out goosebumps on his ropey arms. Gold caught the light at one ear. He glared at me for a bit, then shrugged and raised a hand. *C'mon.*

Still cautious, I crossed to stand beside him.

'I'm Ingo.'

'Verity Fassbinder.'

'The Mistress is waiting for you. Did you bring the stuff?' He had a vaguely Teutonic accent, but it sounded like he'd been trying some American inflections to tone it down. It wasn't a pretty mix.

I shook the hemp bag. I wasn't entirely sure why I'd had to bring all this stuff, but I was working on favours at this point: if Titania Banks had asked for a pony leading an elephant, I'd have done my damnedest to provide.

Ingo took the bag, then *faux*-casually raised a hand in the direction of that nice little house and the glamour shifted so I could see what was underneath. In place of the simple structure was a castle. A genuine freaking *castle*, made of black and grey masonry blocks, with a drawbridge, a moat and four round pointy towers.

'Holy crap!' The words felt punched out of me. I'd never seen a glamour so powerful, so *utter*. It wasn't just that she'd obscured the location; that was pretty standard. It was that she'd made the entire place so *small*, so *boring*, nothing to excite interest. What else could Titania Banks do if she put her mind to it?

'Yeah. This way.'

As we crossed the drawbridge I asked, 'So you do what?'

'I'm a nitromage.'

'And?'

'I blow shit up.'

'Right. What are you doing here?'

'I told you: I blow shit up.'

'But—'

'I live here.'

'Banks is, like, your mum?'

He smirked and didn't reply.

He looked to be in his early twenties, but he could have been much older; Weyrd don't age the same way Normals do. I examined him closely as our footsteps made the wooden drawbridge vibrate a little alarmingly. I couldn't figure out if he was wearing a glamour or not, but honestly, if he was glamoured, he should have done something with his hair. As it was, he looked like your standard young adult slacker, all patchouli oil and . . . oh yes, there it was: *gunpowder*.

He led me through the portcullis and into a paved courtyard with stables at one end. Four *very* tall black horses with fiery eyes stood in the stalls. Or maybe their eyes were just reflecting the burning torches spaced around the walls. Weyrd prefer fire; it reminds them of the old days. They watched us approach, their hooves hitting the stones, sending sparks that matched their eyes flying into the air. My Little Ponies they were not.

'Are there any—'

'There are no unicorns,' he said, and his bored tone made me wonder if he'd once hoped himself.

'Awwww.'

We turned away from the beasts, Ingo pushed open the left half of an arched wooden door banded with iron, then handed me through with the words, 'Watch your step.'

A steep staircase led into a grand hall with a high vaulted ceiling, complete with decorative coats of arms and less decorative swords and shields and battle-axes mounted on the walls. Ancient tapestries covered any spare hanging space. Three long banqueting tables, fully laid, ran the length of the room, looking as if the guests would appear as soon as I turned away, which made me wonder at the lack of people.

'Where is everyone one?' I asked.

'Titania made sure the way was clear for you. Best you not be seen here,' Ingo said as he led me towards a raised dais at the far end and through a door concealed behind another wall hanging. This one featured a much younger Titania Banks, determinedly naked, as Venus in a clamshell, if I wasn't very much mistaken. Then there were more stairs, made for a different age and skinnier people with much smaller feet than mine. Mind you, they didn't bother Ingo, who hoofed it up there like he was born to it. Maybe he was.

At the top of the staircase I stumbled, literally, into a round tower room, mostly empty except for the many candles, dripping wax everywhere. There was a circle painted on the floor in gold, with a pentacle inside it – so far, so traditional – and single candles at each point of the star. Titania Banks was sitting in a Savonarola chair set back against the far wall.

She was tiny, with a shoulder-length fall of sleek dark blonde hair, blue eyes bright against her olive skin and a mouth that was permanently lifted in a smile. Her amethyst dress would make any Romany fortune-teller proud – a very wealthy fortune-teller, for rings glittered on every finger and every seam of the dress shouted 'designer'. Banks had always appeared to find me amusing, but then again, she seemed to find most things and people amusing, so I didn't take it personally.

Sandor Verhoeven objected strongly when I quit my job, but Titania made no negative comment. She and Verhoeven were the longest-serving Council members (although he was the one who held the Brisbane Grant conferring power over the Weyrd community) and while she made no contrary remark, she'd also given no sign of agreeing with him. Theodosia Norn had supported me, as had Bela, if a little reluctantly. Only Udo Forsythe, the newest member of the Five and the most uncertain of his position, had stood beside Verhoeven in his objection; he'd given me a speech about obligation, responsibility and duty to one's people. When I flipped him the bird, he'd called me a half-breed; so much for 'one's people'.

I chose to view Titania's willingness to meet with me as a sign she wasn't entirely inimical to me. I could but hope.

'Ms Fassbinder, what a rare pleasure,' she sang. 'Darling Ingo found you.'

Ingo went to stand beside her chair, leaned down and gave her a long kiss. With tongue. And slurping. So, not his mum. Gods, I hoped not. I heard her murmur, 'Hostage of my heart.'

I cleared my throat, to remind them I was there and that this was really uncomfortable to witness. 'You look well, Titania. Thanks for seeing me on such short notice.'

'The beautiful Jost said you needed help.'

'Yes, and thank you—'

'Sandor is not pleased with you.'

'Nope.'

'Nor Udo.'

'He's kind of low on my care list.'

She laughed. 'So. Aviva.'

'Yes.'

'You need to realise, Verity,' she said carefully, 'that what I will bring back is merely an echo, a sliver of the past. It might not be able to give you what you want. Its memories might not be what you need – they might not be complete.'

'I'll take anything I can get,' I said honestly.

'Did you bring the requested items?'

I pointed at Ingo, who held up the bag. Titania accepted it, opened it and took a deep sniff. She smiled. 'Thank you.'

'What are you using it for in the ceremony?'

'Oh, I'm not. I just ran out.'

'That smudge was expensive,' I started, then snapped my mouth shut.

'Oh, I know. Thank you!'

I'd subjected myself to Merrily Vaughan's questionable company and I strongly suspected been overcharged, just so Titania could amuse herself? I let it go. Necromancy wasn't something to be done on the cheap, I guess.

'Something personal?' she asked. 'Of *hers*?'

'In the bag.'

'Perfect.' She dug beneath the packets of overpriced smudge and excavated the grey cardigan. I'd worn it into the Underworld; Aviva, being dead by then, had not objected.

Titania threw out a hand for Ingo to take and stood, still tiny despite the high-heeled red suede boots, barely reaching her paramour's shoulder. He led her to the top point of the pentacle where a shallow brazier waited. She neatly folded the cardi and placed it within.

'You set everything in place, dear?'

'Most certainly I did, just as you asked.'

'Darling boy.'

Ingo passed Titania an ornate golden dagger – impractical, given how soft gold is, but presumably this one didn't get much hard use

– and she gave him a bright smile, which he returned before loping to the bottom of the circle. I hadn't noticed before that a glimmering powder had been sprinkled over the top of the painted outline of the circle. Ingo took a torch from the wall and knelt, watching his mistress closely. As Titania made a fine, short incision across the palm of her hand, which began closing over almost immediately, Ingo touched the flame to the powder on the floor. The ignition was enthusiastic, fire crackling around both sides of the circle and heading towards Titania, who was busy shaking droplets of dark blood onto the cardi. So far, so easy, and it had only cost me five packets of expensive smudge.

The tongues of flame met in the space just in front of the tips of Titania's boots, then tore up the legs of the brazier to set the jumper alight. In the centre of the circle something began to rise: a smoky form, eight-legged, thick thoracic region, a woman's face on the body, with perfectly coiffed auburn hair.

Eleanor Aviva, sorceress, dealmaker, handbag aficionado, looked confused and hazy as she faded in and out. In that instant before anything happened, I knew *something* was wrong: that unerring instinct that always lets you know *just too late*—

Lightning crackled in the brazier bowl, shooting off the rapidly charring jumper – and it headed in just one direction: towards Titania Banks, travelling, I imagined, along the trajectory of the blood back to its owner. Banks tried to move, but she was caught in a net of silvery bolts, a cage wrapped around her like a jewellery setting, and she lit up like a firefly. I took a step forward, thinking to break the connection – not really thinking at all – and was blown back so hard I hit the stone wall behind me and it was goodnight, nurse.

Chapter Eleven

The darkness didn't last long, thankfully, but I knew the ache in my left shoulder where I'd hit the wall would. The left side of my face felt seared and when I put up a hand I found a fair bit of blood, coming from a thin cut. Just a stinging powder burn, I prayed, and a small scratch. A scar would give me that piratical air so beloved of the modern woman, but . . .

By the time I was able to sit up, the room had filled with all those Weyrd who weren't meant to see me, not that anyone was paying *me* any mind. Ingo was at the edge of the group surrounding Titania and trying to push his way in, but they might as well have been using a Roman shield-wall formation against him for all the good he was doing. He kept wiping away the blood running from a cut along his hairline so it didn't get into his eyes; he looked young and stunned and afraid. When he saw me levering myself upright, he rushed over to help me.

'They won't let me in,' he said urgently. 'They won't let me get to her.'

I gave him a look, but I staggered over to the jostling crowd. 'Oi! You lot, give the lady some air. If you're not actively helping then get the fuck out of the room!'

Some of the Weyrd looked over their shoulders at me: a tall guy with bad dreads, a stocky woman in a tailored navy suit and a very thin bald dude with the tendrils of tattoos reaching up from the v-neck of his grubby white T-shirt. I wondered if his body art meant anything beyond decoration, for many Weyrd didn't approve of using tattoos to throw a glamour or otherwise bolster their natural abilities. It was judged lazy to let something like that do your heavy lifting. But no one actually moved.

'Well, if you want to do things the hard way ...' I slapped my right hand down on the neck of the dreadlocked Weyrd, grabbed him by the scruff and hauled him a foot off the ground. His surprised grunt got the attention of the others as I threw him towards the door – in the gentlest way possible – before grabbing the next one, the be-suited recalcitrant, and giving her the heave-ho too. She went the way of her compatriot with a yelp.

Just a couple more and I had a path cleared to Titania Banks, with Ingo following closely. There was quite a lot of swearing, not to mention some general dissatisfaction from the crowd, but honestly, who the Hell cared? I laid my hand on the last shoulder – and let go pretty quickly when its owner turned to me.

Louise Arnold was a healer, Ziggi's occasional date and a generally nice person. She turned back and bent over Titania, taking her pulse with one hand while wiping the clotting blood from her soft features with the other. She gave me a worried glance, which was never a good thing to see on the face of someone whose talent is fixing broken people, especially when they were as good as Louise, and I should know, having benefited from her talents on too many previous occasions.

'How's she doing?' I asked, then glared at Ingo, who was busy elbowing aside the man who'd been acting as Titania's pillow, making her moan a little as she was bumped in the takeover bid. Louise hissed at Ingo – the only time I'd ever seen aggression from her – but he had eyes only for his lover's red-splattered features. Bruises were already forming on the olive skin, but I couldn't see any burn marks.

'Louise?' I asked.

'As far as I can tell at this point? Concussion, possibly burst eardrums' – she pointed to the ribbons of blood dripping off the delicate lobe – 'and maybe something got in. Whatever was she was trying to bring through?'

'Eleanor Aviva . . .'

Louise went white and I couldn't blame her; I didn't fancy a shade of the arachnoid Eleanor Aviva wandering around Banks' home, or indeed Brisbane, on her eight hairy legs either.

I said quickly, 'But I don't think it got a foothold. She disappeared just before the explosion. It's just a shade, a shell, a sliver of memory. Ingo? Do you remember anything?'

He looked up. 'Will she be all right?'

'I hope so,' said Louise. Her tight tone made me think she didn't like him much and I wondered if any of the castle's other inhabitants or vassals felt the same way. I wondered how long he'd been there, where he'd come from. I'd do some digging later, just as soon as my ears stopped ringing and my skin stopped stinging.

'Can you tell? If something, you know . . .'

Louise pursed her lips. 'Not while she's unconscious. If it's there, it'll play possum, hibernate. When she's awake, *then* I'll be able to tell – it won't be able to stop itself picking around in a conscious mind. We really need to get her into bed so I can examine her properly.'

I helped Ingo carry the unconscious councillor to her bedroom, which involved more narrow stairs and several unnecessarily long corridors before we came to a room decked out with lots of leopard-print cushions and throws, cane furniture and jungle plants absolutely everywhere. It was decidedly steaming in there; I decided then and there that people's bedrooms told you too much about them and I would avoid them in future.

Once Titania was safely tucked up in her tropical bower, I found the bathroom and washed my face. Examining my features in the mirror I could see once the soot and blood was gone that I didn't look too bad. There was swelling and redness, but the cut wasn't deep and the burn maybe wouldn't blister if I smothered aloe vera on it. Louise came in while I was checking my vanity levels. She turned me to face her and as she laid her palm against the injured cheek I felt the tingle of magical healing.

'It'll still bruise,' she warned, gently pulling her hand away.

'Leave it. It'll remind me not to take things for granted, or try to take easy ways out.' The cut was gone and there was much less heat in the burn. 'Do you need me for anything? Obviously it's not ideal for me to be discovered in the home of a councillor when *this* has just happened and I'm already *persona non grata* with Sandor.'

'Go.'

'Text me when you know how she is, okay?'

She led me over to a walk-in wardrobe, reached in and pressed a switch, hitherto concealed by the impressive number of shoe racks. A panel slid aside. When I hesitated at the dark maw, she said, 'There are torches further down. Titania uses it a lot.' She waved me off, her attention already shifting back to her charge.

I stepped into the darkness and tried not to think about spiders or Aviva.

In the back of a taxi smelling like cabbage I went over what had happened, but there really wasn't much to go on: pleasantries, basic blood-letting and cardigan-burning, then, *boom!* The room had been prepared before I arrived and Ingo had obviously helped with the set-up. It had been a surprisingly simple ritual, requiring nothing more than blood and fire and intent, and Titania had acted as though she did it every day; that it was no big deal for her. If nothing else, judging by the level of glamour around her home, summoning a shade should have been a doddle for someone of her ability.

So what happened?

Had someone other than our small band of conspirators known I was coming and made a point of nobbling the evening's activity? Surely the castle had wards against such things? But it was very difficult to set wards to cover all conceivable eventualities . . . A member of the household might have been able to get around precautions.

Or had I inadvertently brought something in with me? I'd been keeping a look-out and as far as I could tell, no one had followed me here. I wasn't infallible, obviously – had something climbed on my back in the darkness outside and hitched a free ride? But that didn't seem likely: wards were generally set to wipe off just such small malignancies.

Had Merrily Vaughan put something in the bag or the boxes of smudge? But she couldn't have known what I wanted it for; I'd not told her it was gift, or for whom. Anyway, why would she do such a thing when her business depended on the goodwill of the Weyrd, and Merrily was very serious about Third Eye Books.

The only thing I could be sure of was that a lot of people now knew where I'd been, so worst kept secret ever. I wondered how long before Sandor Verhoeven sent me a rude message, and how much flak Titania was going to cop. Hopefully, her position on the Council was secure enough that she would get away with nothing more than a slap on the wrist.

I rested my head back against the back seat and sighed, but I kept my eyes open the whole trip home.

★

'*Why?*' I moaned to McIntyre, wishing I'd ignored the damn phone and wondering if it even counted as morning yet. 'Why so *early*? *Again?*' Every part of me ached and I regretted not asking Louise to do something pre-emptive after last night's meeting with a stone wall.

'Because I am a sad individual who finds relief from her own pain in the agonies of others?'

'You know, normally I'd say that comment was a sign of personal growth, but I know you're just taking the piss. I assume there's a real reason for this?'

'Autopsy results on the body over at Laidlaw Street, such as they are.'

'Ah. Okay.' I sat up on the couch and pulled the doona tightly around me against the chill air. Automatically I touched my face and found no sign of roughness or blistering, although there were definitely bruises there. 'Did you get an ID?'

'No such luck. Her fingerprints have been removed somehow. The tips are totally smooth.'

'Doesn't sound like acid, which scars. Besides, that's a Normal thing . . . Who knows what might have been done to her with magic?'

'Yep. Ellen apologises, but she's got no idea. Plus, the woman's teeth are stumps, and badly damaged – I'm not sure any dentist could make sense of what's left. We'll try, but it's hard when we've got no timeline on her, we don't know her name or age or any of the et ceteras.'

'You're circulating photos of her?'

'God, no – you saw her. Our sketch artist did a likeness so she doesn't look quite so horribly dead. Ziggi's got one.'

'Good call. Want to text me one? And the photo as well.'

'Sure, but I have to admit, I am not liking our chances. Someone's gone to great lengths to make it hard for us. It would only have been worse if they'd taken the head.'

'Eew.' I ran a hand through my hair. 'Missing persons reports?'

'Why, Fassbinder, I'd never have thought of that.'

'No need to be so pissy, Rhonda.'

'I haven't had any coffee yet, so there's plenty of damned reason.' She sounded impatient. 'There is one thing, though.'

'Hmmm?'

'Ellen found a tattoo.'

'And?'

'Under the left breast.'

'Okay.'

'A rose, kind of large.'

'Okay?'

'It might something noted down in a file, but there's a ton of them to go through.'

'Can't you yell at someone?'

'I don't think that would speed things up. Constable Oldman is already having her dust allergy medication put to the test once more.'

'Hey, that's more than we had before.'

'Marginally.'

'Your cup's always half empty, isn't it, Rhonda?' I yawned. 'There was something strange about her, wasn't there. The way she looked? That mummified appearance? I wasn't imagining it.'

'It didn't look like an easy death, or like she'd had a fun life for a while.'

'The pyjamas. The design, it was really old-fashioned. The cut of the trousers was like . . .' I scoured my brain, then realised, 'those silky Chinese PJs are like something my grandmother would have worn in her youth . . .'

'What are you thinking, Fassbinder?'

'It was *so* hard to judge her age. I mean the PJs might have been vintage when they were put on her . . . What if . . . she's been kept somewhere for a long while?'

'Then what happened?'

'Whatever left that black soot everywhere.'

I tried to go back to sleep after McIntyre hung up, but my mind was too alert, so instead, I rolled out of bed, showered, ate breakfast and waited patiently for my chauffeur to turn up. By ten a.m. there was still no sign of Joyce, and when I tried her mobile there was no answer and no voicemail. I really hoped she'd not gone and mentioned angels to the Guardian.

At half past ten I gave up on her and called a cab. Turned out, it was a singularly expensive business when you didn't have your own tame taxi driver at your disposal.

Chapter Twelve

The bell above the door of Third Eye Books failed to make a sound when I pushed it open so I called, 'Hey, Merrily? We need to talk.' I took in the wall of books covering such esoteric subjects as magical cookery, *Love Spells That Really Work!*, Wiccan fertility ceremonies, how to improve your fortunes through New Age Spirituality, yoga, meditation, and/or general mindfulness and a demonstrated willingness to throw your money away after anything that might offer a modicum of desperate hope. Three tiny round tables were covered with white lace cloths and set for tea and Tarot, with silver tiered stands displaying luscious-looking pink cupcakes like the ones Christos had served. No matter your opinion on spook shops and their business, this one was *nice*: it smelled good, a charming miniature chandelier hanging from the ceiling threw prisms of coloured light over everything and the merchandise looked shiny. If your taste ran to expensive mood candles, dream catchers, massage oil, incense, wind-chimes, crystals, shawls, meditation tapes and yoga DVDs, you were going to be very happy here.

If you wanted your Tarot read, well, Merrily was a smart reader: she'd give you hints of a happy future, throw in some obstacles that weren't insurmountable for that touch of verisimilitude, and include a damned fine cup of tea to ensure a general feeling of wellbeing. All in all, she was mostly harmless, apart from her resentment that her mixed parentage – like me, she was a Weyrd-Normal mix – hadn't resulted in actual superpowers. When things went wrong it was generally because she'd overextended; her minor magical skills didn't actually require Weyrd blood, just a willingness to perform the ritual steps and pay the red price. She really wasn't too fond of me, for a variety of reasons, but it wasn't as if that put her in a minority or anything.

There was no sign of her in the front of the shop and she wasn't hiding behind the counter, so I turned my attention to the iridescent purple and green curtains covering the entrance to the back room where she kept her stock, a fridge and who knew what else. There was no back way out, so she had to be there somewhere. 'Merrily?'

I was answered by a grunt as I pulled aside the fabric, revealing the dark-haired, dark-eyed proprietor dressed in well-fitting Seven7 Jeans and a creamy lace top with an antique locket and a pair of open-toed gold sandals, despite the winter weather. Merrily swung away from the mirror and I realised she'd been applying make-up to a series of bruises on her throat and cheek.

We stared at each for long moments before saying simultaneously, 'What the Hell happened to you?'

I knew how my own face looked, even with the thick layer of foundation I'd slathered on this morning, and thought ruefully that I didn't look any better than she did.

She grinned reluctantly, then said, 'You first.'

'Thrown against a stone wall by an explosion, thumped cheek on the floor when I fell sideways.' I gestured: *Your turn.*

'Bad date.'

'Does this mean you have terrible taste in men when everything else you do is so well-considered?'

'Jeez, you're at least three different kinds of arsehole, Fassbinder.' She turned to the mirror and went back to applying foundation in expert dabs with a sponge shaped like a teardrop.

'Three at least.' I pointed. 'You missed a spot, on your neck.'

She squinted. 'Oh yeah. Thanks.'

'So, bad date? Did it start off bad?'

She shook her head. 'No – but I should have known he was too good-looking not to be a complete douchebag.'

'Yeah.'

Merrily sighed. 'I met him at Bar Alto at the Powerhouse for dinner. It's all going well, we take a walk along the river to aid digestion, we're chatting, getting along fine, then he asks me about my family. I tell him I don't have anything to do with them, but he keeps asking and I get impatient and say, "Dude, we're estranged" – and I swear, he goes *ballistic*.' She puffed out a breath. 'He . . . he caught me by the throat and started to squeeze, then he slapped me so hard my fucking ears were ringing.'

I felt sick, as if I was actually living through the assault with her. 'How . . . how did you manage to get away?'

'Tased the fucker.'

'The clever girls always know how to accessorise.'

Her grin was genuine, but it faded. 'Fassbinder, I don't know what he was – I mean, I knew he was Weyrd, but underneath? I don't know. I got him in the chest, he went down and I bolted – but he was up and running far too soon. As soon as I saw he was gaining on me, I rolled under a car in the Powerhouse lot – I stayed there for an hour before I felt safe enough to get up.' She took stock of her camouflage work in the mirror, gave a little nod of approval. 'I was terrified someone was going to run me over.'

'Jesus, Merrily! I'm really sorry.'

She faced me, then leaned forward and blended some goop over my bruise. 'You should try this stuff, so much more effective than whatever you're using.'

'Strangely, I don't choose my make-up based on how well it covers my injuries.'

'The way you live? Why the Hell not?'

I had no good response to that. Instead I asked, 'So, your parents?'

She rolled her eyes. 'Mum's been dead since I was sixteen. Dad's alive and awful.'

'Which was which?'

'Mum Weyrd, Dad Normal. Many issues. We fight a lot.' Merrily shrugged.

'Do you think it was anything to do with your father?'

'What could he have done that would interest a Weyrd? He turned extra mean when Mum died and now it's like everything Weyrd is bad and evil.'

'That must have been fun to grow up with.'

'You have no idea.'

'So where'd you meet this guy? Like, Weyrd Tinder? Oh my gods, *is* there a Weyrd Tinder?'

'Nice to be Verity Fassbinder with men falling into her lap,' she said sarcastically, ticking off on her fingers, 'First, eligible bachelor number one, Zvezdomir Tepes, makes you the envy of all the Weyrd maidens; then bachelor number two, admittedly only a Normal, but at least not commitment-phobic, gets you up the duff and then *does the honourable thing*!'

'That's unfair – and only a quarter accurate. Well, half at the most. Life with Tepes was no bloody picnic, I promise.' I put my hands on my hips. 'Anyway, I'm trying to be nice here, which is a strain. So, how did you meet this guy?'

She washed her hands in the tiny sink beside her. 'He came in here and bought a few things.'

'Guessing it wasn't over priced smudge?'

She smiled slyly. 'Crystals. Anyway, we got to talking and he let drop he was Weyrd, but clearly knew I was half and half . . . but he made it sound like I was *exotic*, you know? That he could just *tell*.'

'How would he know that?'

'How would I know? I'm not unknown in the community.' She sounded a little hurt when she said that, then sighed. 'The truth is, I wasn't going to look a gift horse in the mouth. He was *gorgeous* – and how many of those do you reckon I get in here? It's all bored housewives and uni students with too much money. He was tall, *really* good body, dark hair, blue eyes, nice teeth.'

'Well, maybe I'm saying you should just be a little cautious.'

'I *was*! Dinner was in a crowded place, and when we went for the walk . . . well, there were people all around. Of course, by the time he went nuts no one was in sight.' She looked really depressed as she muttered, 'I thought . . . I thought he was okay.'

'Not your fault.' I touched fingers to my face again, feeling the ache beneath my skin, but after Merrily's ministrations it did look a Hell of a lot better. 'But why are you back in the shop? He knows where to find you.'

She grinned broadly, drew back the shiny curtains and ushered me onto the shop floor. 'Because I got a handful of Prince Charming's hair, didn't I? I ripped it out before I bolted.' She pointed to the small chandelier. I had to look carefully, but eventually I picked out a smoky glass globe suspended from the central column. When I squinted, I could just make out it was filled with something which might just have been herbs and fur.

'I thought you said he had black hair?'

'He did: black as night, black as ebony.' She stood close beside me and we both stared up at the golden tufts of fur in the globe. 'Interesting, hey?'

'Very interesting.'

We remained like that for a little longer, lost in our own thoughts. The fetish was like the one I'd made from Joyce's fox fur: very specific, very personalised. Whoever her date had been, he wasn't getting back into the shop any time soon.

'If he turns up again, call me, will you? I mean, yes, I'm not working for the Council, but . . .'

'Who else do you think I'd call if I wanted someone's arse kicked?' She tapped the locket at her throat. 'And I've used some of the fur to ward this too. If he comes within six feet of me, it's the magical equivalent of *pow!-right-in-the-kisser*.'

'You know, that kind of warms my heart.'

'I'm not taking this baby off.' She went over to a silver samovar and checked its temperature. 'So, this has been surprisingly nice, Fassbinder, but I've got a group coming in at twelve. Are you going to be here much longer?'

The not-very-subtle subtext: *You're bad for business*.

'Actually, I came to ask if there was anything special about that smudge you sold me.'

She looked surprised. 'Nope, just my usual stuff, same manufacturer as always. Why?'

I gestured to my face. 'That whole being-thrown-against-a-stone-wall gig? It was when Titania Banks tried a summoning ceremony.'

'I heard about that! You were there? Oh, of course *you* were there' – she leaned forward, hands on knees for support and began to hyperventilate – 'Do they think I . . . ? I didn't . . . *No way* . . .'

I grabbed her shoulder – gently – and said quickly, 'No one thinks *anything*, Merrily – I'm the only who knows where I got the smudge, and in any case, the smudge was not used in any way. I'm just trying to eliminate possible contaminations: it was the only thing I brought in.' *Apart from Aviva's cardi.* 'I was just wondering if maybe it was something new. If maybe you . . .'

'If I thought I might try to blow up one of the Five? Do I look like a moron to you?'

And we'd be getting on so well. 'Not today, no. But I wondered if maybe there was something in there that might interfere with a ceremony to raise a shade.'

'Nothing! I swear—'

'What about your date, when he was in here – was he ever in a position to slip something into the smudge?'

'And redo the packaging before I noticed? Fassbinder, he was *gorgeous*, remember? I watched him the whole damned time.' She gave me a look. 'And anyway, he couldn't have known who I'd sell it to, where it would go . . . and anyway, he was in here *after* you were.'

She was right. I tapped a finger on the countertop. 'Right. So, Ingo, Titania's squeeze – know anything about him?'

'Vaguely creepy dork?'

I snorted. 'Kind of more slacker than anything.'

'Hasn't been here long. He was sent out as part of a hostage swap with German cousins, apparently.'

Ah, so when Titania had called him 'hostage of my heart' she hadn't been kidding. The swap was an ancient habit, designed to ensure the behaviour of rival clans, to honour a treaty, sometimes as prelude to marriage; it was *serious*. If someone fucked you over, you had their relatives in the palm of your hand, for punishment or leverage. I knew the High Kings of Ireland used to blind and castrate their charges if the occasion called for it.

'Well, Titania's certainly taken to her role as hostess.'

'So I heard. And most of her posse are *not* happy about it. Don't get me wrong, they love her, which is maybe why they dislike him so much. P'raps they don't think he's good enough.' She crossed her arms over her chest. 'Mind you, they're probably right.'

'He looks harmless enough. Bit weedy, mind.'

'What if he's not, though? What if he's here to bring the system down from the inside?'

'Calm down, Comrade Lenin,' I started, then stopped. Maybe she was right. On the other hand, I'd've sworn Ingo's distress was pretty darned genuine. But then again, what the Hell did I know? 'Look, let me know if you hear anything, okay?'

When she nodded, I added, 'And keep an eye out when you're going to and from your car, stay near other people, *et cetera*. The locket might only do so much, and you don't know how powerful he might be . . .'

'Yes, Mother.'

Outside the shop, I tried Joyce's mobile once more, again, to no avail. I wasn't sure why I was doing it, because gods knew everything was easier without her looking on and I had things to do, stuff to read, people to annoy and lists to make, so right now, all of that could be undertaken in an orderly fashion. A champagne-coloured Jag pulled up in front of the shop and I heard tapping on the window behind me. A quick glance over my shoulder showed Merrily gently urging me to vacate the footpath – perhaps I was making it untidy? The doors of the Jag opened and a passel of primped-up women spilled out, laughing and releasing clouds of heavy perfumes. I didn't know how they'd not asphyxiated on the drive over. Against my every instinct, I moved off without making either a wisecrack or a rude gesture at Merrily.

Was I mellowing? Rather than examine that idea too closely I made a decision: I wasn't too far from the University of Queensland and it was a nice day. A walk would do me good. Since I had time to kill before tonight's appointment, I'd drop in on the Professor and/or Sophie and see if I couldn't get my paws on that article.

Chapter Thirteen

I like the Cathedral of St Stephen. It's bright and airy inside, which is unusual for buildings usually associated with serious shadows and dim places where a god might rest. The stonework is beautiful, with vaulted ceilings and gothic arches, stained-glass windows and chairs of sycamore. It was also easy to break into after hours if you knew the trick of it.

In the darkness I sat on the garden wall of the chapel across from the cathedral. I ate an apple, peering in the side doors and watching the movement and colour and light of the mass being conducted inside, feeling like the poor kid with her nose pressed up against the window of a house watching the celebration within. Not that I wanted to partake, but c'mon, a party's a party. Faith of any denomination is always simple if you have no real experience of sacred things and if you can convince yourself there's only one god and He's the Boss. But when you know for a fact that there are more gods on this earth than you can – or indeed, would be wise to – shake a stick at, then narrow, inflexible belief systems become less practical or desirable.

I waited another twenty minutes after the last of the worshipful had filed out and the priest had locked the doors before walking across the tidy lawn and down the sloping path that led past the building housing the Catholic Regional Tribunal and took Charlotte Street towards the car park underneath the cathedral. In a dark far corner I fumbled around for the correct brick until I found the one that moved a little when encouraged and pushed. It slid back with that crunch of stone on stone to reveal a doorway. I stepped into the darkness and set the torch app on my phone glowing for all it was worth. The door slid closed without me doing anything, which was vaguely creepy, but I figured there must be a pressure pad somewhere at my feet. The steep, narrow stairs made me wonder if Titania's stonemason had done work here too. I came up in the sacristy and had to resist the urge to rummage through the cupboards – I wouldn't have been searching for anything in particular, just giving in to my inner four-year-old's overwhelming desire to ferret about.

Sitting in the sycamore seats at the very front of the nave, looking as uncomfortable as lions about to be thrown to Christians, were Bela and Ziggi, staring suspiciously at the altar. Though it was only a few days since we'd last seen each other, the sight of them made tears heat my eyes. I fairly launched myself at Ziggi as he rose and my big, broad ginger uncle swept me into a hug and held me so tight that my shoulder objected loudly. I ignored it.

When Ziggi finally let me go he narrowed his eyes at my face, raising a hand to the bruise that was obviously defeating my efforts at camouflage, but was careful not to actually touch it.

'So much for my excellent concealer,' I said.

He said gruffly, 'You think after all this time I don't know every inch of your face, every expression you've got?'

'Under certain circumstances that might sound creepy but I'll take it for the avuncular care it is.' I hugged him again, hard enough that the air rushed out of him and he made a bit of a squeak like an abused squeeze toy.

'Are you sure about this place?' he asked. 'Is it safe? For you, I mean.'

'Honestly? I only know I've been urged to stay away from churches, and urged in equal measure to carry around gifts from the Guardian, so I'm ignoring both bits of advice. I reckon the odds are good he can't see in here, and can't keep an eye on me if I'm not holding something he's given me. Of course, that's all theoretical.'

'V.'

Bela hadn't left his chair. Some dumb part of me thought maybe he'd have changed in the days since I'd last seen him, aged, got some grey hairs, maybe grown a beard, but no, same old Zvezdomir Tepes: coldly, darkly handsome, elegantly attired in very indigo jeans, a perfectly pressed shirt and a charcoal jacket (an Armani Tokyo). Shiny shoes collected a glow from the few lights left burning. He still looked like it was only a matter of time before the shadows claimed him, but not in a victim-y kind of way, just because he belonged to them.

How had I ever thought I could hold onto him? I had no idea where that thought came from.

'Bela.'

'Your family are safe,' said Bela. After a moment he asked, 'Did David's letter help?'

'Some.' I glanced down at my unpolished Docs. 'How is Titania?'

Ziggi made a noise, and Bela's eyes flashed.

'She's not yet regained consciousness,' he answered tightly. 'What *precisely* were you thinking?'

'Ah – ask the questions, get the information, solve the problems?' I said, then regretted it; Titania was his friend and colleague. 'My bad, Bela. Look, Ligeia suggested Aviva might still have answers for me about the Guardian. Olivia told me that Aviva had been the one to come for her body when she was in the morgue – not that she could have delivered my mother, so there had to be some Normal factotum doing that bit of dirty work. You know Aviva collected information for years, Bela, so if *anyone* knew how a broken archangel ended up in the Underworld, it would be her. She'd have squirrelled *something* away.' I thought about what I'd just said. Aviva *couldn't* have seen it in the Underworld . . . so had she seen it at all, or merely heard rumours? Or had she seen it *outside* the Underworld? I filed that away for further investigation. 'And grails – Bela, she might have known something about those.'

'V—'

'Besides, Titania should have been able to conduct that ritual with one hand tied behind her back. I saw Aviva's shade – it appeared quickly, and with very little effort – mind you, that's no surprise when you think about the kind of power she's got to create that glamour around a full-scale freaking castle—'

'V—'

'And another thing—'

'V! Ingo's gone to ground.'

'Shit.' Hostage on the run? 'But Bela, I don't think he did anything . . .'

'It doesn't matter. He ran, which is tantamount to an admission of guilt. Titania's retainers are up in arms and I'm just waiting for Ingo's family to contact me and demand to know what the fuck's gone on and why their son is being hunted.' He ran a hand through his hair, which immediately sprang back to perfection as if it had never been subjected to such an indignity. 'Hopefully, I can find him before anyone else does – or at least before he gets word to his people.'

'Can I—'

'*You* can't be anywhere near this. Some are already saying you had something to do with it.'

I went silent, trying to swallow the ball of hurt in my throat.

He kept on, ticking matters off on his long fingers as he leaned casually back in the chair, almost as if enumerating the advantages of buying an electric car. 'You were there and you don't work for us any more, so it's a small enough leap to think you've turned on the community, V.'

'Do you honestly think I—'

'No, I fucking don't!' Bela yelled. His eyes flashed scarlet, his jaw distended, his very white teeth lengthened and I swear he hulked larger – just for a breath of a second, just for that moment when his temper got the better of him.

Bela had *never* yelled at me before. *Never*. And I was well aware I'd been challenging over the years, like Iditarod challenging, Paris-Dakar challenging, Sydney-to-Hobart Yacht Race challenging. But never, *ever*, had Bela Tepes *yelled* at me.

Girly tears threatened, but I bit them back. 'Okay . . . Okay. So what do you need from me?'

'Just stay out of the way. I can keep them off you for a while, but I've got to tell you, V, Udo Forsythe is out for your blood and he's bending Sandor's ear.'

'Surely Verhoeven knows me better than that? After everything I've done for the Weyrd?'

'Including calling him a sack of shit? Free tip: never underestimate how that sticks in the memory of a fat and powerful man.' He rubbed a hand across his forehead as if to relieve an awful headache. 'I told you this was a terrible idea, Verity.'

'What did you expect me to do? Risk my husband? My child? My mother?'

We glared at each other for a while until he looked away. 'Just keep a low profile.'

I wanted to kick something, but I controlled myself; no point in forcing a vandalism investigation for the sake of splintering one of those pretty chairs. It would make this place harder to sneak into, and I had a feeling I was going to need this sanctuary for a while.

'Bela,' I said after a few calming breaths, 'the tyrant the Guardian wants me to find — is there any chance it's one of the Weyrd? Like one of the old families? Maybe even Verhoeven?'

He stared at me, considering my question, then shook his head. 'I cannot think of anyone whose path would have brought them into contact with an archangel. I cannot imagine an archangel would even deal with a Weyrd—'

'—the Guardian did with Aviva—' I interrupted, and thought, *Tobit with Serena*, but didn't say it.

'—or even one who might have survived such contact.' He amended, 'But for Ligeia.'

'Ligeia had a kick-ass sword, the weapon that did for the Arch, Bela.'

He threw his hands up in the air.

'Right.' I licked my lips. 'So if I ask you for an introduction to a couple of Weyrd families who own grail-type objects, is that going to be a problem?'

He shudder-sighed. 'Who?'

'One you don't need to worry about as I've already met the Nadasys. The other two are the Odinsays and . . .'

Bela give the slightest movement of his fingers, palm facing upwards: *Hit me.*

'. . . the Forsythes.'

He dropped his head into his hands and for a moment I thought he was sobbing. I shot a look at Ziggi, whose expression clearly said, *You've done it: you've broken him.* But then a sound burst from Bela's lips as he sat up and leaned his head back, sending the laughter towards the vaulted ceiling, where it bounced and echoed for what felt like an unnaturally long time.

'Gods, Verity Fassbinder! You just don't quit.'

I sat beside him, leaned my shoulder against his and said, 'Which has admittedly been a bonus for you over the years, Tepes.'

'Can't argue with that.' He took my hand and squeezed it. 'I can fix it with the Odinsays, but I've no idea what to do about Udo.'

'Surely you've got some spy in his household? Someone open to persuasion, just to confirm or deny if there's a grail object in Udo's possession?'

'I'll figure something out.' He put an arm around my shoulders, but that made me uncomfortable. Like holding Callie had made me ache for Maisie, so touching Bela made me miss David more. I patted his leg, then stood up.

'These are the families who are on record as having some kind of a grail vessel in their history? And this information came from whom? Ligeia again?'

I didn't deny it; I didn't want to get Jost in trouble and no one was going to give Ligeia a bollocking, not in her current state – quite frankly, not even if she'd been in full health.

'Fine. I'll get word to you via the Norns – just don't go after Forsythe, okay? Promise me.'

'Scout's honour.'

'Oh, gods . . .'

'How's Ligeia doing, by the way?' I'd left couple of voicemails checking in with Eurycleia but she'd not returned them, not that I'd expected her to.

'Still hanging in, but the deterioration is . . .' He blinked. I knew the old siren's demise was going to be truly horrific.

'Any chance she can . . . make a dignified exit?'

'I don't see Ligeia taking the easy way out, do you?'

'Which brings me to my next point of order: Christos and Tobit, and by extension, Callie.'

'What's up?'

'According to Christos, Tobit has been AWOL for a while now, and flaky well before that.'

'I've got no control over an angel, V – they're not our kind. *You're* the only one he's ever answered to.'

'He's got a crush on you, if you ask me,' said my uncle.

'Shut up, Ziggi.'

'Is that any way to talk to your uncle?'

'Shut up, *Uncle* Ziggi.'

'Much better.'

'The fact is, Christos is worried that with Ligeia dying and Tobit consciously uncoupling from his parental duties, he and Callie are going to be left open to Eurycleia's machinations, and knowing her as we do, I don't think he's being paranoid. She's a wee bit monomaniacal when it comes to her granddaughter.'

'Maybe we should get Eurycleia some kind of substitute – a dog, maybe,' Ziggi muttered, which made me smile, just a little.

'I think that counts as cruelty to animals, doesn't it?' Even though it was cold in the cathedral, I had to wipe my sweaty palm on my jeans. 'Anyway, just . . . you know, be *aware*. Keep an eye on Christos, make sure he's safe. Get someone sitting on the house, maybe.'

'You don't work for me any more,' Bela reminded me somewhat testily.

'Then what *are* you going to do?'

'Get someone sitting on the house.' He sighed. 'Anything else? He asked foolishly.'

'Oh, hey, that body McIntyre called in the other day—'

Bela's eyebrows went up. 'Why do you even know about that—Oh, never mind. What about it?'

'Anything more on it? You know, in terms of Weyrdosity?'

Bela looked at Ziggi, who cleared his throat.

'Something was stored in her, V.'

'*Stored?*'

'As in a spirit.'

'Like, used as a spiritual cookie jar? Was she dead beforehand?'

Ziggi looked grim. 'No, she was alive – she had to be for the *essence*, for want of a better word, to stay in there – to be *contained*.'

'So did she die when it left or did it leave when she died? Have you told McIntyre this?'

'Don't know. And yes.'

'But she was Normal?'

'Yes – she had to be, for something like this to work.' Ziggi looked at me. 'It's not a return, this, it's a *hanging-around*, a *staying-put*, and that needs powerful sorcery and a Normal vessel.'

'But Weyrd magic?'

'Yeah.'

'And the thing that was in her? Weyrd?'

'Possibly.'

'Probably,' said Bela wearily, 'looking at the mess it made, the residue it left behind. Ellen hasn't been able to identify it as anything recognisable so far.'

'But it could be, right? It could be something man-made and Normal, like chemical warfare? We can hope, right?' I paused. 'We're in big trouble, aren't we?'

The three of us were silent for long moments, the only sound was the building whispering around us as the air cooled; even the noise of traffic outside was barely distinguishable.

Ziggi was the first to break it. 'How did you dump your watchdog?'

'Strictly speaking, I think you'll find Joyce is a watchfox.' I scratched my head. 'She didn't show up for work today. She might possibly have seen a photo of Tobit and realised he and the Guardian are the same kind of creature . . .'

'Be careful, V. It's a dangerous game, tearing apart someone's beliefs,' Ziggi warned.

'I've got to start somewhere. She's . . . I feel bad for her. She's lost everything – I know she killed Len and all, but . . .' Suddenly needing something to do with my hands, I tightened my ponytail. 'I just feel like she's not a total loss.'

'Are you drunk?'

'I wish.' I laughed. 'Oh, and Merrily Vaughan?'

'Oh, you have been busy,' Bela said in a way that did not sound as though he was impressed by my industry. 'What did you do?'

'Nothing! I did *nothing*! She went on a date and the guy attacked her. He asked about her family and then attacked her when she told him they were estranged. She was pretty bruised, but she got away – she Tased him,' I said, still impressed.

'*Good*,' said Ziggi with satisfaction.

'She's got the place warded, but . . .'

'I'll get people on her house and shop.'

'Let her know, okay? We don't want her getting spooked by some strange Weyrd hanging around outside. Maybe Mike?' Mike Jones had lost his partner Jerry not so many weeks ago, and I knew Bela was trying to keep him busy.

'Look at you, Verity Fassbinder, all concerned for people you don't like.'

'I like Mike fine,' I grumbled. 'Must be this motherhood shit, making me soft in the head.'

'Just remember, you can't save everybody, V.' Bela sighed and stood, then gazed at me with a kind of fond resignation.

'Anything more on Dusana? Sightings? Piles of bodies?'

He shook his head, but his face darkened and nostrils pinched with anger; nice to know there was someone else he was more pissed off with than me. 'Anything else?' he asked and I knew he was really hoping I'd stop there.

'Yes.' I pointed at Ziggi, annoyed to find my voice trembling as I announced, '*Don't* you get comfortable in my job, Mr Hassman. I'm coming back and I expect the return of my executive bathroom key.' I turned to Bela. 'And Zvezdomir Tepes, I'll be needing an executive bathroom.'

He rolled his eyes and held out his arms. It was a short hug, and I might have seen a look of hurt flit across his face when I broke away. I stayed in Ziggi's embrace much longer; family's family, after all.

He whispered, 'Just keeping your seat warm. Be careful, my little girl.'

Chapter Fourteen

Day Two without Joyce. While there was no doubt her absence was making things a lot easier for me, I was being distracted by a niggling worry about her. If she didn't turn up tomorrow or the next day I might be forced to do something stupid. But those concerns were for another time, so I got on with my day: eliminating the Nadasys as possessors of a grail.

The Ascot House was still glamoured even though Magda Nadasy, the witch who'd bespelled it, was long dead, toasted in the industrial oven she kept in the basement for disposing of the bodies of the children whose tears she stole. My mother had told me not so long ago that it had also been the site of my father Grigor's 'butchery business', back when such habits were indulged in by the Weyrd. After he was gone, new laws were made, including the entirely reasonable prohibition against consuming human flesh.

The last time I'd set foot here it was to find David and finish off Nadasy's husband, Vadim, a very angry mage with a whole barrel of axes to grind. I'd also had to deal with his grandson, Donovan Baker, Dusana's son, who'd morphed irretrievably into a voracious garbage golem, thanks to his grandparents, who'd intended using him as a weapon for vengeance. I could understand why Dusana Nadasy had some issues with me.

I said 'deal with', but I actually set Donovan-the-golem alight, hoping it might take out the whole noisome property, but Bela told me later that the fire had only burned for a while and it hadn't really got out of the basement, where so much evil had been done.

My preference today was for definitely not venturing into the basement; I was praying I'd find something somewhere in the rest of the house, which despite my best efforts was mostly intact, before I had to cross that particular bridge.

I had the taxi driver drop me at the end of the long driveway, ignoring the perplexed expression on his face, and waited until he drove away before I wandered between the enormous camphor laurels forming a canopy over the gravel driveway. The gardens were overgrown and the place, complete with misplaced Gothic windows, looked neglected, the white paint discoloured, and I half expected to see the two storeys, attic, widow's walk and chimney stacks slide off each other like an unbalanced wedding cake. Even after all this time it was slippery to look at; the glamour still held power over the eye of the beholder. Your average Normal wouldn't have stood a chance but I knew what I was looking for – and even I felt like the sight was greasily sliding from my eyeballs.

I took the few short steps up to the verandah, listening to the planks creak beneath the soles of my Docs. The front double door had once had expensive frosted glass panels on either side; I'd broken both of them, but now one of the doors was hanging half-off its hinges too. I pushed it aside, pulled out my phone and hit the torch. Last time I'd been here I'd got stabbed and beaten up, almost lost my lover and my life and found the body of Sally Crown, a street kid, a lost girl I couldn't save.

That step across the threshold was a reluctant one.

I tried one of the light switches but got no response; someone had thought to turn off the utilities at last. There was some natural light, as most of the glass had been knocked out of the windows and the curtains had vanished. Very little furniture remained, just some broken chairs, and charcoal-coloured circles on the once-cream carpet showed where someone had been setting campfires. The long silk rug that once ran up the hallway was gone too. I took the staircase up to what had once been impeccably decorated bedrooms and an office. Once again, the place had been stripped, even the mattresses, and I wondered who'd taken everything – it had to be wandering Weyrd; Normals had no chance of seeing past the glamour. So somewhere in Brisneyland, lucky Weyrds were sleeping on mattresses they could never have otherwise afforded. I was okay with that.

Truthfully, I didn't really know what I was looking for – could have been a cup, a chalice, a bucket, a tub, any kind of receptacle – but there wasn't even a nice crystal vase or a chipped mug, nothing I could pretend was even a remote possibility. Back downstairs, the kitchen was just as looted. The refrigerator's silver doors were hanging open and something greeny-black and bearing a striking resemblance to a primary school science experiment sat on one of the shelves.

Any hope that the family grail was something I was going to be able to just stumble across, Indiana Jones fashion, was well and truly crushed. I wondered if someone was right now drinking cheap wine or bad coffee out of a vessel the Nadasys had spent centuries protecting.

I was taking a breather, wondering, *Where to from here?* when I heard something.

A noise.

A scuffle, a scrabble, a scramble . . .

. . . in the basement.

Of course, it was in the bloody basement. Briefly I considered it might be Dusana, but I dismissed that pretty quickly. She had enough money at her disposal and fussy enough tastes not to want to use this shit-heap as a lair.

I really, *really* missed the Dagger of Wilusa and cursed – *very* gently, and not seriously – the Boatman who'd demanded its return, then sighed and put on my big girl pants.

The basement it was.

The door inside the pantry was gaping open. No electricity meant no light, and the beam that came from my phone looked all too feeble against the encroaching darkness. The concrete steps felt sturdy enough, but when I put my hand against the walls for support, they felt thin, unstable. There was soot everywhere, and cinders, more and more the closer I got to the bottom. The door I'd slammed closed on the burning garbage golem was gone entirely. I stepped out into the space, my heart pounding.

The rows of racks that had once housed bottles of wine made from the tears of Normal street kids were in disarray, mostly burned and buckled, but they formed a laneway for me through to the far end of what had once been a state-of-the-art facility for ripping the joy, sadness and life from children just to cater to very specific Weyrd tastes. Years before that, my father had used this place as a slaughterhouse of a different sort.

In the corner against the far wall was the incinerator used to dispose of the little bodies once the Vintner had wrung everything from them.

In front of it were the ghosts.

There were maybe ten in all, skipping in a circle, ghostly-white. Amongst them was the girl I couldn't save, Sally Crown, the oldest of the group, directing play. Behaving like a child as she never had in life, or at least not when I knew her. I could hear, very faintly, a chant, the old nursery rhyme 'Ring a Ring o' Roses'. I blinked.

It wasn't all of Magda Nadasy's victims, surely, but some: the ones who'd not gone with the Boatman. These were stuck here, or perhaps they'd remained by force of will, or sheer accident, here in the place where they'd died, playing as though it had been a place of fun, of joy.

I stepped forward and said, 'Sally?' as softly as I could so as not to startle them.

Tiny faces all turned towards me in surprise . . . then dissipated, bursting apart like dandelions disintegrated by a good strong breeze. They were all gone, even Sally.

I don't know what I'd expected.

I gathered my scattered wits and gave the area, now even darker without the spectres to shed their translucent light, a thorough search, but there was nothing to be found. It was only when I found myself back out on the verandah, sitting in the sun, that I realised my cheeks were wet.

Back home I had a flask containing the Waters of Forgetting. I'd taken it from the Underworld, from a stream that flowed uphill. It took away your memories so you could pass on to where your heart was weighed and your deeds judged. Only then were those memories returned to you, before you moved on to the next stage. I could come back and try to get them to drink; I'd sent souls home that way before. Or I could let Bela know via the Norns that someone needed to come and conduct a ritual to help these little Normal kids pass on. I had no idea how long they had been there, been lost.

The mobile rang and I wiped the tears from my face, as if the caller would see them when I answered.

It was McIntyre. 'You sound snotty. Are you getting a cold?'

'Worse. I've been crying.'

'Jesus.'

'Yeah.'

'Okay, so your friend Joyce Miller?'

'"Friend" is such a strong word, but go on.'

'You're going to have thank Constable Oldman for this; she did the digging.'

'Good to know she's finally developed some research habits of note.'

'I'll tell her you said thanks.'

'Rhonda.' The slow rollout was getting on my last nerve.

'Calm down. I'm getting to it.' She paused, and it sounded like she was sipping something. 'So, you remember the Beaumont Children?'

'The ones who disappeared from an Adelaide beach in the Fifties? I don't think she's one of them.'

'No, you idiot, I'm using it for context, building a story.'

'I'm ageing rapidly here.'

She grunted, then went on, 'So, they disappeared without trace, never found. A similar thing happened in the early Nineties, your people this time: three babies, triplets, disappeared from their family home just outside of Melbourne. Sibyl, Agnes and Joyce. Weyrd mother Amaya Miller (née Mori), Normal father, Ian Miller.'

'Wow. Dead?' But I was also thinking, *Weyrd-Normal mix, just like me*: hybrids who could walk between, and, most importantly, pass to the Underworld and come back up without the usual Weyrd terror of *never-after*. That explained one mystery at least: there was no angelic intervention to allow them to move where full-blooded Weyrd feared to tread.

'Nooooo!' McIntyre crowed, 'Alive – *both* alive.'

'Shit.'

'Shit indeed.' She paused. 'Are you going to tell her?'

'Not yet. I need . . . I need to make sure she's not in a bad place,' I finished lamely. 'Besides, I also need to *find* her.'

'MIA?'

'Yep.

'I can put out a BOLF – I've got the licence plate here from the traffic incident.'

'Yeah, do that, would you? Finding the car might help. Thanks, Rhonda. But please, make sure no one approaches her. You'll only end up with a neatly sliced platter of constables for your trouble.'

'Why don't you know any nice people, Fassbinder?'

'I do, but they tend to get killed.' I paused. 'Which explains your extraordinary longevity.'

'I don't know why I talk to you.'

'Because I'm freaking delightful.' I laughed in spite of myself. 'Anything more on your corpse?'

'There are a lot of corpses in my day, but I'll assume you mean Laidlaw Street Lady. There's nothing so far. Oldman's still reading reports, looking for any mention of tattoos.' She sighed. 'I think she's up to the Bs. So, what's your next move?'

'I've got a date tonight.'

'I'm sure David will be delighted know you've moved on so quickly.'

'Bite me.'

'You're not my type.'

'I'm babysitting Lizzie. I think I have to watch *Frozen*.'

'Better you than me.'

'Hey, if you have babies, this shit is also in your future.'

'I hate you.'

She didn't even say goodbye.

I was hungry. I called a cab.

Chapter Fifteen

'*Frozen* or *Brave*?' Lizzie looked at me with the level of seriousness only a nine-year-old with a DVD in each hand can muster.

'Well, on one hand: ice, snow, some very neat hair and frocks and a butt-load of singing. On the other hand, wild tawny locks, obstinate behaviour, weaponry and frocks being ruined.' I sat back on the couch, dug into the bowl of popcorn and said, '*Brave*. Let's be *Brave*.'

'Merida!' Lizzie danced her way towards the DVD/Blueray player. I might have been babysitting but she was the hostess. She'd already got the popcorn in the microwave when I wandered in so Mel could head off to meet Jost.

By the time we'd hit the scene with the queen turning into a bear, we were both in hysterics. We'd seen it together half a dozen times before – and all the mother-daughter stuff made me sad for so many reasons – but there's no beating a bear in a tiara trying to fish for salmon for sheer comedy brilliance. The buttery popcorn was gone, but I was responsible enough not to suggest another round.

'Do you miss Maisie?' asked Lizzie when Merida's mother turned into a tiara-wearing bear.

'Of course.' The kid might as well have stabbed me in the heart. 'I miss my mum.'

'You know she's just on a date, sweetie. She's allowed out.' I lifted my arm and she curled in beside me like a little bird. She wasn't baby enough to make me hurt like Callie did; there was nothing to echo my absent daughter.

'I know,' she said, flat and bored. Her body shook with a melodramatic sigh and I had to swallow my grin. I suspected there was some eye-rolling going on too. 'It's just . . . not just *us* any more.'

'Honey, you like Jost, right?' I asked. 'He's kind to you, isn't he?'

'I guess.' She shrugged. 'He's pretty – prettier than the first time I saw him with that guy.'

'Well, he's happier now.' She'd first seen him at my wedding when he was nervous, new to Brisneyland, but that was also before he was a known quantity, before he became a threat to her status quo. I couldn't remember who he might have been talking to then. Nowadays he was happy, I supposed, he was sprucing himself up for Mel (although how you put a bigger shine on a diamond like him, I don't know). Lizzie was a little girl used to having her mother's sole attention. Now someone was asking her to share; even the most well-adjusted kid was going to have her nose put out of joint a little.

'Cut your mum some slack, hey? If you're worried about anything, just talk to her. You know you can, right?'

'Mmmmm.' Lizzie was starting to sound sleepy. She pointed to the television where Merida was hastily sewing up the rent she'd made in the tapestry, desperately waiting for everything to be well once more. 'This is my favourite bit.'

'Yeah.'

By the time the credits were rolling, she was asleep against my side, snoring like a kitten and drooling down my white T-shirt. I'd work myself up to putting her into her own bed, but for the moment it was just nice to be like this, close, relaxed, loved, not home in an empty house where I could still feel the echoes of my lost ones. I rested my head on the back of the couch and my eyes fell closed. *Just a couple of minutes . . .*

I don't know how long I was asleep for but the TV was mostly dark except for the Pixar logo ping-ponging back and forth across the screen. Outside it was fully dark, and when I checked my phone on the sofa beside me, it was eight-thirty, which meant an hour or so before Mel expected they'd be back from dinner. I was hungry; popcorn, however tasty, didn't count as a proper meal. I was gently extracting myself from Lizzie's concrete-weighted body and replacing myself with a cushion when I heard something low-pitched but persistent, as if someone had attached something to a piece of rope and was twirling it around their head. It grew louder and louder and began to circle the house, but Lizzie was showing no signs of waking, so I slid out and moved to the centre of the lounge room, turning and turning, trying to trace the source, trying to work out if it was getting faster. Abruptly, the noise started changing: it slowed down, then sped up and went around the other way. I walked closer to the kitchen and was almost at the battered Formica table when the window over the sink exploded—

—or it *started* to.

The glass bowed, curving inwards, and I could see each individual crack, every fragment and fracture. I threw up my hands in a vain attempt to cover my face, but beyond the initial noise of an impact and the shattering screech of the glass breaking, there was nothing more: nothing hitting the metal of the sink or tinkling onto the linoleum; no shards hit me anywhere, even in my protecting hands . . .

When I cautiously uncovered my eyes and looked up I could see the glass was still in the frame. It looked like a dropped mirror, the crazed glass reflecting me back in a million pieces, sharp against the darkness. On the outside, in the centre of the window, was a viscous vermilion smear.

I looked over my shoulder; Lizzie was still sleeping.

I grabbed a knife from the block on the kitchen bench and swallowed hard as I carefully slid the chain off and opened the back door. I stepped out onto the tiny landing and peered over the railing to where the UFO had fallen, then reached back inside and flicked the switch for the light that was meant to illuminate the yard, but the bulb was blown. Tightening my grip on the knife in my right hand, I pulled up my phone in the left and shone the torch downwards. I could just about make out something off-white, the size of a basketball, bleeding and panting.

'Damn it.'

Every step creaked under my weight, so there was no chance of sneaking up on whatever it was huddling in the gloom. I approached cautiously, nerves singing, until the torch beam hit it.

Sparse feathers, a lot of greying flesh, blood oozing where it had been impaled on Lizzie's bike pedal when it fell (gods, the impact!), neck contorted to the side from hitting the window. The grotesque, bloated thing's beak was twisted and broken. Little crimson eyes glimmered weakly, then went out.

A night-dove.

It was a nasty low-level summoning, something to do damage, make someone's life unpleasant at the least and maim or disfigure them at worst. Generally they didn't manage to kill because their lifespan was limited – in fact, 'life' was pushing it, it was more like an 'appearance-span'. A night-dove sending was a punishment, a torment, meant specifically to leave a bad memory.

And they travelled in fucking pairs.

'Verity?' came Lizzie's wavering voice and I turned to see her silhouetted against the light in the doorway at the exact moment I heard the flap of wings from one of the trees in Mel's back yard. I know I screamed, but I don't recall hearing it, although my throat felt raw for days after. I threw myself back up the stairs, knowing I wouldn't get to her in time.

I saw the night-dove flying straight at her.

Lizzie wobbled backwards.

And the night-dove was *bounced* away from her the moment it tried to cross the threshold into the kitchen. I heard the crack of its neck as it hit an invisible barrier, and the noise that its animating spirit made as it departed. And I heard the little girl cry out as she fell deeper into the kitchen, trying to throw herself away from the dead thing's claws and beak.

I got to the top of the stairs, hurdled the disgusting corpse and knelt beside Lizzie, who was weeping but unhurt.

'You've got to be brave for me, honey, okay?' I murmured, hugging her. 'Just like Merida.'

She looked at me with big dark eyes.

'You're so tough it didn't even get you, did it? You're so tough it died of fright!'

She gave a surprised giggle at that, which I took to be a good sign.

'Wait here, will you? Just for one second, okay? Just one, I promise.'

I returned to the landing and looked at the second night-dove, which was already decaying before my eyes, falling into the component parts someone had kludged together to make it. Even now the one downstairs would be a pile of goo. These were dead things and the maker had to have something of the intended victim – hair, clothing, blood, whatever – to form a link to home in on, but they were easily drawn off course. They might instead go to somewhere you'd *been*, because the pull of that old presence was closer and stronger than where you actually *were*. And Lizzie had been napping against me so she'd have smelled like me, and that would have been enough to draw a not-very-clever-very-dead-bird-thing to her instead of me.

I did wonder who had something of mine – I was always careful about leaving hair, nails and so on lying around – but I guess it's impossible to guarantee you've caught everything. There might be some of my clothes left at the Bishop's Palace after my last sneaky exit; it was entirely possible someone there had got hold of my T-shirt or jeans; or even sold a piece on to someone with an axe to grind. I made a note to check on that when I was back in my old job. *If* I ever got my old job back.

Had one of Titania's crew decided to take matters into their own hands? Or did Udo Forsythe think he was taking care of business? It wasn't Sandor Verhoeven's style: he might be pissed off at me, but he wasn't the shifty sort. If he'd been trying to maim or kill me he'd've been up-front about it – he'd have let me know, just to be polite.

It wasn't the Guardian, either; he would have sent someone to ensure I knew who was behind my latest piece of misfortune. Dusana? It felt a little too hands-off for her too, especially as I knew just how much she was aching to squeeze the life from me with her own fair mitts.

But what about Joyce? I thought long and hard about that. *Maybe*. I couldn't rule her out, especially not after the whole disappearing act.

I kicked the carcase over the edge of the landing and listened to it land on top of its twin with all the elegance of a bag of wet garbage.

Lizzie was asleep again by the time Mel and Jost came home. She'd been woken twice by a nightmare, but had quickly gone back to sleep both times. I didn't bother to school my face when the happy couple came bouncing in and my expression was enough to send Mel running straight to her daughter's side.

I didn't bother to follow. I needed to talk to Jost. 'Night-doves,' I said succinctly.

He went pale under his golden colouring. 'Lizzie—'

'Is fine, but she almost wasn't. I'm assuming it was after me – could it be one of Titania's lot? Or Forsythe's?'

He shook his head: *I don't know.*

'But it didn't get in, did it? Neither of them did – which means a general ward, and a fucking powerful one, judging by the state of that window.' I pointed and saw the flash of pride in work well done. 'Since I sure as Hell didn't do it – I've left only light protections on this house so folk can get on with their living and visiting – I have to assume you're responsible?'

'I did. I thought . . .' He looked at me meaningfully. 'I thought maybe a time would come when they were in danger and I might not be here. And you might not be here either. We can't protect the ones we love all the time, but we can give it a damned good go.'

I pushed out a breath. 'It's a good thing you did, Jost. I . . . I wouldn't have reached her in time.'

Inside, I could hear Mel fussing over Lizzie; the little girl's calm replies belied how scared she'd been. *No, Mummy, I haven't had any nightmares. Verity was here to save me.*

Verity was, my arse. But thanks, kid.

'Keep your ear to the ground and let Ziggi and Bela know what happened.' I ran a hand through my hair. I wasn't going to be in the hallowed halls of the Weyrd any time soon so I added, 'And hey, can you check in the Archives to see if anything from the Nadasy house was accessioned?'

'Anything in particular?'

'You need to ask? They were a grail family, so anything even remotely grail-like – a vase, a spittoon, a gravy-boat. Of course, it might have been sent back to the Old Country, or it might have been a lie to improve their status – or perhaps it was stolen by whoever's been through the house like a dose of salts; the place has been completely stripped. Can you just check for me?'

'Of course.'

Mel was shaking when she came out.

'She's okay—' I started, but Mel interrupted.

'Was it after you?'

The brisk tone hurt. 'I think so,' I answered.

'Right. Of course it was.' Her voice was ice.

I knew she had every right to be pissed off and upset, but it still stung. 'Okay, then. Jost, you explain.' I picked up my jacket and headed out of the back door, only too aware of the foul odour of decaying night-doves, and climbed over the fence. I wasn't sure I'd be using that route again any time soon.

Chapter Sixteen

In addition to the usual Normal fashions, the Weyrd have some other options when it comes to travelling. If you're really powerful, and coded with the appropriate DNA, you can disappear and reappear at will at your chosen destination, although it's exhausting. Bela can do it and so can Dusana Nadasy. Eleanor Aviva could, too. If you don't happen to have that particular sequence of nucleic acid markers in your make-up, you can use a ritual. You do need to know where you're going with *pinpoint* accuracy (otherwise you might end up half-in, half-out of a wall, which is not only unpleasant but also generally fatal). Or you can be transported by someone who has a much higher degree of magical ability.

I had had no choice but to use the third way not that long ago, which had made me throw up. A lot.

If you're travelling to the Underworld and you're Normal (or half-Normal), you have three options. You can (a) die and get a free trip, (b) ask the Boatman nicely if he'll take you there in exchange for the return of his *loaned* super-sharp dagger, which you might have been hanging on to for a tad too long, or (c) you can seek out one of the cracks in the skin of the world that leads *down*.

I was disinclined to (a) and I had tried (b) and could not honestly recommend it, so that left me with option (c).

Having Joyce around to watch my back was starting to feel like a good idea – unless, of course, she'd been the one to send the night-doves . . . but to rule that out, I needed to find her. For the love of all that was holy or otherwise, I couldn't shake a guilty feeling that she might be in trouble, and that it was my fault. She'd been obedient to the Guardian her whole life, so it was entirely possible that she'd not been able to break that habit and had started asking pointed questions about *angels*.

And since I now knew her parents were alive, I thought I should probably return her to them. At some point.

So here I was, (almost) willingly subjecting myself to a trip that I knew would feel like a scary long drop and a scarier short, sharp stop – but this was the only place I could think of to start searching for the fox-girl: 356 Lutwyche Road, also known as the old Windsor Shire Council Chambers, where she had shown me a way *down*. I really hadn't enjoyed that trip, but I hadn't thrown up, so I counted that as a bit of a plus.

I pulled out my spiffy Christmas present from Uncle Ziggi – a top-of-the-range electric lock-pick – and once inside, made my way to the back of an old storeroom now housing nothing more than cobwebs and dust, and a spot where the world's membrane is paper-thin.

I eyed the corner, took a breath to prepare myself, then stepped forward and instantly found myself drowning in marshmallow. I sped through shadows both sopping wet and impossibly dry that were clinging to my skin as if trying to catch me and keep me. Just when I thought the journey would never end, it *did*. There'd been no actual *sensation* of falling, but when I hit bottom it was pretty unpleasant, even though I'd kept my knees bent to absorb the impact, just the way Joyce showed me.

I'd landed in a small alcove not far from the entrance to the Guardian's private space, a huge cavern hidden behind painted silk screens of great value and uncertain provenance. Once I was certain I wasn't going to heave, I tested my walking skills and was inordinately pleased to discover that my gait was only a *little* like that of a sailor trying to find his land-legs. I was planning to procrastinate just a little longer until I heard voices: the Guardian's great rumble and another, lighter, tone, a measured, reasonable voice I didn't recognise. I couldn't make out whatever the voice was saying, either, and the Guardian was monosyllabic in his replies, just '*yes*' and '*no*', with the occasional '*perhaps*' thrown in for good measure.

I crept along, hoping to catch sight of the Guardian's companion. My mother had told me there were others who worked for him, injured, angry people with whom the creature had also made bargains. I realised too late that the voices had grown silent, but for the word 'visitor', which was still hanging in the air when I stepped around the silk screens depicting phoenixes and fire. There was just the Guardian, surrounded by his Aladdin's cave of treasures. And the font. *How could I have forgotten the font?* The Guardian had been talking to someone carrying a gift-link: someone who'd done a deal with it. *Someone somewhere else.*

It – the Guardian was a *he*, I knew that, but I couldn't help but view him as *other* – was mostly burned black, except for the occasional patch of pristine, marble-white skin shining through. There were a few strands of deep russet hair on the skull. The charred wings still bore open wounds, as if a blade had been taken to them; they might not be in any state to bear it anywhere, but they were *definitely* wings. Even broken, it – he – still terrified me.

He was lying in the middle of an enormous bed, staining the sheets where his injuries oozed and wept.

'Why have you come?' he asked, an edge to the tone. 'I did not summon you.'

'I felt bad about being a no-show the other day, so I thought I'd pop in and say hi.' I couldn't admit I was looking for Joyce, because what if she wasn't here? What if she'd done a runner after what I'd shown her? I certainly didn't want to alert the Guardian if she was in the wind.

I didn't go too far into the cavern, which was filled with furniture, carved wooden chests, books, artwork . . . I could have sworn the three jewelled saints moved just a little when I wasn't looking straight at them. I added kleptomania to the list of Things Wrong With The Guardian as I gazed around at all manner of stolen things that wouldn't look out of place in a palace or the Vatican or a high-end museum.

From the mad green stare I could tell I'd not been believed. I gazed at the ruined face, which had decayed even more since I'd last seen it, trying to find words, but all I could manage was, 'How did this *happen* to you?'

'I was betrayed.' The pitch stayed low despite the intense emotion. 'I risked all for the salvation of others, and I was burned.'

'Was it the tyrant who did this?'

'Yes.' The voice was precariously balanced on the knife-edge of crazy.

'What happened to it? I mean, *this*' – I gestured vaguely at the ravaged form – 'had to come at a price.'

'I do not know,' he said shortly, and I knew it was a lie, at least partial one.

'Surely it was injured too?' I pressed. 'I can't imagine that the flames that got you would have left it untouched.'

'It was . . . *different*. Made of flesh and mettle other than my own.'

'And you have no name for it? Not even whether it's he or she?'

'It was never such a simple thing. Its name . . . its name does not remain in my mind but swims away like silvery fish in deep waters. I cannot . . . cannot *catch* at it.' The great head shook so fiercely that splits formed up the side of the throat, displaying crimson flares amongst the black, although the archangel showed no sign of having noticed. 'I have no name for you, Verity Fassbinder. You must uncover this for yourself. Do not tell me my faith has been misplaced.'

'Nope.'

'I certainly hope not. Where is Joyce? You are keeping her busy?' He sounded curious.

So, not down here then. 'She is following a lead on the grail.'

'And the tyrant?' The tone was avid.

'Surely even you must admit that the lack of information you've got makes this a bit problematic?'

The Guardian shrugged, making an annoyed noise at the same time. 'Is she learning?'

'I believe she is,' I said truthfully, then asked, 'Am I the only one you've got working on this?'

'This is my most sacred business. I would not entrust it to anyone but you.'

I did not believe it for a second. 'Oh, that's nice. And hey, by the way, last night someone sent a pair of night-doves after me.'

The Guardian stopped breathing . . .

At last he asked, 'You are unhurt? Your face . . .'

I really was going to have to invest in better foundation. 'By sheer luck, I am unhurt. Can you think of anyone who might wish to get in the way of my enquiries?' I wasn't going to mention the whole 'exploding summoning at Titania's'; he didn't need to know I'd been trying to dig up Eleanor Aviva . . . or maybe he already did. Maybe that *explained* the exploding.

But the head was shaking slowly again, oblivious to blackened skin splitting open.

'I'd better be getting back, check on Joyce,' I murmured in an offhand kind of way. Obviously she wasn't hanging up in the torture chamber or wandering around the Guardian's domain, so she had to be upstairs somewhere. Maybe someone had called in a hit on the BOLF; perhaps McIntyre would have some good news for me. I could but hope.

'Allow me.' Before I could decline the offer – I'd wanted to refill my flask with the Waters of Forgetting for the child ghosts at the Ascot House – an enormous hand had reached out. I felt as if I'd been seized by winter and was suddenly filled with terror, not knowing where it might deposit me. I felt frozen, for ever – then I was back in the council chambers and falling to my knees, shivering hard and vomiting even more violently.

But something stuck in my mind, a whisper I don't think I was meant to hear. I had to scramble for the words, quicksilver against my ears, but at last I had them.

I need more time.

I myself needed food. I needed company. I needed actual useful information.

Chapter Seventeen

Little Venice was filled to bursting when I arrived, with not even a tall stool at the bar standing free. Not that it mattered, as Aspasia wasn't giving me a chance to sit down anyway.

'You're in big trouble,' she said through gritted teeth and a fake smile.

'When am I not?' I asked, quite reasonably, I thought.

'If you won't leave immediately – and when do you ever? – then you're going upstairs right away.'

'But I'm hungry—'

'There's a table in the courtyard currently occupied by Titania Banks' retainers, just in case you didn't notice on your merry way in. And in case you were wondering, *they* clocked *you* as soon as you arrived, Verity Fassbinder, and I can see from here that there are rumblings. No, don't turn around—'

'Kick-my-arse type rumblings?'

'Are there any other kind where you're concerned?'

'I'll go upstairs. I need to talk to Thaïs anyway. Maybe you could bring me a sandwich?'

Her reply was unprintable.

No sandwich then.

Theo and Aspasia shared the second storey and Thaïs had the top floor all to herself. The space was lit only by candles, but incense-burners were working overtime, which made me wonder what the oldest Norn was trying to cover up or be calm about. Most of the room was open-plan; a huge bed sat on a raised platform and only the bathroom was walled off. The rest of the furniture comprised four couches set in laager around an intricately carved coffee table sitting on top of four pillars of small drawers where Thaïs kept all her accoutrements for scrying, fortune-telling, spell-casting and what-have-you.

The woman herself was pacing back and forth in the wide area uncluttered by furniture, which was noteworthy because Thaïs was normally serenity personified (I'm ignoring the time an angel hoisted her several feet off the floor and was slowly strangling her; any loss of *sangfroid* at such a time was entirely understandable). Apart from that, Thaïs had *never* been known to engage in anything that might have constituted exercise, and that including unwarranted movement. She hated it worse than I did. Theo was whippet-thin and Aspasia was voluptuous, but Thaïs was *fat*: tall and round and weighty, like a flesh-and-blood Venus of Willendorf. Her white-blonde hair was plaited into a complicated series of braids and her eyes were Arctic blue against her snow-white skin, which was glowing coldly in the candlelight. Her black caftan had flashes of gold shot through the fabric, which somehow made her skin even paler. With the light catching on the golden threads, she looked like a supernova against the shadows.

Most of all, though, she looked worried.

'Thaïs?' She didn't hear me, so I entered the room and called louder, '*Thaïs?*'

She whirled about, much faster than I'd have thought her capable of. Her face was pulled into a terrifying snarl, ice and smoke steamed from her flesh and hair and frost crackled from her fingers and froze in the air.

None of the Norns had *ever*, in my sight or in *any* living memory I'd ever tapped into, displayed this kind of manifest power. They told fortunes and they could make or break them. They knew more stuff than they ever admitted to. They gathered information and knowledge with the enthusiasm and dedication of a kleptomaniac mediaeval monk with a book fetish. But *never* had any of them shown power like this. I couldn't help but think that if they had, maybe none of them would have borne the quadrate scars they did. Thaïs' was high on her right cheek, still very rosy against her pallor.

When she saw it was me, everything stopped: the frost, the ice, the cold smoke, it all dissipated and she was normal old Thaïs once more, although she was definitely looking at me with a certain level of distress. The spike of ice that had been tearing towards me dropped abruptly and shattered on the floorboards.

'Thaïs — *what the actual fuck?*'

'I don't know! It started a few days ago . . .' She looked as bewildered as she sounded.

'Is it affecting the others?' Neither Aspasia nor Theo had mentioned anything.

'No — but I am the oldest and there is . . . *more* of me . . . Perhaps it will come to them later? Perhaps it will be greater or lesser?' She pulled at her braids. 'I don't know!'

'You weren't bitten by a radioactive spider, were you?' She gazed at me blankly, which I should have expected. 'Okay, right. So apart from the snow-and-ice thing, is there anything else? Any unnatural desire to take over a small nation, invade Asgard or rob a bank? In short, any kind of super-villain tendencies?'

'Are you taking this seriously, strangeling? I am *changing*!' she shouted.

'And I acknowledge that most people aren't good with change, Thaïs. But what I'm trying to establish is whether this is urgent, or something that can be *managed*. Maybe it's just *evolution* and not life-threatening to anyone. We could ask one of the healers to—'

'No healers!' she shouted. 'No one is to know about this.' She stared down at her palms. 'Not until I know what it is. Fassbinder, for the Weyrd, *change* is a sign of weakness – and weakness is deadly.'

'I cannot deny that.' I rubbed my face. 'Do your sisters know?'

'Not yet, but they cannot help but notice something is amiss.'

'What can I do?'

She stared at me for a moment, then said regretfully, 'Nothing, I fear. We shall simply have to see what develops. Why are you here?'

'Aspasia sent me up. There's a posse of Banks' people downstairs glaring at me over their non-fat chai lattes. Also, I wanted to ask you about grails.'

'Grails? Oh, yes, Theodosia mentioned that.' She sighed and made her way over to one of the couches. As I sat across from her I tried not to examine her too conspicuously for pinpoints of icy stars in her hair, her eyes, her skin, but there was nothing.

She clasped her hands in her lap as if that might be the best way to control them. 'So: grails. What do you want to know?'

'Can you recall stories, substantiated or otherwise, of any being brought to Brisbane? I know Normal knights would return from the Crusades with so-called reliquaries or other items of religious value to make *them* special, to bring greatness upon their houses.'

'Indeed,' said Thaïs, 'and thus did many a common man rise beyond his station, pulling his family up the ladder after him. Weyrd families used grails in similar fashion, to bolster reputation and position, to win favour.'

'Do you, you know, *use* them?'

'To heal? Yes. But *mortal* wounds . . . the pull towards death is too strong in such cases; even a grail would be ineffective.'

I nodded, thinking about Frau Berhta and her resurrection by sheer force of will. 'I know there are three grail families here: the Nadasys, the Odinsays and the Forsythes—'

'The Forsythes are liars.' Her face went even frostier with contempt. 'They are newcomers – *parvenus*. Their lineage papers are unlikely to stand up to close scrutiny – you'll probably find they came from the stables and the servants halls, if Udo is anything to go by.'

'That's not very egalitarian of you.'

'They – *he* – is protective of family prestige in the way of those who've come from much lower down the social ladder. Udo is still creating his own story, building his reputation – his continual trumpeting of what he claims to be his Old Country lineage is just so much sound and fury.'

'Which generally signifies a lot of insecurity. So, stories of a grail in the family . . .'

'Highly unlikely.' She sniffed. 'For if he did have one, chances are it was stolen – and since Weyrd families do not tolerate such thefts, Udo and his low-bred brood would not still be extant.'

'Solid.' So Udo was on the back-burner; I didn't need to go near him unless it was *absolutely* necessary. Bela would be *delighted*. 'What about the Nadasys? I've been through the house, which has been completely looted, by the way.'

She frowned. 'Vadim Nadasy was a first-class snob, as you know, but he was also a younger son. His removal to this country carried with it the usual tales of misdoings and exile—'

'Really?'

'Really. He built that enormous home, he threw money around

like water, but he brought with him nothing of true value. Had he something like a grail, it would not have been a gift from his family – such items are not given to lesser offspring – so it would have been stolen, and if that had been the case, he would have been hunted by his own and would never have lasted long enough to make your life difficult last year.'

'Wouldn't that have been nice to avoid . . .'

'Indeed.'

'What was he exiled for?'

Thaïs shrugged as if she didn't know or didn't care and it mattered not at all. 'Some said he was fleeing a dynastic marriage; others claimed he'd wounded a rival's scion. In any case, Nadasy had no true roots in this country. Zvezdomir has perhaps told you he "helped" Vadim come here, but in truth your Bela provided nothing more than a safe haven for someone who had once been a friend, a long time ago. Your father came in the train of Vadim's service.'

'I figured that.' I didn't want to discuss Grigor any more than I had to. 'So that just leaves the Odinsays.'

'A good family – a fine family, the sort who might well have a true grail in their possession. Freydis Odinsay and her husband Egil. Upright, with a great sense of *noblesse oblige*.'

'Well, good on them. So now I just need to talk to them.'

'I believe Bela has that in hand,' she said slyly, but before I could ask what she meant, there was a disturbance outside and the door flew open, thudding against the wall.

Five Weyrd in the process of dropping their glamours to expose horns and pointy tails, talons and fangs, several with ragged wings, burst in.

The dreadlocked guy in the lead – I recognised him from the night of the abortive summoning – lifted a claw-heavy hand in my direction and spat through a lot of very sharp teeth. 'This one comes with us to atone for what was done to the Mistress.'

Yeah, he was definitely the first one I'd tossed around. 'I had nothing to do with that,' I said firmly. 'I just happened to be there.' One thing was certain: the times sure were a'changing if Weyrd were not thinking twice about disrespecting the Norns' space.

'You never were one of us and now you're no longer with us,' a woman with twisted horns growled.

'That's neither nice nor true. I want to know what happened to her as much as anyone.' I slowly rose from the couch, flexing my hands, rolling my shoulders, pointedly reminding them that I wasn't harmless. If they wanted a fight, they would get it, and while sheer weight of numbers might bring me down eventually, more than one of them was going to finish up short a limb or three.

'We have questions—'

'And I'm all out of answers.'

'Then we'll take them in blood!' Someone snarled and, as one, the monstrous regiment took a step forward – and they halted as one as Thaïs' voice ripped through them.

'*Stop!*'

That one word was carried on a gust of rime and icy vapour, hitting at speed, ruffling clothing and tearing furrows into exposed flesh. The temperature in the room dropped significantly and I puffed out dragon's breath as I watched the disbelieving expressions in front of me. I put off thinking about what might have happened to me if Thaïs hadn't controlled herself when I'd entered unannounced; now was not the time for speculation.

'Um, guys? Can I suggest you back out of here, *right now*?' I started.

But Thaïs wasn't having it. 'You have violated the sanctity of my home,' she said, her voice crystal-clear. 'You have offended against the most sacred of our laws. *There is a price.*'

And she pointed slowly and deliberately at the dreadlocked Weyrd. A stream of something that looked like the love-child of lightning and snow shot from her hand, swirling up and over the guy until he was covered and unmoving and only his eyes twitched from side to side. Thaïs, stately as a queen and inexorable as a wave, crossed the floor and stood in front of him, then, with one contemptuous finger, *pushed*.

He hit the floor and shattered, leaving nothing but ruby shards scattered across the polished floorboards.

The oldest and, officially, Most Terrible of the Norns, turned her gaze on the remaining Weyrd and said, very quietly, 'This woman is under my protection. Should anything happen to her, I will seek you out. And should even one of you ever think to cross the threshold of Little Venice again, *let alone* invade my home . . .'

They were all gone before she had finished the sentence, leaving behind the melting crimson shards of their erstwhile leader.

Neither of us said anything for a while.

Eventually, I pulled myself together.

'Thanks for that, Thaïs.' As she graciously inclined her head, I added, 'Mind you, it's going to make keeping things a secret a bit difficult.'

She shrugged. 'They will tell tales, perhaps, go running to whomever sent them here with hate in their hearts. Or perhaps knowing I had right on my side they will keep their mouths shut. This was not just an incursion, it was an *attack*; it was defence of self, defence of home.' I wondered if Thaïs and I weren't related, somewhere in the *way* back. 'They may well think it nothing more than a spell or sleight-of-hand.'

'Maybe.' I looked down at the spreading melting vermilion that had once been a man. 'Maybe.'

On my way down I met Theo and Aspasia, running up, mortified that one of the Banks posse had distracted them with complaints about the soup special, allowing the others to sneak upstairs. I told them they'd need a bucket and mop, but Thaïs was okay, at least for the moment. I also told them to let me know if either of them started to manifest powers.

'They might seem pretty awesome, but only until someone gets their eye poked out,' I said firmly. *Listen to me, being the grown-up.* They looked at me in surprise, but I kept going; Thaïs could explain better than I ever could.

I got outside to find a police car waiting. Constable Lacy Oldman leaned across and shouted through the passenger window, 'You've got a problem.'

How novel.

Chapter Eighteen

'When did you find her?' I asked, following the beam of Constable Oldman's torch down the spiral stone stairs. Our footsteps were echoing upwards as if trying to escape; they clearly didn't want to go any further either. 'And how the Hell did you know she was *here*?'

The Old Windmill Tower, sixteen metres of brick and rendered stone with a cantilevered balcony standing in a nice little park on Wickham Terrace in Spring Hill is a Brisbane landmark. It'd been used variously over the years to grind grain, as a signal station for ships in the river, regulating time-keeping, transmitting early radio and television signals . . . and now it was just a picturesque bit of history that might or might not have ghosts. It's one of those bits of the city's history people don't really notice any more.

It had also been used, not irrelevantly, as a chapel; no one had ever bothered to take off its churchly stamp of approval so it remained consecrated: holy ground.

'Brisbane City Council started getting reports of an inordinately large fox seen in the park – I mean, in London, maybe, but *here*? Anyway, when the animal control guy turned up he found a very drunk, very angry, very *naked* young woman of Asian appearance. Apparently, she tried to bite him.'

'He's lucky that was the worst of it.'

'I didn't think telling him that would be very helpful.' Lacy looked at me in the glow from the beam of the torch. We were walking abreast, maybe because it felt a bit safer. 'Anyway, when she disappeared into the tower, he called it in – because of the whole nudity and the threatened biting. We've got "fox" in the system as a keyword since, well, you know, so it came up as a weird shit basket job and when the boss flicked it to me since I'm her designated shit-kicker, I thought, *Haven't I recently dealt with a kitsune case?*'

'How did you know where to find me?'

'A report of an incident at Little Venice, which is a known hang-out of yours. Trust me, it didn't take a beautiful mind to put two and two together there.'

Was I becoming so predictable?

'I noticed you didn't go inside to check on the incident . . .'

'I'm not stupid!' she protested. 'I knew you'd either walk out, run out or get thrown out pretty quickly – and see? I was absolutely right.'

Not that long ago, I'd had to hoist Lacy Oldman a foot in the air by the front of her shirt to emphasise something in my typically subtle fashion, and since then, she'd become a lot more confident, maybe even reasonable. I really hoped she'd got over the whole bizarro 'sibling rivalry' thing she'd had with me, for some insane reason thinking I was McIntyre's favoured child with no boundaries, whereas *she* had to obey every rule and law *and* bring me answers when Rhonda told her to. Or maybe she'd developed some smarts and was just hiding it better. If she grew up a bit, stopped being bored and lazy, she might just make it as a cop. Maybe.

'*Do* I need to check in on Little Venice?' she asked, almost as if it were an afterthought, but there was a definite undertone of excitement.

For once, I actually thought before I answered. It must have been one of the Normal clients reporting the soup-special-related fracas downstairs – good thing they hadn't seen what was actually happening upstairs; it might have put them off their muffins. 'Nope, you don't need to go to Little Venice. In fact, Lacy, you *never* need to go into Little Venice . . . well, unless you're reporting my death. You are *not* prepared for dealing with the Norns.'

I couldn't work out whether the look she gave me was petulant or just queasy from all the going round and round and round.

For some reason I found myself adding, 'I'm not putting you down or belittling you; it's just that the Norns are special and touchy at the best of times, and right now they are going through some stuff. There's a reason McIntyre leaves dealing with them up to me.'

'Yeah, but you're not working for the Weyrd Council any more.'

'True, but Ziggi Hassman is, so if in doubt, pass the problems on to him. Constable Oldman, all McIntyre does is *liaise* – she does *not* police the Weyrd, and if you think you should be doing that, then you need to reconsider your job choices. Play your cards right, don't get killed and you may well inherit her mantle, but I – well, *Ziggi* – is there as the thin Weyrd line. Don't cross into territory you don't understand and are not part of, okay? It's dangerous.'

Her tone was definitely petulant when she stopped a few steps from the bottom of the stairs and said, 'She's in there, as far as I can tell. I don't think there's anywhere else for her to go.'

'You're not coming with me?'

She pointed at the stone archway and the blackness beyond. 'Not my community, just liaising.'

'Touché.' I held my palms upwards. 'If you hear screaming, I'd advise running.'

I moved past her into the gloom and stepped beyond the beam of her torch.

'Ah, Joyce?' I called before I went in too far, wondering how long she'd been down here. Everything smelled of ferment. I clicked on the police-issue Maglite Lacy had handed to me, a twin to hers, easily big and heavy enough to double as a weapon.

The Maglite was bright as a spotlight, left my mobile phone torch for dead. I waved it around and the beam caught Joyce as she was in mid-transformation, that flicker from human to fox, a shape that was neither and yet both. The fox raised a paw that became a hand to shield her eyes. There was the sound of a bottle tipping over and liquid glugging onto the stone ground and a muttered voice slurred, '*Shit.*'

I angled the beacon away so it wasn't blinding her, but I could still see her outline wavering in and out, in and out, like a reel of old film. 'Jeeez, Joyce. Bender much?'

'Everyone can just bugger off,' she growled, 'and you, of all people, can bugger right off the most.'

'I'm aware there are a lot of reasons for you to feel that way, but is there a specific one relating to this particular situation?'

'You showed me the angel.' She began to weep, flailing her arms about, and more bottles hit the stone floor; some broke.

I wasn't game enough to get any closer to her, but I tried talking. 'I'm sorry, but you had to know.'

'What? That *everything* I've ever done is a *lie*? That the Guardian's been keeping secrets from me? That my sisters died for *nothing*?'

'Well, take your pick, really. Isn't that important to know?' I wasn't unsympathetic, for all I might sound like it.

As more sobbing echoed round the chamber, I tried, 'Joyce, I'm genuinely remorseful. I really am. But now is not the time for wallowing.'

'Really? I'd say it's a pretty fucking perfect time to wallow.'

I ducked the bottle she threw at me and called, 'You're so close to being free. You *want* to be free of the Guardian.'

'What do you know about me, you bitch?'

Another bottle, another quick dodge.

'You went dark – you got rid of everything the Guardian gave you, didn't you, so he can't connect with you, hence the nakedness: no copper bracelet, no weaponry.'

At my words, she curled around herself.

'And, finally, you found the smallest church in Brisbane because you knew he couldn't see in here; he can't *whisper* to you . . .'

As she started sobbing again, I told her, 'Joyce, he's nothing more than an archangel, broken and insane. I've dealt with that kind before.' I began to pace as I started thinking aloud. 'He's outside the will of his God, and said God is, to the best of my knowledge, AWOL. The Guardian hides from the light and his brothers because he's ashamed and afraid.'

'How can you know that?'

'Can you think of any other reason for him staying down *there*? You've seen his condition and you've seen Tobit, so you know how an angel is meant to look. He doesn't *belong* in the Underworld, Joyce; he's a guardian of *nothing*.' I stopped.

After a moment, I asked gently, 'Did you make a deal with him?' She looked blank.

'Like Mike did through you, or the *smågubbar* Wilbur Wilson did? Like my mother did?' I looked at her impatiently. 'Did you make a deal for something? Like revenge on your sisters' murderer?'

'Your mother, you mean?' She lost her shape with a sob, then pulled herself together. There was a long pause before she said, 'No. I've seen what happens to those who bargain with the Guardian. And besides, when we were taken to the Underworld after our parents' deaths we were so young – we didn't know anything about what had happened, not then. We were brought up there; it was all we knew.'

'So he can't whisper to you; there's no Breath of God and all that bullshit; he can't go giving instructions to *crush, kill, destroy*.' I thought of my erstwhile bodyguard, Mike Jones and how, unbeknownst to me, he'd done a deal with Joyce as an agent of the Guardian. Mike had carried one the ruined archangel's 'gifts' which allowed the Guardian to connect to him. It was the threat cast over my loved ones that had been enough to convince me to bargain with the burned monstrosity.

So Joyce was free of that, so all I really had to worry about was that she might be lying; that this was all an act. It was pretty convincing, mind you, although maybe not convincing enough for me to tell her that her parents were alive; not yet. If she had been feeding me porkies and the Guardian *could* still tap into her, then he was just as likely to take out her remaining family members to make her despair, frame me for it and reel her back to the fold. I had quite enough on my conscience as far as the Mori-Miller family was concerned; I'd really like to keep Joyce's parents alive.

'Joyce, get up for fuck's sake, will you? That stone floor is freezing cold, it'll give you haemorrhoids.'

That actually shocked a laugh out of her. I offered her my hand and after a brief hesitation, she allowed me to help her up. 'God, you smell bad.'

'You try wallowing in self-pity and cheap booze for days and see how sweet you come out,' she retorted.

I shone the torch around and could see nothing but bottles; not even her satchel was there. 'You really got rid of everything, huh? Okay, so, first off, shower for you and lunch for me. Also, probably for you. And a lot of black coffee.' I paused. 'Joyce, this couple of days out of contact? The Guardian's likely to suspect you're compromised, understand? So you need to keep an eye out, hey? If he sends someone against us, someone we – *you* – don't know . . .'

As I lit the way back to the bottom of the stairs, I looked for the shine of Lacy's police-issue Doc Martens and when I failed to find them, I stopped.

'What is it?'

'Got a weapon?'

'Nope. The *sai* came from the Guardian.'

'Right, grab a bottle and pretend it's a bar fight. Follow me.' And while the thought of Joyce behind me with a broken bottle pointed at my ribs did not fill me with joy, the idea that something was waiting for us above made me even less happy.

Then I started to wonder if maybe we'd been locked in.

But when we got to the top, lo and behold, no locked door, and even better, no attack waiting, just Constable Oldman standing outside, phone to her ear, kicking at some defenceless weeds growing through the cracks in the pavement. She was clutching a blue police-issue jumpsuit, which she tossed at Joyce while she was nodding, as if the person on the mobile could see her.

'Yes, ma'am,' she said at last. She hung up, breathed a sigh, then said, 'You've got another problem.'

'Can this day get any better?' I turned to Joyce. 'Is the car nearby? That wasn't a gift from the Guardian, was it?'

The body this time was in an unfinished apartment block in New Farm, almost directly across the river from where the first one had been found. She'd been discovered by a carpenter called Edward, who looked pale and shaky and was probably going to need some serious counselling. Most people don't see dead bodies in their life, and certainly not in their place of work, right on the spot where they were about to install some luxury kitchen cabinetry.

There was no mattress beneath her this time, no kindly cushioning; instead, she was laid out on the concrete floor. Like the previous victim, she wore heavily embroidered silk pyjamas, this time of a deep emerald-green, and a worn-thin-with-washing white cotton dressing gown. She had the same mummified appearance, the same black soot in and around her mouth, streaking her nose and chin and sprayed across the unpainted ceiling, the same washed-out look in her eyes. Her long hair was the same mix of dark and silver.

'Another one,' said Joyce, fidgeting in the over-sized jumpsuit. She'd collected the Honda from the secure car park on Wickham Terrace and followed Oldman and me over here.

McIntyre gave her the *Hello, Captain Obvious* glare, then followed up with, 'Did you sleep in a wine barrel?'

'Has Ziggi seen this?' I asked quickly, trying to head off any sparks.

'Your uncle's already been.'

'Did he say anything?'

'Apart from "Shit"? No.'

I knelt beside the body; one of her hands was palm up, open. I pointed. 'No fingerprints again.'

'Smooth?' McIntyre asked.

'As a baby's bottom.'

'Still got her teeth, though.'

'Perhaps he ran out of time?' suggested Lacy.

'Or he's getting sloppy,' Joyce added.

'Both are possible. Or maybe he thinks there won't be dental records around for her.' I leaned closer and tugged at the collar of the dressing gown where I could see some lettering peeking out. 'There wasn't any kind of identifier on the other gown, was there?'

'Nope. What have you got?'

'A label, one of those sewn-in things: St Barbara's Private Hospital.' I stood.

'Wasn't there . . . wasn't there a church-run place over at Waterford?' Lacy asked. 'I'm pretty sure I had an old aunty who was a nurse there.'

I had a passing acquaintance with only one religious place over that way. 'St Barbara's Seminary and Church?'

'That sounds about right.'

'It's been closed for years, I'm guessing, or at least the hospital bit has been.' But I wasn't too worried, because I knew the priest in charge. Father Tony Caldero, ex-exorcist, friend to the Weyrd, would surely be able to help me out with any records. For the first time, I felt a surge of hope.

'Ideas?' asked McIntyre. 'You look happier than you have in days.'

'A couple, yes. The first one is for Joyce to shower.'

Chapter Nineteen

The next morning, Joyce collected me at nine-thirty, which was a nice, healthy compromise. She'd even texted when she'd arrived – I wasn't feeling so Pollyanna-ish that I was going to take the ward off the house just yet.

After our trip to New Farm, we'd gone shopping for clothes, then booked her into a serviced apartment. Seeing to her personal comforts had included a fairly dramatic make-over: she'd chopped off the long black hair she habitually wore in a tidy bun, and I had to admit that for a hack job it didn't look half bad. It was edgy and cool and all I-don't-give-a-rat's-arse-about-anything. Her normal understated Librarian's attire of frock and Mary Janes had been replaced by tight black jeans, a leather jacket and a black T-shirt decorated with a glittery fox. I did not feel I needed to mention that the burgundy Blundstones she was now sporting were my mother's footwear of choice.

'So, what are you doing for a weapon?' I asked after climbing into the vehicle.

'Glove-box,' she instructed.

With some trepidation I opened the compartment to reveal a shiny iron war fan gleaming up at me.

'Oh. Nice!'

A quick bout on Google had revealed that St Barbara's Private

Hospital, which stood next to St Barbara's Church, had been repurposed into a seminary in 1956. And next to the church stood the little rectory that housed Father Tony Caldero and his housekeeper, Miriam Parry, a sweet little old lady whom I suspected was keeping more than his house for him.

After a mere forty-five minutes, only fifteen of them stuck in traffic, we pulled up outside, and the door had opened before I was even out of the car. Miriam must spend her days by the window, waiting to see who arrived – priests don't need watchdogs as long as they've got housekeepers.

Her soft lilac hair was as perfectly coiffed as always, and a pristine apron topped a full-skirted 1950s swing dress in electric blue. When she recognised me, she smiled and called, 'Ms Fassbinder!' She gave me a hug, and then Joyce too.

Joyce wasn't sure what to do about that. It was at odds with her new tough chick image, so I helpfully mouthed, *Lean into it!* and she gave me the finger over Miriam's head.

'How lovely to see you.'

It was nice to hear that from someone who meant it for a change. 'Hi, Miriam. This is Joyce. Is Father Tony around?'

'He's doing pastoral visits, dear. He won't be home until late this afternoon.'

The new grown-up me managed to keep the swears in. I should have called ahead, but oftentimes that just forewarns people when I prefer them to be decidedly *un*forewarned. I'd found you generally got more truths that way. Besides, I'd figured on Sunday he'd be close to home for the performance of Masses and such. Not that I thought Father Tony would lie to me, but I could see no reason for me to change standard operating procedure when it had been a winning formula for a really long time.

'That's a shame. I was hoping to ask him about when this used to be a hospital.'

'Oh, really? Not many people even know about that, and he couldn't help you with that because he wasn't here then. But I was. I've got an hour before I head off to bingo. Won't you come in?'

Even though I'd protested there wasn't time for tea, Miriam was not to be denied. She wasn't going to be derailed by someone like me who had insufficient respect for the niceties. The tea was strong and the homemade biscuits sweet and crisp and I had no reason to complain, except maybe for my questioning time being eaten up by the brewing and straining and the careful and precise placement of jam drops on a plate. I did, however, take advantage of the enforced break to text McIntyre with a request.

Once we were settled in the front parlour, which contained too many chairs, too few of them comfortable, and all had floral teacups in hand, Miriam said, 'What do you want to know, dear?'

'For a start, what happened to the hospital? What kind of patients were here? Were there any – well, you know, any mysteries?'

'It closed because a bigger hospital opened up, with better facilities and paying better wages. I was a nurse then, you see.' She smiled fondly. 'And you remember Sister Bridget? From your wedding?'

How could I forget my favourite militant nun? Like Father Tony, she was also an ex-exorcist; she'd been *Mulieres Bonae*, one of a secret all-female arm of the adjuristine-exorcism squads of the Vatican in the late Sixties. 'Of course.'

'We both started our training here – hers not long after she'd left Rome. Our lives take strange paths, don't they?' She smiled again, this time a little sadly. 'We mostly looked after patients who'd fallen into comas after some traumatic incident or other. When the doctors or their families gave up on them, or the money ran out, we cared for them at St Barbara's. There wasn't much we could do except to be patient and kind, but it was a good grounding for a young nurse, and I learned a lot about the human body – how it operates, how it fades, how it falls away from itself when the soul is gone. But by the end, we weren't needed so much. Fewer people wanted to travel right the way out here, funding was being diverted elsewhere and the Church decided that it was more important to train new priests than to care for the infirm.' She didn't sound at all bitter as she added, 'And you can see how well that worked out.'

The seminary hadn't been able to fill its quota for many years.

'So that was it?' I tried not to sound disappointed. 'It just kind of blinked out?'

'Well, the disappearance didn't help.'

That was music to my ears but I didn't want to show it. 'Disappearance?'

'A woman called Alison Brandt; she was taken from her bed. She'd been non-responsive for five years or so and there was no sign of that changing, but one night she was safely tucked in and the next morning she was gone. I believe it was towards the end of 1980.'

'Did they ever find her?'

'No, dear, and she didn't have any family that we could ever find, so it just sort of died away. The hospital closed a couple of months later. The disappearance just gave the administration the excuse they needed. They said we hadn't been paying attention to our duties, that *we'd* been neglectful.' Her blue eyes turned steely enough to laser through some hapless bean-counter if she'd been given half a chance.

My phone buzzed: McIntyre had come through. I wished it was a better picture, but Ellen had obviously done her best, and quickly, cleaning off the soot, tidying the hair, getting the mouth to close. A green sheet was drawn up to the neck so nothing else showed.

First of all, I pulled up the sketch of the first victim, from the house in Laidlaw Street (*not* the crime scene photo). 'Would you mind looking at something for me, Miriam? It's a bit gruesome, I'm afraid.'

'I was a nurse, dear.'

I handed her the phone.

Her expression registered nothing but sadness. 'I don't know her, Verity. I'm sorry.'

I took the phone again, swiped the new image and turned it to face her. 'One more.'

'I've seen it all, dear.' Then her face went slack, then perplexed, then confused, then anxious. 'Well. Except for that.'

'It's just a dead body, Miriam,' I began gently.

She gave me a look. 'I mean, seeing someone long gone who doesn't really look much different to the last time you saw them. Oh, she's all dried up, but I'd know her features anywhere. I looked at her almost every day for five years. I'd know her skin hanging on a fence post.'

She clicked her tongue. 'This is Alison Brandt, Ms Fassbinder.'

I texted Alison Brandt's name and the very scant details of her disappearance to McIntyre; at least with the name she'd be able to get information a lot faster, and it helped no end that she wasn't – or at least *Lacy* wasn't – going to have to waste hours or days assuming that our dead body was 'modern'.

Which led to my next question: what the Hell was a woman who'd disappeared almost forty years ago doing turning up dead on a building site and why did she not look older, just mummified? I wondered if Ellen could do something about rehydrating the body so we could get some idea of how she'd looked before that had happened so we could estimate her age. I thought of the silver in her hair.

While Joyce drove us back towards the city, I made some calls.

'Third Eye Books, this is Merrily, how may I help you?'

'My, what a nice phone manner you've got.'

'I'm hanging up now, Fassbinder.'

'No, don't. I'm checking in. Any sign of your suitor?'

'Nope, but Bela's got a guy sitting in a car across the road. Kinda cute.'

'That's Mike, who is recently bereaved by the death of his life partner *Jerry*, remember? Please leave him alone. Try not to distract him from actually keeping you safe and watching your back.'

'I'd rather he watched my front.'

I hung up.

'Christos?'

'Verity.'

'How are you? How is Callie?'

'Tobit hasn't responded to my text.'

'That's not what I asked.'

'But you were going to.'

'Sure. But how are *you*?'

'With a client, so how about you let me go and make some money to support my daughter?'

'You are unusually snippy. You know Bela's talking to Eurycleia, right? He's got a guy sitting off your house?'

'Correction, two guys.' He sounded a little more cheerful at that. 'One on the house and one on the shop when I'm here.'

'And Callie's okay?'

'Fine, happy as a clam. Vicki adores her and she adores Vicki. What's the kid got to complain about?'

'And nothing more from Eurycleia?'

'Just the usual.'

'Right. I'll let you go then.'

I hung up and thought a moment, then announced, 'Joyce? Change of plan. We're going to visit the sirens first.' I gave her the address. 'I want to check on Ligeia. The old bird knows more than she's saying, as usual, so it's time to shake some of Tobit's secrets out of her, if I can.' I figured I had a high chance of being bitten, but I didn't really have much choice.

I took a deep breath before I made the next call.

Mel was cool when she picked up.

'Hi – I just wanted to check on you and Lizzie. You know.'

'We're fine,' she said, adding reluctantly, 'She's not been having any nightmares.'

Phew.

'I'm really sorry, Mel. You know I am . . . I'd never expose Lizzie to risk on purpose . . . what else can I say?' My voice trembled, and from the corner of my eye I saw Joyce shooting glances at me.

'Look, it's not your fault, V. I get it. I was just so worried.' She started sobbing. 'And I felt so *guilty* – I was out on a *date* when my little girl was threatened—'

'Mel, you could have been at home and something could have happened that wasn't at all related to me. Shit happens, you know? And please, you need to keep in mind that you're dating a Weyrd now, so *extra* shit is likely to happen now. But hey, Jost had warded the house: he'd thought ahead, looked out for you guys.'

'I know. I know.' She gave a quavering sigh. 'V, I was going to call you anyway. Lizzie and I are going to stay with Jost for a while, just until things settle down with you. His place will be safer, it's . . .'

'Not near me. I get it.' As I understood it, the Archivist had a palatial pad in the Hamilton Wharf Apartments, which meant he was paid a great deal more than I was.

'That's not what I meant!'

'That's okay, Mel. I don't want either of you hurt. It's a good idea. Give my love to Lizzie.' I hung up as she was trying to explain something to me that I already knew: *she was right*. It didn't make it hurt any less, but she was right. I took a deep breath and gathered my thoughts. The next call should be a doddle after that one.

'Sister Bridget.'

'Verity Fassbinder.'

'How are you?'

'What do you want?'

I sighed. 'Miriam tells me you used to work at St Barbara's Private Hospital at Waterford.'

'Yessss?' She sounded surprised.

'I wanted to ask you some questions.'

Silence.

'Specifically about the disappearance of Alison Brandt.'

'Good Lord, why? After all this time?'

'She's been found.'

Sister Bridget said a word not normally used by nuns, which kind of took my breath away for a second.

'I've got an errand to run, but perhaps you might be free for a chat after that? Say about five?'

She hesitated.

'Sister Bridget, are you avoiding me in some way, shape or form?'

'Of course not.'

Yet there wasn't quite enough conviction in her scoff and I heard a voice in the background. 'Have you got company?'

'No. The others are all away.'

'Pilgrimage?'

'Girls' weekend at Jupiter's Casino on the Gold Coast.' Now there was the sarcasm.

'I think they call it The Star nowadays.'

'Whatever. Five-thirty. Bring milk, I've run out.'

Chapter Twenty

I wasn't entirely comfortable bringing Joyce with me. The sirens were private types – they didn't even like to associate with other Weyrd because they thought themselves better than the rank and file. However, I did like the idea of a fox-girl assassin on my team just in case things went pear-shaped. Besides, if she was going to be released back into the Weyrd population at some juncture, she'd need to learn to play nice with all aspects of the community. The war fan disappeared neatly up her sleeve. We parked and I faced the intercom.

I was in luck. The gate opened without me having to offer names or explanations, which I took as a sign that whoever was watching had decided I was legit, as was anyone keeping company with me.

'Trusting,' said Joyce, her eyes wide as we entered the compound and she took in the gardens.

'Yeah, that or it's a trap.'

The gardens weren't deserted, but the sirens were moving differently, slower, as if burdened. None of them were flying, although pearly wings were unfurled as if to catch the sun.

Joyce stared. 'Are they like . . . ?'

'Don't say that to either them or the angels or you'll be for it. They *really* don't like each other. Ancient rivalries, as far as I can tell, with all the maturity of a pair of three-year-olds yelling, "She hit me first!".'

'And yet Tobit got close enough to . . .'

'Yeah. He did.'

She watched as one of the sirens approached, her gait far more graceful than you might expect of a woman whose bare feet ended in claws. '*So* lovely.'

'Aren't they? But prickly. Watch the teeth and talons.'

As I recognised Thelxiope, I noticed something else: the feathers at the ends of her wings were turning black. My eyes widened.

'Verity Fassbinder.' She saw my expression and followed my gaze. Smiling sadly, she said, 'It is but grief.'

'I was worried you'd caught Ligeia's withering.'

She shook her head and repeated, 'It is but grief.'

'I wanted to see how Ligeia was doing.'

'Not well, I'm afraid.' She bowed her head but swept one hand back, indicating we should follow. It was a silent walk, me keeping my gaze straight ahead while Joyce was looking left and right, taking in the sight of creatures as mythical as she herself was. I guess when you grow up in a hole in the ground you don't really see a lot of that sort of thing. It was kind of cool to witness one creature of legend fascinated by another.

We were nearly at the mansion when an amazingly loud shriek went up from somewhere in the building. Thelxiope stilled, then took off at a run that contained none of her former grace; now she was all headless chicken, pushing herself towards the source of the sound through sheer determination.

Joyce dropped to all fours, a rusty-coloured blur, and tore ahead of me. I considered her instinct to run *towards* the sound of a tragedy and decided it probably boded well for her future.

The front door was open and Thelxiope fairly flew in, with us in hot pursuit. Sirens clustered at the base of the steps, staring upwards at the source of the howling, not sure what to do. We charged past the gawkers, running up and up and up, with the sirens behind, their black-feather-tipped wings streaming along as if our passing had broken their trance.

At last we reached the tower and Ligeia's room; even in my panic it was disconcerting to have Joyce shift from four legs to two and appear beside me suddenly taller and considerably less furry.

In the rays of the afternoon sun, Eurycleia, in a long black gown, her platinum hair loose and flowing down her back and over her wings like molten silver, knelt beside the four-poster bed, rocking backwards and forwards, her head and shoulders shaking. In the bed, the covers drawn away from her so every article of her death might be on display, lay Ligeia, her mother, the Exile, the oldest of them, keeper of secrets, killer of angels, eater of flesh: she who'd seen the walls of Troy torn down and Helen dragged back to her husband like a prize, a slave.

The old siren was a blackened mess of flesh and sinew, bone and feathers. The creeping illness that had been devouring her in tiny bites had won, leaving only her face free of the ebony scale. Behind me a great wail went up, a melodic keening because the sirens could never make an ugly sound in song.

As I watched, wondering what the Hell to do, feeling resentful and irrational as a child that she'd broken her promise not to die before I returned, Ligeia began to change.

The blackness that had engulfed her peeled away from her face, moving gradually down to her toes. Her skin turned a healthy pink-white, her hair turned the same platinum as her daughter's, shining, and her wings and legs sprouted feathers, the pearly-white, luminous coverage complete. She looked *perfect*, just as she must have been when first made.

But she was still dead.

Thelxiope stepped forward to stand by Eurycleia. She laid a hand on the heaving shoulder, only the gentlest of touches, but one that had an immediate effect. Eurycleia's fine-boned face lifted, she took in Thelxiope's grieving expression and a look passed between them. One of love.

I was glad there was someone there for her, even if I didn't especially like the head of the nest.

As Thelxiope helped Eurycleia to her feet I thought I heard a creaking and cracking of bones, as if her mother's death had aged her. *We become them*, I thought. *When they are gone there's no one to stand in their place but us.* Maybe one day, when Olivia died, I'd think of this . . . if she ever did. That was a thought for the future: the Guardian had given her powers of speed and strength and she'd already sort of died once, when she threw herself into the river. I narrowed my eyes. What if she outlived me?

My musing was interrupted when Eurycleia turned around and saw me.

'I came to see Ligeia,' I offered, and it wasn't and never would be enough.

Her violet eyes flickered to the bed where Ligeia lay in state. 'Then you have seen her. Leave us to our grief.'

There wasn't much else I could say except, 'I'm sorry, Eurycleia. I really am.'

At the door her voice stopped me. 'She liked you.'

'It was mutual.'

'I do not.'

'Nope.'

'Yet if I were to remove you, someone else would step into the breach, someone less . . . *reasonable*.' That was the first time I'd *ever* been called that. 'My mother pointed this out to me: that you are the lesser of two evils.'

'Oh, of at least a dozen, I expect.' I smiled. 'And then you'd have to deal with Tepes and Hassman – and it doesn't matter that I no longer work for the Council. They're my family, and you know how families work.'

She gave me a smile that was all teeth. 'We must co-exist.'

'That would be best.'

'The little man' – *Christos* – 'is afraid of me.'

'Well, you do go out of your way to be scary.'

'I want to see my granddaughter more often.'

'Stop making Christos afraid and we'll talk.'

'She must begin her education. Though you maimed her' – *took the wings that would have led to her death, you're welcome* – 'she will one day take my place, and she must be prepared.'

I nodded, although I wasn't really sure how much influence I had. Bela had been awfully pissed off with me. 'I'll talk to Zvezdomir about it.' Somehow, I will talk to the person I'm not meant to talk to.

'He will listen to you,' she said. It wasn't a question. Although I suspected people were over-estimating the extent of my influence on Bela Tepes, it probably wasn't in my interests to disabuse anyone of that right now.

'Ligeia's funeral?'

'Will be private,' she hissed, which sounded pretty final until her shoulders slumped in a defeated fashion and she finished, 'but Thelxiope will advise you of details.' She looked at her mother's body once again. 'It will be soon.'

'Wow. She *really* doesn't like you.'

'I did tell you, Joyce, it's a long queue.' My chest felt hollow. Ligeia had been unique and I couldn't – didn't want to – imagine the world without her. All in all, Eurycleia had been *reasonable*, which made me suspicious and not a little nervous, but whatever she had up her sleeve would have to wait, as would mourning for her mother, my friend, because *something* was scratching at my memory.

'But I mean, really *really*?'

'Got a point there?'

'*Really really.*'

'Just drive.' I recited the address of St Agnes of the Mercy Hospital where Sister Bridget worked, then phoned McIntyre.

'Even you cannot expect a result this quickly, so I am going to assume you've got a solution to all my problems?'

'Nah, just a random thought: that cold case? The body you were talking about the day Joyce got me arrested as an accessory to driving like an arsehole?'

'The bag of bones over at Teneriffe? What about it?'

'How long's it been there?'

'The forensic anthropologist Ellen talked to reckons nearly almost forty years.'

'Got an ID yet?'

'Nope, it's a cold case so there's no rush. Besides, everyone I've got is busy cleaning up the current spate of mummified bodies.'

'Two is hardly a spate, Rhonda.'

'Tomayto, tomahto. What's your thinking, Fassbinder?'

'Alison Brandt's been misplaced for almost forty years . . . well, thirty-seven, to be precise-ish.'

'I'm happy to report the body's male. The pelvis is distinctly blokey.' She sighed. 'At least it's not another dead woman being used to store . . . *something*.'

'Right. Oh well, just a hunch. Unrelated then.'

'Yeah.'

I bit my lip. 'I keep thinking about the first body – such care taken with de-identifying it.'

'Yeah.'

'Okay, well, I'm going to see Sister Bridget now, to find out what I can about St Barbara's and Alison Brandt.'

'Keep me updated.'

'Will do.' I clicked off, then began to scroll down, looking for Professor Harrow's number. His office had been deserted by the time I got there the other day and my conversation with Thaïs about grails had reminded me I'd still not heard from either the old academic or his dogsbody.

'So, how does this work? I drive you around all day while you make phone calls?' Joyce sounded surprised, which surprised me.

'Um, yeah, pretty much . . . It was good enough for Ziggi.'

'I'm not Ziggi.'

'Well, *obviously*, because Ziggi and I would never be having this conversation.'

'How am I supposed to contribute to an investigation if you don't fill me in? All I hear is one side of the conversation. It's like a jigsaw puzzle with half the pieces lost down the back of the couch.'

'You don't need to know everything,' I hedged, which meant, *It's probably safer for me if you don't know everything, oh possibly-still-untrust-worthy ally.* 'Besides, it's not like you've been completely honest with me about everything, is it?'

Just a stab in the dark, but it hit home. She went quiet.

I hit dial and waited for the phone to be picked up on the other end.

I waited in vain: no answer. I left yet another message. I wondered if Sophie had another extension, maybe even an office of her own somewhere for when she wasn't sifting through Harrow's papers and books, taking notes while no doubt sneezing and scratching at dust mite itch. Maybe I was going to have to go and find the old guy in the Antiquities Museum again and physically drag him up to his office, then go through everything on my own. I wasn't sure I had the lifespan.

Feeling lucky – or maybe just resigned – I called the rectory in the hope Father Tony might have returned; I wanted to throw a few questions at him, see if he knew about Alison Brandt, add to what Miriam had told me before I faced Sister B. The phone rang out.

'Turn up here, park on the left.' I considered what Joyce had said. 'We're going to visit Sister Bridget. She's a nun, an ex-exorcist, and she's very grumpy. Don't piss her off.'

'I'll leave that to you.'

Sister Bridget and four other nurse-nuns were housed in a two-storey red-and-white-brick residential building at the back of St Agnes of the Mercy Hospital. Bedrooms and bathrooms were upstairs, the common areas on the ground floor. All of the sisters were ageing, and what had once been an exclusively religious staff had been gradually replaced by non-denominational nurses as time crept on. St Agnes' wasn't a Weyrd place *per se*, but those who worked there were used to dealing with non-Normal patients and while not all Weyrd were willing to put themselves in the hands of Mother Church, the sisters had built up considerable trust over the years with their specialised maternity service.

Sister Bridget, in her well-preserved sixties, was the youngest of the remaining residents and her reign of terror was almost supreme. It wasn't that she was *bad*; she was just terrifyingly efficient and didn't take any crap. I liked her but she scared me a bit – not that I'd admit it to *anyone*. But Sister Bridget had been there when I needed her. She'd been the only one willing and able to stand by me, waiting on a cold riverbank like a reliable Orpheus to anchor me so I could come back from the Underworld.

I knocked on the front door and when I received no reply, I tried the handle. The door was unlocked, which I took as a gilt-edged invitation to come in and make myself at home. Inside was a small, tidy hall with scuffed green linoleum, a coat rack holding umbrellas and scarves but no coats, a hallstand with a stack of unopened mail, mostly catalogues. A few steps took us into a large, bright kitchen with a scrubbed pine table in the centre surrounded by mismatched chairs.

At the far end of the corridor was the common room; I could see some impressively brown sofas and armchairs in yellow and orange and overflowing bookshelves. Hearing voices, I gestured for Joyce to follow, but as we approached those voices stopped and when I stuck my head around the doorway, there was just Sister Bridget, a fit-looking plain-clothes nun, sporting a pair of black combat trousers, boots and a long-sleeved T-shirt, looking like she was about to parachute into a particularly irreligious place and maybe arm-wrestle atheists. She was middling height with short iron-grey hair, youthful olive skin and alert blue eyes. The forbidding aura was an optional extra.

'Sister Bridget – did we interrupt anything? You look ready to start operations . . .'

'Hello, Ms Fassbinder. No.'

'Could have sworn I heard voices.'

'Must be imaging things.'

I narrowed my eyes at her. For a nun, she was a terrible liar. I let it go.

'We forgot the milk.'

'Black tea it is, then.' She rose from the armchair she'd been occupying and led us back to the kitchen where I made the introductions.

She looked at Joyce. 'Is she the one who—'

'Yes.'

'Didn't she—'

'Yes.'

'Your funeral.'

'Probably. Although Joyce reassures me she's had a change of heart. Several, in fact.' I gave her a glance. 'She's kind of on probation.'

'Still living dangerously, I see.'

'So, St Barbara's Private Hospital and Alison Brandt.'

Sister Bridget lifted an enormous old-fashioned metal teapot from the Aga sitting in the space which had once housed a proper hearth. She pulled out three mugs and put them onto the table, along with a crystal bowl of sugar cubes, then produced an old orange-lidded Pablo coffee jar filled with Milk Arrowroot biscuits.

'Any butter?' I asked tentatively. Everyone knows Arrowroots are better with a wodge of the creamy yellow on them. Sister Bridget rose in my estimation as she pointed at a dish waiting ready on another counter and slid a knife towards me when I sat down.

She poured tea, dark as a witch's brew, and I buttered biscuits and passed them on. Joyce looked askance at me, but I said, 'If you trust me on nothing else, trust me on this.'

She took a bite and her expression said I'd definitely earned some Brownie points. From the outside we might have looked like three socially awkward friends having a very low-rent afternoon tea.

'Sooooo.'

Sister Bridget sighed and rolled her eyes.

'Do that too hard, you'll see your brain.'

'St Barbara's Private Hospital. What did Miriam tell you?'

'That it was a nice little cottage hospital for traumatised folk in comas.'

'Oh, Miriam! Such a gift for understatement and leaving out the important bits.' She smiled. 'You'd think butter wouldn't melt in her mouth.'

'She wasn't one of you, was she?'

'What? *Mulieres Bonae*?' She snorted. 'Can you see Miriam exorcising *anything*? Except maybe a cupcake.'

'You know, if you say something even *I* think is mean . . .'

She waved a hand as if to dissipate the comment. 'St Barbara's was specifically for members of the clergy who'd fallen afoul of . . . *things*.'

'Things from the dark?'

She sighed. 'It's not always a happy ending for an exorcist, you know. We couldn't have people who'd been so injured in normal hospices or retreats in case something still clung to them, or used them as vessels.'

'St Barbara's was a *containment facility*? An ecclesiastical Area 51?'

'There are more around than you'd think – but yes, essentially. The inmates could be cared for and be kept safe – and the public was safe from them, too. That was another reason it was next to the church, sacred ground.'

'You'd left the squad by then, hadn't you?'

'The squad?' Joyce scoffed another biscuit.

'Adjuristine-exorcism squads. *Mulieres Bonae* was the female wing.'

'Not that it lasted long,' sneered Sister Bridget. 'Anyway, off topic. Yes, I'd left the Vatican; the squads were disbanding and I'd seen enough. St Barbara's was a good place for me to go, a good halfway house while I made up my mind about what I wanted to do next. I was disillusioned, but I hated seeing all those good women and men struck low. Some of the skills I'd picked up in *Mulieres Bonae* were . . . useful.'

'So, did you see anything . . . re-inhabit any of those folk?'

She sighed. 'Three times. The old priest who was there at the time wasn't qualified to handle that sort of thing so it fell to me to do that dirty work.'

I'd get her full life story out of her one day.

'And Alison Brandt?'

'She was a nun from Sydney, no family. She'd gone to Germany after the war to offer aid' – *Helping Nazis get to South America?* I recognised that as an uncharitable thought and didn't let it out for a run – 'and . . . she picked up a "hitchhiker". Originally it was thought to be a poltergeist, but they seldom travel; they're usually rooted to a location. Wherever she was posted, the convent would end up haunted – terrible disturbances, flooding, fires, destruction of property – and poor Alison herself . . . she'd be cut, her hair pulled out, she'd vomit glass and nails . . . It was like the Loudun possessions all over again.'

'Shit.'

'That too, sometimes.' Sister Bridget accepted the biscuit I handed her. 'Eventually she was "cured": an exorcism that's been written up in several very specialised medico-theological journals.'

'That's a thing?'

To shut her up, I buttered Joyce another biscuit too. 'But I'm guessing it didn't go entirely well?'

'No, the haunt was removed, but Alison didn't recover at all – she didn't ever speak again, or not that I heard of. She was brought to St Barbara's and I nursed her there for five years.'

'And then she disappeared?'

'And then she disappeared.'

'Got any theories? Did she walk out of there under her own steam? Was she carried? Did she float out on a malign cloud of magical influences?'

'We looked for her – don't think we didn't. It's in no one's interest for a former possessed person to go on the wander. We had Weyrd run traces to see if there'd been any transit activity or any magic done, but there was nothing.'

'Had there been any visitors to St Barbara's in the days before she disappeared?'

'No strangers came to St Barbara's.'

'That's not what I asked.'

She sighed. 'There was no one unknown to us. There was no one who suddenly dropped off the radar after she disappeared, no one who behaved strangely – believe me, I watched. I tried to find her.'

I pulled out my mobile and pulled up the image of the second victim. 'Miriam said it was Alison Brandt, but it might be hard to tell.'

Sister Bridget took the phone and stared, a range of emotions playing across her face; her blue eyes swam until tears spilled, but she didn't bother to dash them away; she wasn't ashamed of them. 'It's her.'

'And she wasn't Weyrd, was she? Normal?'

'Not a lot of Weyrd with a fondness for the Church, Ms Fassbinder.'

'No, but some of them painted beautifully in the Sistine Chapel.'

'Where was she found?'

'A development over at New Farm this morning. She's the second such body in the same state; the first was over at East Brisbane – Laidlaw Street.' I pulled up that photo and showed her. 'Is this one familiar?'

She examined it long and hard, but shook her head in the end.

'Alison was forty when she came into my care. She was forty-five when she left it.' She took my phone, swiped back to Alison, then shook it in bewilderment as if it had been lying to her. 'Even with the way her skin is . . . this woman doesn't look in her eighties. Her hair's no greyer than it was when I knew her.'

'And she's Normal, no doubt about that.' I tapped a nail against my teeth. 'Okay. If you think of anything else.'

'I will call you reluctantly.'

'That's a level of cooperation for which I have prayed. Thanks, Sister. Take care.' I snapped my fingers. 'Oh, hey. How are your spirit-laying skills these days?'

'I keep my hand in,' she said cagily.

I had a vision of the good Sister performing the occasional exorcism just to take the edge off. Maybe she did some work for Soteria Insurance, a company that specialised in dealing with Weyrd threats to property. 'Okay, can you do me a favour?'

'Last time I said yes to that I nearly got frostbite sitting on the bank of the river at all hours of the day and night.'

'And I and my mother are eternally grateful for that.'

She snorted. 'What?'

'The old Nadasy house at Ascot.'

Her expression darkened.

'There are ghosts there. Children. The ones she—'

'I know what she did.'

'They need to be sent on. I was going to use the Waters of Forgetting, but I don't have enough and I don't know when I'll get a chance to go back.' I swallowed. 'They've been there too long already.'

'Why now?' she asked suddenly. 'Why have they only been seen now? Did you question that?'

I shrugged. 'I don't know . . . maybe because it's been quiet down there for a while? They're not afraid to come out any more because the Nadasys are gone. It looks like there've been some travellers dossing there. The place has been stripped, but I couldn't see any sign of anyone in the basement.'

'Haunted basement. Lovely.'

'Take Ziggi Hassman with you – no, don't look at me like that, I'm serious. Even a nun with your specialist knowledge shouldn't be alone in that place. Besides, there's a chance you won't be able to see it because the glamour's still in operation. I wonder . . .' Magda Nadasy had cast that glamour and she was well and truly dead, but sometimes that didn't affect the spell. But what if it was linked to blood? Dusana Nadasy was still alive; might that be holding it in place? It didn't really matter. I just thought it curious. 'Just promise.'

'Scout's honour.'

'That sounds bad enough when I say it.' *And even less convincing*.

'Nun's honour.'

'Well, okay then.'

'Look,' Joyce said hesitantly, 'what you said about me not telling you everything?'

'Mmmmm?'

'That guy?'

We were back in the Honda and heading up the driveway that fed onto Wickham Terrace. The noise of the city, utterly absent in the residence down in the little hollow behind the hospital, now reappeared. Joyce barely paused before pulling out onto the road; in all fairness, it was unnaturally clear for that time of the day.

'You're going to have to narrow it down.'

'What you said about not being entirely honest?'

'Yeeesss?'

'The delivery driver.'

'He had a name.'

'Len. The one I . . .' *Murdered.* 'You know.'

'Yeah?'

'He wasn't blameless.' She gave me a sideways look and caught my expression. 'Look, I killed him, sure, I own that. But whatever you thought, he wasn't your friendly neighbourhood delivery dude.'

'Well, what was he then?'

'He was working for someone else – and he was asking questions about a grail. He approached us because he'd seen us following you. He asked my sister, Sybil.' She licked her lips. 'We didn't know what it was about – we didn't know the Guardian was looking for it, but Sybil asked and the Guardian—'

'Did you know who Len was working for?'

'Sybil was supposed to find out, then kill him . . . Well, Olivia happened first to Sybil and by the time I talked to him, I wasn't feeling very . . . patient. He was stubborn and I wasn't convinced that waiting would do much good. And I was angry.'

'I thought they were on a date . . .' I frowned. I'd seen Len and Sybil at the cinema while David and I were on a date night; that now felt like a lifetime ago. Maybe it was.

'Nope, he was following you. He'd seen Agnes scoping out your house one day and he followed her and they got to talking about mutual interests.'

'Did he do a deal with the Guardian?'

'No. He never met the Guardian – he didn't ask us for anything like that. He was just hired help for someone else. *He was watching you*, but here's the thing: he was looking for *the grail*. Whoever he was working for had already linked *your* name with the grail, even before the Guardian blackmailed you into looking for it.' She took a deep breath. 'And there's something else you need to know.'

Later on, I realised that I'd seen the black Mercedes GLE 350d waiting in the side street as we drew level, but it didn't really register because I was too busy digesting Joyce's revelation. It was *fast*: it ignored all the other traffic and just T-boned us. I watched the driver's side door buckle inwards, saw Joyce thrown towards me in slow motion. There was the breaking of glass, the crush and shear of metal and the pop of airbags.

Then there was darkness.

Chapter Twenty-One

I'm sitting in the Boatman's low, dark craft. I was in it not that long ago so I recognise it. I don't like it any better this time.

We glide through the tenebrous waves; they shine strange and oily beneath the hull, yet throw up no reflection when I lean out. These waters only *take*. There's mist all around, thick and heavy and damp and cold. Last time I was in this boat, spirits tried to prise open my mouth, to get inside because I was alive and didn't belong, yet I feel no trace of their fingers now. I glance over my shoulder at the oarsman, who's paying me no attention but stares straight past me; I catch the glimmer of his obsidian eyes.

Ligeia, radiant in the glory of her death, sits in front of me. She smiles, all teeth and sublime dangerous beauty and I think lovers wouldn't have cared that she was going to kill and eat them in the end because, in her first days, her loveliness was so overwhelming. I wonder how Helen of Troy compared to her; did she look like a dowdy cousin, the girl you'd go with when the cheerleader wasn't interested in you? Or if you didn't want to shuffle off your mortal coil just yet, would you bed Helen and dream of Ligeia?

I think of everything I'm leaving behind: strife, searching, lies – and mysteries, all the damned time, everyone telling me fibs instead of just coming straight out with the truth. I think of the burdens of love and caring: of Olivia and David and Maisie and Ziggi and

Bela. I think of Rhonda and Ellen. I think of Joyce and Lacy. I think of Dusana Nadasy, who's probably had something to do with this; she's got her wish and I'm gone: honour satisfied, accounts cleared. I think how easy death can be, the memories and obligations left behind. I think how much better off my family will be without me. My mother will look after David and Maisie and they'll have normal lives. They'll be safer without me around.

What will my heart weigh? When the memories are taken so I can travel on, do I get to choose those I want to leave behind? Will I wave my hand like I'm being offered another slice of cake? *No, thanks, had enough.* The outline of my fingers is shifty, not solid.

My body feels light.

The Guardian will find another idiot to do his dirty work . . . then again, with our bargain unfulfilled, will he go after Olivia, try to draw her back? Will he wait for my daughter to grow, to become whatever she will be, then hunt her down and take her in beneath his cinder-blacked wings? Will he whisper in her mind, make her a machine for killing? Take away David, her father, to make her hurt and hard? Her grandmother, will she be gone too? Will he come for Bela and Ziggi? Will someone else find the grail for it – and will the Guardian then be reborn, healthy and crazy? And the tyrant: what about that? What if it's worse than the archangel of the Underworld?

I think of those whispered words last time I saw him, words not meant for me: *I need more time.*

What if . . . ?

What if . . . ?

I open my mouth and manage a sound, a croak really, then I remember that only the dead have their voices taken from them. I try again. I say, 'No.'

Ligeia smiles – then pushes me out of the boat.

I hit the waters and they close over me like a too-thick blanket. So much for being weightless. I sink like a stone.

There were distant murmurs, blips and pings, the rustling of sheets; somewhere, further away, were footsteps, soft-soled shoes. It was cold, as if I'd dragged the weather of the other place with me, then I remembered not only was it winter in Brisneyland, but it's always cold in hospitals. I rolled onto my side, feeling something pull in the back of my hand, and opened my eyes. A cannula was attached with that medical tape that always gave me a rash. *Thanks.* But I could move; apart from a pervasive ache of bruises and jangled bones, I couldn't feel anything broken. There were no casts around my limbs, no bandages to indicate bad cuts.

There were two beds in the room and on the other one Ziggi slept. Bela sat upright, not sprawled, in an armchair, eyes closed. My heart clenched. There was no sign of Joyce.

Is she— Did she—

'You shouldn't be here,' I croaked.

Both Ziggi and Bela woke immediately.

'Really, you shouldn't be here.'

'Good to see you didn't hit your head and suffer a pleasant personality change.' Ziggi sat on the edge the bed and pulled me up into a hug.

'Ow,' I protested, but he didn't apologise, just let me go and pressed the button to tilt the bed. 'Where's Joyce?'

'ICU,' said Bela. 'She'll probably be there for a while. The driver's side was totalled. She might not even get out.'

'Damn it.' I closed my eyes and leaned my head against the pillow.

'Indeed.'

'The Guardian must've figured out by now that she's turned.' I swallowed, feeling sick. 'Which means it might well consider me suspect too . . .'

'Don't worry. I've checked in at Ocean's Reach and everything's fine there – everyone's a little more alert, just in case, and they're ready to move out fast if needs be.' He held up a hand to quiet me and I sort of wanted to snap a couple of his fingers off. 'In addition, I've got Velma on Joyce's door and Septimus is doing the rounds of the perimeter. Besides, I don't think it was anything to do with the Guardian.'

'Why not? Who else would it be? I couldn't see who was driving the Merc but not Dusana, surely? That's pretty unsubtle.' I frowned. 'Or was it one of Titania's crew? But Thaïs scared the shit out of them . . .'

'V, it was Mercado White,' said Bela with a sigh.

I stared at him. Mercado White, disgraced ex-Councillor, purchaser of wine made from the tears of children, most definitely not the head of my fan club – and apparently a gold medallist for holding a grudge. He'd escaped custody last year and had stayed off the radar ever since. Obviously he'd returned to seek revenge, but even so, this felt like a bit of an over-reaction.

'What in the name of . . . what's he doing *here*?'

'Cooling his heels in the morgue downstairs – McIntyre's people will collect him tomorrow,' Ziggi said.

Bela frowned. 'I suspect he was working for Dusana. You said yourself she needed new minions. He hates – *hated* – you with a passion. She gave him the chance to get his own back.'

'This is a little extreme. I mean, running your car into someone else's car?' I shook my head. 'Did *he* make it out alive?'

'Nope,' said Ziggi. 'Went straight through the windscreen. Wasn't wearing a seatbelt.'

I frowned. 'Doesn't that strike you as a little risky for such a fastidious little man? He *never* took risks – he didn't like direct dealings with *anyone* for nefarious purposes, did he? Doesn't this seem a little hands-on?'

'Maybe?' said Bela.

'Maybe?' said my uncle.

'Well, I'm glad we've cleared that up.' I took a deep breath, then lost it at another thought. 'Do *not* tell David and my mother about this. You won't be able to keep them away. You didn't, did you?'

'I wanted to,' grumbled Ziggi.

'And I wouldn't let him,' replied Bela. 'We have enough complications, don't you think?'

'Glad one of you is thinking straight. Can I have some water, please?' The jug beside my bed was empty; Ziggi took it into the bathroom for a refill.

'Bela, you guys have to get out of here and *I* have to get out of here.'

'V, you are remarkably unscathed – and by *remarkably*, I mean *miraculously*. The damage to Joyce looks all out of proportion when compared to yours. How do you explain that?'

'I'm lucky?' But I considered my lack of real injury and thought about Thaïs shouting at the invading Weyrd that I was under *her protection* . . . if that was one of her new superpowers, it was pretty damn impressive. But I wasn't going to say anything, not yet, not if I wanted to keep the Norn's secret. Besides, who knew how long it might last?

'Very.' He looked unconvinced. 'But if you think Sister Bridget is going to let you walk . . .'

'Oh. Um . . . maybe you two could cause a distraction?'

'No way,' was Ziggi's emphatic reply. He'd always had a healthy fear of the nun.

'Not even a little distraction?'

'When Hell freezes over.'

'Given current events, that might be more of possibility than you'd like to think.' I pouted and resigned myself to a night in a hospital bed. 'Bela, one other thing: just before the "accident" Joyce told me that Len—'

'The delivery guy?'

'Yeah, him: he was working for someone else. He was looking for a grail – asking about it before I'd even *heard* of it.'

'Not working for the Guardian?' Ziggi frowned.

'Definitely not, according to Joyce, which was one of the reasons he was killed: clearing away the competition. At the time I thought it was just to send a message to me and Olivia – well, it was, but to someone else as well.'

'And of course we don't know who he was working for?'

'Of course not.'

Bela rubbed his face with both hands, a sure sign he was tired. 'Ligeia's funeral?'

'I'll be there.'

'As will we.'

'Just don't talk to me.'

'V, a lot of the Weyrd will be there tomorrow, Verhoeven and Forsythe included. Do you really want to do this?' Ziggi asked, although his tone suggested he was speaking more just to get his comments on record, not because he thought I'd reconsider.

'Yes. I will pay my respects.' I didn't mention seeing Ligeia in the dark boat, or her final act of tipping me over so I had to come back; she could take that secret with her because I would never want my family and friends to know how easily I might have left them. 'I promise I'll start no punch-ups. I will blend into the background. You'll never see me.'

'Fassbinder, you'd defeat an invisibility cloak.' Bela sighed and shook his head. 'Just . . . oh, I give up.'

'I'm sorry.'

'No, you're not.' He rose, and he and Ziggi headed to the door. 'Just don't start any trouble here tonight. Get some rest.'

'You know I can't promise either of those things.'

'Fassbinder?'

I'd just failed to finish what was easily one of the worst meals I'd ever had (which included most of my own cooking) when Rhonda appeared in the doorway to my room. Mind you, I didn't really have much of an appetite after visiting Joyce. The fox-girl was a wreck. I was surprised that her human shape was holding; maybe that was a defence mechanism? She had cuts and bruises, her skull was bandaged, there were tubes leading into and out of her, her left leg and right arm were in casts. Checking in with Velma, the Weyrd who was watching ICU, meant trying not to stare at the nictitating membrane randomly uncovering her green eyes while we spoke. It was about five minutes before Sister Bridget found me and shooed me back to bed.

I went meekly, I had to admit.

'Rhonda! Can you get me out of here?'

'And hello to you, too. Sister Bridget has already spoken to me quite sternly about that sort of request.' She smiled. 'The answer is no, by the way.'

'All my friends are arseholes.'

'Maybe you should start by not calling them arseholes.' She reached into her handbag and pulled out a burger wrapped in greaseproof paper. She eyed the remains of my chicken surprise – the surprise being it contained almost no chicken – and offered the alternative, then extracted another, sat herself in the armchair and proceeded to picnic.

'How were you not followed by every dog in the neighbourhood and every patient, human and Weyrd, in this hospital?' I asked.

'I was. Had to fight my way through. And yet you call me an arsehole.'

'You're my favourite arsehole?'

'Yeah, yeah, bet you say that to all the girls.'

'Untrue.' I waved the half-eaten burger. 'Thanks, Rhonda.'

'Did you learn anything more about Alison Brandt?'

'I should have known there was an ulterior motive for this visit. '

'Look, I can bring food *and* extract information, okay?'

I relayed what Sister Bridget had told us, then shared what Joyce had told me about Len. 'Did you look into him much after his death?'

She shook her head. 'There was no family, no person to contact in case of emergency. He lived alone in a rented one-bedder in West End. Work colleagues said he was, and I quote, "a nice guy".'

'Well, maybe not. Wonder if his unit's been leased out again yet?'

'That's something I can get Constable Oldman to look into.'

'Maybe I could go with—'

'You're not going anywhere tonight.'

'No, I've come to terms with that.' I finished off the burger. 'All it needed was a bit of food to make me easy to get on with—'

'—I *wish* it was always that simple—'

'But as you know, I am down a driver. So, tomorrow, Constable Oldman could come and collect me and we could go and check out Len's flat – if it remains unlet – because it would be safer to travel in pairs.'

'I'm sure Constable Oldman would be delighted to spend a morning with you.'

I grinned. 'Anything new on body number one?'

'Still nothing. Wonder if she was connected with St Barbara's as well?'

'Sister Bridget said there was only ever one disappearance from there; any more than that would be kind of hard to cover up, I'd think.' I screwed the wrapper into a ball and gave a happy sigh. 'Rhonda, I'm getting tired.'

'Well, you had a big day, car crash and all.' She rose, took the greaseproof paper from me and threw it with hers into the bin. 'Sleep well, don't leave this bed, try not to annoy the nun.'

'Do my best. Would you mind turning the light out?'

She gave me a brief hug and left.

I pretended to sleep for about twenty minutes, enough time for Sister Bridget to come and check on me, then wander off, convinced I was mostly harmless.

Chapter Twenty-Two

I have no great fondness for morgues. I'd managed to avoid the police one out at Coopers Plains for quite a lot of months, so it wasn't lost on me that I was wandering into *this* one of my own free will, and at midnight too.

St Agnes' mostly dealt with maternity cases, but they did deal with other women's health needs and sometimes there were deaths, of mother or baby, or battered wife or girlfriend who didn't want to hang on any longer, which is why they had their own small but perfectly formed morgue in the basement. As soon as all three blue-clad RNs had their backs turned to check charts I snuck past the nurses' station and took the stairs down. I'd wrapped an oft-washed, thin and very soft dressing gown around my standard naked-backside patient's attire, but my feet were bare and I was pretty much chilled all over. In truth, I hadn't warmed up since Ligeia pushed me out of the boat. Whether that had been dream or reality, I had no idea, but the cold stuck.

A line of blinking fluorescent lights revealed a white corridor, pale green marbled linoleum with a line in the centre and, at the end, a set of double doors with windows set at head height and the word *Morgue* painted on the outside in cheery red. I pushed my way in and let them swing shut behind me.

A bank of freezers filled one wall, sink and stainless-steel tubs another. Three steel tables were neatly lined up in front of metal shelving, which took up most of the room. Only one table had a sheet over it. I thought about what Olivia had told me, about how all those years ago she'd been laid out on just such a cold bed after trying to drown herself, her soul still stuck inside, the essence of who she was not on its way to the Boatman and the last ride but instead trapped in the cage of her body, waiting for the knives and saws, waiting for her scalp to be peeled back and the top of her skull popped off like a boiled egg.

Waiting.

I shuddered.

I didn't really know why I was down here. Bela and Ziggi would hardly lie to me about Mercado's death, but it seemed such an *unlikely* demise – surely if you're trying to take out your nemesis, the ultimate aim is to survive yourself? Otherwise, what happens to all the accompanying dancing on graves, et cetera? Surely taking out me *and* himself was not his optimal plan? I didn't know what I expected to see that no one else had, but I couldn't stop myself from coming down.

The sheet felt thick between my fingers, too coarse for still-living skin but nothing to trouble the dead. I threw it aside quickly, like tearing off a Band-Aid.

Mercado had been a thin, nervous man, his wispy blond hair always carefully styled to make it look thicker than it actually was. He was still thin, although there was no sign of the nervousness, what with his current state of deadness, and his hair was so full of dried blood it was more like floss than fluff. I guessed he'd be transferred to Ellen's tender mercies at the police morgue some time tomorrow, but there didn't *seem* to be any surprise about what killed him: his chest had been stoved in by the steering wheel before he head-butted the windscreen. There were cuts to his face and brown smears clung to his dreadfully snowy skin. Oddly, it was the fragments of white where his ribs had broken through his torso that were truly dreadful to behold. His head lay at an angle that indicated shattered vertebrae.

I thought I caught a whiff of something, and even though I *really* didn't want to, I leaned closer. Yeah, I was getting more than a whiff now.

In fact, it was quite strong and I had to step back to stop myself gagging, as Ellen got pissed off about people throwing up on her corpses. Or maybe this was also evidence?

This was *proper* decay, not fresh: not hours old but *days* dead, maybe even a week. Mercado White was already in full rot-mode, which meant he'd either decided to be an over-achiever for the first time in his life – well, *death* – or he'd been dead for a good while before he'd jammed his foot on the accelerator of the black Mercedes and tried to total me.

He'd been driving the same car I'd seen Dusana driving – she'd made a point of letting me see her, trying to intimidate me, make me nervous – but maybe she'd also been trying to distract me? If she'd had Mercado working for her, following me, then where was *she*? Was Dusana ruthless enough to kill her minion and then reanimate him, just so he could take me out?

It didn't feel right. I could see she'd use him to do her dirty work, maybe a bit of assassination admin, but Dusana wanted *personal* pay-back. Not to mention that from what I knew of Mercado, he'd never been your hands-on avenger. Dusana Nadasy definitely wanted to take me out, but like she'd taken out Eleanor Aviva: when she came for me, it was going to be up close and *very* messy.

No, Dusana would never have used Mercado this way, and he would never have consented to be used in such a way.

So . . .

When Mercado sat up on the table I was *really* happy I'd gone to the loo before starting out on my little expedition. I was less happy, however, about the dead guy reaching for me. I took a step backwards and stumbled, my foot slid out from under me and I crunched down on my knee, then fell to the side, which *hurt*. So apparently Thaïs' protection only extended to when *other* people tried to hurt me. Good to know.

Mercado didn't waste time being graceful. He didn't bother swinging his legs over the side of the trolley, just kind of tipped himself off and landed right in front of me on the tiles with the wet slap of a fish crashing onto the deck of a boat.

I scrambled away on my bum, my hands and feet grasping vainly for purchase, desperately trying to get up and run before Mercado could get his broken fingers on my flesh. At last I felt one of the doors give behind me and leaned back, pushing it open, hoping to get out – just as the other door swung inwards and I saw a pair of black leather trousers and scuffed biker boots take two steps into the room, then the right foot swung past me to connect with Mercado's bobbling head. The force sent him tumbling back into the morgue.

I looked up, taking in the Rammstein T-shirt, now under a long black coat, and watched as my saviour threw something at the body as it fetched up against the steel lockers.

Really shiny dust . . .

Or at least, it *looked* like dust, until my saviour shouted a command that hurt my ears and the powder coating Mercado exploded and the dead body erupted in flames.

As I watched, a crabbed thing smaller than a baby prised open Mercado White's silent lips from inside and tried to escape the burning cage of Mercado's body. Its grey-green skin rapidly charcoaled, but I could see the bald head was round, with eyes that ran vertically from the tip of its nose to the top of its forehead. Its teeth looked horribly sharp, like needles.

It made a shrieking sound as the orange flames overwhelmed the form until it gave up, shrank back into Mercado's mouth and disappeared.

I breathed a massive sigh of relief as I looked at Ingo. 'Nitromage, hey?'

He shrugged. 'I did tell you I blow shit up. Listen, I didn't do *anything* to Titania – you've *got* to believe me, Ms Fassbinder . . .'

His heroic deed done for the day, Ingo, smelling of body odour and burned things, collapsed into tears and began maundering on about the only thing that mattered to him.

I'd read about resurgence imps, but I'd never seen one myself. Like 'serkers, monstrosities who liked their meat bloody and screaming, they lived in the darkness between the light and the not-so-light worlds. Sometimes they came through on their own, found thin places to pass, but they didn't tend to reanimate corpses on their own – they didn't really have a lot of initiative like that. They were generally *summoned* things, brought in by a mage for a specific purpose. So Mercado's corpse was just that: an empty shell someone had filled after his soul has taken its last ride. But *who'd* done the summoning? Who'd thought to use him this way? *Dusana?*

Before I could start putting my thoughts in order, Sister Bridget started handing round steaming mugs of hot chocolate. I hugged mine gratefully as Ingo got straight back on topic . . . *his* topic.

'Listen, as I was trying to tell you, I didn't do *anything* to Titania.'

'Ingo—'

'I mean I *did* something, but not intentionally, not to *her*.' He grabbed one of the nun's emergency stash of Arrowroots, broken out only because I *begged* in a most undignified manner, took a huge bite of buttery goodness and tried to talk through it. Whatever Titania saw in him it surely wasn't his table manners. 'I stuffed up the formula, okay?' he admitted miserably.

'What?'

'For the powder-mix for the ceremony – I stuffed it up. I was lazy and didn't measure properly – that's why shit blew up.' He ran a hand through his messy hair, which badly needed a wash. In fact, all of him needed a wash. 'And then—'

'And then the household turned on you.'

'Every single one of them,' he said indignantly.

'So here's a question: had you actually made an effort to make friends with anyone other than Titania? Anyone at all? Or did you just suck up to the mistress of the castle and basically lord it arrogantly over people who'd served her faithfully for a metric fuck-tonne of years?'

Somehow his shamefaced look came as no overwhelming surprise.

'Yeah.' I tugged the blanket Sister Bridget had given me tighter around my shoulders and tucked the bottom edge under my bare feet. *Still cold*. 'And not that I'm complaining about the timely rescue, but how exactly did you know I needed it?'

'I've been following you for days, trying to get your attention, but there's always someone around and I kept having to break off to hide or get food. I couldn't get near your house – those are some wards.'

'I do my best. Didn't try to send a night-dove or two as a courier pigeon, did you?'

He looked horrified. 'What? *No!*'

'Can you think of anyone who might? From Titania's crew?'

'A lot of them. They're old and powerful.'

I thought about Mercado crisping, then dissipating. 'So what exactly did you throw on Mercado?'

'Gravedust, gunpowder, some other stuff.'

'You didn't use fire to ignite it this time? Just a spell?'

'I told you—'

'Yeah, yeah, you blow shit up.' I took another biscuit and delicately nibbled an edge. 'So, when did you notice him? You had that powder ready pretty quickly.'

'Two days ago, when I was following you. I knew he was dead.'

'Driving while dead: that has to be against the Road Rules, doesn't it?'

'I figured he'd make his move at some point, then I could . . . well, help.'

'A warning might have been nice,' I grumbled. 'But you know what, now's not the time to complain – thanks, Ingo. I do appreciate it.'

'Now you'll help me, right? I've *got* to see Titania – I need to make sure she's all right.'

'That's going to take some doing' – I held up a hand to forestall any complaints – 'but it's not impossible. You just need to be patient, okay?'

Before he could start complaining again, I went on, 'First thing we need to do is let Zvezdomir Tepes know you're here—'

'But—'

'Ingo, trust me: Tepes is your *only* safe option. Remember how you're on hostage exchange, which is just like school holidays but with a slightly higher chance of horrible death? Well, Zvezdomir Tepes is the *one* person with your best interests at heart. Now, please tell me you haven't told your family what's happened . . .'

'Tell my father that I fucked up and put *Titania Banks* in a coma?' He sounded incredulous, but I felt hugely relieved; at least Bela wouldn't be blaming *me* for causing internecine strife.

'So I'll take that as a *no*. Sister Bridget? I appear to have left my mobile in my other backless hospital gown.' It was in my room, actually.

'I'll call Tepes. Ingo can stay here tonight if it's the safest place.'

'Thank you.' I closed my eyes, listened to the massive ache that was my body telling me it wanted a big sleeping pill, fluffy pillows and a really long sleep. 'Sister Bridget, you're sure there weren't any other disappearances from St Barbara's?'

'No. Alison was the only one.'

I considered Mercado's reanimation and the state of his body and compared it to Brandt and the unknown woman, but neither of them stank of decay – it was pretty clear that even after all the decades Brandt had been missing, she must have been alive pretty much up to just before her corpse had been found – there simply hadn't been time for her to start rotting the way Mercado had.

'Well, I guess I'd better go back to my room.'

Sister Bridget glanced at the back corner of the kitchen; she'd done that several times since we'd arrived.

'Sister, are you seeing ghosts?'

She looked startled. 'I—'

'You're staring off into corners like a bloody cat,' I grumbled as I stood. 'Ingo, don't run again, okay? Got a mobile?'

We swapped numbers, then I warned him, 'Stay out of the hospital – there are loads of Weyrd there, especially around Joyce. If you need anything, call me. And you can trust Tepes, and Ziggi Hassman too, okay?'

I stepped outside, wincing as my bare feet hit the concrete and the winter air immediately started biting through the blanket I'd neglected to surrender. *Hot shower when I get back to my room*, I promised myself. *Hot shower and sleep*. I *really* needed to sleep.

Halfway across the courtyard my legs stopped moving. I dropped my head back and looked up at the sky, winter-clear and cold, the stars bright as bright could be. I thought about David and how he'd know just what to say. I thought about his arms around me, his stubble against my face as he kissed me, how I never felt cold with him. I thought about Maisie, the weight of her, the warmth, her tiny fingers pulling my hair, exploring my face, the smell of her. I thought of Olivia, still a stranger to me, but returned and then taken again. The memory of her caring for my husband and daughter when I couldn't made me shake.

I thought about the holes they'd left in me.

And the agony of it became so acute I thought I was having a heart attack, that I was expiring properly and this time I wouldn't have the will to dredge a voice out of the depths of myself and climb back to the world of the living. I feared my knees would buckle and I'd collapse onto the concrete, that I'd start to howl and maybe this time I might not be able to stop.

Then I thought about how much I had to do. I thought about how I'd said *No* to the boat ride; that I'd kept my voice, as the dead do not. I put steel back into my legs and I straightened. I held the blanket tighter around me and I walked on, swallowing the sobs, telling them they'd get their run at a more appropriate time.

Chapter Twenty-Three

'McIntyre said you'd need something,' Constable Oldman said as she handed over a plastic bag.

'Thanks,' I said, peering in uncertainly. My own attire had been cut from me after the accident – yet another pair of favourite jeans sacrificed in pursuit of my job. Lacy had brought me newly purchased knickers and bra and tights (disconcertingly, the right size) and a long-sleeved red woollen dress of hers which *almost* fitted. It was a bit tight across the shoulders and my new mum boobs, and while it would have reached her knees, it skimmed me at mid-thigh. I looked like it was Eighties date night and I was determined to get lucky.

On the plus side, it did have pockets.

At least my Docs were intact and my winter coat had only a few splashes of blood, barely noticeable now they'd soaked into the weave. Anyway, I'd had baby spit and other unidentifiably noxious substances on my clothes for the last month, so a bit of crimson barely registered.

'I'll get the dress back to you as soon as I can.'

'It's okay. I haven't worn it since I was eighteen.'

Great. 'Well, thanks.' I watched the city speed by; you really did go faster in a police car, even in a sixty-kilometre zone. 'So no one's been in this apartment?'

'Apparently not. We did have a look after the death, but since it was a Weyrd case and you knew who did it, we weren't really looking for evidence, just for family, someone to contact.' She whistled, a surprisingly off-tune squeak, then added, 'The landlord's going to meet us there.'

'Cool.'

The unit block was so old and falling apart that I wasn't sure how the landlord was legally allowed to keep letting it. It looked like a firetrap for a start, and surely that was a sinkhole about to open up out front? I couldn't help but think it might be better for all concerned if it did just slide into the earth and was never seen again.

The block had eight apartments: three units each on the first two floors, with the last two sharing the top floor; I was willing to bet the landlord charged a premium . . . Len had rented one of those top-floor flats. Joyce had killed Len, stolen his van and then lured my mother to it with threats and lies . . . which made me wonder.

'His van – did anyone go through it?'

'Yes. It's still in impound, but there was nothing out of the usual there other than all the mail he hadn't delivered. I'm pretty sure that got released and sent on.'

We pulled into a car park beneath the building, but I didn't like the weight of the building above us and when I asked Oldman to move out onto the street she humoured me.

'I take it you're no longer on traffic duty?'

'Current events have postponed my learning experience.'

'Ah.' I got out of the patrol car. 'Come on.'

'But the agent's not here yet.'

'We can meet him at the door, have a look around. You know, do some actual *investigating* . . .'

Some guy rode by on a bike and wolf-whistled, so I did the only thing acceptable in the circumstances and flipped him the bird, which set Oldman off; she was still laughing as we made our way up the rickety stairs, me trying desperately to pull down the hem on my dress.

Standing in front of Number Seven, we both caught our breath. I reached for the doorknob—

'What are you doing?' hissed the well-trained constable.

The door opened with very little effort at all. 'Look: *unlocked!*'

'*Fassbinder* . . .'

'It's not a crime scene, it's not currently rented out and the door's open. Technically, it's barely even breaking and entering. In fact, if you say the door was already a little bit open, there was no breaking involved at all.'

I went in.

'I hate you,' Lacy muttered, and followed.

The place was neat and tidy and pretty much empty. 'Did it look like this last time you saw it?'

'Nope. This has been cleaned.'

'And emptied.'

A loud, unfriendly voice came from behind us. 'What the fuck are you doing in here? I said I'd meet you outside.'

Constable Oldman pulled out her ID, just in case her police uniform wasn't hint enough, but neither had any appreciable effect on the amount of respect the new arrival was giving either of us. She began, 'Mr McGee—'

'Honestly, you fucking cops think you can get away with anything and everything. I'll be complaining – I will contact a current affairs programme.'

The landlord was big and aggressive and wearing a suit that might have cost more than the entire building. He'd clearly spent a lot of time in the gym and a lot of money on his short dark hair; he was a muscle-bound, handsome arsehole. I was willing to bet the car he'd left outside would be some hot European import that I'd find it hard to resist keying when I left. I couldn't tell if he was Weyrd or not, but that was par for the course.

'Mr McGee, is it?'

He looked at me as though he'd just noticed my mini-dress: Lacy was short and petite; I was not.

He eyed me as if he couldn't decide if it was too late to try and be charming or not. 'Hi. I'm Greg.'

'Sure you are. Mr McGee, did you have this place cleaned out? Any idea where the previous tenant's personal effects are now?'

'I need to show this place – the lease is up at the end of the month so the rent stops. I'm sure you understand, Miss—'

I didn't offer anything except a raised eyebrow and he decided it wasn't worth the effort. 'Look: clothes to St Vinnie's, furniture repurposed in my other properties and anything I couldn't sell was burned – letters, notes that sort of thing.'

'You absolute arse.'

'Look, I think you've taken up enough of my time, so why don't you both bugger off out of—'

He didn't finish the suggestion because I had him up against the wall, his feet off the ground, kicking fruitlessly while I watched him turn a nice shade of reddy-purple. Constable Oldman looked on, grinning. She'd been in a similar position once before and I had no doubt that she was taking almost as much pleasure in not being the one dangling from my fist as in watching an arsehole get his highly deserved come-uppance.

'You're a very rude man, Mr McGee,' I pointed out.

He managed something that might but probably wasn't 'fire truck' and I had to admire his determination. But I didn't have time . . .

'One thing you should know about me, Mr McGee, is that I'm *not* a cop. I don't answer to anyone. So I can pretty much do what I want to you.'

His eyes twitched towards Lacy.

'Oh, really? You really think the good constable here's going to help you out? When you were so very ill-mannered to her?'

Oldman barely managed to suppress a snort. After a moment, I let him go and he dropped to the ground, his bum hitting hard while his legs shot out in front of him so fast I had to sidestep swiftly. We watched him gasp for breath for a bit, until he gradually lost the bright beetroot colour.

'Now, let's start again, shall we? Been on any dates lately?'

'Are you hitting on me?' he got out.

'I think I can safely say that if there were millions of women and you were the very last man on Earth, we'd be dying out as a matter of choice.'

I stepped away and looked sternly at him. 'The other night a nice lady called Merrily had a really bad date with a handsome dark-haired stranger with appalling manners. Was it you?'

'I don't know any Merrily – I *swear.*'

'And let's keep it that way.' I took my phone from the pocket of the coat and snapped a picture of him, which I texted straight to Ms Vaughan. 'Now, you said the rent's still being paid?'

'By a boyfriend, maybe. Len signed the lease, but someone else paid his rent. Some bloke was always here – I thought it was his sugar daddy, except he didn't look old enough.'

'What did he look like?'

He sneered. 'Handsome dark-haired man.' He saw my expression, considered the proximity of my Doc Martens to his crotch and said quickly, 'I don't know his name but there's a company that pays the rent. I will give you those details, just don't hurt me.'

'You know, that would be so helpful,' I said sweetly. 'Send the info to Constable Oldman, would you? If you don't have her mobile or email I'm sure she can rectify that.'

'No, no, I got it.'

'Good. Now, please don't get up until we've left. I don't like you enough to promise I won't knock you down again.'

As I walked away, Lacy said gleefully, 'Thank you for your time, Mr McGee.'

There was an expensive penis extension in the driveway: a silver Maserati Ghibli S Auto. I was proud of myself for not keying it, though it was desperately in need of some runes, or perhaps something small and pornographic.

Oldman and I sat quietly in the car for a few minutes. 'Don't start the engine yet,' I said quietly, and sure enough, McGee's head appeared over the balcony. He saw us still sitting there and rushed back inside; I smiled as I imagined him scurrying back to the wall like a good boy.

'You know, you raining down the whoop-ass? So much more fun to witness than to experience,' Lacy pointed out.

'Like so many things in life.' My phone buzzed with a negative response from Merrily; I didn't bother to answer her second text, *Is he single?*

It had been worth a shot, but I realised me wishing him to be Merrily's weird date was as much to do with wanting to kick him in the nuts as solving the mystery. 'So, once he sends those account details through . . .'

'We might be able to find a name associated with the company.'

'Are you okay to do that research?'

She nodded. 'I'm getting used to it. My dad told me I needed to get my shit together and change if he was going to be proud of me.'

I laughed. '*My* dad told me change transforms, makes things both *less* and *more* – well, different – and we all adapt in our own way.'

'My dad's an arsehole who withholds affection and approval.'

'Mine was a murderer and butcher of children.'

'You win.'

'Hey, both our dads were arseholes: we both win.'

'Yay.' Oldman started the engine. 'Where to now?'

'Can you drop me out at UQ? I need to check on something. I can get myself home.'

Professor Harrow wasn't in the Antiquities Museum and the young man who kept staring at my legs couldn't recall having seeing the old guy for a couple of days. I kind of wanted to slap him and yell that I was old enough to be his mother – I wasn't, but I felt like I should have been, or at least be telling him to make better life choices. But Hell, he was working in a museum, how much better could it get?

I took the lift up and knocked on the door of Professor Harrow's office. Sophie answered quickly. She was dressed all in black, her eyes puffy in a pale face. She didn't look delighted to see me.

'I got your bloody messages.'

'Is the professor around?'

'Look, he's gone.'

'What?'

'He died – he died two days ago. At home, in his sleep.'

'Oh no – I'm so sorry, Sophie.' And I was – the old chap had seemed harmless and nice. 'Is there anything I can do to help?' I made the offer knowing there was nothing, shrugging as I said it and she shook her head, but looked mollified.

'Look, I know you want that article — and I have been looking, but I haven't found it. I'll get to it, I promise. I've got to clean all this out anyway now.' She looked behind her at the stacks of books and papers and said wryly, 'Should only take me a couple of years.'

'I'm . . . well, you already know I'm sorry. If there is anything?' I couldn't actually think what that might be, but it seemed polite to repeat the offer.

'Put a match to this lot?' She jerked a finger at the contents of the office. 'It's just been a rotten few days, you know? First that stalker, now the professor . . .'

'Stalker?'

'Some guy's been following me from the office to the car park — three nights in a row.'

'Oh crap. What does he look like?'

'I don't know: I just hear his footsteps and see a shadow. He doesn't say anything.'

'Do you get the—'

'—security shuttle now? Yep. No more walking through the campus in the dark for me.'

'Okay — listen, give me a call if you think of anything or if you see him, will you?'

Out in the Great Court I wandered aimlessly around while the gargoyles and grotesques laughed down at me. Idly I wondered how many of them had been Weyrd, how many had sat for the sculptor and sniggered afterwards about how closely or otherwise their 'portrait' resembled them, if the artist had managed to tap into what lay beneath the surface.

My mobile beeped: a text from Aspasia, demanding my presence at Little Venice as quickly as possible.

How nice to be wanted.

Chapter Twenty-Four

I wished I could say no one looked at me when I walked into Little Venice, but at least no one was dumb enough to whistle. Thankfully the crowd was small, and I couldn't identify any of Banks' people. Hopefully, they'd been banned for life.

'You've got legs,' said Theo, as if it was a possibility that had never before crossed her mind.

'Forget you ever saw them. Is Aspasia around?'

'Upstairs. She's feeling . . . poorly.'

The way she paused made me very nervous. I eyed Theodosia closely, trying to detect if she was feeling 'poorly' too, but I couldn't see much different about her.

'Hey, how's your cute little fox-girl? Ziggi said there'd been an accident. You look pretty good for a crash-test dummy.'

'*Not mine*. She's in a coma still: lots of broken bits. And apparently I've got a fairy godmother or something.' I waved my hand vaguely, as if Joyce's state didn't hurt me. I'd been wondering whether I should have McIntyre contact her parents – what if she died? Would it be better for them to know one of their girls *had* been alive? Or what if she got through this, lived, but by telling them, I put her parents in danger? What if the Guardian found out they were in play and came after them to punish Joyce?

Too much thinking.

'You should go and visit her. Take grapes.'

'You said she's in a coma.'

'Yeah, but you'll need a snack.' I headed towards the door that hid the stairs. 'Plus, they say it helps if you talk . . . surely you could annoy someone into consciousness?'

Theo and Aspasia's rooms on the second floor of Little Venice were jewel boxes of antiques and artworks. I'd noted a Weyrd (not to mention the Guardian's) tendency to hoard and I wondered if it was a need to have part of their own ancient past within proximity – a reminder, a touchstone. Every time I visited the Sisters Norn I wanted to start opening drawers and chests and cupboards, like trying to locate more buried treasure, but so far I'd managed to restrain myself.

I raised a hand – and remembering Thaïs' icy welcome, instead, I stepped smartly to one side of the door, *then* I knocked.

I heard a muffled reply of 'Come in!' through the wood.

The small lounge was cluttered by the three velvet-covered chaises longues, which took up a lot of space around the expensive-looking silk rug depicting the fall of Adam and Eve. The colours were as rich as if no one had ever set foot on it, although I knew they did; somehow the weave stayed pristine, like it was coated in mystic Teflon. There were bookshelves filled with leather-bound tomes, statuettes and assorted things that might have been votives or trophies. Aspasia was lying on one of the couches, an arm draped over her face, the skirt of her emerald dress trailing on the floor.

'Very Dame aux Camélias.'

'I hate you.'

'You and everybody else. What's wrong?'

She sat up took her hand away from her face. She was grey with worry.

'Jeeez, Aspasia! You look really sick!'

'I feel sick – and it's not just the flu, although I think I'm getting that too . . .' She looked at the rug then back up at me. 'It's *this*.'

On the glass mosaic coffee table in front of her was a bonsai tree in a long, low rectangular pot. It was a pretty thing, bright green with red flowers like drops of blood. Aspasia pointed at it, then, her palm facing the ceiling, she jerked her fingers upwards as if signalling.

The plant lifted out of its soil. Particles of dirt were suspended in the air as the bonsai hovered a foot above its nest. I could see the root system shivering and shuddering with shock at this sudden relocation.

Aspasia looked at me with wide dark eyes.

'Shit . . .'

'I accidentally uprooted three paving stones out in the courtyard this morning,' she whispered. She lowered her hand and the tree dropped back to the planter, landing perfectly.

'Paving stones' was downplaying the size of those things; they were *head*stones – they'd come from a church that vanished *years* ago.

'Wow! First Thaïs, now you,' I said unhelpfully as I sat across from her. 'Any sign of this happening with Theo?'

'No, but she always was slow to develop.'

'Snarky. Now, are these powers actively causing difficulty? I mean, apart from you surprising yourself by involuntary earthworks?'

'Well, no, it's just . . . *disturbing*, you know? Unexpected.'

'Right. Okay, so currently I've got a few other things that have to take precedence, so until this becomes an *actual* problem, it's on the back-burner – and Aspasia, I *promise* you I'm not just being an arsehole.'

'Jury's still out on that,' she said resentfully, but she sighed in resignation. 'Bela's set up a meeting for you with the Odinsays. Tonight, in the cathedral, same time as last time.'

'Thanks.'

'The Odinsays?'

'Yeah?'

'Very . . . formal.'

'Stick-up-the-backside formal?'

'Try a whole forest. They're Old Norse – they claim they can trace their ancestry directly back to some godly hanky-panky when Odin was still around, blah blah blah.'

'Nothing like a converted Viking.'

'The fact is they used to eat horsemeat and burn families in their houses to teach them a lesson.'

'Duly noted.'

'Oh, and another thing. Titania Banks is awake and she wants to see you.'

Titania Banks was looking very small, pale and weak in her very large bed, like a kitten deprived too long of milk. Even the jungle foliage was a bit wilted. When I entered the room, Louise was just removing a golden goblet from Titania's hands. A drop of dark red trembled on the pale lips, then was wiped swiftly away by a soft linen square. I hoped it was something pharmaceutical, but the odds weren't good; somewhere one of her retainers was likely sitting quietly with a bandaged arm or wrist and a large glass of whisky in front of them.

The retainer who'd met me on the street and escorted me as Ingo had once done looked familiar. As she stood aside to let me pass, I realised the stocky woman had been wearing a navy suit on my first night here; she'd been one of those who'd charged into Thaïs' sanctum at Little Venice, only to watch her colleague get turned into shard and then slush.

When I glanced back at her, she bowed and muttered, 'My apologies.'

Having Thaïs scare the Hell out of people had its advantages.

'Titania. How are you?' I asked, even though she looked like crap.

She gave me a frail smile. 'Well enough, Ms Fassbinder, but rumour has it I'm not the only one in the wars.'

'I'm amazingly resilient.'

'Yes.' She gave a smile, which quickly faded. 'Ingo—'

'He didn't do it on purpose,' I said quickly. I could at least do that for him. 'He's just a dumb kid.'

'Oh, I know that. He's arrogant and I treated him too well – unwisely, as it turned out, and to the distress of my own people.'

'Will you have him back? He'd need to make amends to your folk, be humble and penitent.'

'Perhaps.' She smiled. 'I would dearly love to see him again.'

'I imagine Bela will take care of that.'

'Sandor is likely to forbid it.'

'What say does he have in it?' I asked, genuinely curious. 'From what I can see, your powers shit all over his. Why aren't you in charge?'

'Sometimes leadership is not merely a matter of the ability to shit from a greater height than another.' The corner of her mouth rose.

I laughed and admitted, 'I'm pretty much *persona non grata* there so I've got no influence at all.'

'Indeed! I believe he is bordering on hatred.'

'Bordering? That's actually a step up for me.'

'Udo Forsythe has no love for you.'

'He barely knows me,' I pointed out.

'All joking aside, Verity, he does not think you belong.' She frowned, and I saw that talking was exhausting for her. 'He believes you have wielded too much influence for too long in our community.'

'He's been on the Council less than a year!'

'It doesn't appear to matter – and remember, Ms Fassbinder, he is not the only one to hold or have held such opinions.'

'I know.' I dragged a chair over to her bedside and she winced as it scraped against the polished floor. 'But truly, it is a little over the top for someone who barely knows me. I mean, I've never even sworn at him.'

'Ah, but you did at Sandor.'

'And believe me, it is on my increasingly long List of Things I'm Living to Regret.'

'Udo is not . . . of as old a family as he would have others believe. Position is important to him. He looks for pawns to sacrifice.'

'Thaïs called him a *parvenu*. I think that's French for cashed-up bogan.'

She didn't rise to the bait but said quietly, 'Ms Fassbinder, despite your rough edges and your insistence on being obnoxious, *you* hold a position of power and influence. People *listen* to you. They are afraid of you.'

'Well, I *had* a position . . .'

'Indeed: and the moment you let that go, Udo began his campaign against you. He sensed a shift in the dynamics of power and, more importantly, an advantage for himself. It began in small ways, but has become as fast-moving as an avalanche.' She *tsked*. 'You are on occasion your own worst enemy, Ms Fassbinder.'

'Do you really think you're the first person to point that out?'

'Udo has spent his time on the Council seeking and finding weaknesses, exploiting them where he may, filing them away for later use. He's a *whisperer*, dear Verity, and his words find their way to many ears and to many delicate egos. It is my observation that he works more effectively on men than women – but not your Bela.'

'*Not* my Zvezdomir, Titania.'

'Or your Ziggi.'

'Him, mine, sure.'

'Theodosia Norn does not listen to him; she actively turns away when he speaks, which is a matter of great frustration to him. She should watch her back.'

I made a note to warn Theo, just in case she'd not noticed. She probably just didn't care. Well, if my sole purpose in life was to be a warning to others, so be it.

'More worryingly, he has spent many months pouring small poisons into Sandor's ear. Sandor and I have known each other for centuries; you saw he considered Aviva a friend, even after her betrayal. He was a forgiving man . . . but since Udo, Sandor is more aware of his position, more alert to insult.'

And I'd played into that with my smart mouth. *Good one, Fassbinder.*

'Thanks for the warning, Titania.'

'And now to the other matter: Aviva.'

'I wasn't going to mention that.'

'An unusual subtlety for you.'

'You know, people never give me enough credit for the stuff I don't mention.' I pulled the hair away from my face, feeling a little overheated in the jungle room. 'Louise was worried it had hitched a ride with you.'

'I cannot feel it, there have been no signs and dear Louise can find no trace.'

'Then it just went back wherever it came from?'

'One hopes. What I can tell you is that things were going well – before the explosion at least. I summoned her shade with ease and I can do it again, but I must rest a few days longer. I will take care of the mechanics myself so there can be no mistakes made by arrogant children.' She smiled ruefully.

'If you're sure?'

She inclined her head. 'You still have questions, and besides, it is a matter of pride. I believe Aviva has things to share with us, whether she knows it or not.'

'Why are you being so helpful when it was me who got you into this mess?'

'I believe you are needed – and that you will help get me *out* of this mess. My stock is very low with Sandor.'

'Thank you.' I looked at my watch. 'I have a meeting in the city, so I'd better head off before the traffic becomes a trap and no cab will pick me up.'

'The Odinsays?'

'Seriously, do I have no secrets nowadays?'

'Bela asked me to intercede. As you know, I have been otherwise engaged,' she said wryly. 'Their prestige is important to them. You would do very well to practise being respectful and not flippant.'

'But disrespectful and flippant is pretty much all I've got.' I raised my hands in surrender. 'Joking! Thank you, Titania. Take care of yourself.'

'There are others to do that.' She smiled. 'I would dearly like to see Ingo again.'

Thus proving once again that there's no accounting for taste or love.

'And I know he is desperate to see you. I'll see what I can do.'

Outside the door of the room Louise waited.

'How is she really?' I asked.

'She was badly wounded, but she is recovering. Slowly.'

'Keep an eye on her, will you? She's offered to finish the ceremony.'

'If Aviva is piggybacking, or there's some shred of her left behind, it might not be Titania's idea.'

'Oh, good. She said you'd not found any trace of Aviva . . .'

'. . . and I didn't, but she was always tricksy.'

I scratched my head. 'Is there *any* way we can tell if something hitched a ride?'

'Wait and see?'

Chapter Twenty-Five

They looked like gods: *very* unhappy gods.

Bela was late, and I had never been much inclined to small talk.

Freydis and Egil Odinsay stood in front of the sanctuary area of St Stephen's, although not so close that they were up cheek-by-jowl with the altar; there were limits. They were around eight feet tall, which was surely not something they'd let Normal folk see; I figured glamours had been let loose especially for me, so I'd appreciate who I was dealing with. They were both that peculiar blond that comes of Weyrd Norse blood, both with eyes like a winter sky, and both were perfectly beautiful, with icicles gleaming on hair and lips and the same kind of frost sifting off their skin as Thaïs had displayed. Egil's beard was a thing of true magnificence, plaited and hung with tiny silver birds and intensely blue glass beads. If he lost an eye and had a raven on each shoulder he'd be a shoe-in for the next Odin look-alike competition. Even if their claims to be related to the Allfather were nothing but puffery, looking at them as I sat in the front pew, I could truly believe they had gods' blood in their chill veins.

Freydis wore a long dress of pale blue with a belt slung low on her hips and a chatelaine that appeared to be made of ice. A silver necklace with a raven-shaped pendant hung at her throat. An argent ring on Egil's left hand bore the same device. His trousers and shirt looked home-spun; the shirt was open at the neck as if to show that the cold didn't bother him one little bit. Freydis had a wool cloak of pure white, but it was flung back off her shoulders to show she didn't really need it, thank you very much. She had the same haughty look as Dusana, which might have made me a little twitchy if I hadn't reckoned it was too obvious: if this *was* a disguise, it wasn't a very good one.

They'd brought no attendants, so either they didn't think they needed them or they didn't want anyone else to know they were in a *church* and meeting *me*.

I was being very mindful of Titania's and Thaïs' warnings, so I just sat there and stared at them politely. What had Titania said to convince them to come? Chances were blackmail had been involved, which led me to consider what she might have on them.

After a while, the silence got to Egil.

'What do you want of us?' His voice rang like thunder through the space, a startling effect.

Freydis' expression made it clear he'd let the team down by making the first move.

'Who me? Oh, hello. Only you didn't acknowledge me when I arrived so I didn't know we were doing the talking thing.' *And I'm out.*

'We are here at another's request,' chimed Freydis coolly.

'Yes, you are. And I appreciate it.' I wondered what chance I had of clawing back ground. 'I was wondering about the legend of your grail.'

They exchanged a look and I guessed neither Bela nor Titania had thought it wise to mention the purpose of the meeting before they got the Odinsays to agree to see me.

I hurried on, 'Three families are listed as having grails as part of their swag.' Even I winced at that. 'The other two have been eliminated' – one quite literally – 'which leaves your very fine selves.'

'I cannot tell if you're being facetious or not when you say such things,' exclaimed Freydis.

'I don't know either, half the time.' I shrugged. 'But the fact is, claiming you've got a grail is one of those lies that's really easy to sell: set up a nice vase or goblet under glass and tell everyone it's the source of your family's fortune – you know, a cup of plenty, a chalice. It's a pretty impressive thing in times of peace, when no one expects you to use it . . . but the days when your armies march to war, when you need to put the thing to the test and revive the fallen? It's pretty hard to maintain the fiction then.'

I lifted one palm upwards, the other down, like two sides of a scale. 'But nowadays? How often do the Weyrd armies muster and mobilise? How often would such a claim need to be validated? Infrequently enough to perhaps make it worthwhile to fib?'

Again, that exchange of looks.

'However, a family like *yours*? You came here willingly. There's no exile in your past—'

'We like the weather.'

'—and it agrees with you: your standing in the community is *impeccable*.'

Nice hair, good teeth.

'You've got *lineage* – you don't need to lie about *anything*. If word on the street says you've got a grail, then I'm willing to put money on you actually having a grail.'

'I do not know what Titania sees in you,' sniffed Egil.

'She finds me amusing,' I explained, 'but if you know her at all well, you'll know she's got a pretty quirky sense of . . . well, *everything*.'

Freydis gave a little tip of her head that might have been agreement.

'And if we do have such an item? What then?' asked Egil, puffing himself up to look even bigger; but he kept looking at her, at Freydis. It was like he was throwing stones to distract me so *she* could see how I'd react.

'Then I'd like to see it.' Once I found the damned thing, I'd have to work out what the Hell to do next, as giving it to the Guardian certainly wasn't on my to-do list. But I also needed to find the tyrant and work out if it could be used *against* the Guardian — or if I was just going to end up with double the trouble on my hands.

'Perhaps you want to steal it.'

'Nope. Not me.' Not *me*.

'Perhaps you're more trouble than you're worth. Perhaps we should get rid of you.'

Ah, we were on to the war talk; the formulaic insults would come next, possibly even some kind of pissing contest.

'Or perhaps you might remain civilised, Egil.' Bela materialised out of the darkness and I wondered how long he'd been standing there. Probably the whole time, most likely waiting to see if I managed to stay polite. I guess the jury was kind of out on that. He had the patience of a rock and the presence of a shadow that might smother you if you put a foot wrong. Egil Odinsay, enormous as he was, stepped back as Bela moved into the light. Maybe it was something to do with the fact that darkness clung to my ex-boyfriend. Say what you will about his commitment phobia and tendency to send me into dangerous situations, the man knew how to make an entrance.

Looking at him still made me miss David.

'Tepes.' Freydis tilted her chin regally and offered her hand. Bela bent over it in chivalrous fashion, his lips barely touching the ice-gleamed skin.

There was no contact with Egil other than stiff-necked head nods at fifty paces.

I kept my mouth shut; it felt wise.

'We appreciate your attendance upon us.' Bela managed to make it sound like they were supplicants and not the other way around: a verbal bitch-slap so subtly done it would be impossible to complain without seeming childish. For a moment Egil looked inclined to give it a go, but Freydis put a hand on his arm and he was subdued.

Oh yeah, *she* was very definitely in charge.

'Verity and I do not wish to waste your time, or keep you over-long in this . . . location.' All three Weyrd threw their glances up to the vaulted ceiling and the crucified son, all the trappings of a religion that had done its best to wipe them out. It couldn't have been lost on them that said religion had failed quite signally to finish the job. 'If you will kindly answer her questions, you may be on your way.'

Boom.

Freydis looked at the stones underfoot and Egil looked at Freydis. She pursed her lips, breathing out. A snowflake the size of my head formed in the air, beautiful and intricate — then she flicked it with her finger and it dissipated.

'Once . . . once we did have just such an item. It was taken from us,' she said, her voice clear as bells.

'"Taken"? Stolen? Or removed from your possession as a punishment?' I asked.

'Stolen,' said Egil shortly, but Freydis was shaking her head.

'Taken,' she corrected. 'Our son took it.'

'Where is he now?' asked Bela.

'Our only child.' Freydis looked upwards again and I thought perhaps there were frosty tears in her eyes. 'We did not report it as a theft for we did not wish to . . . pursue him.'

'So it could be anywhere,' I said, rising; I couldn't feel my backside any more (so much for comfy sycamore seats). On the upside, I couldn't feel much of the aches from the car accident either.

I started pacing, thinking, then asked, 'What was your son's name?'

Freydis looked surprised. She blinked and opened her lips as if the name hadn't crossed them for a long time and she feared what might come when it did. 'Harmsorgi,' she said at last. 'It was my father's name but we should not have used it. It means grief, sorrow.'

Maisie wasn't looking too bad now. 'When did he disappear?' I tried to keep my tone sympathetic.

Egil made a show of thinking about it, but I was sure that was an act; such a date would be carved into his heart. Dates of loss always are.

'April 16, 1980.'

See? 'And the cause of the argument?'

'You pry.'

'Yes, I do: because the more information you give me, the better my chances of finding him – and finding your grail.' I smiled. 'Would you not like to see your son again?'

There was so much *longing* in Freydis' expression that it hurt, but Egil just looked stoic. He couldn't care less, or at least that was the impression he wanted to give us. The boy had obviously defied him and stolen the family's honour; he was good and gone and best not ever mentioned again.

'Freydis?' I said softly.

'His choice of lover,' she answered, equally softly. 'A Normal woman – a Normal woman, to taint the bloodline.' She looked away as if embarrassed to say such a thing to me, who had Weyrd and Normal blood running in *my* veins; whose child was also mixed.

As if it made us lesser.

'And what happened to that woman?'

'She left,' said Freydis, then corrected herself. 'She disappeared – before he did. Harmsorgi accused us of having orchestrated it, ruining his life.'

'And did you?'

She glared at me. 'We made our displeasure known to him, for all the good it did us, but she was gone and there was nothing that could be done about it.'

'And he left soon after?'

'A week,' whispered Egil, as if giving up a long-treasured secret.

'What did the grail look like?' I asked, and got a strange look in return. 'Well, if I'm going to find it, I need to know what I'm looking for so I'll recognise it.'

'Beautiful,' said Freydis longingly. 'White as bone.'

'You will not find it,' said Egil shortly, his brief vulnerability gone. 'It is as gone as is Harmsorgi – it is beneath the earth, surely. If *we* could not find him, then what hope have *you*?'

'Well, for a start, he doesn't know I'm looking for him. He would have known what you'd do and doubtless he'd've taken steps to avoid your people – he knew your habits, your tendencies, your minions . . . I'm betting you didn't bother hiring anyone who wasn't known to him?'

Their expressions told me I'd hit the mark.

'And I'm presuming it's a long time since anyone's hunted him? So he's likely grown to think himself safe and forgotten. He might have started to leave traces.' I crossed my arms over my chest. 'Especially if he's spent all this time looking for his lover. What was her name, by the way?'

'Ava,' said Freydis, and the word came out as though it was somehow dirty. 'Ava Montclair.'

'Do you know anything else about her? Like where they met?'

Egil looked away: *No, of course not.* They didn't want to know anything about her so they'd stuffed themselves up with wilful ignorance. I flipped a card out of my pocket and offered it to Freydis – if any help were to be forthcoming, it would be from her. After a hesitation, she took it.

Egil's face stiffened, but I didn't think he'd have much influence over her.

'If you can think of anything else . . . ?'

They were gone very quickly, heading off into the darkness together. Bela and I listened to their footsteps fading and the thud of the heavy door to the sacristy closing and settling in the frame. We sat back down in the front pews, one seat between us, and stared up at the beardless crucified man in front of us.

'How much are they not telling?' I asked.

Bela shrugged. 'Hard to know. The Normal woman part . . . I felt like they were telling us the absolute minimum they could get away with. Something else happened, but as to what it was . . .'

'Hmmm. Agreed. Is that name familiar to you? Ava Montclair?'

'Can't say it is, but that doesn't necessarily mean anything.'

'I'll see if McIntyre can find something.' I rested my elbows on my knees, leaned forward and put my head in hands. 'Did you know Harmsorgi Odinsay? Hear any scuttlebutt?'

'Before my time, V. There might be something in the Archives, but if they didn't report him doing a disappearing act . . .'

'I wonder how Jost's programme of familiarising himself with the holdings is going? Oh, do you know if he found anything grail-related in the Nadasy stuff?'

'You mean, was I aware my Archivist was still working for you despite clear instructions to the contrary from Sandor Verhoeven?'

'Sure, phrase it like that if you must.' I glanced at him; his profile was stark as bone against the shadows in the cathedral. 'Well?'

'No, nothing. I'll ask him about Harmsorgi, but *please* don't trouble him. I'm concerned about Jost. He's . . . *distracted*.'

'He's got Mel and Lizzie staying with him.' I told Bela about the night-doves and the fallout and he made an irritated noise.

'Why wouldn't he tell me that?'

'Because he's still new enough to think he can keep secrets from you?' I watched as Bela rubbed hard at his face. 'You're going to start taking skin off, you know.'

He laughed.

'And I don't know if Lizzie is too keen on him,' I admitted.

'She's used to having her mother all to herself. It's only natural.'

'That's what I figured.' I sighed. 'Jost will need to work his love-life out on his own.'

'Speaking of which.' He fished his mobile out of his jacket pocket and pulled up an image.

It was my family: David and Olivia in the garden at Ocean's Reach. My mother was glaring at the camera – now I knew where I got that from – but David wore a goofy-serious grin: *amused but patient*. Our daughter was on his knee – our daughter who at one month was the size of a one-year old! – and all that strawberry hair she'd got from the Fassbinder side of the family was starting to turn into curls too long for the brief time she'd been away from me. I wondered if it would darken, if she'd start to look more like me and less like Ziggi at some point. She had green eyes, like her father's and mine, and her round little face was screwed up in an intense stare while pudgy little starfish hands reached towards Bela. At David's feet – or *on* them, if I wasn't mistaken – was a German shepherd pup, all soft fur and irresistibly cute nose and ears and paws.

Apparently my family had a dog now; just no *me*. I swallowed a couple of times before I managed, 'You were there?'

He touched my hand. 'You can't be there for them, V, but . . . this is what I can do for you.'

I brought my knees up and curled around them and began to cry, the sobs dissipating into the gloom of the cathedral, then bouncing back to us. Bela shifted over one seat and put his arms around me. I'm pretty sure he kissed my hair at some point.

Eventually I unfurled, dried my tears and muttered, 'I just miss them.'

'I know.' He self-consciously shuffled back to his original spot.

'And my daughter's a giant.'

'Weyrd blood. Olivia told me you had the same growth spurts.'

'She did?'

'She did.'

'Where's Ziggi?' I sniffled.

'At St Agnes', giving Septimus and Velma a break. There's been no sign of anyone looking for Joyce – you might just have got away with it.'

'For now.'

'For now. Do you still think the Guardian is likely to go after your fox-girl?'

'He's certainly been voted Mostly Likely to Fuck Up Former Employees.'

'Great.'

'But he'll work through agents and minion, Bela. He won't – he *can't* – come against her directly. You just need to keep everyone on alert.'

'Noted. What next?'

'I need a shower and a change of clothes.'

'Nice dress.' He eyed Oldman's cast-off sweater-dress and I punched his arm.

'Shut up. Sleep. I need sleep. Tomorrow is another bloody day.'

Chapter Twenty-Six

My day began in the winter dark at 4 a.m., with Lacy Oldman –
against whom I'd not had the foresight to ward my house – banging
on the door.

'Fassbinder! Fassbinder!' She wasn't yelling precisely, but at some
point the neighbours would realise there was a low-frequency racket
running beneath their sleep and get *very* pissed off. I rolled off the
sofa and answered the door in T-shirt and doona.

Oldman drew back when she saw me by the glow of the sensor
light on the porch. 'Whoa.'

'This had better be good.'

'Another body – *and* we think we've got whoever is doing this
cornered.'

'Where?'

'Lindsay Street, Hawthorne.'

'Not far.'

'Not far at all.'

I stepped out and went to pull the door shut behind me.

'Ah, you sure?' asked Oldman. I looked at her blankly until she
said, 'Trousers? Shirt? Shoes?'

Five minutes later and closer to properly attired, I joined Oldman
in the patrol car.

'You good to go just like that?'

'What now?' I huffed.

'Well, your hair is kind of . . . you know what, never mind.'

There was no traffic, unsurprisingly, just the occasional shift-worker returning home, no need for sirens or lights on the eight-minute trip, no need to wake the slumbering populace – you're welcome, Brisbane.

'So,' said Constable Oldman as we sped onto Wynnum Road, 'I knock on your door at four a.m. and you just come out. That's pretty funny.'

'As opposed to?' But she was right: I had got into Oldman's car very easily. There'd been no text from McIntyre, which was unusual, but if there was a containment situation, I could see she might have her hands full.

'To how roughly we started off – that's all I'm saying. Now, it's like *Starsky and Hutch*.'

'I feel you're a little too young for that pop culture reference.'

'No! You know, Ben Stiller and—'

'I have to stop you there.' Watching the original TV series with my grandfather remained a fond memory and I would not have it ruined. I ran my hands over my face, worked some sleep out of the corners of my eyes. My breath would have slaughtered an elephant. 'Do you have any mints?'

'In the glove-box.'

'Thanks.' I offered her one too. 'So, wait. Why are you taking me over there? I'm not Weyrd any more.'

'You'll always be Weyrd.' She grinned. 'You're closer, and besides, Hassman's looking after your fox-girl—'

'Again, *not* my fox-girl.'

'—and Tepes is apparently otherwise engaged.'

Leaving Muggins here to schlep out to a cold crime scene and possible nastiness in the early hours of the morning: Muggins who was *not* meant to be doing Council work; Muggins who'd automatically wandered out into the freezing cold just because she was asked.

Well, not really: *really*, it was because there was a chance the perpetrator was within reach and I would happily strangle whoever it was if given even half a chance.

'Where's the body? How was it found?'

'In a small house on Lindsay Street.'

'Inhabited?' I asked sceptically.

'Nope. Belongs to an old lady who moved in with one of her daughters yesterday – apparently the girls live next door to each other a few streets away, so it's easy for family visits. That's nice, I think.'

'It is, Lacy, it is.' I paused. 'So the finding of the body . . .'

'Right, so: a neighbour saw a light on in the house – he's an early riser, apparently, and he's used to the old lady being awake at the same time and used to pop over for a cuppa. He thought she must have accidentally left a light on and didn't want her to get a nasty shock with her bill, so like the good neighbour he is, he nips over to turn it off. He knows where the spare key is, but the door's already unlocked, which makes him suspicious, so he sneaks in – and sees a woman's body laid out in the front room. She's wearing red silk embroidered pyjamas. He hears someone moving around and sneaks out to call Triple 0. Mention of the pyjamas got it passed straight up to us.'

'And let us bless keywords. And?'

'And the place is surrounded. No one's come out, but there's definitely movement inside.'

'And normal cops don't go in to situations like that.'

'Nope. You do.'

'Right now I really wished I didn't.' I cracked my knuckles. 'If I die, I will come back to haunt both you and McIntyre.'

'Noted.' The patrol car swiftly ate up the distance between us and 54A Lindsay Street, Hawthorne.

'Hey, did you ever manage to trace the owner of Concord Holdings?' She looked at me blankly until I said, 'The Honda CRV Joyce was driving until recently.'

'Oh. No, sorry – but not for lack of trying; it's just shelf company after shelf company. Someone's covering their tracks.'

I grunted. 'I'm also sending a bill for this. This is well out of the range of "Hey, Fassbinder, how about a little favour?"'

'Agreed.'

'Why *are* you being so agreeable, Constable?'

'Because you're going in there alone and I'm hoping your last moments will be pleasant?'

And at last I realised that Lacy Oldman was trying to be *friends* with me. Well, it was four o'clock in the morning . . .

'So, you know that bad things happen to my friends, right?' I started. 'I mean, there's a whole range of stuff: exile, beatings, stabbings, drowning, down to occasional burns and bumps that are hardly worth mentioning. Oh, and car accidents! Let's talk car accidents.'

She looked hurt. 'I just . . . I just want to learn from you.' She blushed. 'You're cool.'

'*Really?*'

'We're here.'

We pulled up a few houses down from the scene, next to where two patrol cars had formed a roadblock. At the far end of the street I could see the lights of Hardcastle Park and the Hawthorne Ferry Terminal gently rocking on the Brisbane River. McIntyre was leaning wearily against one of the vehicles. I knew how she felt.

'Anything new?' I asked, taking in the chain-link fences, which were at odds with the stucco walls in front of the renovated-to-within-an-inch-of-their-lives houses on either side of the little cottage at 54A.

She shook her head. 'Just a shape moving past the windows; that's pretty much it. It's big, Fassbinder, and male, as far as I can tell. I don't think he knows anyone's here – I'd imagine he'd have done something about leaving before now, rather than meandering about in leisurely fashion.'

'Yeah.' I pointed at Lacy Oldman's waist. 'Would you mind lending me that?'

She touched the telescopic baton on her belt, then handed it over with a brief smile.

I gave it a flick and it extended nicely with a good, solid *snick*. Joyce's fighting fan would have done more harm, but this was good too. With my strength behind it, it would give me a bit of arm's length to manoeuvre and cause some damage.

'Well, wish me luck.'

'You know what they say about needing luck?'

'If you need it, you're already fucked?'

'Close enough.'

'Pull your people back, will you?' I said to McIntyre. 'I don't want anything unnecessary on my conscience.'

'Be careful.' McIntyre stepped aside so I could get by; as her head dropped, I couldn't help but think of someone letting the dead man walking pass. That was *not* a comforting thought.

I concentrated on what I knew: three bodies so far, three dead women, and the cause of death might be unknown but it was obviously unpleasant and the same in each case. The perpetrator was in there and *I* was going in there. And I really shouldn't have been.

Don't get killed, Fassbinder, you'll be in a world of trouble.

I made it up the five wooden steps onto the narrow verandah

without making a sound, which was itself an achievement in such an old house. The blinds – proper pull-down fabric blinds, not Venetians or lacy curtains that I might be able to peer through – were drawn, but I could see his silhouette behind the one on the left, which I figured was probably a lounge. Then he started moving again, heavy footsteps sounding down the hall inside, not coming towards me, as I'd feared for a sharp second. The front door was still ajar, but obviously the intruder hadn't noticed that anyone else had been around. I pushed it just enough to slip by.

The blue-and-white lino in the hallway had faded to oyster from the scuffing of shoes over the years. I saw a black sneaker at the end of the hall disappearing into another doorway, maybe a kitchen. The house was tiny; perhaps it was a bedroom down there? Hard to know, so I guess I just had to find out.

I hefted the baton, feeling a bit uncertain about how light it felt now.

I tiptoed down the short hall, paused a couple of feet from the door, then took another step – and stopped as a creaky floorboard blared like a klaxon. The noises of someone rummaging through kitchen drawers in the room next door ceased and I expected to hear . . . well, I don't know, but *not* what I heard.

It was the noise of demolition: of a large hard body hitting and passing through plaster and wood. There was no hesitation either, no sound of a second or third hit needed to break through, just one thoroughly good *bam!* done right the first time.

I stepped into the doorway.

Sure enough, there was a big hole in the wall, straight through the timber and plasterboard and what I hoped to Heaven wasn't some kind of asbestos insulation. I strode to the hole and peered out into a tiny backyard. There was the thud of the front door banging against

the wall which I guessed was the cavalry in the form of Oldman and/
or McIntyre coming to the rescue.

Someone or something scrambled over the wooden back fence –
maybe it had used up its quota of wall-walking? – but all I got was
an impression of bulk. *Fleeing* bulk.

As Oldman was saying, 'What the f—' I resigned myself and
jumped through the breach.

I jammed the baton into the waistband of my jeans, then clawed
my way up the fence, almost regretting not accepting the Guardian's
offer of my mother's speed and strength. Instead, my own muscles
got me over the top and into the next garden. My only guide was
the crashing of my quarry, scaling another fence ahead of me. I still
couldn't get a proper sight of it: there was grey and black and maybe
gold flecks in the moonlight, but of its entirety I couldn't tell.

I kept going.

Another yard.

Another fence.

Another yard.

Another fence.

I wished I'd got my act together and bought myself a Taser.

Whatever I was chasing was heading towards the river. I noticed
it was avoiding the street and keeping to the shadows despite the
challenges of the built-up environment. My ribs were aching as I
watched my prey vault the last fence – the fucker didn't even have the
grace to look puffed – and dropped down onto the floating walkway.

I followed: up and over, jarring knees and ankles, now heading to
the right, and I kept running until there was no sound behind me . . .

. . . and then there was no sound of footsteps in front of me, either.

It had led me away, put on just enough speed to keep me thinking
I'd got a chance of catching it.

I slowed to a stop, sliding the baton into my sweaty palm. I listened hard, caught the merest whisper of a laugh before something a full head taller than me tore past, its shoulder lowered to knock the breath out of me. I struck out with the baton as I went down and heard a grunt, then a splash as it went into the river.

I felt like I'd broken a rib as I lay there on the boardwalk, staring up at the stars and telling myself I really needed to make better life choices until McIntyre, outpacing Oldman despite her youth, dropped to her knees beside me and started shouting and shaking me.

'Christ! Fassbinder – Fassbinder, are you all right? Oh God, Bela will kill me.' Pause. '*Everyone* will fucking kill me—'

'*I'll* kill you if you don't stop fucking shaking me! *Ribs*, Rhonda: *ribs*.'

'Oh, thank you, God! Oldman, give me a hand.'

They helped me to the Hawthorne stop where the CityCat docked, then along Lindsay Street and back to the crime scene, where the SOCOs were starting to dust handles, doors, walls and windows for prints.

In the little front room was the third body, her red pyjamas like blood on the lino. I knelt beside her, wincing at the pain in my ribs and thinking I should have words with Thaïs about the gaps in her protection . . .

Brunette hair struck through with silver; eyes white, dead marbles. I looked at her broad forehead, the high cheekbones, the shape of the nose beneath its coating of soot, the mummification . . .

'Okay, the absent bits of face from victim number one notwith-standing . . . does it strike you that they're all a bit alike? I mean, I could be imagining it, I'm still pretty oxygen-deprived and this poor thing's messy but . . . there are three now, and it's looking a bit . . .'

Lacy and Rhonda both loomed over the body and I could see from their expressions that they were halfway convinced already.

'Not related, though, not siblings,' said Rhonda.

'No, I don't think so. But someone's picked them because they're alike enough to look like one woman?'

Lacy just nodded and Rhonda asked, 'So where does that get us?'

I sighed. 'In a lounge in Hawthorne looking at another corpse with not a sausage of a clue between us.'

I rose to more wincing and a couple of impressive grunts for effect.

'Oh, hey, this is yours. Thanks.' I'd retained the baton despite the shoulder-charge. I offered it to Lacy – then stopped and examined it more closely.

In the joins of the shaft extension were tufts of hair . . . no, *fur*. *Golden fur*.

The same shade, if I wasn't was much mistaken, that Merrily Vaughan had plucked from her assailant.

Well, well, well.

Chapter Twenty-Seven

Due to McIntyre's inexplicable unwillingness to let me borrow a police car, I had to call a cab around ten a.m. so I could return to St Agnes' Hospital.

Oldman had dropped me home just before dawn cracked the sky and I'd stumbled inside for a shower and some food – well, a couple of wheatmeal biscuits and a tea. I must have fallen asleep despite my best intentions, because I was woken by the buzz of a text. I was half-sitting, half-lying on the couch and the first thing I noticed was that the car-accident ache had been replaced by a major shoulder-charge ache. Thaïs' protection clearly had limits and I made a mental note not to push my luck.

The text was a summons from Sister Bridget and I figured I could also stick my head in to see if there was any change on Joyce before heading over to Third Eye Books. I wanted to do a compare-and-contrast between the fur McIntyre'd let me have in a plastic evidence bag last night and what Merrily had stuffed into a glass jar like some atavistic souvenir. Then I'd get ready for the afternoon's obligation.

I dropped in to the ICU first, hoping to chat with Ziggi about last night's adventure, but the shift had already changed. Septimus was a ginger Weyrd, but he wasn't a *Jäger* like my uncle. He looked up casually from his book when I opened the door, which made me peeved.

I didn't bother to hide it. 'Not very alert, Septimus.'

He blushed that shade only gingers can manage. 'Last time I checked, you weren't my boss.'

'True, but I can and will tell on you.' I stood at the foot of Joyce's bed. 'Any change?'

He carefully put a bookmark between the pages before he rose and looked down on the fox-girl with something like fondness. 'No. She's sleeping like a baby.'

'Or a head-injured car-crash victim. Have either you or Velma seen any sign of watchers?'

'Look, I really think you're being paranoid—'

'Septimus, exactly what are the *ill* consequences of you taking extra care with your job?'

He looked at me in surprise. 'Er . . . nothing.'

'And what are the ill consequences of you half-arsing your job?'

He glanced away and muttered, 'Got it. I haven't seen anything, but I'll keep an eye out.'

'That's all I'm asking. I don't want to come back and find her dead because you were too wrapped up in *War and Peace*.'

'Understood.'

'Thank you.'

I took a last look at Joyce and noticed there was a Styrofoam container on the bedside table, stamped with 'Little Venice' on the top. It looked suspiciously like a cake carrier.

In a fit of observation, Septimus caught the direction of my gaze. 'Theodosia has been in a couple of times.'

I was glad to hear it. I hoped Joyce was okay in there. Still, I gave Septimus a final glare, wondering if the lax attitude was something creeping through the Weyrd ranks; they were so used to being powerful and feared that they stopped fearing much else in a world that didn't believe in them. Had me being around for a long while, doing what I did, made them complacent? If I managed to get through all this, managed to take my job back, some things were going to have to change. Bela and I were going to have words about the rank and file of the brute squad. Next stop, Sister Bridget. I didn't bother to knock, but as I walked past the kitchen, Ingo called out to me. I was surprised he was still there, but then, maybe it was the safest place until things settled down back at Casa Del Banks.

'Hey, Verity.' He had half a loaf of bread in front of him and judging by the crumbs, it looked like he'd been loading slices into the toaster for most of the morning. I'd be willing to bet Sister Bridget wasn't going to be too happy being eaten out of house and home by the equivalent of a stray shaggy dog. But hey, that was Ingo's lookout; I'd not be getting between the nun and her target under any circumstances.

'How's it going?' I asked, helping myself to the toast as it popped up.

'Neat. Good reflexes.' He offered me the butter knife. 'So, do you know how long I'm going to be here? Only, I kinda miss . . .'

'Titania feels the same way.' I slathered on butter, followed by a healthy dollop of jam. I honestly did not want to listen to an emo monologue. 'But Tepes will keep you here as long as he deems it necessary. There are some matters to be settled, Ingo. You made kind of a mess, you know.'

He hung his head. 'I know.'

'There's all manner of diplomatic stuff needs to go on between people with more manners and sticks up their backside than little old me. And as for the Council itself . . . well, there's some politicking too, so just be patient, okay? Don't do anything stupid – in fact, don't do anything but help out here. Don't give Sister Bridget a reason to bite your head off.'

'She's kinda . . . strange,' he said hesitantly, then followed up quickly with, 'Don't get me wrong, I'm used to *strange*, and she's very nice, although a bit prickly. But . . .'

'What?' I tilted my head, curious.

'She talks to herself a lot. And I mean, *a lot*. I walk past any room she's in – except maybe the bathroom – and she's talking to herself.'

'What about? Sure it's not praying? It does go with the whole nunly thing, you know.'

'Well, I guess . . . she asks a lot of questions, about fire and falling and broken promises. I kind of thought maybe she's talking to her god . . . or an imaginary friend.'

I frowned. Was Sister Bridget somehow communicating with the Guardian? And if so, why?

And if that were the case – *Jesus!*

I shook myself firmly. *No, no way.* If Sister Bridget had gone to the dark side, Joyce would have had her plug pulled by now and Septimus would have had his backside kicked. As a former exorcist, Sister Bridget had more than one coping strategy and her wiry frame gave no indication of her hidden strength, not to mention a good deal of cold, practical blood flowing in her veins. Once again I wished I could ward the hospital, but St Agnes' had too many Weyrd patients and staff for that to work. Half the doctors wouldn't be able to get inside the doors.

Sister Bridget had memories she probably didn't want. She'd told me not so long ago that once upon a time she had basically been me. If the way she dealt with her own demons was by talking out loud with them, well, fine by me; she could do so to her heart's content.

'Cut her some slack, Ingo. She's seen some stuff, you know.'

'But she's a *nun* . . .'

'Oh, you dumb-arse *child*! You think nothing and no one existed before you accidentally popped into being? People had lives and histories and tragedies and joys long before you arrived. One day some snot-nosed kid is going to look at you and say, "Hey, Granddad, you've never lived!"' – mind you, with extended Weyrd life-spans, that might take some time – 'and you'll remember this moment.'

'Sure, sure.' He ducked his head, as if hoping I wouldn't slap him over the ear. I was tempted, but reined my desire in.

'She in the sitting room?'

'Yeah.'

'Don't worry, Ingo. I will get things moving for you with Tepes – just be patient, okay?'

'Sure. Thanks.' He refilled the toaster.

'And go easy on the bread: try not to eat the good Sister out of house and home.'

As I approached the sitting room with its symphony of orange and mustard and brown furniture deemed too hideous even for the less fortunate, I could hear Sister Bridget's voice once again, low and urgent, like she was telling beads, praying the Rosary. And as usual, she fell silent just before I could begin to make out individual words.

Sticking my head around the door, I saw the nun half-reclining on a sofa that had seen better days. She was in jeans and a long-sleeved T-shirt and she looked exhausted. Her eyes were closed and her short iron-grey hair was a mess.

'You need to sue your hair stylist,' I said.

She opened one eye. 'Hair stylists not really deemed essential for nuns.'

'Quite frankly, they should be.'

'You're the one to talk.'

'Fair call.' I picked an armchair across from her and felt the seat springs just readying themselves to leap and bruise my backside. I might have groaned when I sat.

'Bad night?'

'Chasing a *something* through back yards at Hawthorne and another woman's body found – same condition as Alison Brandt's – in a house there. And no, I did not catch the *something*, but it gave me a good whack in the ribs.'

'Any ideas?'

'Something furry.'

'Okay. I went to the Ascot house early this morning.'

'With Ziggi?' My tone was sharp.

'*Yes*, with your uncle.' She rolled her eyes. 'I got them, sent them on their way.'

I sensed a 'but'. 'All of them?'

'Almost.'

'Ah.' I had a feeling . . . 'Wouldn't have been a thin girl of about fourteen? Pale, flossy hair, maybe in a pair of green Converse sneakers and a too-short skirt?

'Ziggi said you'd known her.'

'Sally Crown. Poor Sally.' She'd been a street kid, lost and alone, who'd helped Magda Nadasy source other street kids for her wine-making activities. Sally hadn't been brought up so much as dragged up by the scruff of her neck and she hadn't any benevolence to spare for anyone else, not when it had been in such short supply for her. I wondered if I was the first person to be kind to her; she'd given up the Winemaker to me, then enough information to track down those who'd been happy to buy wine made from the tears of children. When Vadim Nadasy, Magda's husband, had found her, it had cost Sally her life, and she'd died hard, had Sally.

'Did she say anything?' I asked at last.

The dead who travel with the Boatman lose their voices for the journey so they don't cry out, beg for mercy or call down spells to overturn Fate. But sometimes the dead slip away from the Boatman and wander, become ghosts, corpselights.

'She just said your name. I tried to send her twice.'

No wonder Sister Bridget looked exhausted. Laying spirits to rest was hard enough without having a spirit who just didn't want to go.

'It's okay. I'll head over there.' I still had the flask with the Waters of Forgetting. If I could convince Sally to drink, she'd go. She'd have to have her heart weighed and her sins tallied, and there had been a fair few of those, as far as I could tell, but she'd come good at the end and I hoped that would be enough. 'Anything else I need to know?'

She just shook her head.

'Have you spoken to Father Tony lately?'

'Not since last week. Why?'

'He's proving elusive.' I'd tried to phone again last night; no answer. 'I have questions.'

'Do you think those things might be connected?'

'For a nun you're very prickly.'

'I don't know where you got your ideas about nuns from . . .'

'*The Sound of Music*?'

She just stared at me until I said, 'Any sign of recovery for Joyce?'

'Not yet.' She smiled. 'But I always have hope.'

That was unnaturally perky for Sister Bridget . . . 'And is everything okay with your houseguest?'

'There's basically a ravenous monster in my kitchen. Do you have any idea how much bread he gets through? And he creeps around.'

'He's basically a teenage boy. Apart from that?'

'It's okay.'

'Good enough for me.'

'Easy for you to say.'

Mike Jones was tall, with the overly muscled physique of someone
with too much time and not enough to do. Beneath his dark-haired,
pleasant-looking glamour his eyes glowed carmine and he had
leathery black wings, a negligible nose and ears not much more than
depressions in the side of the skull. Oh, and let's not forget the coat
of spiky black fur all over him. I used to think of him as Monobrow
Mike, but ever since he'd lost his partner Jerry protecting my family
I'd tried to be kind – I'd even been understanding about the fact that
he'd later been unable to resist Joyce's conniving and made a deal with
the Guardian that put my family at risk.

He was sitting in a red Jeep opposite Third Eye Books, looking
tired and bored. When the cab dropped me off outside the shop, I
crossed over to him. He sat up straight when he saw me, but didn't
quite manage a smile.

'Hey, Mike.'

'Fassbinder.'

'How's it going?'

'All's quiet on the Western Front.'

As far as conversations went this wasn't going to be the highlight
of any literary salon.

'How are you feeling?' *And winner of the stupid question of the year
goes to . . .*

He didn't bother answering that. 'I haven't seen anyone, at least,
not who I was told to look out for. And she's fine – a little hyper, if
you ask me, but fine.'

I figured now was not time to ask if he was open to dating again.

'Okay, thanks. I appreciate it. Mike?'

'Yeah?'

'I really am sorry. Let me know if you need anything.'

He just grunted as I walked back to Third Eye Books. Mike had been through a lot of mood changes in the past month, which was understandable. He'd been a typically arrogant member of Bela's brute squad, confident in his size and Weyrd abilities, afraid of nothing – until Jerry was killed by a water eidolon, taken in place of my daughter and leaving Mike suddenly very aware that there were some things that couldn't be stopped by brute strength. He'd been variously apologetic, angry and grief-stricken, alternating between self-blame to blaming everyone else, especially me, which in my view was completely fair. I didn't know when I'd be able to say anything to make a difference. If ever.

Never was looking like a distinct possibility.

Or maybe next Tuesday would be different again; who knew?

Merrily was in fine form when I walked in; she was wearing a very floaty feminine dress and black boots, her dark hair wildly and casually curly in a fashion that could only have taken a long time to achieve. Her perfume wasn't her usual pleasant floral scent but something more in the line of 'bludgeoning a man until he thinks he's being seduced'.

My doubts must have been clear on my face because she said defensively, 'Baiting my lure, Fassbinder.'

'Oh gods.'

'I'm not distracting him – I'm mindful of what you said. But when all this is done – and when will that be, by the way? – *then* it will be time for a date.'

'I told you, Merrily, Mike's in mourning.'

'But one day he won't be, right?'

'I know he dated Aspasia once, but I think that was the last time he was interested in, you know, vaginas.'

'Can't hurt to make an impression.'

'You're an extreme optimist, Merrily, and I have to admit, that's kind of admirable.' I looked around as if he might appear at any moment. 'Any sight or sign of your less-than-chivalrous erstwhile suitor?'

'Nope. You came all the way over here to ask me that?' She gave me a doubtful look.

'Can't I just come and hang out?'

'What do you want, Fassbinder?'

'Okay, so last night I chased a something or a someone – long story, yadayada, but the end point is this.' As I pulled the evidence bag from my pocket the golden fur caught the light from the chandelier and we both looked up at the fetish she'd hung there.

'Now, that *is* interesting.' She pointed. 'Can you grab that? Go, on, stretch – saves me having to climb on a chair.'

I did as bid, wincing at the strain. Although there was less in her container than I remembered, the two samples looked identical to me.

'Interesting indeed,' I said. 'And you're sure there's been no sign of him?'

'None. Mind you, I haven't checked the security camera this morning.'

'Okay, let's look at the tape.'

'You know it's not tape any more, right?'

'Shut up.'

In the little room out back, we huddled in front of the monitor. The film was short – Merrily was smart; the camera was triggered by motion, saving us having to fast-forward through hours of endless nothing – and there was really only five minutes of four dogs, two cats, seven ringtail possums . . . and one man.

And not the man who might have been expected: not a tall,

handsome, dark-haired chap with strangler tendencies, but a more unexpected visitor: Professor Tiberius Claudius Ulysses Harrow, considerably less dead than advertised, in granddad jeans and a wind-cheater, his silver ponytail flowing over his hunched shoulders.

Chapter Twenty-Eight

'I was just about to call you.' McIntyre sounded unusually excited. Merrily was printing out a screen-grab of Professor Harrow so I had proof of date, time and life. 'We've got something.'

'On last night's body?'

'Not that one – the first one.'

'How did that happen?'

'You remember the tattoo I mentioned? Under the breast? Ellen was looking at it – the tattoo, not the breast, obviously.'

'Rhonda.'

'Anyway, she realised it wasn't just a rose. The rose was fading, but what was underneath it wasn't – and no, I don't know if it's from being in the freezer or something magical and Weyrd and I don't care. I'm just thankful it happened.'

'So if it's not a rose, what is it? Don't keep me in suspense!'

'It's a *bird*, Fassbinder, which gives us something more to work with. We can't figure out when the rose was laid over the top, but maybe there's mention of the original tat in the missing persons files. At any rate, it gives Lacy something else to work with. The rose might not have made it into the files if it was inked on after the initial disappearance.'

'That's great, McIntyre.'

'Huh. You don't sound impressed.'

'I am, I promise, just distracted. Can you send me a picture?'

'Ellen thought you might ask. Emailing now.'

'Legendary. Later, Rhonda.'

While I waited for my phone to buzz, I called, 'Merrily, you know that old guy?'

She stuck her head out through the shimmering curtains. 'Sure, he comes in here every couple of weeks. Goes through a lot of smudge.'

'That's all he does? Buys smudge?'

Turning back to the printer she said lightly, 'He's a sweetie.'

'Strange.' My phone buzzed with an incoming email, which took a while to open, but when it did finally come into focus, I felt a shiver, as if someone had danced a jig down my spine in icy-soled shoes.

It was a bird, all right: a raven.

A raven bearing a remarkable similarity to the sigil on the necklace and ring worn by Freydis and Egil Odinsay.

I let out a low whistle. 'Merrily, you supply a lot of the Weyrd homes with mystical crap, don't you?'

She came out of the back room waving a sheet of paper to encourage the ink to dry before it got handed over. 'If you mean, "I provide specialised services and goods required for the prestigious Weyrd lifestyle", then yes.'

'You deliver stuff?'

'Yes.' Now she looked curious.

'So, impressive address book, you'd say?'

'Oh no.'

'Merrily, I need a favour.'

'Oh no.'

'Look, how many people have Verity Fassbinder in their debt?'

'None, because they all die before they can collect.'

'Not entirely true.' I sighed. 'Merrily, I need an address: a Weyrd address. I mean a *High Weyrd* address.' And if I asked Bela for it, there would be delays, formal requests, Byzantine politics and refusals.

'You're killing me, Fassbinder.'

'No one will ever hear it from me.'

Her shoulders dropped in defeat. 'Oh, all right – and then just promise you'll go away. I knew your visits were going too well.'

'They were, weren't they. Sorry about that.' And I kind of was.

'So whose day are you going to ruin?'

'Freydis and Egil Odinsay.'

'Oh sweet mother of crap.'

'Yeah.'

It turned out the Odinsays actually lived quite close to Bela's maximally expensive, minimally furnished apartment in Highgate Hill. Three houses away, in fact, close enough for me to feel a little paranoid when I got out of the cab. It took all my will not fold into a crouch and run towards the gate like I was in an eighties action movie.

They lived rather like Bela, too, hiding in plain sight. The enormous four-storey house had what looked like electronic shutters over lots of tinted glass. There was no garden, not even a tiny patch of lawn. I could detect no glamour, but that didn't mean one wasn't operating. A closed-circuit camera was set up over the driveway entrance to a subterranean garage and who knew how many other basement floors.

I hit the buzzer three times because I was peeved.

The door was answered by a very large, very bearlike Viking. There was another one looming in the hallway, which made me wonder if they came in matched pairs.

'Yes?' A slight accent, a breath of northern snow and ice.

I smiled. 'Hello. I'd like to see the Odinsays.'

'You have an appointment? I don't believe so, as there is nothing in the diary.' He extended a massive hand to his twin in the hallway, who slid an iPad onto a palm the size of Finland. Thing One tapped a few buttons and the device *booped*, possibly objecting to the rough treatment. 'No, you do not.'

'I don't work well with schedules. At least, not other people's.'

'You must make an appointment.'

'Please tell your employers that Verity Fassbinder is here to speak with them.'

'It does not matter who you are.'

'Tell them it's about their son.'

He blinked at that but began shaking his head, which was when I grabbed hold of his wrist (it was like manhandling a tree), dragged him towards me, and dislocated the finger he'd used to tap the screen so violently. In my head, the iPad cheered. The Viking went down on his knees, mouth open in a surprised scream that hadn't managed to yet become audible. Thing Two looked like he was about to leap at me, but I held up a warning digit. '*You* get a dislocated shoulder.'

Wisely, he stopped, but it was a near thing and I really hadn't fancied having to deal with the bear-weres I suspected they were. I carefully popped Thing One's finger back in – and *that* made him scream properly. I patted his head and walked into the entry hall. I closed the door behind me because I'm nothing if not well-mannered, then looked at Thing Two expectantly.

He led the way into a Viking longhouse interior-designed to within an inch of its life: a lot of honey-coloured wood and skins from a variety of animals from colder climes (I wondered how Thing One and Two felt about that). I couldn't imagine the expensive-looking furniture bearing Egil's weight, let alone the help. My guide led me at last to a chamber on an upper level where a ceiling of glass surmounted the log walls. It hadn't been visible from outside, so it was not entirely unglamoured. This was obviously the Odinsays' sanctuary: long benches covered with more animal skins; a pit in the middle of the room with a roaring fire, the smoke obediently trailing up to a hole in the ceiling. There were totems, mead kegs, even a loom. Freydis sat in front of a tapestry, picking out stitches like Verðandi. Egil stood at her shoulder, glaring at the doorway as soon as Thing Two ushered me in.

I waved. 'Hi. Got a couple more questions for you.'

'Tepes will hear about this,' snarled Egil.

'Yes, he will.'

'We have nothing to say to you.' Freydis sounded as if she really wanted to believe it; as if saying the words often enough would make them true.

'You can tell yourself that all you want but I am not leaving until I get answers. And I am quite capable of incapacitating this one' – I pointed at Thing Two – 'just as I did his mate.' I looked Egil up and down. 'And you – in fact, I'm more than capable of sitting on your heads until you give me what I want.' *If they didn't ice and snow me first, of course, which was always a risk.*

Reluctantly Freydis waved a hand at Thing Two, who didn't bother to hide his relief at the dismissal. When the door had closed behind him, I marched straight over to Freydis and sat in front of her on one of the long benches.

'Your son had a girlfriend of whom you did not approve – whose name, by the way, was *not* Ava Montclair.' McIntyre had found no trace of anyone by that name. 'So, you got rid of her?'

Neither of them answered. I retrieved my phone and pulled up the image of victim number one – not the rather kind sketch, this one, but the proper photograph of her ruined face. I got closer to

Freydis than I really wanted to, but I needed to hold the screen so she couldn't help but see it. I watched the shock shiver across her features, then shifted so her husband could get a good view of the devastation.

He remained impassive.

'You see, there's not much of her face left, which has made identification somewhat problematic. But' – I took a moment to swipe to the next photo – 'she has *this* on her, and despite someone's best efforts, it's still there.'

I took in their faces as they saw the black raven tattooed on the woman's chest.

Freydis closed her eyes in a long blink; Egil looked away.

'As you can see, a special effort has been made to conceal her identity. But you knew her right off, didn't you?' I smiled, but I didn't mean it. 'Such a special effort, which tells me she's *important*. Did you have anything to do with this?'

'Not . . . whatever has happened to her is in recent times,' said Freydis.

'My dear—' Egil's tone was warning, but she ignored him.

'Her name was Vaughan Carpenter. Our son – our only son, only child, the last scion of our house, our future – fell in love with a Normal girl and brought her here so that we might *approve*.'

'What happened?'

'She was *pregnant*. She lived here for six months and we kept it secret . . . for the Odinsays to have such a family *incident* . . .'

'Right. Then?'

'The child died,' said Egil quietly, with more soft regret than I'd have thought him capable. 'The child died and our son disappeared and we were left with this girl . . .'

'She had a stroke during the birth; she was left comatose,' Freydis said. Her voice was a whisper of snow in the pines.

'You didn't think to get a healer to her?'

'We did! We did, but she'd gone too far within herself . . . the trauma . . .'

'And what happened then?'

'Harmsorgi did not return, although we waited . . . we waited as long as we could, and then we had her sent away.'

'*Away?*'

'It was arranged by our steward. We had no choice.'

'Was it Thing One or Thing Two?'

They looked confused, then Freydis understood. 'Neither Bjarni nor Brandr but Erik Alhström, a dead man now.'

'How'd he die?'

'A blood-feud,' she said casually, adding, 'not one of ours. He was careless in his dealings with . . . others. He had left our employ by then.'

'So you don't know where she was sent?'

'We do not know what happened to her after Erik arranged for her removal,' she confirmed. 'And we have never seen Harmsorgi again in thirty-seven years.'

None of these women looked the age they should be – oh, they looked older, but not in their eighties, like I knew Alison Brandt was. So *where* had they been kept and *what had happened to them?*

'And you've got no idea where she was taken?'

'In those days there were sanatoriums . . .'

'Bills would have had to be paid.'

'Do you honestly think we will have copies of invoices from so long ago?'

That was unlikely. And anyway, they'd wanted Vaughan Carpenter gone and that was it.

'If you're lying, I'll be back.'

'We'll be ready,' said Egil. There was no mistaking his threat.

I grinned. 'Bring it on, Frosty.'

In the cab I texted Vaughan Carpenter's name to McIntyre, which would give Oldman a nice bump-start. In return, Rhonda gave me the third victim's name. Shirley Ignacio, a Normal who'd disappeared from a hospital in Bundaberg in early 1981. Her fingerprints were intact – either because the captor was getting lazy or because I'd interrupted him before he could do anything about them the other night – and they were on file because her disappearance had actually been reported. Like Alison and Vaughan, she had dark hair and delicate features — and she was comatose when she was taken.

All three of them had been in a state of being dead-to-the-world in the deepest sense. I wondered how empty they'd been when whatever was stored in them had been poured in. What had happened to their own souls – both when they'd been filled, and then emptied, crushed up inside a body they couldn't control? Or did they sleep there too, in the core of themselves, with no sense of being trapped, hijacked? I was becoming more and more convinced they'd been used until they'd worn out, then been discarded like empty bottles.

How had these women been found? *Sourced?* Two were from Brisbane, one from Bundaberg, five hours' drive away – were they crimes of opportunity or was there a pattern here, even if I couldn't yet discern it? And if the bodies being dumped had reached the end of their usefulness, were there other women out there being used to replace them? There was yet another awful thought.

I closed my eyes and hid in the darkness for a few moments, then I decided that was probably what Alison, Vaughan and Shirley had experienced for a *really* long time, so maybe I wouldn't close *my* eyes.

I took a deep breath and focused. I had to get ready for a funeral.

Chapter Twenty-Nine

Black tailored dress, black leather boots with enough heel to give my legs a nice line but not so much that I walked like an arthritic sailor, charcoal mid-length coat, unobtrusive handbag, brushed hair pulled into a bun in a fit of optimism, as if all those little wisps weren't going to make a break for it within seconds and turn back into what my grandmother used to called kiss curls. Oh, and make-up.

Tidying myself up was the least I could do for Ligeia, even though she herself had been no great respecter of sartorial matters. But I'd be amongst a bunch of sirens and looking like a shipwreck had no appeal at such a time. Besides, Eurycleia didn't need anything else to hold against me.

The taxi let me off at the now-familiar gate to the sirens' compound and I joined a long line of visitors being vetted by Thelxiope and two younger women. Thelxiope gave me a weary smile, but her helpers exchanged a look I couldn't quite fathom. Directions were given and I followed a crowd of people. I vaguely knew some of them, but there was no one close to me. There were some glances – I was an object of curiosity as a matter of course, which never failed to annoy – but no one approached me.

The wide expanse of the lawn in front of the mansion had been covered with two banks of fold-out seats arranged in rows. There was no sign of Eurycleia, but at the far end of the avenue between the chairs was a bier, an intricate network of wood and brush the distinctive colour of driftwood. And atop it, draped in the sheerest of veils, was Ligeia, lying in state.

Usually I'd just take a seat at the back to watch everyone else, but I felt compelled to go forward and see the old siren one last time. She was an omega, the last of her kind – oh, there were other sirens, but she was a *nonpareil*, unique. The glimmer of her skin lit the gossamer fabric. Death certainly became her.

On the other side of the catafalque the sirens were gathering. I heard footsteps behind me and turned to let the next mourner pay their respects, only to come face-to-face with Sandor Verhoeven and Udo Forsythe. Both wore dark frock coats, top hats with mourning crepe wrapped as a band and elaborately tied cravats, Sandor's in wheat, Udo's in electric blue. Udo's outfit was complimented by a silver lion-headed cane I was fairly sure he didn't need for walking.

Verhoeven was corpulent, urbane and calculating. He was intelligent, too, which made it hard for me to believe Forsythe had really managed to weasel his way into the old man's good graces. I'd have thought Sandor could spot a bullshit merchant at fifty paces, but maybe he'd become isolated. The loss of three Council members last year, all of them to ultimately violent deaths, had had a seriously destabilising effect. Maybe he'd just found Forsythe's constant siding with him supportive and comforting at a time when everything else appeared to be built on shifting sands.

Where Sandor's spread was mainly horizontal, Forsythe went vertical. He was thin, dark-haired, wiry, with the greedy look of an ascetic. Just because you deprive yourself of things doesn't mean you cease to want them, it just means you fuck yourself up a little more every day. He had piercingly pale green eyes, cadaverous cheeks and a blade of a nose poised above a slash of a mouth that pinched even tighter at the sight of me.

'Sandor,' I said with a nod. I ignored Forsythe, even though I knew using his first name would have irritated him, which would have made me happy.

Sandor nodded, but said nothing. He looked almost sad, but maybe that was because of the occasion of the funeral not because he thought of me as some difficult lost daughter. As I moved past them Forsythe muttered, 'Half-blood!' but I restrained myself. There was no point in attacking a Council member at a high-profile funeral when you're no longer employed by said Council and don't have Zvezdomir Tepes to run interference for you. Plus there's probably a limit to the number of times he can say, 'Yes, she's a little unorthodox but she does get the job done.'

Two more steps and then his voice, snaky and reedy, sounded again. 'What is *she* doing here? She relinquished her place amongst us.'

I stopped, sighed, and turned on my heel; no one could say I hadn't tried. Four steps took me right back to Udo. He was a head taller than me so I stared for a moment at the antique yellow pin in his cravat before lifting my gaze. I did my best to ignore his flaring nostrils, the cold coming off him and the faint whiff of something like formaldehyde and spoke into his face.

'I am here to say goodbye to a *friend*. I'd suggest you postpone the pissing contest until afterwards, unless you wish to make an undignified exit over the cliff there.'

'There will be no conflict this day.' Eurycleia had joined the throng. Her voice was weaker than I'd ever heard it and when I looked at her it was clear she was ill. There was no colour in her face, although her mourning black didn't help. Her hair was lacklustre, as were her

'Well, it's true you're quite the social pariah, but in this case you're not entirely to blame. But hush, it's about to start.'

Thelxiope walked the avenue carrying a burning brand. Eurycleia took the torch from her, hesitated a moment, then touched it to eight points, one after the other, on the woven wood. The massed sirens standing in a semi-circle on the far side of the bier began to sing a dirge. The words were unrecognisable, to me at least, but the meaning was clear. The fire quickly ate Ligeia and it was very quickly all over and the sirens were moving back towards the house while the Weyrd stopped to pay respects to Eurycleia, who was hunched in Thelxiope's arms, clutching at her chest as if it troubled her. Then the Weyrd too moved off, including Verhoeven and Forsythe, who gave me one last withering look of contempt. I was tempted to ask Theo to incinerate him, but I didn't want to abuse our friendship.

When everyone else had disappeared – there was no wake – Theo and I made our way over to Eurycleia and Thelxiope. Theo gave her condolences from behind dark glasses, then gave me a hug and extracted a promised to come and visit as soon as I could. Even I could admit that three Norns with superpowers officially counted as an emergency.

'Come into the house,' Eurycleia said.

It was only then that I realised that I'd not seen Bela nor Ziggi in the crowd.

They'd not been at the funeral.

By the time we got inside, Eurycleia was limping badly, curling in on herself in pain. Thelxiope took her right arm and I propped myself under her left shoulder; neither of us was comfortable with that degree of closeness, but Eurycleia didn't really have a choice in the matter. We hobbled to Eurycleia's study, a round room lined with bookcases. It was in the centre of the house and there was no natural light, just lit torches. There was just one armchair, and one desk chair at the enormous bureau; this was a space for contemplation . . . contemplation and plotting.

We helped her to the armchair, then Thelxiope went straight to the desk and picked up something.

'I should . . . I should have given this to you immediately, as she asked.' Eurycleia, gasping in pain, tore at the high collar of her dress, popping buttons and shredding fabric, revealing bloody, peeling red flesh. There were holes in her neck and I thought I could see worms moving in the gaps. 'This . . . this is all over me.'

'Eurycleia . . .' I swallowed hard. When I'd kept the Dagger of Wilusa from the Boatman for too long, a similar thing had happened to him. I said again, 'Eurycleia . . .'

She waved her hand in annoyance. 'And the letter, Thelxiope. Make sure she gets the letter.'

Thelxiope came back to us. In one hand was a long dark object, in the other an envelope with my name scrawled on the front in a jagged script. She handed them first of all to Eurycleia, who didn't look strong enough even to hold them. I tried to intervene, but Thelxiope said sternly, 'No, *she* must give them to you.'

So I waited while Eurycleia caught her breath, gathered her remaining strength and sat up straight. 'This is for you, Ms Fass-binder: my mother's last gift, her bequeathal. It will be owned by none but you.' She handed over the items and, shaking the long one like an act of war, begged, 'Open this, open it now.'

I did as I was told. I put the letter in my jacket pocket and turned my attention to the black leather sheath with an ebony hilt studded with gold protruding from it.

I drew Ligeia's sword. The blade was engraved with swirls and curlicues and the last time I'd seen it she'd been moving through a crowd of angels like a farmer with a reaping hook, cutting them down and evening the odds for her sisters. She'd stuck it through the Arch's back, then eaten his heart as if it were a rare treat.

'This can't be right,' I said.

Eurycleia, breathing more easily now, laughed with relief and pain in equal measure. 'That's what I thought, believe me. My mother gave instructions, which I was determined to ignore. That sword . . . she's had it all my life. I should have borne it too.'

'That,' I said, pointing at her throat, which was mending itself at speed now matters had been rectified, 'that happened to the Boatman when I kept the Dagger of Wilusa too long.'

She nodded. 'Yet there was no physical effect on you, was there?'

'No. None.' I frowned. I'd done the wrong thing when I'd hung onto it, yet there had been no toll taken on me, no punishment at all, as far as I could see. The Boatman, who'd let me have it, had been the one to suffer.

'No, of course not. My mother said you are meant to wield both weapons, but the Boatman stepped out of line and gave you one before it was time.'

'What—?'

She held up a hand. 'I know no more than this: that such things are often forged in pairs. That one day you will bear the God-Slayer and the Reaper into battle.' She shrugged. 'Perhaps there's more in her note.'

I'd forgotten the letter. I laid the sword across my lap, then tore open the envelope. The letter was every bit as brief and cryptic as I had come to expect of Ligeia.

There are truths I cannot tell because they are not mine to share, little strangeling, but ask Tobit. It is time he spoke. Ask him about the broken god.

'I know that I cannot go against you, not if this is the price.' Eurycleia laughed. 'Consider yourself and the little man safe. I will take what time I am allowed with my granddaughter and be grateful for it. You, Verity Fassbinder, are clearly not to be trifled with.'

Chapter Thirty

I couldn't concentrate, not least because there was an enormous sword on my lap in the back of the cab. Ligeia had disguised it, most of the time, like an umbrella, but I didn't have that facility. However, I would need to make some kind of arrangement because carting a deadly – however awesome – weapon around in plain view was just asking for trouble. I divided my time between staring at it and looking out the window, all the while replaying Eurycleia's words in my head.

One day you will bear the God-Slayer and the Reaper into battle.

I wasn't sure I had time in my schedule for that.

The only thing I was sure of was that I needed to talk to Tobit.

A broken god . . . the tyrant the Guardian was hunting . . . it wasn't such a leap, was it?

I needed to risk calling Bela, not only to ask where he and Ziggi had been, but also to discuss this unexpected inheritance. When I got no answer, I left a message. 'Hey, it's me. I really need to talk to Tobit. Any chance you can draw a bead on him? I've got something to do at the Ascot house. Call me.'

I left Christos a similar message, hoping he'd heard something and just forgotten to tell me; although that was pretty unlikely.

The taxi dropped me at the Nadasy house and as it was driving off, my phone rang.

'Ms Fassbinder?'

'Hi, Sister Bridget. I'm taking care of Sally Crown right now.' I was aware I sounded a bit like a kid claiming I *was* cleaning my room, but the Waters of Forgetting really were swishing around in the flask in my handbag; it would be just enough for one mouthful.

'That's good of you, I'm sure she'll appreciate it.'

'Maybe, maybe not. It's always hard to tell with Sally.'

'That's not why I'm calling, though. Your friend has woken up.'

'Joyce is okay?'

'Well, she's pretty broken, but she asked for you.'

'A lot of that going around.'

'Ms Fassbinder . . .'

'Okay, okay.' Truth was, I felt relieved. 'I'll be there as soon as I've dealt with Sally.'

'Be careful on your own.'

'Oh, don't worry about me.' *I'm some sort of Chosen or other.* I reminded myself I didn't have the dagger, though. 'I won't be long.'

I walked under the canopy of camphor laurels and up the steps to the verandah. The afternoon shadows were getting long; I hoped I hadn't lied to Sister Bridget, that I *wouldn't* be here long. I was thoroughly sick of this place. I wondered what my chances were of getting it demolished. Technically it belonged to Dusana, as her parents' sole heir, but as she was in even deeper shit with the Council than I was, perhaps I could put in a bad word with Bela. Or maybe burn it properly this time.

I made my way down the basement stairs by the light of my phone – I really wished I'd hung onto Oldman's Maglite – and into the big open area littered with debris and fire-damaged remains, broken pieces of wood with nails protruding, shards of glass. I wondered if Sally was lonely without her playmates. I wondered why she'd stayed behind and what she could possibly have to tell me.

I walked further into the darkness, the beam of light picking out shapes and shadows that weren't real but looked like things they weren't, ordinary junk became monsters.

Something scuttled in the gloom.

'Sally?'

No answer.

I swapped the phone from my right hand to my left and replaced it with the sword, still sheathed, but an impressive bludgeon if required. In one corner was a glowing figure, wearing the same too-short denim skirt and grey singlet with a few remaining sequins clinging to its front . . . although now the colours were as muted as she was, washed out by death.

'Sally?'

She turned and a smile appeared on her face. She came towards me, hesitantly at first, then faster, and tried to throw her arms around me for a hug – which was my first sign that something was wrong. She wasn't a hugger, our Sally; a biter, a kicker, but not a hugger.

Not unexpectedly, she passed through me like a wave of ice-water.

'Oh, don't do that.' I shuddered and pointed the torchlight directly at her.

But she wasn't Sally any more.

It was a gradual process, and not pleasant – and in this very basement I'd already seen Vadim Nadasy peel off a skin suit made of the old Archivist Ursa – but gradually her shape settled into something with an entirely different centre of gravity: Eleanor Aviva's shade, echo, whatever. The sliver of her past self that Titania had summoned, that Louise Arnold had feared had slipped *through* untethered, stood before me with perfectly coiffed auburn hair, a swollen thoracic region and eight legs, uncertain on its feet, shifting as if blown by a breeze I couldn't feel.

Sally Crown hadn't hung around when Sister Bridget sent her away; Sally had gone. But Aviva, made of stronger and stranger stuff, had stayed and taken the girl's shape to set a lure.

'Eleanor. How did you get here?'

'You called for me.'

'Yes, but here? Specifically *here*?'

'Ah! I rode the dullard boy as he fled when Titania's followers hunted him. They tell tales of this place, you know?'

'That's why they couldn't find you in Titania.'

'No.' She looked around, then repeated, 'You called me.'

'I did. You left me a note.'

'I did?' She sounded genuinely puzzled.

Titania had said the shade might not have all the memories of the living being so I was prepared to believe that was case in this instance. I wondered *when* this sliver might be from. I needed to be careful about my questions. 'About the "3-in-1".'

'What happened to me? I remember you, Verity Fassbinder, but I don't remember what happened to me?'

Honestly was probably the best policy. 'Dusana Nadasy happened.'

The spectre frowned, her face rippling with doubt, then clearing. 'I remember her husband and her parents. I remember her expression when I sealed her in that mermaid statue. But . . . nothing else.'

'No,' I said. 'She got out of her prison and she found you.'

'Ah.' The sound was soft, not understanding the precise details, with no lived memory, but knowing that action had resulted in her end.

'*Why* did you come here?'

'Why not? I spent many happy hours in this very room, watching your father work.'

My stomach churned. Grigor the murderer, the butcher of children. 'Why would you . . . ?'

'Because the Nadasys and I weren't always enemies, of course. They found me useful once upon a time. I helped source meat for your father's tender mercies, for all those fine Weyrd tables, all those High Weyrd too fussy to get their own hands dirty.' She leaned a little closer and faux-whispered, 'I was young and I needed the money.'

'You collected my mother's body from the morgue. You delivered it to a thing calling himself the Guardian of the Southern Gate of the Underworld.'

'Now that I *do* remember. Poor Olivia, such sweet meat for the Guardian, but you know I couldn't have delivered her, not to the Underworld.' She narrowed her eyes. 'Although I must say, that thing looked a lot like a wounded angel to me.'

'You *saw* him? Where?'

'Above.' She fluttered her hands at the ceiling as if indicating the lounge over our heads. 'At night, in parks, forests. But he's not been seen much in recent years; I don't think he likes to go out. I think he's been deteriorating for a long time.'

So the Guardian hadn't always hidden away. He had walked on the earth until his decline, however slow, had taken its toll. 'How injured was he when you saw him?'

'Very, but there were still healthy patches of flesh, quite large ones. Is it . . . is it no longer the case?'

'No longer.' I thought about the Guardian, as crispy and black as Ligeia's death had been. 'What work did you do for it?'

'Collections, deliveries, rarities. Angry mostly dead women like your mummy.'

'Little fox-girls?'

'Well, it's so hard to keep track of everything, though they definitely weren't mine, dearie.'

'Why them?' I said more to myself.

'I'd imagine something to keep your mother occupied and yearning for you less. You were a terrible distraction.'

I bit the inside of my mouth; she was trying to rile me.

'What did you get out of these transactions, Eleanor?'

'The same thing I always did: money. Lifestyle. A buttress against a harsh future. You've no idea what poverty is like.'

'Didn't do you much good, did it?'

She shrugged as if it didn't matter. 'It was fun while it lasted.'

I said slowly, 'Were there other things you delivered? To someone other than the Guardian?'

'Many things, many clients, many deliveries,' she almost sang.

'How about the bodies of comatose Normal women?'

'Perhaps.'

'Vaughan Carpenter, Alison Brandt, Shirley Ignacio.'

The shade smiled broadly, then said confidentially, 'Beware the wolf of the borders.'

My brain was so sluggish, trying to digest everything, trying to ask the right questions, and when at last I understood what she was saying, I felt sick. 'Jost Marolf', as Ziggi had told me not so long ago, meant 'border wolf'.

'He's been here quite a while, little Verity, moving in the shadows.'

'How long?' My throat was suddenly parched.

'Oh, long enough. I remember him from the eighties, but who can say how many years he's hidden?' There was a sharp intake of breath. 'Or does he no longer hide himself away?'

'No, he does not.' I cleared my throat, trying not to show she'd scored a hit. 'You took Sally's shape. You didn't want to lay to rest again?'

'Not when there's so much to do here.'

I reminded myself that this wasn't actually Aviva's soul; that was long gone. This was just a sliver, a memory of what had once been. This was something that had hitched a ride and was clinging on. The thing was, I didn't know how to send it away; it wasn't like a ghost or a spirit. 'So, the note you left me mentioned the "3-in-1".'

'Ah yes. Something fell. Something broke.'

'Right.'

'Split into three.'

'Right.'

'Well, at least that's all I can recall.' The shade was swinging between genuine confusion at its Swiss-cheese memories and pleasure at having wasted my time.

'Got any plans I should know about?

'I have no need of plans.' Aviva's echo smiled. 'Besides, *she's* here now.'

And so she was: Dusana Nadasy was stepping through the wispy substance of Aviva as though the spider-woman was nothing more than a hologram. For a person who'd spent fifteen-odd years in a bronze mermaid, she packed one Hell of a punch.

I hadn't expected her to come at me like this. Blades, sure, maybe a crossbow, something old-fashioned and out of a weaponry museum. But the right hook? Nope, not expected.

I lost my grip on both sword and phone and tumbled arse over tit across a floor made rough by rubbish. I let out a fairly undignified noise through my split lip as I fetched up against a wall, then quickly rolled to my feet, trying to gauge my chances of getting the sword back. I could see it in the light of Aviva's glow, but it was also right next to Dusana's right boot, although she didn't appear to be paying any attention to it.

I spat blood, thinking a tooth might be loosening. 'She brought them here, you know.'

Dusana made a swoop at me, and sharp nails raked the bodice of my dress. It was an *expensive* dress; I was clearly not meant to have nice things. I needed to get a grip on her, get my hands around her neck and pop her head off before she did too much damage with those damned talons. 'Your mother. She brought children down here.'

Dusana's expression flinched for a second.

'This was the place where my father butchered them, years ago. Then *your* father rebooted the old firm.' Another incursion into my space, another slash. This one put holes in my *very* expensive coat *and* me. I could feel blood oozing; clearly I'd definitely over-estimated the protection of Thaïs' benediction. On the upside, I'd been able to move away from the wall so my chance of getting to the sword was a little improved. And if I got the sword, I had *reach*, which meant I could keep her away from me, which was a worthy aim. 'Innocent children, as powerless as your son.'

The direct hit to her heart that showed in her face and she swung wildly, stumbled and ended up against the wall, sagging as if her energy had been sucked away. I got closer to the sword, where Aviva's shade was hovering. 'Did you grow up here, knowing what they did? Your parents, my father? Did you sleep well, knowing what happened down here?'

'I didn't know what they did!'

'They showed the same level of contempt for your son, you know. Your own parents turned him into a *thing*, a golem made of *garbage*, Dusana, because they thought your little boy was disposable.'

'Shut up!'

'Do you know what he looked like when he died? Your baby? He stank like old wine and piss. Rubbish was embedded in his skin, his hair, his head. Your parents did *that* to your son and now you're fighting for an ideal of *their* honour?'

As she charged at me with a terrible shriek I managed to sweep up the sword and step aside. There was no time to unsheathe it; as she rushed by I used the flat edge to slap her in the back of the head and she landed face-down, slid a foot or so and banged her head into the wall.

Dusana wasn't moving, but I didn't trust her. I picked up my mobile, relieved to find it unbroken, and scouted around for an old length of wood.

I found what I was looking for fairly quickly: nails protruding from the end of a broken plank. I pulled them out with my fingers; they looked old so there was a good chance they were made of iron – at any rate, it was all I had if I didn't want to kill her.

When I rolled her over, I saw her face was grazed and sooty, very different from the Weyrd princess who'd sworn to kill me. I placed one of the retrieved nails at the joint of each shoulder and drove them in with neither mercy nor second thought, ignoring her shrieking. It was, after all, what had been done to my father and to Eleanor Aviva. Iron would stop her from either transporting herself to somewhere else or using magic in general against me. And if they weren't iron? Well, she'd still have a delightful time trying to fight with those things in her.

I turned my attention back to Aviva's echo, who was staring at me in disbelief. 'I can't believe you . . .'

Slowly, I drew forth the sword and its blade shone in the dimness. 'Now, you're a shade and I don't know what this will do to you, but I'm happy to find out.'

I swung at the floating spectre. The blade slowed down on its journey through her as if it had met resistance, and as it sliced into her, a rent appeared in her strange flesh and she *deflated* until in no time at all there was a torn puddle of glittering mess on the basement floor. It was still helping to light my way, however.

It wasn't a soul and there was nowhere to send it; it was just an echo plucked from the air.

Released from the need to stay upright, I sat down heavily on the concrete floor and gulped in breaths, trying not to think about vomiting. The silence was very loud for a few moments, then the sound of boots running along the corridor upstairs made their way to me. As I heard them hit the stairs, I struggled to my feet, tightened my grip and waited, sword in one hand, mobile phone in the other.

Three figures materialised: Bela, Ziggi . . . and, with blood on her face and clothes, my mother, Olivia Fassbinder, who was supposed to be keeping watch over my husband and daughter.

Chapter Thirty-One

What I meant to do was ask my mother what she was doing there. What I actually did was fall down, because if Olivia was here and *not* with David and Maisie, then something was very wrong indeed and I knew it and my knees knew it, which is why they decided to give out. In fact, *everything* decided to give out, and I was soon producing tears and snot by the bucket-load, whimpering and trying unsuccessfully to replace everything with actual rational sentences.

Olivia knelt beside me and now I could see the cuts on a face so like mine. Those in her hairline had stopped bleeding only because they'd been sealed by a thick gooey crust. Both cheeks were bruised, and when her jacket flashed open I could see a significant tear in her green shirt and a wound beneath peaking through.

She cupped my cheeks to hold me steady, but she started crying too. 'Verity, you need to be strong.' Her voice trembled; her words had the power to destroy me, because I might never recover from what she told me; I was shaking so hard I didn't think I'd ever stop. 'You need to stay calm.'

'Where are they?' I screamed. Turned out, staying calm was difficult.

Your husband and child are dead.

Your husband and child are lying cold.

Your husband and child have gone where you cannot.

'They were taken. Verity,' said my mother, and she steadied my head again; it felt so heavy I thought it might drop from my shoulders. 'Verity, they're alive: I absolutely believe that because David and Maisie are no use against you if they're dead.'

I knew so little of my mother other than she was dangerous and had been vengeful, she had dark depths, and a steely will to do what was needed. But I did know, truly, looking into her dark green eyes, that she'd stand with me no matter what I had to do. My blood would be with me; we'd find David and Maisie – and if they weren't alive, Olivia Fassbinder would wade through a red tide with me until we'd had our fill. But it didn't stop me from asking, 'Why are you here? What *happened*?'

Her eyes clouded and her expression twisted with pain. 'Wanda and I were inside and David and Maisie were in the garden. Maisie loves the pilgrims' path, she likes to play there, walk it with her feet on her dad's. Sulla and Jacquetta' – the look she threw at Bela was not friendly as she spat the names of their bodyguards –'were outside too. I heard Maisie cry and David yelled.' She closed her eyes, swayed, then straightened her spine. 'When I got out there, Sulla had herded them to the centre of the pilgrims' path and Jacquetta was running interference, but she took so long to die that they had time to transit before I could get to them. Whoever moved them knew where they were, had a pick-up organised and a set destination.'

'Who knew where my family were, Bela?' I asked, even though I knew the answer.

'The Council,' he said quietly. He wasn't looking at me but staring at Dusana with her scraped face and the blood seeping through the holes I'd made in her with the nails. Maybe that's all he could do when one ex had beaten up another ex who was trying to kill her; when he'd made a really big mistake. 'Only the Council.'

'And who recommended Sulla and Jacquetta for this detail?'

'I picked them.' His tone left something unsaid.

'But . . . ?'

'They came from Forsythe's house,' he said quietly. 'Sandor asked me to show some faith in Udo, to allow this *honour*.'

'It didn't occur to you to change the guard when you realised good old Udo was whispering against me?'

'In case you hadn't noticed, I've been busy . . .' He stopped, swallowed hard. 'V, I'm so sorry. I'm so bloody sorry.'

'If I don't get my family back, you really will be, Tepes.' I struggled to get up and Olivia helped me, although it couldn't have been easy for her, wounded as she was. I pointed at her injuries. 'This?'

'Jacquetta.'

'How many pieces is she in?'

'A lot.'

'Good.'

I bent and collected my sword.

Olivia whistled. 'What's that?'

'This? This is my inheritance from the siren Ligeia. Apparently it's called Reaper.' But I didn't tell them about the rest of Eurycleia's pronouncement, not about the battle I'd wield it in, nor that the Dagger of Wilusa would be returned to me.

I glared at Bela and Ziggi, both of whom looked ill; bloodstained and bruised my mother still looked better than they did. 'Any idea where my family is?'

Bela's expression said he didn't want to answer but he knew better than to keep information from a woman whose child and husband had been snatched. 'I've not been able to contact Sandor since he and Udo left Ligeia's funeral. We were supposed to talk.'

'Was that why you weren't at the funeral?'

He nodded. 'When Olivia called, Ziggi and I went to Ocean's Reach and tried to back-trace the transit spell, but the tracks had been well and truly covered.'

'And you failed to let me know.'

'Would it have done any good?'

'It might have helped me to still have a little bit of respect for you remaining, Bela.' He was one of my oldest friends; we'd stayed close, despite our past, but at that moment I was having trouble finding any fond feelings for him. It would pass, I was sure, but if anything irreversible happened to David and Maisie . . .

'This isn't helping,' interceded Ziggi. 'We've not been able to make contact with anyone in the Bishop's Palace either, V.'

'A coup?'

'Looks like it.'

'Is Verhoeven in on it?'

'Unlikely,' said Bela, 'but not impossible. I think it more likely he's either dead or being used as pawn or hostage.'

'Great.' I bit my lip. 'Do you think my family are there?'

'Nowhere else would be safer,' said Ziggi.

'Okay, so we need a plan of attack. We need to figure out how many of our people are in the Palace, not just David and Maisie. There's going to be blood spilled, but let it be the *right* blood.' I looked at Olivia. 'And I think my mother needs to go to the hospital and be seen to.'

Olivia began to protest, then thought better of it. Nothing would have made me happier than marching on the Bishop's Palace right then and there, but that felt like a good way to get a lot of people killed.

'I need to talk to Sister Bridget, too. She's another one who's been holding out on me.' I rubbed my face. 'Oh, and speaking of betrayals?'

Bela looked at me.

'Jost Marolf.' I told them what Aviva's shade had imparted. 'And I haven't been able to get Mel to answer her phone for a couple of days. I just thought she was still pissed off with me, or enjoying being all loved-up.' I swallowed hard. 'But . . . what if Jost's found his new spiritual cookie jar? So where are they – and what's he done with Lizzie? And *why* is he doing this? What's he *storing*?'

'I'll have his apartment checked.'

'Is there anyone still on our side?'

'Of course!' Bela looked highly offended, a grandee offered insult. 'I still command loyalty. Forsythe's *bought* his troops, he's new and ambitious and those who have accepted what he's offered are mercenary.'

'I hope you're right, but, Bela, you know as well as I do that the Weyrd tend to wait to see who's upright when the dust settles. You might not find too many willing to stand beside you.' I pointed at the lump of Dusana Nadasy on the floor. 'Ziggi, can you please carry that?'

'No,' said Bela. 'She's not going anywhere.'

'Well, I'm not fucking leaving your other ex-girlfriend here so she can escape again, Bela.' Colour me bitter.

'She won't escape. The murder of Eleanor Aviva means Dusana is to be summarily executed. No trial, no hearing, no chance at a defence. She threw those rights away. May I borrow your sword, Verity?'

'No!'

'Ah, you don't want your new toy dirtied.' I watched as he flexed his right hand and the nails grew to talons. He walked to Dusana's side. 'Perhaps this should be personal, after all.'

'Bela! No – not like this.'

'I have no choice. This is the law I am sworn to enforce – as are you. Or were.'

He'd always been considered, controlled – this was a different Bela, the cold creature I'd only occasionally caught shadowy glimpses of when he came close to losing his temper.

'There's another way,' I said, not really believing what I was doing. I looked at Dusana and saw she'd regained consciousness and was watching me with those blue, blue eyes.

'No, there's not.' He raised his hand as if to get height before he plunged his talons into Dusana's chest.

'The right of vengeance,' I said quickly, and he froze. 'Under the right of vengeance, which is a law I am fairly sure no one in the Weyrd world has ever thought to repeal, I am the injured party for her attempt on my life. Which means I'm entitled to *her* life.'

Ziggi let out a breath as if he'd been punctured, then said in warning, '*V*—'

'Am I right or wrong, Zvezdomir Tepes? Right or wrong? She can be my thrall or my victim.'

He let his hand drop, the talons replaced so quickly with ordinary but very shiny nails that I could almost have doubted I'd seen them. His hand was shaking. He'd loved her once; surely there was some feeling left? 'You have that right, but I would advise—'

'Don't care. I, Verity Fassbinder, officially claim right of vengeance against Dusana Nadasy.' Before I thought better of it I turned to her and said slowly, 'You will be my thrall until such time as I deem you to have expiated your crime against me, to wit: attempted murder. Twice.'

'Twice?' She spat blood that spattered my boots. Honestly, it had not been worth getting dressed up today.

'Having Mercado T-bone the car Joyce and I were in.'

'I haven't seen Mercado in days – why would I want him to get all the enjoyment of killing you? Why would I ask him to do something so clumsy and unsatisfying? Why would I deprive myself of the pleasure of watching the life go out of your eyes?'

'You are not making a good argument for my having just saved your arse, but you do have a decent point.' Or maybe she was just lying; maybe she didn't want to be tarred as the kind of employer who killed and reanimated her henchmen by means of a resurgence imp. I sighed. 'Look, you've got a choice: you can accept my proposal. Or you can accept Bela's proposal. But right now I need to concentrate on getting my family back. You promised me you wouldn't hurt them, that you had no interest in doing so.'

She narrowed her eyes.

'I can either kill you or knock you out properly, but no one's going to remove those nails any time soon and we all know you can't take them out either. Or we call a truce, you come to the hospital with us until we can work out where to store you, and then when all of this is over you can go back to plotting how to kill me. How does that sound?'

'You are only delaying the inevitable.' She glared at me. 'But your proposal is acceptable.'

'Uncle, my thrall, if you would.' I faced Bela as Ziggi helped Dusana to her feet. 'Forsythe?'

'Yes?'

'How sure are you of his support base being weak?'

'Fairly sure. He has been in power for a relatively short time, and despite his best efforts I believe most of my people are loyal, Verity, no matter what you think of my opinions.'

'If you're right, then he's got something else up his sleeve. He must have. You don't stage a coup with no back-up, do you? Taking hostage Sandor Verhoeven, who's been in power for almost two hundred years and holds the Brisbane Grant? That's pretty bold, and so's moving against me and acting as though you're irrelevant. So Udo thinks he's got an ace up his sleeve.'

'I'm inclined to agree with you.'

'Come on, Mum, let's get a Band-Aid or twelve on you.' I paused and looked at my ex once again. 'Zvezdomir?'

'Yes, Verity?'

'I promise you that if anything happens to David or Maisie I will kill you.'

'I know you will try.'

'Just so we're clear.'

'And I'll hold you down,' said Olivia through gritted teeth.

'You won't need to,' Bela answered quietly and propping his shoulder under my mother's arm, we both helped her out of that basement of that house I was going to burn to the ground properly, first chance I got. I'd bring marshmallows, make a day out of it.

Chapter Thirty-Two

Ziggi had called Louise Arnold and she was sitting on the edge of Joyce's bed and holding the fox-girl's hand when we arrived at St Agnes'. Healers weren't perfect and they weren't fast cure-alls; it all depended on the level of injury. There was stuff that needed to get better on its own – but someone like Louise could help speed things along. Joyce's face was all kinds of black and blue and there were a lot of bandages wrapped around her, not to mention the arm and leg casts, but the swelling around her eyes had gone down and she could see us when we walked in. Specifically, she could see Olivia, and the transformation was startling.

Her shape shifted into something a lot more vulpine, but she couldn't hold it; it hurt her. I could see that when she snapped back into solidity.

'Hey, Louise, would you mind taking this lot elsewhere for a while? Olivia needs some attention.'

Louise gave me a look, but she did as I asked.

I took her place on the edge of the bed and stared down at the distressed girl. 'Good to see you awake.'

'You look fine.'

I pointed at the split and swollen lip. 'Ready for my close-up. Obviously I was on the lucky side of the Honda.'

'Typical.'

I filled her in on everything she'd missed – Mercado, the resurgence imp, Dusana, Aviva, the Odinsays – and she listened in silence until I paused for breath. Joyce pointed over my shoulder where the hilt of Reaper was visible. 'And you got a new toy.'

'An inheritance.' I rubbed my face, wincing. 'So, I know you're still pissed at Olivia—'

'Don't say it so *casually*! Don't say it like she stole my last biscuit or my seat on the bus!'

'I'm sorry – *I'm sorry!* I know . . . Look, I *am* sorry.' I closed my eyes, squeezed them tight for long seconds. 'I know she killed your sisters. And I know the Guardian told you Olivia murdered your parents – but she didn't.'

'How can you know that?' she scoffed, and it felt as if any camaraderie we'd developed had been burned away by the sight of my mother.

'Because McIntyre found a report from years back of three young girls disappearing. Their parents were – *are* – Amaya Mori-Miller and Ian Miller. She's Weyrd, he's Normal. No trace of the little girls were ever found . . . until they started following me around, trying to flush out Olivia Fassbinder, who'd come to her senses and deserted the Guardian's cause.' I took a deep breath. 'Aviva told me the Guardian might have had you and your sisters stolen to give my mother something to look after. And she did do that, didn't she? You've known her all your life. The fact you all turned into such excellent and obedient assassins was just a big bonus, really.'

'What difference is that supposed to make? She still killed my sisters!'

'Yes, Joyce, and you know what? She will *always* have killed your sisters – but your sisters were trying to hurt *me*, both times: her own *heavily pregnant* daughter.' I narrowed my eyes and gazed at her. 'What would you have done to me to try and get her attention? Cut the baby from me? Tortured me until I screamed loud enough to bring her running, just so you could drag her back to the Guardian and he could take her heart out for his own amusement?'

'I . . .'

'Yes? Go on, do tell. You and your sisters came at me with *weapons*. You came with blades unsheathed and murder in your hearts. Tell me, Joyce, *what should my mother have done*?'

She was silent, but I had not finished. 'You let your own hurt at her perceived abandonment embitter you. You believed whatever lies the Guardian told you about Olivia because you *wanted* to. You thought that justified doing *anything* to hurt her back.'

'But—'

'You are *always* going to have that pain in your heart, Joyce. Nothing I do or say – nothing my mother can or will ever do or say – can take that away, so you need to work out how you're going to deal with it. I'm not interviewing for the position of arch-nemesis right now, what with Dusana Nadasy' – currently locked up at Sister B's residence – 'pretty much admirably fulfilling that role. So here's the long story short: I do *not* want to be looking over my shoulder for you.'

'You don't get to pick and choose your nemeses, you know.'

'No, but I *am* asking for a break.' I could feel a headache coming on, a big one. 'At any rate, things have changed for me. My family's been taken by Udo Forsythe's people and Forsythe has staged a coup against Sandor Verhoeven. Those two things are connected. The Guardian knows you've gone rogue, so I suggest you stay here where the guard on the door can keep an eye on you.'

'Where am I going to go like this?' She gestured to the cast on her left leg.

'*My* point is that this is probably the safest place for you right now. And it's where Theodosia keeps delivering the cake.'

She blushed deeply and I puffed out a breath instead of giving the grin I wanted to. 'The thing is, Joyce, your parents are still alive.'

She stilled like water frozen mid-fall; she even seemed to stop breathing. Her eyes on mine were huge and the expressions that ran across her face were myriad.

'*My parents?*' Her voice was whisper-faint.

'Are alive. Yes. And after I get the current mess sorted out, I promise you – my untimely and hideous death notwithstanding – that I will bring them here. In fact, I'll instruct McIntyre to do that in the event of my not making it through the next twenty-four hours. What you do from that point onwards is your affair.'

'What about what I did to . . .'

'Len? I've told Bela about him. The Normal cops aren't going to go after you; you're not their purview. And it does look like he was working for someone else. You can meet your parents, move home and have a long-delayed teenager-hood or whatever you want to do. Just leave my mother alone, okay? Because she'll just kill you, and frankly, I think Olivia's got enough on her conscience.' Which admittedly appeared to be a pretty flexible object.

Joyce stared at me. She didn't nod but she didn't shake her head either. I rose and went to the narrow cupboard meant to keep patients' possessions safe. I found what I was looking for and held out my offering: her war fan, retrieved from the wreckage of the Honda.

'So, this is for strictly self-defensive purposes only, okay? That is, it is *not* for use on my mother. Promise? Just for the next twenty-four hours. Just let me get my family safely back, just promise you won't try to stab me in the back even though it would be an ideal time to give it a go. I need her.'

She took the fan, then used it to point over my shoulder at the hilt of Ligeia's sword. 'I'd rather have that.'

'Yeah, no. That's "prise it from my cold dead fingers" territory. Just . . . take care, okay?'

I'd done what I could. I just hoped it was enough, that Joyce was of no real interest to the Guardian at the moment, that Udo Forsythe had no interest in her, and that she wouldn't take it into her head to try and hurt Olivia. Because, quite frankly, I was pretty certain that would only mean a third dead fox-girl.

I'd made it into the corridor when my mobile rang.

'Fassbinder, how are you holding up?'

'Not dead yet, Rhonda. How about you?'

'Got some news for you. Oldman said you'd had her drop you out at UQ to talk to some academic?'

'Professor Harrow.'

'Well, here's the thing: remember that cold case I was looking into the day you were in the holding cells?'

'A day I'll not soon forget.'

'So, an ID came through on that body: one Professor Tiberius Claudius Ulysses Harrow, formerly of New College, Oxford, who came out here in 1978 to pursue a career in the University of Queensland's Classics Department. Now, correct me if I'm wrong, but hasn't the prof just finished up a distinguished career?'

'In more ways than one! He's supposedly dead and yet, as you know, I saw him in security footage at Third Eye Books.'

'Now, that is strange. Some might even say *Weyrd*.'

'Yeah, I get the message — but you do recall I'm not currently working for the Weyrd, right?'

She gave a sigh and said, 'Fassbinder, you'll be working for the Weyrd until the day you die, and maybe then some.'

'Well, now I'm depressed.'

She hung up.

I'd hoped to slip into Sister Bridget's without anyone noticing but Ingo was in the kitchen. Again. I put my finger to my lips, gave him big 'shut the Hell up' eyes and tiptoed along the corridor. I wished I had my Docs on instead of my fancy funeral boots, but I wasn't sure I'd have been any quieter. Sister Bridget's voice stopped before I got within two feet of the common room door.

'Hello, Sister.' I stepped over the threshold and looked carefully around, trying to find the spot where the air was a little bit broken, a little bit shimmery, but nothing really showed up against that symphony of yellow and brown and orange. 'Talking to yourself again?'

'Well, you know what they say, when you're after intelligent conversation . . .'

'Sure, sure. How long's he been hiding out?'

'Who? You know men aren't allowed in here.'

'I'm not accusing you of throwing wild parties, Sister, but of harbouring an angel. Tobit, you chicken-shit, make yourself visible.'

And to my mild surprise, he did.

I'd been racking my brain, trying to figure where the angel – no, *arch*angel, for that's what he was – might be laying low. He had no great liking for living on the streets or hanging about cathedral spires, and no allies in the city apart from me, Ligeia and Christos, and he wasn't letting us in on any secrets he might have been keeping. But Sister Bridget . . . I should have recalled her look of awe when she'd met Tobit at my wedding: a living, breathing sign that what she'd devoted her life to was, in some way at least, true. I should have thought of it sooner. The residence at St Agnes' made perfect sense, especially with the other nuns away: what better place for him to find faith to feed upon and a sympathetic ear?

He looked terrible – maybe not as terrible as Ligeia had, but still pretty rough. Still beautiful, though. He took up two of the sofa cushions. I noted he was dressed in full angelic regalia.

'Didn't see you at Ligeia's funeral. Were you there?'

'Yes.'

That explained the outfit. Even if he wasn't seen, he'd frocked up out of respect for the old siren.

'Hidden.'

'Yes.'

'You might recall that at the wedding I asked to discuss archangels in general, crazed ones in particular, with you. You've been avoiding me since.'

'Yes.'

'Ligeia left me a note.'

'Yes.'

'Is that all you've got?'

He didn't answer.

'She left me a gift, too, and I *know* what it can do to an archangel.' To emphasise matters I jerked my thumb at the sword on my back.

He gave a slight grin at that; I was an ant threatening a bear. But I strongly suspected that what I had was heaven-forged; my current theory was that it and the dagger were meant to be used to keep some kind of balance. The details were a little sketchy so far – as with many of my theories – but I'd add evidence as I went.

'Ligeia's note said that it was time for you to tell the tale of the broken god.'

He dropped his head into his hands.

'Not to be pushy or anything, but I'm on the clock here: my

family's been taken, there's been a coup at the Bishop's Palace, and there's a thing beneath the earth calling himself the Guardian of the Southern Gate of the Underworld, but he's basically a broken archangel. He's seeking a grail and a tyrant.'

At that, Tobit started.

'I need to know what – *who* – the Guardian is. I need to know what the tyrant is. And the grail . . .'

Tobit began with the grail. 'There are many such things in the world . . . I cannot help with that; I know not which he seeks. Many of them would not work on angelic flesh . . . many will not work on Weyrd flesh . . .'

'The Guardian, then.' *Hurry it up*, I wanted to shout.

He took so long to reply I thought I was going to have to start with some serious foot-stomping, but at last the tale came out, staccato as blocks dropped on a wooden floor.

'Once he was called Ramiel. The Thunder of God. The Angel of Those Who Rise; the Archangel of Resurrection. My . . . brother. The one I trusted above all, except for The Deity. So I did not see the treachery growing in my brother's heart. I did not see how far he had fallen from Grace. And so I did not protect our parents when he used the Dagger of Wilusa against them . . . I did not . . . suspect how far he had strayed.'

'God's *dead*?'

He shook his great head. '*No* – no. Fractured. Broken. You cannot entirely destroy such a being, but you can damage it. Ramiel did not understand that, as he did not understand so many things. He saw heresy everywhere. He saw in The Deity's weariness a failing and a faithlessness. He was ever judgemental, my brother.'

'And you, Tobit? What were you?'

'I was the one who failed. I failed to see the Fate that was coming . . .'

'Why are you here? Why Brisbane?'

'When Ramiel . . . did what he did, he burned, but The Deity was not of our substance: more friable, more brittle. It fragmented and shards of it fell . . . I have followed its echoes for hundreds of years, trying to piece those pieces back together, but . . . I can never quite grasp them. Sometimes a fragment feels so close, like a vibration or a whisper in my ear, and then . . . there is nothing. It's as if the fracturing has rendered it unknown to itself, unidentifiable, so that even we who knew The Deity so well can no longer see it.' He closed his eyes, but tears seeped out, liquid silver. 'I can hear the presence some days, feel it like a humming in my bones. But I can never find it; I can feel it but never see it. Brisbane . . . Brisbane is the place I have felt closest to it in the past century . . . in the longest time.'

I thought about fragments and echoes, of the flesh and bones of a god rent asunder and raining down across the world, being embedded not just in the earth, in sacred groves and mountains, in places where centres of worship might grow up, where healing shrines and wells might develop, but also in humans and Weyrd who might be hit by the debris scattered across heaven and earth.

I thought about what the Guardian had given me: a piece of blindingly white bone he said would shine when close to either the grail or the tyrant, and I wondered if the Guardian had pulled that fragment from his own flesh after he fell. The reliquary, which I had sitting in a box in a dark cupboard so the Guardian couldn't use it to track me, was the only thing I'd carried with me from the Underworld. It was the only change I'd made on earth that might have upset a delicate balance.

I thought about the Norns and their new powers. They had begun developing only after I'd brought the reliquary to the surface. Thaïs was the first affected: she was the eldest, and there was more of her to work on. Then Aspasia started, and finally Theo. Was godly flesh recognising godly bone close by? Was that proximity beginning the process of re-knitting? I wondered if the Norns had any inkling of what they had been before the fire, so violent it all but destroyed an archangel, had broken them in three?

If I brought the reliquary close to them, would it glow? Would they get stronger? Was the waning of my 'protection' from Thaïs connected somehow to my distance from her – or the increased influence of the reliquary?

And Aviva's '3-in-1' – how the Hell had she known? She was renowned for having a finger in every pie, a breath in every mouth, a whisper in every ear; it was just the sort of thing she'd discover or piece together over the years and hang onto until she could make the information pay. She'd not let it go with her to her grave, though: she'd *wanted* to tell me. I'd never know why; maybe it was just to fuck up someone else's day. Anything was possible with Aviva.

I voiced none of this to Tobit or Sister Bridget. The only thing of which I was certain was that no one else needed to know about this – not yet, maybe not ever. What might a fanatic, a crusader Weyrd or Normal do, to gain a broken god, to bring it back to itself, to make it whole again?

'Tobit, I need you to pull on your big-boy pants and buck up. I'm going to need your help in about three hours. When I call you, you'd better answer that fucking phone or so help me . . .'

He nodded, a simple defeated motion.

'And you, Sister Bridget, go and get Ingo, please.'

'Why?'

'Because I need him to blow shit up.'

Chapter Thirty-Three

Little Venice was closed when I arrived, which was unusual in and of itself; it operated with very little respect for legislation relating to such matters as opening and closing hours. Still, it was so late that Ziggi got a parking place right out front; I suggested he stay in the purple gypsy cab and enjoy it, just in case we needed to make a quick getaway. It wasn't that I was unhappy to have the band back together, but I needed to talk to the Norns alone.

I thought about busting the lock on the front door, just for fun, then figured it was an unnecessary level of destruction even for me – who says I'll never evolve? – so I took the side alley and hauled myself over the fence, which was fun in a dress. My stockings already had more ladders than the Roma Street Fire Station; who was going to notice a couple more?

I paused in the courtyard before showing myself in the gap where a sliding door would have been closed and locked if there'd been any kind of security and called out, 'Anyone home? Don't bolt-of-lightning me, it's Fassbinder.'

'Who else would be dumb enough to make that much noise sneaking in?' A tired-looking Aspasia appeared, a mug of steaming something-or-other in her hand. Her black locks hung lank and her skin had lost its sheen. I swallowed, considering the deleterious effects the reliquary was having on them, and wondered if their individual personalities were going to ultimately blink out. I wondered if they *really* knew what was happening to them.

'So, how are we doing here at Superpower Central?'

'We haven't set anything on fire yet or buried anyone in dirt or frozen anyone else. Does that count as a success?'

'My bar is so low nowadays, I'm going to call that a win. Is Thaïs around?' In the bar area I could see Theo was pouring herself a stiff drink.

'Where else would our dear sister be, Fassbinder?' Theo made a fairly sloppy gesture with her glass that made me think it wasn't her first. I doubted it would be her last.

'Rhetorical question, sure. Come on, I need to talk to all three of you. You guys go first. I don't feel like being a moving target again for a couple of hours at least.'

'She's entertaining a gentleman caller,' said Aspasia with a degree of bitterness. She caught my look and continued, 'Oh, not that sort. This is the kind of thing from your past that you really would prefer had stayed well and truly in the past.'

'Oh, goody. Someone else getting messed with makes me unaccountably cheerful.'

We trooped upstairs like a ragtag band. Aspasia tapped on the door to Thaïs' third-floor sanctuary, then opened it without waiting for permission, as only a sister would dare. I followed them, figuring they'd be excellent cover should Thaïs decide to throw a snowstorm or some such – then pulled up short.

On one of the sofas sat Thaïs and Professor Tiberius Claudius Ulysses Harrow, who was not only looking remarkably alive and alert, but considerably younger. The air of the old dodderer was gone; he sat straight, shoulders back, hair still in a ponytail, but now blond as a Viking. And the body was no longer soft-looking, but sinewy and lean and *dangerous*, as if all the tension in him was coiled like a snake. *This* Professor Harrow was handsome, with a square jaw and strong nose, a man who could look after himself in a bar fight, thank you very much. Granddad pants and chambray shirt had been replaced by tight indigo jeans, a long-sleeved black T-shirt and a slim-cut olive-green pea coat. There was nothing *avuncular* about him at all.

A basin filled with dark water sat on the coffee table between them.

'Hello, Professor.'

He gave me that eye-flick the Weyrd have perfected for dealing with their lessers and I sighed.

'What's your real name?'

He said instead, 'I knew when you turned up that thirty-seven years of refuge was done.'

'Destroyer of refuges, that's me.'

He looked at Thaïs, mildly annoyed. 'I thought this place might be safe at least for a while.'

'Do you really think anywhere is safe from *her*? She walked the earth of the Underworld and came out alive. She rode with the Boatman and returned. She's borne the Dagger of Wilusa and now' – Thaïs pointed to the sword-hilt showing over my shoulder – 'if I'm not very much hallucinating, she bears the Reaper. I told you long ago that no sanctuary is for ever. You've had a good run, Harmsorgi, but it's time to pay the piper. She's right there.'

'*Harmsorgi?* As in Harmsorgi Odinsay, infamous disappearing son of disapproving parents who got his Normal lover up the duff and is currently giving me shit for being a mixed-blood? *That* Harmsorgi?'

'I'm going to have to kill her,' he said casually to Thaïs, who, much to my relief, rallied.

'No one will harm her under my roof. Besides she's very hard to kill, like a cockroach.'

'Aw, I love you too, Thaïs.'

She ignored me, much as he had. 'Harmsorgi, if anyone can find a solution, it is Verity Fassbinder. I helped you disappear years ago, but this is beyond my aid. It might well be – in fact, mostly likely will be – painful, but it will be a solution nevertheless.'

The false professor looked me up and down as if calculating how much trouble I'd be either way, then said, 'I don't look down on you for your blood, Ms Fassbinder, but because you're a pain in the arse.'

'Well, isn't that a nice change?' I took a seat across from him.

'Maybe it's better you didn't die in the car accident,' Harmsorgi said reflectively. 'Perhaps you can be of use after all.'

'Did you just blithely admit to trying to murder me?' I glared at Thaïs. 'Did you know he'd tried to kill me?'

'Of course not! Do you think we'd offer asylum to one who would bring you down on us?'

'Were you— Did you— Mercado—' I couldn't get the questions out, but he understood.

'I noticed that little ferret following you the first time you came to visit me – I could see him through the glass, hanging around outside the museum doors. I'm surprised you didn't spot him.'

'Me too,' I admitted.

'I thought he might be useful, so I kept an eye on him. When I realised you were bothering my daughter, I decided it was time.'

'*Daughter?* Mister, I've been bothering a lot of people lately so you're going to have to be more specific.'

'Merrily.'

Merrily.

Merrily Vaughan.

Vaughan Carpenter. Not such a stretch, really.

'Wow! She looks really good.' I'd assumed Merrily was younger than me, but Weyrd blood can keep you young-looking and it had obviously done that for her. 'Does she know you're her father?'

He shook his head. 'I'm the nice old man who comes to buy smudge that he doesn't need and to have his Tarot read badly, just so he can spend time with her.' His shoulders sank. 'She doesn't know who I am – she doesn't know what she is. She thinks she's some sub-par hybrid with no abilities at all.' He smiled brokenly. 'She looks so like her mother . . .'

'So what is she if not a sub-par hybrid, to use your less than edifying description?'

He looked at Thaïs, who said, 'The truth is the only way.'

Harmsorgi looked at his hands as if there might be an answer there. There wasn't. Eventually he looked at me. 'The paper you sought from me?'

'However unsuccessfully, yes.'

'It hinted that a *person* could be a grail. That a matter of breeding might produce such a result.' He closed his eyes tightly, opened them again. 'You know that the Odinsays are a grail family, Ms Fassbinder, but unlike others, it's not something we acquired . . . my family *breeds* their grails.'

I cleared my throat. 'But you're not the real Harrow, so why would you write such a paper?'

I didn't. It was Tiberius' first paper, part of his Ph.D. at Oxford – his only original idea, if truth be told – and it gained him a teaching position at the university, but after a couple of decades he'd produced nothing further and he was under pressure. He'd known Vaughan when she'd been one of his students, so when he finagled the position at UQ, he reconnected with her.

'At first I was jealous, but I came to like him. He was extremely charming and persuasive. We all became closer and I . . . I spoke too freely, too often ... I gave him secrets about the Weyrd and my family that should never have passed my lips. By the time Vaughan was pregnant ... he ... he'd written it all down and was editing it into a new journal article.'

Harmsorgi clasped his hands tightly, the knuckles whitening. 'I'd given him the information he needed to make the leap from his first thesis. He was going to expose our world for the sake of his own career advancement, tell everyone how a human grail had to be the right mix of Weyrd and Normal – not just any hybrid would do; it had to be a place where two things met, to form a gateway between life and death. Such a combination might be thrown up just once in one, two, three hundred years.'

'Did he *name* you? Make the family traceable?'

'He didn't need to. All anyone with eyes to see and mind to understand would have had to do was to find *him*. He was a Normal; it wouldn't have taken much to shake the information from him and then my family would have been targeted. Whether it was believable to the majority was irrelevant: it needed only one or two open minds to go digging.'

'Surely some people knew the truth about the Odinsay grails anyway?'

'There was a great cup of carved bone that sat above my mother's throne – I imagine it still does. Whenever someone asked, *Where is the grail, the family luck?* that's what they would point to. But only a very few know the truth, the ones who can afford to purchase what we produce – and such people do *not* share that sort of information.'

'So it was all just a set-up? You wanted Vaughan to breed?' I felt ill.

He shook his head vehemently. 'No! Absolutely not – but that was why my parents tolerated the relationship, despite their *shame* – they had hopes that another grail might be born to us. And she was, but at great cost.'

'Your parents said the child died.'

He hung his head. 'Vaughan had a stroke during the birth and the attending doctor said she was unlikely to recover. But the child was delivered to term. My daughter was safe.'

'And so you . . . ?'

'I knew what my parents would do with her: she would be sold to the highest bidder, to win wars or to keep old men and women from death. She'd be used until she was empty. So I took her and disappeared. I knew they'd assume I'd run far away, which is why I stayed here. I gave her to adoptive parents – I kept watch and as she grew up, I began to visit in my guise as the harmless old academic.'

'But what about the real Harrow?'

'He'd earned his fate. Luckily, he could be useful to me in death. By taking his place, I could hide in plain sight.'

'So you killed him?'

'It was not my first instinct, but yes, in the end. He had had enough chances. I have spent *my life* destroying that infernal first paper, erasing every trace of it, except for the idea of an honourable reputation. It's always the first crumb in the trail. But just when I think I've succeeded, something pops up on the damned Internet, or Verity Fassbinder darkens my doorstep and brings everything crashing down.' He rubbed his face. 'How did you hear of it?'

'Brisbane's Archivist had a note of the title but no copy. He pointed me in your direction.'

Harmsorgi made a noise of irritation, like steam rushing from a pipe.

But as I said it, something about that sentence made my brain itch; something wasn't quite right. What if – just *maybe* – Jost did have a copy after all? He'd spent months and months going through the holdings in the Brisbane Weyrd Archives as part of his job and that was a locale protected by a butt-load of spells formulated precisely to stop things like erasures working on inconvenient records – that was why Vadim Nadasy had had to impersonate Ursa, Jost's predecessor, to enter the Archives in order to physically tear pages from registers to cover his tracks.

So what if Jost had been mixing personal goals with professional ones, looking through all those old papers and books for *that* article, maybe one of the last copies in existence? What if he'd *found* it? He wouldn't have given it to me: that would have made matters too easy. But putting me on the scent but without any actual detail had set me on Harmsorgi's trail. So Jost had applied me like a pressure pack to someone he couldn't or wouldn't approach himself. After all, asking the wrong questions got one killed; Jost was clearly smart enough to stay at one remove from such things.

While I tried to figure out what to say next my mobile rang and saved me the trouble.

'Bela?' I kept my tone neutral.

'Jost is not answering his phone, nor is he to be found at home, but Ziggi and I have been through his Hamilton apartment,' Bela told me.

'And?'

'There is no sign of Mel or Lizzie. I'm sorry, V, but . . .'

I suppressed the feeling of nausea that bubbled up. 'What? No point in sugar-coating things.'

'There are three hospital beds, all empty, and IV drips and other paraphernalia for keeping the comatose alive.'

'Oh, Bela.' Neutrality gone, distress on full display. 'He's been . . . what – *who* – has he been keeping in them?'

And what might someone like Merrily Vaughan mean to whatever his long game was? Did he know she was the one he'd been looking for? I paused. Had *Jost* been her bad date? She'd said he was dark-haired, but the fur she'd pulled from her suitor had been golden . . . I'd never seen Jost without his glamours, so maybe he had more than one layer working on him? I remembered Sophie, Harrow's assistant, saying she'd had a stalker following her; she'd had no description to give, but what if . . . what if Jost had been following both Merrily and Sophie? What if he didn't know who he was looking for but had figured *something* out? Perhaps he'd been playing a hunch that Harrow was more than he seemed and he'd realised that one of the two dark-haired young women Harrow spent time with was of *significant* interest to him?

As I said all this aloud to Bela, I watched Harmsorgi's face empty of all colour. When I hung up, I ignored his questions and asked, 'Who could possibly know what Merrily is?'

'No one,' he said.

'Really? Think carefully before you answer. *No one*?'

He stared into his hands. 'My parents' steward at the time helped take care of Vaughan. He arranged for her to go to a respite home.'

'Actually, nope, he did not. He contacted Eleanor Aviva to get rid of the vegetative problem and she sold Vaughan on to the highest bidder.'

'*What?*'

'The bodies of Vaughan and two other comatose Normal women who fell through the cracks around the same time in the early Eighties have all turned up in recent weeks. They've been used, as far as we can tell, as vessels for keeping something . . . or some*one*.'

'Who's doing this?'

'Jost Marolf, who's clearly been here longer than anyone's known.'

'Jost!' said Aspasia in shock. '*No—*'

'Although perhaps not surprising . . .' Theo mused.

'Why?' I asked.

Thaïs sighed. 'The border wolf had a great love affair with a daughter of Byzantium, the Lady Aelia. She died, and he was inconsolable for many years.'

'Inconsolable? Try *insane*,' Theo broke in. 'Fassbinder, Jost was not capable of rational thought for a century or two. For many years he was . . . he was kept in a place where he could be safe from himself. Gradually he was brought back from the brink. He disappeared for many years and when he came here – well, when we thought him newly arrived – he seemed *well*.'

I remembered him saying to me that he'd loved and lost, that he'd known the pain of it. That he wouldn't hurt Mel . . . but what if he didn't see what he was doing as *hurting* her? People in pursuit of a goal often suffered from tunnel vision, not to mention a moral compass seriously out of whack.

'Who was she, this daughter of Byzantium?'

'A scholar of note, a sorceress of considerable power. She died in the great city in the tenth century, during a siege.'

'She was Weyrd, so she should have passed on, gone with the Boatman.' I thought about Frau Berhta, defying a god who gave in to her will and sent her back to life. The Byzantine princess clearly wasn't the same calibre as my ever-so-great-grandmamma, but Jost might well have shared Berhta's determination to cheat death. 'The bodies of the Normal women: could her soul have been stored in them?'

'But the strain on the body would be *immense*,' Harmsorgi started.

Theo said, 'But if there were three of them and he was moving her around regularly? The Normal flesh would provide both an anchor and a hiding place for a Weyrd soul.'

'That would explain why they all came to ruin around the same time. She burned them all out.' I gulped a breath. 'She died in the tenth century? How many Normal women has he used in this way over the years?' Having asked the question, I avoided doing the maths because I just didn't want to contemplate it.

'And he used my Vaughan for this?' asked Harmsorgi in a low voice.

I nodded. 'So, I ask again, who else might have known that your child survived?'

'Only my parents' steward.'

'You parents said he was dead. An Erik Alhström.'

Harmsorgi laughed, a great bitter snort of a thing. 'Dead? Not at all. And Erik Alhström? What is it with my mother's love of false information and made-up names? Perhaps he paid them to say that, or to simply not tell anyone he once was a servant, no matter how elevated. Udo Forsythe was in my parents' employ, though it suits him to forget it now.'

I closed my eyes, kept all the swears inside, then said evenly, 'Udo Forsythe has staged a coup. He has stolen my family and as far as we can tell, he has the Bishop's Palace in lockdown.'

'*What the actual fuck?*' Theo looked stunned.

'Bela is currently running the numbers to see who he can count on for support. But for the moment, he's keeping this little bit of intel quiet. You might want to follow suit.' I rubbed my face. 'You're here, Bela's still working, Banks is not in the best condition. That leaves Udo and Sandor – and we're not yet sure if Sandor is a hostage or complicit.'

'What could Sandor gain from this?' asked Theo. 'The Brisbane Grant was entrusted to him two hundred years ago. This is hardly the place to launch a comeback for the Old Country.'

'Nope, but if you've got a peasant's lineage, ravening ambition and a chip on your shoulder? This is the perfect place and way for *Udo* to start establishing himself. You know bloody revolutions are still considered a valid form of regime-change amongst the Weyrd.' I sighed. 'I'd advise any and all Councillors not siding with him to stay the Hell away before he decides he has some other incumbent for your seat. That will be the next thing he does.'

'The Weyrd won't—'

'Going to stop you right there, Theo. The Weyrd have a history of waiting to see where the cards fall before they make decisions. Bela is ridiculously confident of finding folk to rely on, but I'm not convinced. There are those who've taken Forsythe's coin; there will be those who'll quietly leave town – but those who will stand and fight? I'm not willing to calculate those odds.'

I was depressed – if unsurprised – that no one gainsaid me. Something else was digging its heels into my brain and I muttered, 'Lizzie said something the night I babysat for her and the night-doves came.'

We'd been talking about Jost and she'd said he was pretty: *Prettier than the first time I saw him with that guy*. I hadn't been paying enough attention: if she'd seen him, where had that been? Before my wedding – and who had he been talking to? *Len?* According to the revolting Mr McGee, Len had a sugar daddy paying his rent. Had Lizzie seen them in my yard? Len had been looking for the grail before I'd ever stumbled into the Guardian's lair, so who else would be looking for the grail before then? Jost in his dark-haired disguise?

'Night-doves? For you?' Harmsorgi sounded uncertain.

'Do you know something about that too?' I asked, exasperated. 'What did you do?'

'Not me. Merrily. When I went to visit I found her constructing them with the fur she'd taken from her attacker.'

'There's a nice daddy-daughter project. The fur – I thought there was less in the fetish! The doves went to the place closest to where they could feel its presence. It wasn't *me* at all! But Jost had been spending a lot of time at Mel's . . . Well, that *is* a nice change.' I dropped my head into my hands, thinking furiously. 'It was Jost on the date, wanting to know about her family. He'd seen you with her and with Sophie, but he couldn't work out which was his target – if either were.'

'Is Sophie all right?' he asked.

'I'm going to assume so. She told me she had a stalker, but I'm willing to bet she's been safe since he worked out Merrily was his goal.' I ran a hand through my hair. 'At least he can't get into the shop, or to her, not with those wards she's made. Still, I'll be happier if we can get her somewhere safe, somewhere Jost can't get at her. I'll call Bela.'

'That's why I'm here, Ms Fassbinder, seeking *their* aid, or trying to beg it of old friends.'

'I cannot find her, Harmsorgi. She walks not on the surface of this earth.' Thaïs' tone was sad; she gestured to the water-filled basin on the table in front of her. 'I've scried and can find no trace.'

'She's already gone,' Harmsorgi said to me, his eyes wide, his voice hitting a high note of distress. 'She's been taken from her place of business. My child is gone.'

'Shit.'

Chapter Thirty-Four

I asked Ziggi to deliver Harmsorgi Odinsay to Bela, who'd set up his War Room at Sister Bridget's place, then come back for me. I'd told the false professor what I expected of him and promised I'd do my best to save his daughter. What worried me, although I didn't feel the need to share, was that if Thaïs couldn't find her on the earth, then she was probably already *under* it – which didn't necessarily mean death, because her value lay in her as a *living* thing. But I thought it mostly likely that the Guardian had got hold of her – there was no way Jost could have got through those wards – although I didn't know *how*.

I was obviously worried for Merrily, but at least there was a better-than-average chance that she was not dead yet, which was always a cause for celebration. My hope didn't extend to poor Monobrow Mike, who wasn't answering his mobile. Bela told me grimly that his car was empty and the engine cold, and a small amount of blood had been found on the driver's seat. I just hoped he would find his way to Jerry as soon as he could, that they'd be together again.

When I returned from handing Harmsorgi into Ziggi's custody, the Norns and I took a sofa each and sat quietly for a few moments, me gathering my thoughts, them trying not to tear apart the fabric of time and space, or so I imagined.

Then I said, 'Okay then. Superpowers.'

They gazed at me expectantly. Theo let little sparks leap from her fingers, frost crackled out from Thaïs' head like a halo and Aspasia's expression said she'd be happy to flip a table or a plateau at a second's notice. I breathed in and out a few times to gain a little time.

'When I first came back from the Underworld, the Guardian gave me a gift – he's big on gifts, is the Guardian. The only reason I took this one was because he said that when I was near either the grail or the tyrant, this reliquary – it's a crystal with a bit of bone set in it – would glow, because all three were made of the same substance.'

'And where is this item, strangeling?' asked Thaïs.

'Hidden in a box in a cupboard at home. Gifts: that's how the Guardian gets a line to his minions, those he does deals with, those who work for him: they carry around some object that came from his big old burned hand. My mother had the sword and the magic mirror, Joyce had an antique tantō and Mike found a pocket watch on him, remember? That way, the Guardian can use a little technique he likes to call the Breath of God, which is just a poetic term for screwing up someone's day. Pretty soon I'm going to have to go and get that reliquary and that will draw the Guardian down on me.'

'Why? Why draw it out?' Thaïs' voice rose well above her usual calm timbre.

'Because at some point I'm going to need to draw it into the open. And quite apart from that, I have a theory of mine that I should probably confirm.'

'Which is?' asked Aspasia quietly.

'That if I hold that reliquary anywhere near you lot it will light up like the sky on fireworks nights.'

'No.' Theo mostly swallowed the word.

'No,' said Aspasia, even less certainly.

Thaïs was silent.

'See, the way I figure it, the changes in you began when I returned. Even though I've had the thing hidden away, since it's been above ground it's had an influence. Four and a bit weeks? That's enough time for it to be influencing matters. Thaïs, when did you begin to notice the changes?'

Her sisters stared at her.

'Perhaps three, perhaps four weeks . . .'

I'd wondered if her sheer size could be why it had affected her soonest, and perhaps it was a sign of something more: whether her refusal to leave the third floor of Little Venice was a sign of *too much knowledge* of what the world outside held – if she had more memory than her sisters of what they had been; if she was the repository of, quite simply, *more*.

'What do you remember, Thaïs?'

'Nothing,' she said brutally. She shook her head and icicles flew from her hair and skin.

'You do, I think. You remember what your sisters don't.'

A curl of frozen lightning reached out for me, but stopped short. Thaïs gave me a warning glance.

You'd think she'd forgotten who she was dealing with. 'You can turn me into an ice block, sure, but it won't make the truth any different. It won't put the genie back in the bottle and your sisters won't stop asking you questions. And there's no point in having a cat-fight between you because with your superpowers returning you'll just leave scorched earth behind.'

Thaïs rose and loomed over me like a localised ice-storm just waiting for a chance to let loose. Aspasia and Theo also rose, and they planted themselves between us. I could feel the heat coming off Theo, and Aspasia smelled like freshly turned earth. Part of me wanted to curl up in a ball on the sofa; the other part of me would never let that happen.

'What happened, Sister?' asked Theo quietly.

'If you carry our memories, we are owed them. We've wandered so long, making new remembrances, pretending we knew our history, but always, *always*, there is a place that is blank and empty.' Aspasia held a hand out towards Thaïs; it was the gentlest tone I'd ever heard from her.

'I remember fire,' whispered Theo. 'Or I think I do. Perhaps it's just a dream.'

'If we fell—'

'We did *not* fall!'

'*When* we fell—'

The moment stretched long and taut as a bowstring, then Thaïs slumped back onto her sofa and the tension left her sisters' bodies.

'I – *we* – were tired. *So* tired. If we had not been so tired, perhaps we would have noticed Ramiel's discontent; we might have seen his anger. But there were so many demands, so many prayers; the constant importuning of humanity and angels, other gods pressing their claims . . . We were so very weary.' She lifted her hands in despair. 'We did not pay sufficient attention. We turned our back on many things. We did not try to rein in the tide of disbelief – why would we do that? If they are created to make their own choices, why would we try to change that? – and we turned our back on Ramiel. And Ramiel turned a weapon on us that we had once helped to forge.'

'Fire,' whispered Theo, a hand to her throat.

'There was fire and we fell, broken, fragmented into we three, and soon we were only a memory and a myth, a persistent legend.' Thaïs closed her Arctic-blue eyes, then opened them and looked at me. 'I gathered my sisters, who remembered nothing of our travail, and we wandered. I wondered, sometimes, if we were pursued, but we remained unfound.'

'Tobit followed you. He's been following you for a very long time, but he didn't recognise you.'

'We were broken, no longer the same, so we could not be easily located by anyone who had known us.'

'And you hid here.'

'The latest of many refuges. This was a small place; we could fit in with the Weyrd, not stand out. Our breaking had emphasised all the things we have in common with them. We could be involved enough not to excite talk, but distant enough to be independent. The angels, those we'd raised high, they would never have accepted us as we are now.'

'And when I mentioned the Guardian to you, you didn't make any connections? Like, how many burned and broken archangels have you left in your wake?' I gritted my teeth. 'You didn't think, maybe, to volunteer any information that might have made my job easier?'

She didn't answer me but I already knew what she would have said: *I like my life now. I don't want to go back. You can't make me. If I bury my head under the blankets this will all go away and this tiny, safe little world I've made for myself and my sister-selves will stay just as it is and nothing will change.*

No matter that Ramiel had betrayed them and broken them; I suspected his true gift had been to give them an unintended peace, if only for a time. Part of me understood that and ached for the Norns at having that taken away.

Part of me was just mightily pissed off.

'And the irony of an angel trying to kill you last year because you wouldn't give it information doesn't strike you at all? Might you have said something then? Like, "Calm the fuck down, crusading angels, I'm here. I've been here all along." No?'

'You witnessed them: do you think they would have believed us? We are *fragmented*, sundered from what we were. The fault lines in our being render us *different*, invisible. And we are now so *very* female.' She hissed out a breath of frustration. 'When the first one came, I did wonder . . . then when one tried to kill us, with no sense of what we were . . .'

'Okay, so here's something else I don't get: if Merrily is a grail, then part of her is god's flesh: she's half and half. The Weyrd aren't *godly*, surely.'

Thaïs licked her lips. 'When we fell, fragments were expelled from our person. Some were lost; some shards embedded themselves into those nearby. It is my belief that one of the Odinsays' ancestors was thus pierced; that from that moment on something slept in them until the right combination was made. But I cannot be certain.'

I thought about that, a fragment of the Norns lying dormant in someone's veins until a Weyrd and a Normal made a baby and that shard was for some reason activated, just like a recessive gene. What might Weyrd and Normal alike do if they knew about the Norns? About what they were, what their flesh could do?

'And you never thought to say anything to Tobit, even knowing how he suffers?'

'We all suffer,' she sneered. 'Why is his self-pity at his neglect of our safety any greater or more important than anyone else's?'

'Because you can *see* it. He's close by – he's not some random person out of your line of sight. And he was something to you once, when *you* were greater.'

Her sisters at least looked ashamed, even though the shame was not theirs to bear for they didn't know.

I leaned forward, resting my elbows on my knees, and wished I'd had a chance to change into jeans and Docs; I could smell my own sweat mingled with the horribly distinctive scent of the Nadasy basement embedded in the fabric of an expensive dress I wasn't ever going to be able to wear again. 'Here's the thing: I need your help. If the grail is in the Underworld, what will happen to Merrily? Will the Guardian wear her out? How long have we got? *He* doesn't know about you – no one does, and nor will they, if I get my way. You're safe. However, I don't think anyone else in this city will be if the Guardian is healed and goes on the rampage. I will need your powers combined once again.'

Thaïs shook her head.

'Oh, come on! The only reason Ramiel got to you was because he stabbed you in the back!'

'We have been separated too long, strangeling . . . we do not have all of our pieces. All of those shards and fragments embedded in other bodies, other lives? We cannot take them back. It would wreak too much destruction.'

'And a crazed archangel won't?' But I could see her point. 'But you can do *something*.'

'We cannot.' I could tell from her tone that what she meant was, *We will not.*

'I am owed more than this. This city which gave you sanctuary deserves more. My family deserves more.' I rose and glared at all three of them. 'You won't see me again here. I've rendered all the assistance I ever will to you – and if my family dies, then I will do everything in my power to ruin your lives.'

I kicked open the front door on my way out and settled in to wait for Ziggi's return.

The phone rang while I waited. 'Not the best time, Rhonda.'

'I won't take long.'

'You don't have long. You might want to consider some kind of city-wide disaster planning.'

'Your Lizzie? She's been found.'

'*Where?* Is she okay?'

'She's fine, but she's weeping for her mum.'

'What—'

'She was dropped off outside Roma Street Headquarters. Oldman was there when they brought her in. She's okay physically, she's been fed, she's clean, but upset. Keeps asking for her mum – and you.'

'Where is she now?'

'Asleep in the spare bedroom at mine. Ellen is practising mummyhood.'

'Oh good. Did she say anything?'

'Just that Jost promised Mel would be okay. That they'd all be together soon and though Mummy might seem different at first, she'd get used to it.'

'Oh, shit.' I outlined for McIntyre the story of the lovelorn border wolf and his series of preservative jars. 'This really sounds like the next level, doesn't it?'

'Oh, *shit*.'

'Just keep Lizzie safe, okay? When she wakes, tell her I'll bring her mum home.' I'd made that promise before and I'd done it. I wished I was certain I'd be able to do so again.

I stood undecided for a moment, then headed back into Little Venice, giving the door another good kick as I did so.

Upstairs, the Norns were in the same positions as when I'd left: not talking, not moving, just sitting.

'Yes, I'm aware I said you wouldn't see me again and that as a storm-out this leaves a lot to be desired, but Jost Marolf has Mel and if I'm right he's going to try to put Aelia into her. If he's doing what he's done before, he'll be looking for other women to use as vessels.'

'Mel isn't comatose, Verity, at least not that we know of,' said Theo slowly. 'This is different.'

I swallowed hard. 'Do you think he might be . . . ? He told Lizzie that Mel would be returned, even though she might seem different.'

'If he thinks the grail has been found, he can use it to make the transfer permanent, to repair the damage to the Lady Aelia, to bind her soul into a body once again. He thinks it will make her whole again, proof against the pull of death,' Aspasia said.

'Will it?'

Thaïs heaved a great sigh. 'Perhaps. Or perhaps it will simply tear both Aelia and Mel's souls *and* bodies apart.'

'What can I do to stop it? I need to know how to get rid of whatever he's putting inside her. How can I pull the stray soul from Mel and restore her?'

There was a long pause as the Sisters exchanged a look. Then Aspasia said, 'You need something infused with our death.'

'But you're still alive.'

'The death of what we *were*, strangeling,' said Thaïs. 'The death of the *before*. The death of a god.'

She sighed, then told me what to do.

Ziggi was still waiting at the kerb outside and the sight of him and his awful cab made me very happy in spite of everything. I unbuckled the sword – which I was pretty sure was going to get me arrested sooner than later – then slid into the back. Relaxing against the slightly sticky, peeling, uncomfortable faux-leather, I couldn't help but grin. My husband and daughter had been kidnapped, my mother had been used as a pincushion, Mel was probably being used as a canopic urn for a Byzantine witch, the Norns were a god and a very uncooperative one at that, Merrily Vaughan was missing and probably with the Guardian, which could in no way be pleasant, and Joyce Mori-Miller was in a hospital, all banged up with broken limbs and a lot of mixed emotions.

But I was here, where I belonged, where I needed to be, and my uncle was literally in the driver's seat. Something at least was right with the world.

I reached forward and patted him on the shoulder; he gave me a stare with all three eyes; the one in the back of his head, beneath his thinning ginger hair, was particularly cynical. 'I missed you.'

He grunted, which I knew meant he loved me and he'd missed me too. I ran through the highlights of Jost's activities, the truth of the bodies, most of the details of Merrily Vaughan's actual identity and nature, and what I thought Mel was going to be used for. The stuff about the Norns I kept to myself; even if they weren't going to help, I wasn't prepared to let the truth of what they were get out in any way, shape or fashion. An unholy war was exactly what Brisbane – and I – didn't need.

'So, what are we going to do?' he asked at last.

I sighed. 'Something stupid.'

'That always works.'

I didn't reply but pulled up Jost's number in my mobile, took a deep breath, prayed to a god more reliable than the one I'd left at Little Venice and hit *call*.

Pick up, pick up, pick up, motherfucker.

'Verity.' Jost's tone was neutral; he didn't know what I knew. He didn't know whether Lizzie had been found or if she'd spoken to me. He didn't know if I knew about Mel. Hopefully, he didn't know Merrily was gone – that was the biggest risk of all.

'How're things?' I asked, equally casually.

'Mel is fine, if that's what you're asking.'

'Well, I guess it is. When you say "fine", do you mean "for a person with a Byzantine witch about to be jammed inside her chest"?'

A long hesitation. 'It won't hurt her.'

'I don't think that's really the point.'

'Verity, I'm begging you to be reasonable. You've got something I need. If you don't give it to me then Mel will just end up another empty shell.' He sounded sly now, playing his ace. 'This way, at least some of her will be preserved.'

I let him hang for a bit, as if I were seriously considering it, as if I had no choice, then I stepped off the cliff. 'I've got the grail.'

'Who is it?' He tried to sound disinterested, but the tremor in his voice gave him away.

'Merrily Vaughan.' I lowered my voice. 'But then, you suspected that, didn't you? Her rather than Sophie?'

'I knew there was something not quite right about Harrow when I couldn't locate that article of his.'

'You found a copy though, didn't you?'

'The Archives are a veritable treasure trove.' He laughed, then sobered. 'It was pure luck, I must admit. It was the difficulty in finding it that made me look closely at Harrow. He's smart, though; he didn't drop out of character at all.'

'So you set me on him.' I tapped my fingers against my thigh.

'You do have the effect of shaking things loose.'

'When Aviva offered you Vaughan's body, did you know who she was?'

'Who she was?' He sounded genuine.

'Harmsorgi Odinsay's lover. Merrily's mother. Vaughan Carpenter.'

The long pause told me *no* before he did. 'I . . . never knew their names, the women I . . .'

Which made me feel extra enraged. He didn't even think of the women he used as people.

'How strange a coincidence . . .'

It was time to get back on track. 'You promise me this won't hurt Mel?'

'I promise. The process will be like falling asleep. When she wakes, she won't even remember what happened.'

She won't be Mel any more. She won't remember herself. 'And do you promise that Merrily will be okay afterwards if I let you use her?'

'I've never played you false, Verity.' But I noticed he hadn't actually answered my question.

'Except for the bit where you lied to me? Where you shoulder-charged me over at Hawthorne? Attacked Merrily Vaughan?'

'Exceptional circumstances – I needed your help, but you'd never have agreed, would you? And Merrily . . . I became frustrated and lost my temper. You must believe me, Verity, this is all done from love.'

I managed to keep the laughter from my voice when I asked, 'Where are you?'

'Where are *you*?'

I closed my eyes, prayed. 'Just leaving St Agnes'. I had to check in on Joyce.'

He bit. 'Then just come home. I'm at Mel's.'

'Safest place for you, I guess. Who'd have thought to look there? I'm on my way.' I paused. 'Jost?'

'Yes, Verity?'

'This had better work.' I disconnected before he could answer.

'Those are some pretty big cheques you're writing,' observed Ziggi. 'And I know how little there is in your bank account.'

'You should have a little faith, Uncle. Just drive towards home. We're going to have to coordinate a few things, and when we leave there it's going to need to be fast.' My finger hovered over another a contact in my phone. 'Oh, how are your glamour-casting skills these days?'

Chapter Thirty-Five

Ziggi dropped me down the street from my place and I'd walked back carrying the sword, then snuck down the driveway, and up the stairs, letting myself in the back door. It felt like an eon since I'd been home.

What I wanted to do was sink onto the couch, have a good long cry about the current circumstances, screaming and railing, letting my agony about David and Maisie *out*. But instead I screwed it up in a ball and jammed it in that hollow spot in my chest where the pain would sometimes just sit quietly when I told it to. I kicked off my ruined fancy boots and got into my Docs, which raised my spirits probably more than was reasonable, but I left on my grotty torn expensive dress and coat. I wanted Jost to think me beaten down.

I wanted my daughter and husband back; I wanted a shower; I *really* wanted the Norns not to be so damned flaky. I wanted my friends safe; Hell, I even wanted my frenemies safe. I wanted the Guardian dealt with. I wanted Jost bleeding and I wanted Udo Forsythe wearing his balls for earrings.

I wanted a lot of things.

Then I went into the library.

Before I opened the cupboard, I considered the sword, all nicely wrapped in its fancy sheath. It wasn't like I needed a weapon against Jost or most folk, thanks to my Weyrd strength and all, but there was something comforting about Reaper that made me feel I'd like to have it around. Then again, that's how I'd felt about the Dagger of Wilusa and it had become something of a crutch. It probably wasn't in my best interests to confront the Archivist armed, whether he recognised the weapon or not; that would be like throwing down a glove. I'd been looking forward to using it on Jost Marolf, but I needed him to think me beaten and acquiescent. Reluctantly, I opened the door and slid the sword onto the top shelf. I'd retrieve it before the next challenge.

My hands feeling suddenly very empty, I reached deep into the back, behind the jumble of books and winter jumpers and stacks of general crap I stored there until my fingers curled around the little midnight blue velvet box. I barely looked at it, just in case even that minor attention was enough to spark the Guardian's Spidey-sense. It sure as Hell wasn't getting opened until it absolutely had to be.

There was a lonely banana just clinging to life in the fridge; I grabbed it and wolfed it down as I went down the back stairs. Going over the fence added some more tears to my dress, some lovely grace notes to my down-and-out expensive-gone-to-shit hobo style. I paused on the little landing outside Mel's back door, then knocked. I was pretty sure I could still smell the scent of decaying night-doves.

I immediately heard the sound of hurrying footsteps and the door was pulled open, leaving Jost silhouetted against the kitchen light. He stepped aside to let me in.

'Verity, thank you so much for coming,' he said, as if I'd dropped in for tea.

I had a choice?

'Jost,' I said, sizing him up.

He no longer looked perfect.

It was the most casually attired I'd ever seen him, but maybe 'casual' wasn't the word; maybe it should have been 'wrecked'. His distressed hipster jeans had mud around the ankles and shins; there were soot and bloodstains on his pale blue T-shirt and he wore no shoes on feet that were enormous, covered in golden fur and with long toenails that clacked on the polished wooden floors like a dog's. His face was bruised and there was a bald patch on his head where I was willing to bet Merrily had yanked out his hair, and a long, thick mark where I figured I'd got him with the tactical baton. Small wonder I'd not seen him in this shape since he'd attacked Merrily. There were tuffs of fur along his jaw-line and his outline wasn't staying solid.

I'd noticed that before in the Archives, but I'd put it down to the lighting there, but now I figured it was because he was holding three forms, one over another: the border wolf at his core, the perfectly urbane blond Archivist and the handsome dark-haired man who'd gone on a date with Merrily Vaughan. And with the magics he was having to maintain to keep three vessels alive as places to lock down a Weyrd spirit being pulled towards death, it was amazing that he could walk and talk at the same time. But the toll being taken was well and truly on display now.

'Where's Mel?'

'Where's Merrily?'

'Almost here. Ziggi had to go and collect her. He's the only one Mike would hand her over to without questioning him.'

'Ha! Mr Jones, the watchdog,' he sneered. Clearly Jost didn't know about Merrily's disappearance or Udo's coup, or anything else that wasn't connected with his own plots and plans. 'Harmsorgi Odinsay's daughter.' His eyes were bright with want and madness, as if proximity to his goal had loosed wolves in his head. 'Who'd have thought?'

'You've been in Brisbane a long time, haven't you?'

'In one guise or another. I came here – to this ridiculous country town! – to speak to the Odinsays about their grail – one of my rare personal appeals.'

'Not looking like this, though.' I gestured to the blond hair.

He shook his head. 'Dark and different – but I'm sure Merrily told you about my disguise.' He grinned, unsurprisingly wolfish. 'I learned soon enough to hide behind others. But I arrived too late; their son had already disappeared and they said he'd stolen the grail.'

'And by then you needed new vessels?'

'As I would now, with my three worn through, if not for these fortuitous circumstances. There have been many over the years, of course. Aviva was always there to help, for the right price; she found me what I needed.' He grinned. 'That she'd sell me the grail's mother and not tell me . . .'

'I'm guessing you didn't bother to ask for names.' I managed to keep most of the disgust out of my voice.

He looked contrite, but I didn't know if there was any truth there, if he still retained some long-buried skerrick of compassion reactivated by my prodding, or it was just part of that self-deprecating charm thing he'd found worked for him for the longest time. 'So, you came out of hiding when . . .'

'. . . when the Archives position came up. It was such a chance, to dig through all those records – and ultimately, the chance to get close to you . . . to put you to work.' He grinned again. 'You'd dealt with Aviva by then: she was locked in the depths of the Bishop's Palace, so I knew there no chance of recognition, and then Ms Nadasy finished her off . . .'

'All very convenient for you.'

'I've always been lucky.'

'Apparently not.' I took a deep breath. 'Or your Aelia, at least, ran out of luck.'

'No.' And there it was, something genuine: grief, absolute and inconsolable. He grabbed a hank of hair and pulled at it, so hard I thought it might come out.

'But why me? When we met I had no idea about grails . . .'

'No, but I was quite sure there was some way I could utilise you, Verity. You're determined: you bring to light matters others would prefer remain in the shadows. Although I had no specific plan for you, I was sure you could be put to good purpose.' Jost lifted his hands; the nails were almost as long as the ones on his toes. 'Secrets don't stay dark near you for very long, Ms Fassbinder.' He looked both admiring and resentful. 'It's been difficult maintaining my disguises.'

'I'll bet. But you had Len poking around . . .'

'It is so frustrating, having to wait upon others to do my work for me. Asking too many questions gets one noticed, as poor Len would attest. All he was supposed to do was watch you, but he saw those fox-girls and decided to show some initiative . . . I was enraged when he told me he'd asked them about the grail. So sloppy.' He grinned. 'He liked you. I told him he'd be looking out for you.'

'Kept you out of the picture, did your dirty work for you.' I rubbed my face. 'When I came back from the Underworld asking about grails you must have thought all your Christmases had come at once.'

He just smiled.

'Jost, people aren't just disposable.'

'Some are, Verity.'

'Like Vaughan Carpenter and Alison Brandt and Shirley Ignacio?'

'They were . . . they were not going to serve another purpose in their life.'

'You can't *know* that. You don't know that they were never going to wake up.'

'The only miracles I believe in are those I make for myself.' Having an Ozymandias moment, he gestured around him to the kitchen, the house, as if it was all his doing: *Look on my works, ye Mighty, and despair.*

'Jost, where's Mel?'

'You must understand, Verity, that she will be different, but her existence will be much enriched: imagine the life we can give Lizzie, the three of us together. Believe me, I'm terribly fond of your friend.'

I like her so much I want to splice her with my dead girlfriend.

'This whole thing about using women as receptacles, Jost . . .'

'I promise, she'll be *fine*. There will be just two of them in the one body. Verity, I chose Mel *because* I liked her so much – and she looks much like Aelia did in life, so it will be even easier to love her. The fact that I found her and that the grail has surfaced now, after all these years – doesn't that tell you that this is *right*?' His smile was a brilliant thing. 'Don't you understand, Verity? I'm doing all of this out of love.'

'Serendipitous,' was all I could manage. I began to move away, stepping backwards into the lounge area. 'Where's Mel?'

'Where's Merrily?'

Before I could answer, there was a knock. *Nicely timed, Ziggi.* Jost strode into the room.

'That'll be her now. Promise me, Jost, that Mel and Merrily will both be okay after all this.' I stood in front of the door, as if trying to stave off the moment when I had to hand the grail over.

'Verity, it's too late. If you don't allow me to use the grail to bind them together, Mel will remain a vault with Aelia's soul inside.' He smiled gently down at me and put a hand on my shoulder and I let him move me out of the way. 'She won't even know about it.'

'Okay.'

As Jost opened the door to welcome his guests, I began to back away, towards the hallway that led to the bedrooms. A sick feeling roiled in my stomach: what if Mel wasn't there? What if he'd been lying all the time?

Peering past Jost's back I could see Merrily Vaughan, stepping over the threshold, stiff and vacant-looking, in an outfit she'd never be seen dead in: a long-sleeved red woollen dress that was a bit tight across the boobs but the perfect length for someone not my height. Behind her was Ziggi, hovering and glaring.

'Merrily, welcome. I've waited so long for you.' Jost's tone was gentle, melodic. It gave me the spur I needed to turn on my heel and run.

To my immense relief, Mel was in her room, laid out on the bed, dressed in a highly embroidered and embellished dress of royal purple. The gown covered her from neck to toe. The collar was high and round, the sleeves tight and the cuffs fringed in gold. I imagined Jost had been hanging onto the frock since, well, the Fall of Byzantium, preserved by magic – or maybe he was a dab hand with a needle and thread. Her hair had been woven into braids and pulled into a bun on top of her head. Heavy earrings of what I guessed were rough-cut diamonds and emeralds set in gold hung from her ears. All in all, it was a look I didn't think she'd care for, even if it hadn't come free with another soul.

I pulled the velvet box from my pocket, flipped its lid and tried to open Mel's mouth.

Her teeth were clench tight, so I tried prising, then rubbing the hinges of her jaw, but I was wary of breaking facial bones – she wouldn't thank me for that – and by that time there was a ruckus in the lounge. I guessed my little deception had been discovered, as Jost was sounding more like an enraged wolf than an urbane Archivist.

Saying, 'I guess you'll forgive me for this one day, Mel,' I punched her in the stomach, which had the desired effect: a gasp, an open mouth just long enough for me to jam the crystal in before those bloody teeth clamped down again, taking some skin off the tip of my right index finger.

For a moment nothing happened and I cursed the Norns for telling me that the reliquary was imbued with the truest of deaths, that it could break through all of Jost's magics, crack the sanctuary of Mel's body and cast out Aelia's soul, too long kept from its final journey.

Then at last Mel began to shake, a fifteen on a Richter Scale that only went up to nine, and I kept firm hold of the reliquary's chain, worried she'd bite through it, that the crystal and shard of godly bone would choke her. Black smoke began to pour from her nose and ears and mouth – the Norns had failed to mention *that*! – and I thought with terror of the soot left on the first three women and their surroundings. Mel's abdomen swelled as if she were pregnant, as if something was clinging to her from the inside, determined not to depart . . .

Then her eyes flew open to show a swirling mist of reds and purples and yellows. I held my breath: a cosmic battle was being fought within her body and soul and there was nothing more I could do. Now it was all down to Mel.

At last her eyes cleared and she gave a great heave, expelling the last of the black cloud. It hit the ceiling, spilling across the white moulding like fire, roiling for a moment until it looked like it was pulled away by a powerful exhaust fan, out through the gaps in the window frame.

Death had finally got hold of the Lady Aelia. I hoped the Boatman was feeling super-alert.

Mel sat up, coughing, spat out the reliquary and threw up on the fancy antique dress, which made me happy.

'Mel, are you okay? The near-body-snatching notwithstanding?'

'What the fuck did that *prick* do to me? Where's Lizzie?' Her voice was husky, as if she'd been strangled, but she was good and angry, which made me think she'd be fine.

'No time to explain beyond "Not marriage material", and Lizzie is with McIntyre; she's safe.'

I helped her off the bed and supported her out to the lounge.

Jost was lying prone on the polished wooden floor with Ziggi sitting on his back. Lacy Oldman, no longer wearing the Merrily Vaughan glamour but definitely still wearing her eighties dress, was re-arming a non-regulation Taser.

'Good work, Oldman. Definitely no more traffic duty for you.'

Any reply she might have made was lost in Jost's scream of rage as he realised Mel was *Mel*, not some super-hybrid Byzantian/Brisbanian. I guessed Ziggi had probably been a little *laissez-faire* in his attitude towards the handsome Archivist, thinking him not much more than a pretty boy, but through the tears in Jost's T-shirt I could see where he'd been tattooed. The intricately designed patterns and words in a tongue I couldn't understand running across his skin suggested Jost wasn't averse to getting some mystical body art to do some of the heavy lifting on his spells. My uncle definitely should have wrapped the border wolf in the silver chains as soon as the Archivist was on the ground, but he hadn't yet; they were still by the open front door.

With a mighty roar, Jost threw off Ziggi and as he rose, he transformed until he was fully-furred and lupine. Oldman showed a flash of extreme good sense and threw herself out of Jost's way as he charged towards me. I shoved Mel after Lacy, then waited for what felt like the longest, dumbest seconds in the history of everything before stepping aside and throwing my right arm out horizontally

– and Jost ran into a stiff arm of which a professional rugby player would have been proud. He kind of swung up and then fell straight down onto his back, gasping for air.

Who needed a sword?

I took a couple of steps and kicked him in the ribs.

Mel got a bit of a run up and kicked him in the crotch.

I think we both felt happier.

Ziggi, on his feet again and vaguely embarrassed by being so easily tossed, got the shackle on Jost's right hairy wrist. The fur there began to smoke immediately and the border wolf added a thin scream to his gasping. Ziggi looked around for somewhere to anchor the other end of the chain.

'The back landing,' I said.

He dragged Jost through the lounge and kitchen like an unwilling puppy, kicked open the door and wrapped the chain twice around the metal rails before securing the lock.

'Fuck!' I'd abandoned the reliquary in Mel's room. I hurried back, but both the midnight blue box and the crystal were still there. As quickly as I could I wiped the reliquary clean on my ruined dress, then thrust it back into the box and snapped the lid shut. I sat on the floor, shuddering, my back against the mattress, listening for the sound I'd heard only once before, the terrifying noise of an angel's wings beating the air.

One minute.

Five . . . ten . . .

Ziggi and Mel and Lacy all waited silently in the doorway, watching me, waiting.

Nothing.

Nothing landed on the roof.

Nothing ripped through the house.

Nothing tore my friends apart and shrieked at me for breaking faith.

Whatever had the Guardian's attention, it warranted more than I did.

For the moment I'd take whatever reprieve I could get.

Chapter Thirty-Six

The nuns' residence at St Agnes' was *not* a hive of activity when we arrived. Lacy had taken Mel to McIntyre's and I'd made them promise to hunker down there until I told them it was safe to do otherwise. Ziggi warned me while we were en route that Bela's faith in the Weyrd of Brisneyland had been sadly misplaced – although it wasn't so much an active betrayal, more simply a refusal to show up and fight. As if that made it any better. *Wait and see*, was the community mantra, so Bela shouldn't have been surprised. No group so often run out of town survived by going gung-ho into every fight that came up. Still, I felt sorry for him; it had to be a blow.

I'd taken five minutes to shower and change. If I was going to die this day, I didn't want it to be in my funeral frock, no matter how appropriate that might have been. The midnight blue velvet box was in the pocket of my leather jacket with the silver flask and Reaper was slung across my back.

Dress for the job you want, in my case: Being Not Dead.

Apparently I still looked like shit, even in clean jeans and T-shirt, because when we walked in, Ingo, who was yet again on toast-making duty, told me, 'You look like shit.'

Sister Bridget softened the blow by handing me a jammy slice, then said, 'You really do.'

You'd have thought someone who had a major black mark beside their name for hiding Tobit would have been a little bit more circumspect. One day very soon we were going to have a little talk about that – although as Ziggi did point out, I'd never actually *told* Sister Bridget I was looking for the recalcitrant angel, and she wasn't, as far as he knew, a mind-reader.

'Thanks for the positive reinforcement, guys. Ingo, are you all prepped?'

He nodded.

'Got your formulas right this time?'

He grinned goofily. 'Yeah. Pinpoint-accurate.'

'Better be.' I finished the toast, gestured for more, even remembered to say *please*. 'Where's Bela?'

'Sulking in the common room. He's with Harmsorgi.'

He'd keep. 'Only to be expected. Ziggi, do you wanna . . . ?'

'Not really.'

'Just go.' He did with much grumbling; apparently without me there as a buffer Bela and Ziggi's interactions had become a little rough. Something else I'd have to deal with. 'Now, where's my mother?'

'Upstairs, talking to Joyce.' The nun was a little stingy with the jam this time.

'Sister Bridget, *why* is Joyce not in her hospital bed?'

'They had to move her due to the incident.'

'What kind of an incident?' I almost didn't want to know.

'The kind where Joyce removed someone's hand from their arm with a Japanese fighting fan,' said the nun lightly.

'Then your mother, who was in the next room – *amazing* hearing, by the way – removed his head from his shoulders with a sword,' added Ingo with relish.

'Yeah, she does that.' I closed my eyes. 'Who was it?'

'There was a lot of blood.' Sister Bridget looked at if she couldn't decide whether her tone should be admiring or censorious. 'Why don't you talk to them?'

I rolled my eyes but no one was giving me anything else. 'Fine.'

Upstairs, I found the room they were in on the fifth try. Olivia was sitting on the edge of Joyce's bed. Joyce didn't have her leg in a cast any more – Louise's quality work, I'd bet – but there were still plenty of bandages. She and my mother were holding hands and they were both crying. It was all very cosy.

I leaned in the doorway. 'I'm relieved to see you're both intact. I hear someone else isn't.'

Olivia rose and came to me and for a brief moment that space in her arms was the nicest, safest place in the world. 'Verity. Are you okay?'

'Yep. One border wolf dealt with, Mel rescued from becoming a duplex personality with a Byzantine witch-princess, plus I had jammy toast.'

She narrowed her eyes. 'I meant about—'

'I know what you meant, but I don't have any answers about them yet. And I really need to concentrate on something else or I'm going to cry and if I start I don't know if I'll stop.' I filled them in on the useful bits of my meeting with the Norns and Harmsorgi Odinsay, how we'd rescued Mel and how Jost Marolf was currently cooling his heels on a very small back landing in Norman Park.

'They'll be alive, Fassbinder,' said Joyce through bruised lips. 'There's no value in them dead.'

'That's what I'm hanging onto.' I let my mother go and dragged a chair over to Joyce's bed, sitting carefully so I didn't get the sword caught on anything, especially not anything that was *me*. Olivia returned to her previous position. 'So, what happened?'

'It was Mike, Verity,' Olivia said softly.

'Monobrow Mike? As in *Mike Jones*? But he was . . . wasn't he killed or MIA? He's been on duty at Third Eye Books . . .'

'Well, we think he's the one who took Merrily.' She gave Joyce a sidelong glance and my stomach twisted.

'I . . . did something bad,' muttered Joyce. That was going to be a long list. I rolled my hand at her: *go on*.

'I . . . the Guardian told me to bring him back into the fold.'

'*Shit,* Joyce! Whatever happened to the whole collegial let's-defeat-the-crazed-archangel-together deal?'

'This was *before*. This was before you showed me what *he* was, before . . .'

'*So why the fuck didn't you say something before now?*'

'Um . . . you might recall I tried to, in the car just before we got T-boned?'

'Moments, Joyce, choose your moments!'

'I did not know we were going to be the victims of an attempted assassination-by-Mercedes.'

Mike, still desperately hurt and grieving, not thinking straight and determined to have Jerry back at any cost, no matter how many times I told him there was no coming back for the Weyrd . . .

'Mike came into the hospital – V, he took out Septimus' – I'd had that awful feeling Septimus was never going to find out how *War and Peace* ended – 'and then he came for Joyce.'

'So the Guardian's tying up loose ends. Joyce, did you know what was going to happen to Merrily?' I asked.

She shook her head vehemently. 'No – I didn't know anything about her when I made the offer. When he accepted, I just told him who to report to.'

'Which was?' I closed my eyes.

'Udo Forsythe. I *promise* I didn't know what happened after that, who was being targeted. I didn't know it was Merrily.'

I thought about hearing the voice from the baptismal font talking to the Guardian when I'd gone looking for Joyce in the Underworld. Of course Udo, with his lust for power and position, was precisely the sort the Guardian could seduce, someone already with a hole in their soul.

'The Guardian and Udo: a match truly made in the Underworld.' I scratched at my scalp. 'Udo doesn't like me, but is that really enough reason to do all this — just to fuck with me?'

'You are polarising, darling—'

'Thanks, Mother.'

'—but I do tend to agree.'

I sat in the chair beside the bed. 'Udo's after power, the Guardian is after the grail. Just because he never had you two hunting for it, that doesn't mean there wasn't someone else before me. Udo's relatively new to power and he wants more. And folk with something to prove, especially those who are convinced there's a blot on their bloodline, will do a lot to try and make it go away: to make themselves and others forget. The Guardian finds people with *wants*, and Udo took my family because the Guardian told him to . . . which means the Guardian suspected I'd been playing him false.'

I felt sick. But there was still a chance they were safe in the Bishop's Palace. Udo wouldn't give up all his trump cards at once.

'How did Udo know about Merrily, though?' Olivia asked.

'He was the Odinsays' steward back in the old days so he must have known they bred their grails. Maybe he saw a photo of Merrily — she looks a lot like her mother, Harmsorgi said. Bela would have had to have told Sandor that he was putting a security detail on Merrily, and Udo's been sticking to Sandor like glue for weeks.'

'What's the plan then, Fassbinder?' Joyce shifted against her pillows as if about to leave the bed.

'The plan is for you to stay here with Sister Bridget – no, don't give me that look. What are you going to do with a broken leg?'

'I can throw my fan,' she grumbled.

'Which is not a boomerang, so it isn't going to come back to you. You're a liability.' I crossed my arms, set my jaw. 'You're staying here – not least of all because if anyone tries to sneak in here, Sister Bridget can deal with them.'

'She's really scary.'

'I know.'

'Then?' asked my mother.

'How are you feeling, Mother-mine? Up for an incursion? Some minor bloodbathery?'

'Have you met me?'

'I don't know why the Guardian hasn't come for me yet – I used the reliquary, which must surely have sent out a signal. So I can only assume he's still . . . healing, using Merrily however he needs to.' I dropped my head into my heads; I was bone-weary. 'My priority is to get David and Maisie. Forsythe has closed the Bishop's Palace so I'm willing to bet they're there. It'll be warded like a fortress, which means any full-blooded Weyrd not already inside its walls can't get in. Yet I, unworthy mixed-blood mishmash that I am—'

'Don't listen to them, darling.'

'Thank you, Mother. However, *I* can walk through most wards without triggering them. I'm not enough of one thing or the other to excite eldritch attention.' I grinned. 'And I have a theory about you.'

'Which is?'

'You were changed by death and the powers the Guardian gave you. You're not Weyrd, but you're not Normal either.'

'That might be the nicest thing anyone's ever said to me.'

'I'm willing to bet you won't sound any alarm bells either.' I rose, felt the weight of the midnight blue box swing in my jacket pocket. 'Okay, I have a couple more people to talk to, but I'll count you in for the storming of the castle.'

'Before you go, darling,' Olivia said, 'maybe you need some lessons?'

'In storming castles?'

'No, with *that*.' She pointed over my shoulder to where the hilt of Reaper was showing.

I heaved myself up the ladder, right shoulder hurting like nobody's business after half an hour of instruction in the use of a sword – which as far as I could tell had had no discernible effect on my skills – to find Tobit out perched on one of the low walls running around the edge of the roof, threatening to crumble it beneath his own weight.

'Come to any decisions about your life choices yet?' I called, and groaned. There was a real chance that the pain in my shoulder had rendered me more likely to be killed than do any killing. It wasn't that I was totally unfit, but the motions of swashing and buckling weren't ones my muscles were used to.

Tobit's wings flapped, startled by my sudden appearance, and the breeze threatened to knock me off the roof. 'Oi!'

'Sorry.'

'No, you're not. Jeez, you angels have the best PR machine ever. Everyone thinks you're fluffy and helpful but you're really just arseholes with wings. You're like . . . cuckoos – or cats.'

'Did you run out of people to annoy inside the building? That's unlikely, even for you.'

'It's a very small crowd.' I sat next to him. 'So, what are my chances against an archangel who's had all powers restored unto him?'

'Not good. Even with Reaper.'

'Oh, ye of little faith.'

'I've got faith, just . . .'

'Not in me. I get it.' If we'd been higher up I'd have looked at the city skyline, but buried as we were in the hollow behind St Agnes', I just stared at the red brick of the hospital wing across from us. 'I need help. The Norns . . . I don't think they'll come.'

'Why would they? They've never risked themselves as long as I've known them.' His tone was bitter, which was pretty rich for someone who'd made a point of taking care of no one but himself.

'I'm looking for something in terms of a superpower. See, I remember a year ago, when the Arch came to St Mary's looking for your daughter, I remember you being dragged along behind him like a whipped dog. But I also remember this: he was no bigger than you.'

'He came with legions.'

'Yeah, well, no. He came with five lesser angels, any and all of whose backsides could have been handed to them on platters. By you, not by me, obviously; I only managed to take one out and that was by accident.' I smiled. 'But you? Now, you're a different matter.'

'Don't.'

'A Prince of Heaven no less, right hand or left pinky of God itself: greater than Lucifer, blessed and favoured. Mightier than Michael or Gabriel or Uriel. Yet you trusted Ramiel. You didn't see what was coming . . . Or did you? You've got some guilt on you, Tobit: some mighty burden *way* beyond simply letting down the Lord.' I steepled my fingers. 'You let the Arch catch you and beat you when you could have beaten it. Or you could at least have tried to fight, but there were no defensive wounds on you and no marks on any of the Crusaders to show you'd fought back. You keep sinking into despond with depressing regularity. You're guilty because you were complicit.'

He said nothing, but his wings quivered.

'Here's the thing: I don't need to know the details, but I do need you on board. I need you because my husband and my daughter are in danger and you are my last hope. Even if the Guardian, Ramiel, whatever he wants to call himself, is healed in body, I cannot imagine he will be in spirit. He was nuts before he burned and fell and it's worse now, because he will just be nuts inside a healthy body with no conscience and the moral compass of a pinwheel.'

I leaned close to him and my nostrils filled with the floral scent of him. 'Oh, and if I lose David and Maisie because of your self-pity? I do not care how long it takes me but I will make you regret the day you were born, created, hatched, whatever the fuck happens with angels. And before you say something whiny like, "Oh it's too late, Verity Fassbinder, my life has been a vale of regret since I let my brother carry out his plan all those centuries ago", remember this: *I have Olivia Fassbinder on my side*. And if you think I'm bad? She's *angel-enhanced* worse.'

He gave me a long look. 'What do you want me to do?'

I pushed myself away from my perch. 'I want you to pull your pretty head out of your arse. I want you to start being a decent father to your daughter and a support to Christos. I want you to be a better angel to this city. But most of all, I want you in the air and close to the Bishop's Palace. You're not going to set off any alarms because you're not Weyrd and anyway, you can do the whole Romulan cloaking device thing, which is handy.

'I want you to have my back when Ramiel comes for me.' I sighed.

'Do all this, Tobit, and I will tell you where your broken god is – and better still, I'll never tell it what you did.'

I headed back towards the ladder. I could feel his silver eyes boring into my neck. At the door I turned and said, 'Oh, and set your mobile to vibrate.'

'So, where is he? The Guardian?'

In the common room, Bela was eating non-buttered Arrowroot biscuits – he really didn't know what he was missing. Ziggi handed me my third coffee; it was instant and truly awful, but I'd only managed to grab a forty-minute nap and tea was just not going to cut it. My eyes felt gritty and my feeble sword arm ached, but I didn't have the luxury of giving in to exhaustion, no matter how much I wanted to.

'I don't know. Harmsorgi was kind of vague about how long it might take the grail to repair a seriously destroyed archangel – you know, oddly, there's not a lot of data on that sort of thing – but he thought it might take a couple of days for a human or a Weyrd, depending on the extent of injuries.'

'So what do *you* think?'

'I think we're going to be in trouble as soon as I bring out the reliquary again. That's what he's looking for; that's what he will home in on. I used it on Mel, but I think maybe he was still being repaired and wasn't in a position to come after me. But even if he's fine now, I don't think he will appear until he knows where I am. He knows I played him false, so he will want to hurt my family in front of me. And on that cheery thought: where will they have David and Maisie in the Palace?'

'My guess is the cells, probably Aviva's. Forsythe would consider it easily defensible, not to mention an insult to put them there.'

'Nice.'

'You'll need a key.'

'I'll break it. Remember? I pulled the door off the Archives. Gods, you're going to have to recruit for a new Archivist.'

'Let's clean up the current staffing mess first, shall we?'

'Good plan.'

Bela hesitated before saying, 'Are you sure you want to go through with this?'

'The alternative would be?'

'Okay. We'll be ready and waiting for your signal.'

'You know, I wish I could trust Dusana – I could really use her casting skills . . . but I guess we're on our own.'

'We've got Titania and I think she will more than make up for any lack of Dusana's abilities.'

'Really? Is Titania well enough?'

'Since she didn't have to do a second summoning of Aviva for you, she's spent the time resting, and Louise has been watching over her. She'll do. And she's the only one of the Weyrd who heeded my call,' he added morosely. In the corner Ziggi rolled his eyes.

'Excellent. Maybe we've got a chance.'

'I doubt it.'

'Bela? Look, I'm sorry they let you down, you know. I'm sorry they—'

'You said it would happen. I should have listened to you.'

'It doesn't make me feel any better, you know, to see you brought low.' I touched his cheek, thinking how angry I still was with him, and swallowed it down for old time's sake. 'We'll deal with that later, and I promise I'll stand with you. Okay, I'll go and get my mother. Ziggi, be a dear and bring the car around? Fassbinders United: you break it, we'll make it worse, and all that.'

'V?'

'Yep?'

'Be careful.'

I gave him a double thumbs-up and headed for the bathroom, where I promptly threw up everything in my stomach.

Chapter Thirty-Seven

The Bishop's Palace was perched on the high ground at Hamilton, a glamoured nineteenth-century sandstone building which housed Sandor Verhoeven, his aide-de-camp Guillaume, half a dozen servants and a fairly large corps of Weyrd bodyguards. I wondered how Forsythe had managed to circumvent them, as they'd always appeared to be impressively loyal to Sandor. Maybe Udo'd gradually replaced them with his own people, and Sandor hadn't even noticed it happening.

Beneath the pretty rooms with their antique treasures and coats of dust – Sandor Verhoeven was notoriously unfond of change and, apparently, dusting – were the specially constructed and warded cells in the basement. Eleanor Aviva had spent the last part of her life in one until Dusana Nadasy had ended it. There was a good chance that Dusana would spend quite a few years there herself when – *if* – the whole coup business got sorted out. Then again, having cunningly saved her life in what might prove to be the dumbest way known to man, I would probably have to think up some alternative for her now she was my thrall.

The Palace faced Annie Street behind a high black metal fence. A small redbrick gatehouse guarded the driveway, and according to Ziggi, a lot of the security detail gathered in there. There were houses on either side and across the road, big ones, with equally big yards and densely planted gardens that allowed the very rich to yell at each other in privacy and not bother the neighbours.

If you were cunning and knew what you were doing, you asked your uncle to drive to the very end of Langside Road, which was well and truly behind the Palace, and got him to wait there with Louise the healer, whose skills were very probably going to be needed before the night was out. Then you and your mother could creep along what anywhere else in the world might have been called a bridlepath, but because this was Brisneyland, it was known as 'one of those sneaky little spots' that went between houses while not quite trespassing on their yards, right to a blind spot in the fence around the Bishop's Palace.

I'd known about this blind spot because it's precisely the sort of information I sought out, hoarding it away for ages until it was needed in order to do my job.

It was still winter-dark, but dawn would be on us in maybe half an hour. Ideally, we'd be in and out with my family before then, but in the event of the unexpected – and let's face it, no battle plan survives contact with the enemy – I'd have to improvise.

That always went well.

There were no footholds on the smooth metal railings and nothing low enough for me to grab and haul myself up, so Olivia linked her fingers into a step and gave me a lift. In fact, she put a little too much effort into it and I ended up dangling on the other side, wrenching a shoulder already made sore by sword-practice. My mother, super-soldier, made it over in one leap, then helped me down.

So far, so undignified.

'Well, that was graceful, dear.'

'Shut up, Mother.'

I was grateful for the thick foliage and groundcover between the spreading jacaranda and poinciana trees. We were quick and quiet and made it to the edge of the kitchen garden without attracting any undue attention. That wasn't to say there weren't any Weyrd around, but if you're used to looking for them you can pick up the gleam of eyes in any number of brilliant colours, and the flare of cigarettes, the telltale smudge of exhaled smoke against the darkness. I knew some of the faces, but I didn't know who I could trust.

I pointed to the back door leading to the kitchen and we both squinted, trying to make out who was slumped against the frame, taking a drag on a cigarillo, beneath a small lamp casting weak yellow light. It was not a large Weyrd by any means; slight of form and nervous of movement. Only when he lifted his head to blow away the smoke did I recognise Guillaume, Sandor Verhoeven's personal secretary, aide-de-camp, what-have-you. He was beautiful, with cheekbones that looked like they could hold up vaulted ceilings, but he did *not* look happy. I signalled for Olivia to stay where she was; if I was making a mistake, she could still save the day.

I made a little noise approaching him so he wasn't startled into a shriek that might bring back-up. I let him see my face in the sickly light, made no threatening moves, held my palms up, but I was very aware of the length of the sword across my back. Guillaume stared at me for a few seconds and then something sparked in his eyes. Was that *hope*?

'Please tell me you're here to help?' he whispered urgently, and when I nodded, he murmured, 'Your family is in the cells – they're safe for the moment. Sandor is with them. Udo . . . he hurt him badly trying to get him to sign letters to the Councils of Europe, transferring power to him, to Udo. Sandor refused and Forsythe won't let me call a healer. He's holding it out like a carrot, but I don't know how long Sandor will last.' Tears welled in his eyes. 'Save him, Ms Fassbinder, please. Don't leave him.'

'Don't worry, no Weyrd left behind. There's a healer not far away.' I waved Olivia over. 'Guillaume, is there anyone I can rely on inside?'

'No one else is in there but Udo and that fucker Sulla' — Olivia's face hardened at the mention of the name — 'and they're in the library, looking for the Brisbane Grant. Everyone else has been banished to the grounds, although most of them don't know what's happening — oh, they know something's up, but no one's prepared to do anything, risk anything. I'm only allowed in because I can work the coffee machine and find paperwork for him.'

'Except the Brisbane Grant.'

He smiled. 'As far as he's concerned, I've never seen it, let alone handled it. That was the aide before me. Sandor won't tell him, and it's worth more than my life to defy Sandor . . . besides, once Udo gets that parchment, he doesn't need us any more. You know how power passes amongst the Weyrd.'

'Is it easy to get your hands on it without drawing attention?'

He nodded.

'Then grab hold of it and get the Hell out of here. I can't guarantee there won't be some, ah, accidental fire.'

He paled but said, 'Just make sure you burn Forsythe with it.'

'Can do.'

Once inside the kitchen, Guillaume disappeared into the main body of the house and we went down the stone steps to the basement. It's a bit difficult to be totally quiet while wearing Docs or Blundstones, so by the time we got to the bottom, our presence had been noted and the abuse started fairly soon after that. The cells ran along opposite sides of a long room, four to the left, four to the right. Although he couldn't actually see who it was, Verhoeven was clearly continuing a conversation, insulting either Udo or Sulla or both, and in a variety of colourful terms.

'Is that any way to speak to your rescuers?' I appeared in front of the bars of the cell at the far end where Aviva had once been imprisoned.

Sandor's face was a picture when he saw it was me.

As was David's.

The councillor was reclining on the large bed, but facing the bars so he could project his anger in the right direction. There was blood on his chin and the front of his vast white shirt. David was sitting in one of the armchairs. The sight of his face, patterned with dried blood and contusions, made me see red. He limped when he came towards us. I wrapped both hands around the handle on the barred door and pulled with all the rage bubbling inside me. I belatedly hoped the tearing of metal wasn't audible above, but then it didn't matter because there was nothing between us.

His chin was rough with stubble, but his green eyes were steady. I tasted iron when we kissed, and held him gently as he grunted. Broken ribs? Bruised at the very least.

'V.'

'David, I'm so, so sorry.'

'They've got Maisie.' And in his voice was all the guilt of a father who hadn't been able to keep his little girl safe. 'They took her as soon as we arrived – I was busy throwing up from the transit. Christ, V, I'm so fucking sorry—'

'Not your fault, none of this is your fault.' I pressed my forehead to his. 'I'm going to get her back. I'm going to get her now and I'm taking Forsythe's scalp to hang over her crib.'

'You're terrifying. I love you.'

'Love you too. But I'm going to need you to go with Olivia and Sandor here, as is traditional in a jailbreak.'

'I won't go without—'

'My love, you are in no state to help me. I can't look out for you while I'm scalping someone and fighting off his henchman, and Olivia cannot get Sandor out of here on her own. I need you to trust me. This is not the time to get all bolshy and blokey on me.'

'A man with a less healthy self-esteem might feel emasculated by this.'

'Good thing you're not that man. You're a vastly superior beast. Trust me?'

'With my life.'

'I love you. This will be over – well, soonish.'

We kissed again and for a moment nothing else existed beyond us, but I knew we couldn't stay in that place where only two could live, not just yet. When I finally pulled away, I went over to the bed where Sandor was lying and looked down at him, wondering if he was in any fit state to move. 'So.'

'Ms Fassbinder.'

'Been listening to gossip about me, huh?'

'A mistake I will not be making again.'

'Can you walk? Up the stairs and out the back. Oh – how are you going to get over the fence?'

He looked offended. 'Ms Fassbinder, if I cannot blow a section of metal out of a fence I personally set the wards on, then I do not deserve to hold my position in this community.'

'Fair enough. Can you walk with help?' I wasn't sure how much use David was going to be in supporting a heavyweight like Sandor, but he looked determined, like he always did, and I couldn't doubt him. Besides, Olivia needed both hands free if she was going to lead them out of the house. Any fighting needed to done by her; she'd make short work of anyone dumb enough to come against her. 'Louise Arnold is waiting with my uncle. You just need to make it to the end of Langside Road, okay?'

He nodded.

'Who's Udo got on his side? Anything I need to know?'

'You must make sure he doesn't get hold of—'

'—the Brisbane Grant, yeah, all in hand. Guillaume will meet you outside.'

Verhoeven smiled at that. 'Such a fine lad.'

'So again: anything I should know?'

'Udo pays his people; there's no true loyalty there. The fact that of his liegemen he's only allowed Sulla to remain in the house should tell you all you need to know.' Sandor pursed his lips. 'But there is something . . . he keeps talking to himself. I come into a room unexpectedly and he is rubbing that tiepin of his and talking to himself quietly. It is . . . disturbing.'

'Oh, you have no idea.' Most angelics couldn't bear to bring themselves to deal with Weyrd, but this one . . . this one would do anything. 'Don't suppose you happen to know if Udo changed the wards around this place at all? I ask purely because you're the only Weyrd walking out of here now, but if you're going to set off alarm bells . . .'

'He's done nothing more to them. Everything is as I made it almost two hundred years ago. I'm sure he'd have loved to rework things, but first he'd have had to ask me to *un*make the protections and *that* would have made me suspicious.'

'*That* would have done it, huh?'

'I understand that we're going to being having quite the talk when this is all over,' he said in resignation.

'Damn straight. Mum?' Olivia looked up from examining the cuts on David's face. 'Get them to Ziggi.'

'Will do, then I'll be back. I don't think David's ribs are broken.'

'They feel it,' he said, a bit resentfully.

'I know, dear boy.' My mother patted my husband on the shoulder. Good thing he had the calm and balanced nature he did.

'Oh, and V?' he said in that nonchalant tone of his.

'Hmmm?'

'You might want to take him too.'

I followed the direction of his finger to a cell across the way.

Father Tony Caldero sat on a narrow cot in a much smaller, much less fancy cell, staring at the floor like he was regretting booking the economy package. Clearly he'd had good reason for not returning my calls. Apart from being a bit scruffy and beardy, he looked remarkably unharmed in comparison with David and Sandor. Maybe he'd given up his secrets — whatever they were — more easily.

'Father Tony?'

He looked up at me.

'Whatcha doing?'

'I'm so sorry, Verity. It's my fault.'

'Okay, I just really need you guys to get out of here as soon as possible, so let's do that first, then the festival of recriminations can begin. Come on, people, I'm on the clock here.' I 'unlocked' the cell and reached in to heave him to his feet.

'I don't deserve mercy.'

'Look, that's between you and your god, and maybe me if I find out anything really, really bad. But for the moment, let me rescue you. You can give a hand with Sandor, share a bit of the burden with David.'

He followed meekly as a lamb and waited while I went back to help Verhoeven off the bed. As I passed her, I whispered to Olivia, 'Keep an eye on him.'

She gave me a scant nod.

Father Tony looked like he'd been here a while, but Miriam hadn't reported his disappearance — or at least, not to me. Maybe she had told Ziggi or Bela and they hadn't thought to mention it? *Hmmm.*

Leaning over Verhoeven, I asked quietly, 'How long's he been here?'

'He said five days, but he refused to tell me why.'

'Has anyone been to talk to him?'

'I don't know. I . . . didn't know he was here until they brought me down after Ligeia's funeral.'

'So they pretty much put you in here as soon as my family arrived?'

He nodded. 'All subterfuge was done with then.' He grabbed my hand. 'My sincerest apologies, Ms Fassbinder.'

'Yeah.' I helped him up, thankful for my Weyrd strength. 'Be careful.'

I helped Verhoeven up the stairs before handing him off to David and Father Tony.

I hugged Olivia, and she said, 'Don't start the party without me,' and squeezed me tight. I kissed David one last time, wishing we were anywhere but here, any time but now. Then I stepped away from him before I started crying.

I watched them disappear, then took five minutes to give them time to make it to the far end of the garden and collect my thoughts. Hopefully, Verhoeven's making-a-hole-in-the-fence spell would be a quiet one. Finally, I took a deep breath and stepped out of the kitchen into the corridor that would lead me to the marble-tiled foyer and the staircase that curved up to the first floor and the library where Udo Forsythe and Sulla were no doubt plotting plots and scheming schemes.

Chapter Thirty-Eight

Yet again I was struck by the state of living decay in the Bishop's Palace. Guillaume had once explained Sandor Verhoeven's antipathy to change, so I imagined the young man spent a lot of his time maintaining the perfect balance between chaos and stasis. The Palace was half ruin, half preserved archaeological site. There was a room filled with newspapers, which still freaked me out; any stray sparks would light it up like a bonfire . . . but then all the beautiful books would burn too. I made a mental note to do my best *not* to start any conflagrations.

I paused on the landing to take in the panelled walls with their grim-faced paintings of Verhoeven's ancestors and other High Weyrd. The ceiling fresco populated by naked winged babies, women in diaphanous robes and armoured warriors riding clouds was still flaking, one lacy fragment of gold leaf or tempera at a time. The chandelier suspended over the marble floor looked to be holding on by cobwebs alone. I kept moving along the Persian-carpeted corridor, past loveseats and mother-of-pearl-inlaid tables, hat-stands, candelabras, vases of crystal, suits of armour, bronze busts, Ormolu clocks, leather and gold-embossed books.

A number of doors were open but voices and paper-shuffling came from only one, so that was where I stopped and listened, one hand resting on Reaper's hilt.

There was a rustling, then the sound of something being thrown in a temper, followed by profanities and some hissing.

'Where would he have put it? That fat *shit*. Where would he put it?' Udo did not sound like a happy camper.

'The old bastard's smart enough not to have trusted anyone else with the location.' That would be Sulla, gravel-voiced, matter-of-fact, thoroughly bored, if I wasn't very much mistaken. 'And he doesn't care if you tear one of his people apart because his power is more important to him. While not impervious to pain, he certainly does absorb a lot of it. I don't know what else to do.'

'Find me the fucking grant, Sulla! Why else are you here?' There was smashing, a sound suspiciously familiar to something going through one of the stained-glass windows I knew lined the library. 'Go and get that child.'

'Udo—'

'Take the child down to the cells and see how Mister Fucking Lord High and Mighty Councillor Verhoeven likes watching a piece be carved out of *it*. See how its father likes it. If nothing else, it will set them against each other . . .'

Sulla said nothing else, but I heard booted footsteps crossing the floor. If I could find Maisie before anything else, I would do so. I swallowed and backed away, slipped into one of the other rooms but left the door open a tiny crack and watched. Sulla was a head taller than me, shaven-headed, muscular, with scars on his face and neck, wearing navy combats and a black T-shirt, no jacket. Tattoos wound their way up his arms but they didn't look like anything more than artwork, nothing to strengthen his magics or keep an extra-strong glamour in place. I waited until he walked past the landing and had turned left at the end of the corridor before I followed.

There was no sign of him when I rounded the corner, but I kept moving, listening, feeling sick. I didn't want to have to wait until he came back with my baby in his arms – even I wasn't that irresponsible a mother. Eventually, though, after far too many twists and turns, I found at the very end of the hallway, away from everything else, the makeshift nursery as imagined by someone who'd never actually met a small child. It was a bedroom, filled with antiques and more dust. On the musty embroidered green quilt of the four-poster bed, pillows had been laid out in a laager apparently meant to keep a baby from rolling off the mattress. In the middle of it lay my little ginger ninja, wide awake, quiet as a mouse, with a teddy bear I didn't recognise held in a vice-like grip. And yes, she had definitely grown.

There was a distinct lack of Sulla, however, and anxiety made me careless. I crossed the threshold and took three steps into the room . . . and then he was behind me, pressed hard against my back, the length of Reaper between us and a cold blade against my throat.

Fuck. It. All.

'Easy now,' we said simultaneously.

Cue: quiet pause of surprise.

There was even more surprise when Sulla let me go, slowly, and pushed me away gently, leaving Reaper in my possession. I moved off equally slowly and gently and, resisting the urge to rush to my daughter, turned to face him.

Sulla held his dagger up, showing he meant no harm, or at least not much, then slid it back up his sleeve.

'Okay?'

'Udo's lost the plot. I don't think his carriage stops at all the stations.'

'To put it mildly.'

'He thinks he's going to get away with all this? That the European cabals are just going to let him blithely take over this backwater?'

While I bridled at the term 'backwater', I did realise it wasn't the time to argue appropriate semantics. 'Realistically, they probably will. Power taken is power kept.'

He shrugged. 'Look, I don't mind hurting adults. I don't want to hurt your child.'

'The child and I appreciate that. So, what *do* you want?' I knew little of Sulla; he'd been part of the package deal with Forsythe's house, employed by him alone.

'A place after he's gone. Working for the Council. Immunity.'

Plus a nice shiny unicorn. 'Were you the one who hurt my husband?'

He nodded. 'Yes.'

'Refreshing honesty. What about Verhoeven? Did you injure him?'

'Nope. Udo wanted that pleasure all for himself.'

'Right.' I rubbed my sweaty palms on the thighs of my jeans. 'I can't promise anything, except that I will ask Bela for clemency. Even then I'm not sure how much influence I have.'

'What about the damage to your husband?' He looked pained. 'I kind of like him; he's a nice guy.'

'Which is why *he* probably won't punch you out – but I will, when all this is done, just to teach you a lesson.'

'Fair.'

There was a noise at the door: Olivia, with a glint in her eye that I didn't like and a sword in her hand that I liked even less. 'Mum, no!'

She did hesitate, I'll give her that. Maybe it was the use of the word 'Mum'. I wondered how much of her rage was wounded professional pride: Sulla had kidnapped her grandchild and son-in-law on her watch.

'This piece of shit betrayed us. He was trusted, and he stole David and Maisie away.'

'That's true, but I've given my word.' Plus, I definitely didn't need the noise of a fight alerting Forsythe that all was not well, nor did I want Sulla turning on me. His scruples about child mutilation aside, I didn't really trust him. He was only looking out for his own skin, having discovered Udo's brand of crazy a little too extreme even for his tastes. 'Don't mess with my professional reputation, Mother.'

She glared at me, then at Sulla, but put her sword away and *at last* I turned and picked up my little girl, who cooed and wrapped her little fingers through my hair, her tiny lips resting against my neck. The smell of her was heavenly, so familiar and yet so heartbreakingly foreign after our time apart. Although it seemed impossible, she was bigger, pudgier, her hair longer, her eyes greener, her skin even more peaches and cream. It wasn't just the hormones taking over, making me stupid; she had definitely grown like a weed. Was she going to be six feet tall by the age of five? She was heavy and damp in my arms, with a wet nappy, and I didn't care at all: she was *mine*.

'Mum, how'd she get so *big*?'

'Vegemite on toast?' Olivia suggested, then thought better of it. 'Weyrd blood. You did the same. She'll stabilise, don't worry.'

'I don't want to interrupt this charming reunion, but Udo will be expecting to hear screams pretty soon.' Sulla sounded genuinely apologetic.

Reluctantly, I handed Maisie over to my mother. My daughter looked displeased, but she didn't cry, and that made me proud. 'Take her to David, Mum. Get her away from here. And I know you want to argue with me, but please don't. Responsible mothers don't take their children into eldritch battles.'

She frowned, but she really wasn't in a position to debate parenting strategies with me.

'You,' I pointed at Sulla, 'are coming with me.'

Olivia took off, Maisie in her arms, and Sulla and I headed back to the library where Udo Forsythe waited to hear my child's screams. At the entrance, I stood back and let Sulla go in first, which turned out to be a wise move.

He pushed the door open and stepped into the breach . . . then I heard the sound of something thudding into his body and the *whoosh* of breath leaving him. He tipped backwards over the threshold, landing half-in, half-out of the library. I looked down at the surprised expression on his face and took in both the silver filigree dagger sticking out of his chest and the dead eyes staring up at the painted ceiling at all the cherubs that might not actually sing him to his rest.

A strangled curse inside the room told me that *this* was not the intended outcome, which might have made Sulla feel better about it, if he'd known. Or maybe not. I risked a quick look around the doorframe. Forsythe was standing behind an enormous mahogany desk covered with tomes, scrolls and scattered papers. Towers of books had been overturned and slid in fans across the floor. A leather armchair was lying on its side, as was a small coffee table; what looked like a Victorian footstool had had its needlepoint cover ripped off – presumably by the knife now embedded in Sulla – and the stuffing torn out. There was no fire in the hearth – maybe Udo shared my distrust of paper and flames? – and the room was very, very cold.

'That was unfriendly.' I stepped inside.

The way his hands were clutching and clenching told me he had no weapons left. His first throw had been his only toss of the dice.

'Why did you do that?'

'I thought it was you. *He* said you would be coming.'

'The Guardian?'

'He said he sensed . . . *something*.'

That would have been the use of the reliquary on Mel.

'He's waiting, isn't he? For me?'

He nodded, smiled nastily. 'He doesn't like traitors. He's not too fond of your mother either.'

I strode quickly to the desk, leaned across and tugged his tiepin from his cravat. The fabric ripped with that sort of shrieking protest only *really* expensive material gives. I dropped the yellow-stoned thing on the carpet and ground it beneath my boot. When it was utter dust I asked, 'Was that the only gift the Guardian gave you?'

His wide-eyed, open-jawed stare told me yes, and that without it, without his means of speaking to the Guardian, he was lost.

'How long have you been a minion for an archangel?'

'I am no minion!'

'I beg to differ, Udo. Let's face it, you *specialise* in being a minion: you were one for the Odinsays and I've no doubt for many other families before them, each time working your way up to bigger and better minioning, until one of the Guardian's other minions approached you. Then you came back here when you had enough power, figured enough people had forgotten you were once an errand boy. That's why you chose Brisbane, isn't it? It's a nice little place to make your own, no grand cadres or cabals to deal with like in Europe – no one cares about this spot.' I gestured as though the library was *everything*. 'You start here, go on to bigger and better things later. Or maybe not. Maybe a tiny empire is enough – better than no empire, after all.'

He said nothing, just glared.

'How did you know? About the Guardian?'

He smiled, a slick reptilian thing. 'Aviva. She locked up downstairs and happy for the company.'

'Did you promise her clemency when you'd taken over from Sandor?'

'What else? And money and position. She was a simple creature.'

'What a bugger when Dusana took her out.'

'An inconvenience that it was sooner than I'd have preferred, but Aviva was ever the schemer. Once let loose from her cage, I couldn't have trusted her to keep faith with me. She'd have been negotiating with the next assassin, the next insurgent.'

'You'd have had to get rid of her eventually.' A thought occurred to me. 'I bet you own Concord Holdings. The Guardian says, *Get Joyce a car . . .*'

'My reach is long.'

I grabbed him again, by the throat this time, and pulled him across the desk, dislodging more books, more papers. 'As is mine. So: Merrily Vaughan.'

He blinked.

'The grail.'

When he grinned, understanding dawning, I realised I really wanted to see some pink on his teeth, so I slapped him a couple of times without moderating my blows. He looked surprised, but he probably shouldn't have been; then again, probably no one had manhandled him in a long while.

'Where is Merrily Vaughan?'

'Delivered to the Underworld, to the one who needs her.'

'And how do you know that? You can't go there; no Weyrd can. You need a Normal for that. And surely you've noted that Mike Jones hasn't reported in for a while.'

His eyes slid to a corner of the library and I followed his gaze.

Crouched on a stool like a turtle, curled in shame, was a little lilac-haired woman. *Miriam Parry*. Tears had carved gaps in her make-up, her normally immaculate hair was dishevelled and her dress dirty. I gave Udo a good shake even as I said, 'Oh, Miriam.'

'They took my Antonio.' She began to cry.

And there was the answer to my long-time suspicions about the true nature of her relationship with Father Tony Caldero. Now I understood why Father Tony had been apologising to me; he knew how Miriam was trying to save him. 'You needed a Normal to ferry things below. The Guardian seeks out grief. Miriam, what happened?'

'There's talk of closing St Barbara's,' Miriam sobbed, 'and Antonio returning to Rome, to the Vatican – and where would that leave me? They'd *never* let me go with him.' She hiccoughed. 'I tried to help when I sent you to Bridget; I knew you wouldn't let things go. I tried, but I was so scared they'd do something to Antonio if I didn't do what they told me to . . .'

'Miriam, get up. Come over here. No, don't look at him: he can't do anything to you any more. Father Tony is safe, okay? I freed him. Now, I want you to go out the back way, through the kitchen. Out the garden, to the left as you leave, okay? Go to the back fence, you'll find your way. Father Tony will be there, okay?'

'Thank you, Ms Fassbinder—'

'Don't tell me you're sorry. Hurry along now, Miriam.'

I waited as she pulled herself together and scurried past me.

I looked at Udo Forsythe, wondering what to do. 'You were going to carve slices off my child.'

He didn't answer.

'You have betrayed the community that not only gave you a home but also a position. You have dealt with a creature determined to wreak havoc – why do you think the Guardian would keep his word to you? Why would you think, when healed and powerful – although still as crazy as a shithouse rat – the Guardian would have any honour?

He's an *archangel*, Udo. He will chew you up and spit you out. You know how much they hate your kind.'

From my jacket pocket I pulled the last thing I'd thought I'd need, but couldn't quite bring myself to leave behind: a silver flask holding the final drops of the Waters of Forgetting. I didn't know what it would do to a living being, but the Boatman had warned me not to drink it. What I *wanted* was take Udo's head off – but this was the next best thing, at least until he could be dealt with by Verhoeven and Bela. I could think of no more fitting punishment than for someone so obsessed with name, reputation and position than to forget his entirely.

'Drink.'

'Poison?' he asked scornfully.

'Fan though I am of the classics, no. Just drink.'

I don't think he believed me, but when I reached for Reaper – I didn't get it more than a couple of inches from its sheath – he took the flask and drank down the dregs. I watched as his stare grew dull, his expression slack and child-like. I still wanted to kick the shit out of him, but it was a credit to my restraint that I didn't.

'Who am I?' he asked in a small voice.

I shook my head. 'I don't know.'

I led him down the stairs and out the back door, telling him to go and sit under the trees until I came for him. Once I saw him settled, I went back inside, then moved through the house to the entrance hall once more. In the foyer, I unsheathed Reaper although I was horribly aware that I was so grossly underqualified in its use that it was a joke. From my pocket I drew the midnight blue box and with a sigh I flipped open the lid.

The reliquary shone like a beacon.

I slid the chain around my neck, feeling like I might as well be walking through a safari park with a big juicy steak in my hands.

At the front door, I needed three deep breaths before I could force myself to turn the handle and step outside. I was greeted by ten pairs of eyes, all of them belonging to the Weyrd security Udo had banished from the palace.

Chapter Thirty-Nine

All those brightly coloured eyes were glowing at me as the last wisps of night were burned away by dawn's light. There were sparks of recognition in their faces, but none of them went for weapons, even if a couple were already half-shifted into things with fangs. I stood on the front step of the Bishop's Palace, my sword held hipster-level casual, so as not to appear a threat, and said, 'So, this coup is over and done with.'

'Where's Mr Verhoeven?' asked one woman, and it was heartening to hear her enquire after the old lord and not the new.

'He's safe, being seen by a healer.'

'And Forsythe?' another chimed, the tone aggressive.

'Sitting in the back garden last time I looked. Here's the deal: any moment now, things are going to get messy, so I'd like to suggest you take off. By all means, stay and fight an archangel if you wish, but if you'd prefer to get out of here . . .'

There was a pause of uncertainty – until a thunderous crack split the air. It wasn't what I thought it would be, however; a quick glance towards the front gate showed a small figure outside the fence, dressed in a Stevie Nicks skirt and an off-the-shoulder top in deepest purple, curls flying wildly in the breeze made by her magic as she rained spells against the wards surrounding the palace. Titania's efforts lit up the sky like a storm, shuddering through a palate of colours as each layer of protection came away under her attack. After this, the Weyrd were going to be questioning not only the efficacy of their wards, but looking sideways at Councillor Banks and her incredible powers. The neighbouring properties were far enough away that any noises and bright lights could be passed off as an unseasonal fireworks display. Besides, McIntyre would already have put out a bulletin to warn no cops to respond to any disturbances in the vicinity of the Bishop's Palace tonight, where 'exercises' were being conducted.

When the final glow had faded, a tall, skinny figure stepped up beside Titania and raised his hands. There was an explosion and the gate simply fell off its hinges. Even from a distance I could tell Ingo was proud of himself.

'I'd suggest you head that way, and fast. But later on, we're all sitting down for a nice chat about loyalty.' No sooner had the words left my lips than the security team were gone, leaving nothing but dust behind. They passed Bela, Ingo, Titania and Harmsorgi Odinsay on their way out. Titania looked as though she was considering throwing a few thunderbolts after them. Bela, heading determinedly towards me, made a point of not looking at the fleeing Weyrd, but I knew he'd have each face burned into his memory.

I raised my voice before he got too close. 'Bela, get everyone back to the entrance.'

'V—'

'Just do it!' I yelled because I had begun to feel vibrations beneath my feet. Bela did as he was told, but Harmsorgi continued to my side.

'Where is she?' he asked. 'Where's my daughter?'

'She was delivered to the Guardian. I swear to you I'll go down to Underworld as soon as this is over and I will bring her back. I just need to finish this first.'

The tremors in the ground were getting worse, stronger, more destabilising. I wrapped one hand around the reliquary as if that might help and tightened my grip on the sword. The rumbling turned into something that sounded as if a giant drill was coming through the centre of the earth to break through the crust.

There was no breaking, however; the Guardian simply shifted through the dirt as if his molecules could not be bothered to deal with anything so trivial as an organic substance. He just kind of *appeared*, shooting up through the grass as if it didn't matter at all until he was hovering some twenty feet above the ground. The slight form of Merrily Vaughan was hanging casually over his left arm. She looked small as a doll, and as limp as one too.

Beside me, Harmsorgi hissed, then made a noise like the clacking of a bird's beak, the chatter of a crow, until I glowered at him and he shut up. I returned my gaze to the Guardian.

He had been transformed.

The blackened thing with burned, split flesh was no more. The archangel was about nine feet tall, muscular, marble-fleshed, wearing a black chiton. A plain silver breastplate covered his chest; he wore silver boots on giant snowshoe feet. The magnificent fall of auburn curls springy as a shampoo advert had grown back to highlight a face as lovely as a Pre-Raphaelite model, complete with pouty cupid's-bow lips, soaring cheekbones, straight nose, definitive eyebrows, eyes like emeralds.

Ramiel was certainly prettier, but I was afraid he didn't look any saner.

He looked down at me and smiled a terrible smile.

I reached into my pocket for my last trick, clearing my throat while doing it in hope of distracting the awful creature. 'How about you put the grail down?'

The smile got even wider, then he threw Merrily aside with a contemptuous flick of the wrist.

My breath gone as if punched out of me, I watched her fly higher and higher, all fluidity because she was either unconscious or dead, floppy-doll relaxed. I couldn't tear my eyes from her to look at Harmsorgi beside me, even though I heard a new noise: a tearing, a flapping and a caw. The biggest raven I'd ever seen flew into my field of vision, then up and up until it caught Merrily in its claws before she began her descent.

I thought of the tattoo on Vaughan Carpenter's chest, of the raven jewellery sported by Egil and Freydis Odinsay.

The Guardian lifted a massive hand to swat Harmsorgi from the air.

I had the charge Ingo had prepared for me in a small calico sack, its blood price already paid for by Ingo in its construction. All I had to do was throw it and speak the words he'd made me memorise. The thing was so small, I wasn't sure it would be any help at all.

The effect was spectacular – so spectacular that both the Guardian and I were tossed about in the blast, him cart-wheeling through the air and I along the ground like a heavy tumbleweed. Harmsorgi faltered mid-flight but recovered enough to hightail it out of there. Of course, that meant I was the only thing left to draw the Guardian's attention when he stopped spinning.

Excellent.

'You are as faithless as your mother. I will find her, and your family.'

'I'm sure you'll give it a damned good try.' He couldn't know how close they were. Or, I hoped, not so close at all now: I *really* hoped Ziggi had driven them away at speed to anywhere that wasn't here.

'You will learn the price of defying Ramiel the Archangel, the Thunder of God.'

'Oh, so you've remembered your name now? No more of that "Guardian" bullshit? No more idiots to bilk or convince to take your shitty corrupted deals?'

'I cannot understand why they all fear you so, you *scrap*,' he sneered.

'Look, are you just going to keep talking or do you think you might get around to trying to destroy me some time soon? Because I have places to be.'

He dived at me.

I, idiot that I was, did not move out of the way but brought up the sword with absolutely no hope or technique whatsoever – I held it a bit like a baseball bat, if I'm totally honest. I watched the Archangel Ramiel speeding towards me and braced for impact.

But just when Ramiel should have hit me, when I could feel the cyclone conjured by the flap of his wings, the Thunder of God bounced away as if he'd hit an invisible trampoline and tumbled arse over head halfway across the manicured lawn towards the Palace, where he fetched up against the front portico and knocked out several sandstone bricks, two columns, and four heavy pot plants.

I looked at the sword and threw a glance over my shoulder at Bela, who shrugged.

Me or the sword?

The sword, surely? Ligeia's last gift? The reason none of the angels had been able to touch her last year? Or maybe Thaïs' protection was still working? How long might that last?

A god's blessing – and surely a god beat an angel, even an arch, hands down.

Ramiel rose and dusted himself off, growled, and charged again, propelled along on the storm of his wings. I braced myself again—

—and got the same result.

He rolled back against the house and more bricks were dislodged, more bits of roof tumbled down. I couldn't help but feel a little cocky. When the archangel got to his feet this time, I turned slightly so he'd be bowled off in a different direction. Who knew physics could be so much fun?

Well, right up until Ramiel finally realised that there were witnesses to our clash and that if I couldn't be damaged, the Weyrd by the gate were soft targets who could. With a flick of those enormous wings, he went speeding towards Bela and Titania and Ingo.

Oh, I could be damaged, all right.

I ran like I have never run before, screaming '*Move!*' as if that wouldn't already have occurred to Bela.

Of course, I wasn't ever going to be fast enough. Titania was weaving up a spell, but she wasn't going to be fast enough either.

As I watched Ramiel bowling towards Bela, I felt everything twisting in my gut, all the regret I never thought I could feel for giving him a hard time about anything and everything. He could have winked out, transited instantly to somewhere else in Brisbane or anywhere in the world, but that would have left Titania and Ingo vulnerable. He had no weapon, no shield, just those long glassy talons that grew when needed, and those fangs that weren't designed for drinking blood or rending flesh, only for self-defence.

Ramiel wasn't going to bounce off Bela Tepes, and one of my oldest, dearest, most complicated friends was going to die. And Bela wasn't going to move or run because he was stubborn and still smarting from being let down by the Weyrd and from my comments about their unreliability, their cowardice – and about his responsibility for my family's kidnapping.

I was still trying to get between Bela and Ramiel when two things happened.

Firstly, *Tobit* happened, materialising in the space I'd been aiming for, sweeping out an arm to backhand his brother across one perfectly pale cheek.

I did take a moment to think that Ramiel must have been getting thoroughly sick of being smacked down by then. At least there was no rolling and tumbling this time, just a beautiful arc of an enormous body, which landed with a thunderous sound.

Secondly, an ancient cream and navy FJ Holden pulled up in the street with a screech of brakes – and possibly the time-space continuum – and three familiar figures piled out to appear in the gap in the front fence. How many years had it been since Thaïs, a broken god hiding from duty, had been outside the walls of Little Venice? I thought she might have been shaking, just a little, but perhaps that was my overactive imagination.

I skidded to a halt beside the Sisters and puffed out, 'So, what's the plan?'

Aspasia made a noise of frustration. 'You mean you don't have one?'

I held up the sword. 'Do I look like a woman with anything other than antique weaponry?'

Thaïs pointed to Tobit. '*He* has a battle to fight first.'

'Is this just a delaying tactic to avoid doing something?'

'Do you know what it took for me to get here?'

'Okay, okay.'

Thaïs waved a hand at Tobit: *Go on.*

Tobit looked at me, puzzled, as if wondering why he'd take orders from the Norns, and I nodded back at him. I wasn't sure there was any real comprehension in his gaze, not yet, but he moved obediently to where Ramiel was rousing itself.

'Brother, surrender. Accept your punishment.'

Now if it had been me, I'd just have pounded him. But Tobit had lost, if he'd ever even had it, the killer's instinct. Ramiel, however, had never suffered that fate and he flew at Tobit, driving him back with a flurry of the kind of swooping blows one might use to clear away rocks or mountains if one happened to be, say, a giant or a Titan. They were blows to show contempt in a Biblical fashion, one archangel bitch-slapping another.

And, in the end, it was Tobit who was lying there bleeding and unable to get up, and Ramiel was clearly enjoying himself far too much to stop. I winced as he landed another hit on his brother's face.

I looked at Thaïs, who bowed her head and pointed at the reliquary around my neck. 'It won't be enough for long. Too many pieces are gone – but perhaps there are enough for a little while.'

I handed over the reliquary, still glancing at Ramiel. Surely those fists must have been getting tired?

Thaïs hung the reliquary around her own neck, then offered a hand to each of her Sisters. Theo and Aspasia looked resolute.

'Step back, strangeling.'

I did as Thaïs instructed and watched, keeping one eye on the Norns and the other on Ramiel, who was still wailing on his brother and showing no sign of getting bored or tired.

The transformation was slow at first: a glow like a phosphorous fire flickered, then caught, and soon the Norns were enmeshed in a firestorm of such brilliance that I had to shield my eyes. When I was able to look again, there was now just one figure: a brown-robed, dark-skinned woman, shorter than me by a foot, hair a mix of blood and ebony and snow, eyes like raisins and a mouth like a plum, ugly and beautiful, old and young, with a face that shifted between rage and joy, pain and elation, amusement and grief. The reliquary was gone; absorbed, I guessed, into the whole. Her outline shimmered, making an effort to stay together; I really hoped there was enough of her original matter to make a difference. Her feet . . . her feet had three claws in front and one at the back. I almost lost my breath.

I wondered if I'd done the right thing.

Ramiel had noticed the change and recognition burned in his eyes.

Ramiel screamed.

I offered the Norn composite my sword, but she shook her head with a smile. 'That's yours now.'

Ramiel screamed again and came towards us.

The Norn Collective raised her hand and began to speak in an ancient language – Aramaic, Hebrew, all languages, or maybe none – and the words floated through the air like petals on a storm wind. I could actually see them, silvery-thin pearls, travelling to the archangel. Her lips continued moving as she spoke to her murderer – well, attempted murderer, at least – but soon there was just a roaring in my ears.

I heard the archangel begin to weep. He was almost immobile now, hunched on the ground in an aching arc, held in place by a magic he had once tried to destroy. Yet somehow Ramiel managed to move, crawling forward, kept on coming in spite of the power of the broken god, until he was close enough to strike out with one great hand and knock the god high into the air. When she landed, she broke apart and there were three non-moving Norns and a reliquary – which immediately burst into flames – lying on the grass.

Thaïs had been right: there wasn't enough of them and they'd been separated for too long. With the Norns unconscious or dead, I didn't like my chances against Ramiel. I was willing to bet Thaïs' protection had winked out when she had, but I had no choice.

I was the last line of defence.

The Thunder of God rose and flexed his shoulders, stared at me for a full ten seconds – I counted – and then came at me at a steady clip, the true meaning of the word *inexorable*; after all, we both knew I had nowhere else to go. I raised Reaper in a two-handed grip and held the sword out in front of me, as if Ramiel would be stupid enough to just charge onto it. I imagined my mother and Joyce shaking their heads as they watched me ignoring everything they'd tried to teach me.

Ramiel laughed as he closed the distance. 'All these years and *that* is the best that you can do? That It – *They, She* – can do against me? That is *all*?'

'Not quite all,' I muttered, and braced myself, ready for the impact, as Tobit rose from his battering. His face was running with crimson and silver blood and one eye was swollen almost shut. As he bore down on his brother, I prayed he would be fast enough. He hit Ramiel in the back with the full power of his angelic momentum, which thrust Ramiel forward onto the tip of Reaper, then bore him down, down, down onto the hilt. The weight was so great I nearly lost my grip on Reaper as the muscles in my shoulders and biceps strained. Death notwithstanding, I was going to be sore tomorrow.

Ramiel was close enough to kiss. I watched the light go out in his mad green eyes. I could smell flowers on his skin. A line of silver ran from his perfect mouth – then he coughed and a spray of angelic blood hit my cheek. *Nice.*

'Tobit?' I grunted, struggling to keep Ramiel upright. 'Not much finesse in that, but thanks.'

Then I realised Reaper was so heavy because there were *two* bodies impaled on the blade, not one.

Two archangels for the price of one.

I let Reaper go and watched both bodies slide to the grass. For long moments it felt as if time had been stopped by the brotherly demise.

I was still staring at Tobit's glazed silver eyes as he lay there, his arms wrapped around his brother, united in death as they'd not been for so long in life. I was still staring at the wreckage around me, the still bodies of the Norns, the sum of failures, when Bela came and put a hand on my shoulder and I felt like I had permission to weep.

Chapter Forty

The afternoon was warm and spring was only five minutes away. David and I sat on the back deck, watching Olivia play with Maisie and the puppy, which was apparently now part of the household. Wanda Callander had come up from Ocean's Reach to drop off Harold (although 'poop machine' was a far better name, in my view) a few days ago, saying she didn't want Maisie to miss him. I reckoned it was more that *she'd* got tired of scooping up puppy crap, although I couldn't prove it. For a woman trying to get back into my good books, she had a strange way of going about it. At least she'd kept the kitten; I guessed that was a better pet for a witch. But Maisie loved the damned dog and if the price of my daughter's happiness was me getting used to a bright pink pooper-scooper, then I was happy to pay it.

This was the first day I'd actually let Maisie out of my arms, and that was only because Mum had said, 'If you don't let her down, she'll never learn to walk and you'll be schlepping an eighteen-year-old around.'

So David and I sat in the deckchairs and I tried not to twitch as I resisted the urge to keep leaning over the railing to see my daughter's every move, not to mention being ready to leap to her defence in the event of *anything* coming anywhere near her. It didn't matter that my mother was there: my mother who'd retained her powers even though Ramiel was dead and gone; Titania suggested it was because they had been a gift and so only the archangel himself could have taken them back from her. I guess Ramiel had been too busy dying.

In any event, I remained paranoid about losing my family. I suspected I'd be that way for a while.

David's bruises were fading and Louise had confirmed no broken ribs, and he and Olivia were sharing cooking duties again, which was another bonus. And Maisie's growth spurt had settled down; she was the size of an eighteen-month-old, and very strong: she was sitting up on her own and watching everything with those big eyes. At least she wasn't talking yet, which was something of a relief; I'd had about enough development milestones for the moment.

I had my family back. Ziggi would be around for dinner, dragging a bitter Bela with him; I wasn't sure how long it would take him to get over the lack of support from the Weyrd in our time of need. We were going to have to talk about morale at some point, and about how a change in attitudes might be achieved. I suspected a bit of arse-kicking would be involved.

The Norns . . . the Norns. I'd kept the knowledge of their past incarnation to myself, and apparently the burst of light as they recombined had blinded the watching Weyrd so no one else had seen their joining. Part of me wished I'd at least been able to tell Tobit who they really were, to ease his suffering before death. But he'd gone to wherever archangels went, and I had no idea what truths might be given to him there, if any. He and Ramiel were buried in the crypts beneath St Stephen's.

I'd tried to talk to the Norns about what had happened, about what they remembered of their remaking, but only Theo and Aspasia were in any condition to have a conversation, and neither of them had any memory of the incident. Despite their brief reformation, none of their sister's knowledge of their past had flowed back to them – or if it had, it hadn't stuck. All of that was still locked in Thaïs' head and she was in a coma. There was no telling how long that might last; maybe she was hiding, maybe she was travelling. Maybe she was preparing to die because everything was a mess that she didn't want to clean up.

So I was guarding their secret, as I had promised. I wouldn't even tell David. I didn't want to imagine the new Crusades, or what the Weyrd might do if they discovered the Norns weren't *quite* the same as them after all – not just of different matter, but the god who'd been used as an excuse to hunt and murder the Weyrd for hundreds of years. And as for the thought of angels, arch or otherwise, deciding that *their* Deity must once more be elevated over all the others . . . or be cast down for being corrupted, too close to Weyrd, too female, too fractured . . .

Mel and Lizzie were back home, now that the carpenter had repaired the back door and the railing on the landing. When we'd finally returned from the Bishop's Palace, it had been to find Jost Marolf gone. Unable to break either the manacles or the metalwork, he'd chewed through his own limb, and kicked a hole in the door as he'd done so. We found a wolf's forepaw, gnawed off at roughly the spot that would have been a man's wrist.

Both Mel's house and mine now had matching wards using Jost's left-behind fur, just like Third Eye Books and Merrily's apartment.

Merrily and Harmsorgi Odinsay had presented themselves to Bela at the Bishop's Palace as the clean-up got underway and since then there'd been a meeting with Freydis and Egil. I gathered it hadn't gone especially well; it was unlikely the prodigal son would be moving in with his parents again, nor would Merrily's grandparents become a source of soft toys, lollipops and cuddles. I suspected Harmsorgi was going to be watching over Merrily like a hawk – or a raven – for the longest time, so how the Hell Merrily was going to keep dating with her dad living at home was anyone's guess. I probably shouldn't have found that as funny as I did.

Harmsorgi couldn't tell me if his daughter was still a grail or not. It wasn't like they were a single-use item, but healing an archangel was never the intended purpose for her kind. He couldn't tell if she'd been drained of her ability, and he wouldn't subject her to any eldritch tests. I could understand that: better not to know for sure than for anyone to get wind of her potential. Merrily said she didn't remember the experience, which was probably for the best as well, all things considered. Harmsorgi had agreed to accept the judgement of the Council over his murder of Professor Harrow – and just as soon as the Council had the right number of members, it would be debating that very matter.

The doors on the cells in the Bishop's Palace had been repaired and now Dusana Nadasy and Udo Forsythe were neighbours. I still hadn't worked out what to do about Dusana, although she'd been asking to speak to me. Similarly, Verhoeven couldn't decide what to do with Udo: he'd planned a coup, killed people quite happily, would have sliced up my child and had beaten up Sandor himself, but as he retained absolutely no memory of any of it, the Councillor couldn't quite bring himself to execute someone who had basically reverted to a child. None of us knew how dangerous Udo was or might be in the future – how long did the Waters of Forgetting last? They were designed, as I understood it, to remove memory only until you passed from the Underworld to a place of judgement, so might their effect wear off? It would probably have been better for all concerned if I'd just run him through when I'd had the chance and the burning desire to do so. Maybe I'd done something worse by leaving him alive and lost. Verhoeven clearly thought so, anyway; he'd decided I was utterly ruthless.

Maybe that was why he'd asked me to become a Councillor, what with there being a vacancy and all. I told him if he let Ingo stay with Titania, I'd think about it. Then I asked if there was an executive washroom key with the job and I think I might have lost some cred there. But Ingo *was* back in the Banks' enclave, wisely behaving in a humbler fashion; his assistance at the Palace hadn't hurt either. There appeared to be some doubt as to whether or not I'd continue to do investigative duties for the Weyrd if I was a member of the Council; neither McIntyre nor Oldman were especially happy about the thought of having to deal with anyone else, which was amusing for all concerned.

Bela told me that all was not well with Father Tony and Miriam. The priest was not at all grateful for her efforts on his behalf. I was going to have to talk to him soon about the basic tenets of his faith, like forgiveness. I got that he felt her betrayal of the Weyrd community as a personal affront, but he'd been her life for the better part of forty years; what would he have done in her place? Let her hang? I didn't like the thought of getting an answer to that question, in case it changed my opinion of the good father. If others could forgive far greater trespasses against themselves, then surely so could he?

Others like Joyce, who had made her peace with my mother, although she would not be with us for dinner. She was with her own parents, the Mori-Millers, under the watchful eye of Wanda Callander at Ocean's Reach. My fox-girl was still recovering and getting used to an existence not in the Underworld under the rule of a psychotic archangel. She'd probably have to get used to not killing people, too. I hoped she'd adjust sooner rather than later. Theo said she was planning a visit when matters settled down at Little Venice, which I took to be code for when her bruises healed and she looked pretty again.

There was a knock on the front door. David and I exchanged glances.

'You know,' he said mildly, 'I would really, really like to not open the door to anyone ever again.'

'Which I understand. But it's Ziggi, and he is bringing the pie.'

'And Bela?'

'I put him in charge of wine.'

'Okay. He's old, he knows vintage. How wrong can he get that?' He rose and went inside.

As soon as he disappeared I gave in to the urge and leaned over the railing to watch my mother and daughter. I thought about Ligeia and how she'd embraced death. I thought about Tobit and the conversations he'd had with Sister Bridget – and how I was going to be having a chat with her some day soon about those chats. I thought about the sword I'd pushed into the back of the cupboard, the sword I was supposed to carry into a great battle, and I wondered when that would be, when the Dagger of Wilusa would be returned to me. I wondered when I'd see a man with no right hand staring at me with mad wolfish eyes. I wondered how long I'd get with my family.

Then I decided not to worry about it.

All our days are numbered, but you can waste your life pondering what that mysterious number is. Or you can just live it as hard as you can, make good memories, good friends, love your family by blood and choice, and those who stand by you.

Acknowledgements

Thanks to:

My family for their patience as I tell wild stories.

My BFF and Brain, Lisa L. Hannett, for cheerleading.

My beta readers, Peter M. Ball and Alan Baxter for reading very ugly early drafts.

Ron Serdiuk and Alexandra Pierce for once again being my first readers' readers.

Pulp Fiction Booksellers for All of the Things.

Jo Fletcher for her exquisite editing skills, her openness to discussion, and her infinite patience.

Stephen Jones for your professional advice and steadfast friendship.

Ron and Stef for the sanctuary and dogs.

Dennan Chew for making me think about what I do.

Lois Spangler for the lessons in swordswomanship, which I will use in the next book!

Olivia Mead of JFB/Quercus for her unfailingly excellent author support.

The lovely folk at Hachette Australia.

Ian Drury for helping to get me this far.

Meg Davis for the next part of the journey.

Brisbane Square Library and its wonderful staff for hosting all my Verity launches!